CLOSE TO ME

CLOSE TO ME

MONICA MURPHY

Cover design: Enchanting Romance Designs

Editor: Mackenzie Walton
Proofreader: Holly Malgieri

PLAYLIST

"hot girl bummer" - blackbear
"Nightmare" - Halsey
"Lights Up" - Harry Styles
"Pure Water" - Mustard, Migos
"boyfriend" - Ariana Grande, Social House
"Miss Americana & The Heartbreak Prince" - Taylor Swift
"Back At It Again" - Yella Beezy, Quavo, Gucci Mane
"Close to Me" - Ellie Goulding, Diplo, Swae Lee

Find the rest of the **Close To Me** Spotify playlist here:
https://bit.ly/CTMplaylist

We were
   Just friends
   That spoke like lovers
   And that seemed to be enough for
   Two teenagers who were scared to love one
   another.
   (k.a.t.)

PROLOGUE

There are significant moments in life, ones you can't help but keep tucked into your memory banks. Even if you don't want them, they're in there. Lingering. Reappearing when you don't want to remember. Making themselves known during a particular time, almost as if to say, "Ha, told you so."

Those are the worst.

Mostly, when I look back on those times, I think, *That's where it all changed.*

I've had moments like that with one person in particular. I didn't want him in my life, though he was always there. I ignored him, which wasn't easy considering the small school we both attend. Pretending someone doesn't exist doesn't mean they're invisible, though.

I still saw him. How could I not?

And it doesn't mean I was invisible either. He still saw me.

He saw right through me.

FRESHMAN YEAR

CHAPTER 1

I met him the first week of school.

I was mad.

Pissed at my parents. Pissed at the world.

A fourteen-year-old girl with a grudge and a fuck-you attitude is the worst thing ever. Trust me.

But deep down, I was alone and sad and I had no friends. We moved to this small, nowhere town the summer after eighth grade, and the resentment built within me, slowly but surely, with every day that passed. I felt it grow, until it threatened to choke me, consume me by the first day of school.

I show up on campus, no one paying any attention to me, and that hurt. The high school was small, cliquey. Most everyone had gone to school with each other since the dawn of time, and I was an outsider. After being there for a couple of days, I could tell they weren't really interested in me.

Except for one.

I'm waiting for my mom to pick me up after school when I hear someone speak.

"What's your name?"

Those were the first words he said to me. This boy is older, I can tell. A junior, I think. Cocky, confident, *hot.* During lunch, everyone called him JT and I heard someone mention he was the quarterback of the varsity football team. That should've been my first clue, but at the time, I was clueless.

All I cared about was that he actually spoke to me.

"Um." I stand up a little taller, tossing my hair behind my shoulder with a careless flick of my fingers. "Autumn."

He smiles, revealing bright white teeth. "Well, Um Autumn, it's nice to meet you. I'm JT."

When he extends his hand out toward me, I stare at it stupidly for a moment, not sure of what to do next. Dumb, right?

"Hi." I finally take his hand and shake it, a little too enthusiastically.

The moment he releases my hand he takes a step back, slipping his hands in the front pockets of his jeans. He's tall and lanky and has dirty blond hair and blue eyes. He's the most popular boy in school and no one had to tell me that.

I just knew.

"Maybe we could hang out sometime," he says with a shrug and a little smile, like no big deal.

This is a *huge* deal. Maybe not to him, but definitely to me.

"Um, sure." I nod, shocked and pleased he would say such a thing.

"We should talk on Snap," he continues.

My parents won't let me have Snapchat. Dad says I'm too young, but he's so overprotective, it's ridiculous. Mom thinks he's being too strict, and I agree with her.

"I don't have Snap," I admit, feeling like a little girl when I see the surprise etched all over JT's face.

"You should get it. Let me know when you do." He smiles and starts walking. "Bye, Um Autumn."

"Bye," I call, watching him leave. A sigh escapes me once he rounds the building and disappears, and that's when I hear someone laugh.

A boy.

Glancing over my shoulder, I glare at the guy who's sitting on the cement bench, head tilted to the side as he contemplates me, hair dark as coal falling over his forehead, covering one eye. I don't recognize him, but that's no surprise considering I've been at this school for only three days.

"You really think Jonah Taylor wants to hang out with *you?*" he asks, as if he had been listening in on our entire conversation.

I'm instantly pissed. A constant mood for me lately, yet I'm still not quite used to it. I've always been the good girl, and I definitely don't tell people how I really feel.

Turning to face him, I rest my hands on my hips. "Who the hell are you?"

My outburst surprises me, but I remain cool. Anger is power, I remind myself.

Besides, I have nothing to lose.

"I'm your new best friend who's going to tell it to you straight." He leans back against the bench, flicking his hair out of his eyes.

"I don't need a new best friend." I sound sulky, and maybe I'm feeling that way too. I didn't want this guy to burst my JT-induced happy bubble.

"Then let me offer up a word of advice." He hesitates for barely a second. "Jonah Taylor could give two shits about you."

"Gee, thanks," I say sarcastically.

He shrugs. "Just trying to keep it real."

"Are you friends with him?" Doubtful.

The boy snorts. "Not really."

I knew it. "If you're not friends with JT, then I really don't think you should be offering me any advice about him." I turn away from the jerk, eager to head for the pickup/drop off line where Mom is most likely waiting for me, when he says something that stops me dead in my tracks.

"They made a bet about you. The whole varsity football team. Whoever's the first one to get a pussy shot from you on Snap or Insta or whatever wins one hundred bucks."

Say what? Slowly, I look at him over my shoulder once more. "What did you just say?"

Another shrug. He doesn't bother looking at me. Instead, he pulls a matchbook out of the ratty backpack sitting next to him, tearing a single match out before he runs the red tip across the roughened cement side of the bench. The match catches fire, and he brings the flame to his face, his eyes narrowing as he studies the orange glow. He's holding the match so close, I'm afraid he might burn himself if he doesn't watch it.

I'm starting to think he's a complete idiot.

"They know who your dad is," he offers casually, still not looking at me.

Unease slithers down my spine. This means the boy knows who my dad is, too, and I hate that. No matter where I go, I can't get away from the fact that my father is retired NFL superstar Drew Callahan.

Sometimes it's really annoying.

"Do *you* know who he is?"

The boy nods, remaining silent.

"Are you in on this pussy shot bet?" I can't believe the word *pussy* fell from my lips so easily. I don't think I've ever said that word out loud before.

He finally turns his focus on me, those big brown eyes meeting mine. "No."

I don't believe him. "How do you know about it then?"

"I hear talk." Another shrug. "In the locker room."

Great. Just great. They're talking about me in the locker room? "You're on the football team too?"

I find this hard to believe. He doesn't look like a football player. He's not big enough. Too skinny.

"JV."

Junior varsity. Maybe he's making this up. "What position do you play?"

He shakes out the match and lets it fall to the ground. Thin tendrils of smoke rise from it before disappearing into the air. "Quarterback."

Nope. Nope, nope, nope.

Forget this boy. Forget JT too. They're all quarterbacks like my dad. Meaning they all want to get close to me *because* of my dad.

Never because of me.

Without another word, I turn and walk away, praying I never have to talk to him again.

I didn't ask his name, and he didn't ask mine, but he knew who I was.

Eventually, I'd know who he was too.

SOPHOMORE YEAR

CHAPTER 2

I'm spying. I'm good at it, better than my brother Jake, who crashes through a room even if there's nothing to bump into, and then there's my little sister, who has the biggest mouth EVER. Ava is eleven and a total pain in my ass. Mom says it's because she looks up to me, that's why Ava follows me everywhere.

Whatever. She's always getting in my business, digging through my room, going through my makeup, my face wash, my freaking tampons. Trying to steal my clothes, even though she's smaller than me. It's annoying.

She's annoying.

And then there's the baby of the family, Beck. He's six, and he looks *just* like my dad, even more so than Jake. As in, Beck's the actual spitting image of my father when he was the same age, and that melts our mom's heart. Combine that with him being the youngest, and he has Mom wrapped tight around his dirty little finger.

His finger is dirty because he's the boy-est boy of all boys. When we moved to this house in the mountains, Beck's heart filled with absolute joy over the fact that he had acres of land to explore. He's always digging up something, even old animal bones, which is freaky. Falling and hurting himself is part of Beck's daily life—he broke his arm last year and it didn't even faze him, though I thought Dad was gonna flip out. Can't wreck his throwing arm, you know.

What Beck really is, is totally lovable. Even I can admit that.

I'm veering off topic when I should be listening to what my dad is saying to my mom. They're having a big discussion, and I'm praying it has nothing to do with me.

"...I thought we moved up here to get away from it all. So we could just focus on our family and nothing else," Mom says, sounding mad.

Wait, not mad. Just irritated. And I rarely hear her sound like that toward Dad.

"I know. And this shouldn't take too much time away from us," he says, making Mom snort.

"Drew, be real right now. You'll throw yourself into this project. You will become the best offensive coordinator that high school has *ever* seen. Do they not realize how lucky they are that you're even considering this? You played for the NFL! You won two Super Bowls! You were a commentator on TV!"

"Yeah, and that's all behind me now. What else am I going to do with my time?"

"Oh, I don't know, maybe spend it with me and the kids?"

Dad just totally stepped in it.

"They're all in school. Even Beck. And now his time is tied up with football practice just like his brother," Dad points out.

Beck is in youth football, as is Jacob. Beck's on the peewee team and Jake's on the senior team since he's in the eighth grade. Next year he'll be at the high school with me, and honestly?

I'm not looking forward to it.

"If you're going to coach anyone, coach Jake's team. He's your son," Mom stresses. "He needs you."

"He doesn't. My son is amazing. So is his team." The sincerity in Dad's voice rings true. Jake is an amazing football player, even I can admit that. And their team will most likely win their league championship. "The high school needs me more. They're so close to being good, but they're not quite there yet. Besides, Jake will be at the high school next year," Dad points out.

"And you'll be coaching the varsity team."

"It'll bleed over into the JV team and you know it. Come on, babe." I'm not looking at them, but I can tell he just pulled her into his arms. My parents are very affectionate with each other. Sometimes almost *too* affectionate, like when they kiss and stuff in front of us.

It's gross. Who wants to see their parents act like that? They're so old.

"Does this mean I have to go to every game?" Mom asks on a sigh.

Look at how easily she gives in to him. I'm surprised. She's always trying to protect his time, especially since he retired.

"Aren't you already going to be at every game because of Autumn?" he asks.

"Yeah." She sighs. "True."

There's no more talking, which tells me Dad convinced her it was a good idea and now they're making out like teenagers.

And that's my cue to leave.

I slip down the hall in pure stealth mode, back in my room with the door closed in seconds. Mom has to go to the games because now they're my games too.

I made the cheer team last spring. After fumbling around

the first month of my freshman year like a lost little puppy, I actually made friends. Lots of friends. A couple of them were on the cheer team and they convinced me to try out for next year with them. So I did.

And I made it.

Doing dance for years helped, I'm sure. The fact that my dad is a football legend has nothing to do with it, which feels really good. For once I did something on my own, and I like that. I think Dad's shadow hangs over Jake, so he always has this need to prove himself to everyone he meets. I'm guessing Beck will end up the same way, though maybe not. That kid has major swagger and he's in the freaking third grade.

Within minutes of me being back in my room, there's a knock, and then it's my dad walking through the door, a barely there smile curling his lips.

I sit up straight on my bed, blinking up at him. If you didn't know him at all, you'd say he was intimidating. He's big. Tall and broad with dark hair and laser-focused blue eyes. Eyes that see everything, which is a little scary sometimes. My parents always say you can't pull anything over on them. They've seen and done it all. Stuff we couldn't begin to comprehend, Mom always adds, almost like it's a threat.

I don't know exactly what they mean, but I believe them. They scare me. And not because they abuse me or anything like that. I love my parents so much, and I know they love me too, but I'm secretly terrified I'll disappoint them, and that is the worst.

We remained in San Francisco for a few years after my dad retired from the NFL, and he's still considered a celebrity there. He couldn't escape the fame, even though he wanted to. Living in such a big city, my parents eventually got tired of it, so they decided to pick up and move us somewhere quieter. A smaller town with a good school district and not as much traffic and crime.

We may have moved to this small town to get away from everything, but everyone who lives here knows who my dad is, especially all the boys at my school. Of course, they do.

"Hey princess." That he still calls me princess is a little irritating sometimes, because it makes me feel like a little girl and I'm not. Not anymore. But whatever.

"Hi Daddy." See? I slip into little girl mode when he says stuff like that.

"I have a question for you." He sits on the edge of my mattress.

"What is it?"

He leans back all casual like. "Would you care if I was one of the coaches for the football team at the high school?"

Kind of, I want to say, but if he were to ask me why, I probably couldn't come up with a good answer. So I just nod and shrug. "It doesn't really matter, I guess."

He actually looks hurt by my words. "It wouldn't matter?"

"I don't know," I say carefully, not wanting to say the wrong thing. "I suppose it would be nice to see you while I'm cheering on the sidelines." Though I don't know how much I would actually notice him.

"It wouldn't bother you that I'm there? That I would be at practice a lot with the team? Boys you go to school with?" he asks, his voice curious.

"I'm at practice too so…" I shrug. Him being there really won't make a difference in my life.

"I just don't want you or your brothers and sister to think me doing this will take time away from the family," he says as his gaze drifts around my room. "Did you move your furniture around again?"

I do that a lot, rearrange the furniture in my bedroom. I'm constantly wanting a new look, and I know it irritates them sometimes. Dad says I'm going to scratch up the wood floors, but I never do. I'm always careful.

I decide to change the subject.

"Are they paying you? The high school?" I ask, wrinkling my nose. We have enough money, I think. We live in a huge house in the most exclusive part of town, with a gorgeous view of the lake. We have a dock on the lake too, though we don't own a boat yet, despite having lived here now for a year.

At first I thought it was isolating, living on the lake. Now I realize it's a coveted spot, and lots of kids party near my neighborhood, which really isn't a neighborhood at all, not like we used to live in. Everything's so spread out, and everyone owns so much land, including us.

There's a spot on the ridge, though, just above us, where everyone goes on the weekends. I haven't been invited to go yet, but when you're a freshman, they all ignore you.

I'm going to be a sophomore now, and a cheerleader. That has to give me some sort of cred.

"They're giving me a stipend, but I'm not doing this for the money. I'm doing it for the kids. For the boys on that team. I get the sense that they need some sort of leadership," he says, and I can see it in his eyes that he means every word he says. My dad only wants to do good for people. Sometimes too much. Mom says his kindness gets taken advantage of sometimes, but she's more wary. Not as trusting.

I guess they balance each other out.

"The boys have a lot of potential," Dad continues. "They have a great quarterback."

Yeah. JT the dick, who tried to get me to send him naked pics last year.

"And the one who'll replace him next year is amazing. So much raw potential. He's just—troubled," Dad finishes, a dark look on his face.

My entire body goes tense. I know who he means.

Ash. Asher Davis. Does he play with matches because of his name?

That's how I always figured it. Who knows if I'm right? I don't even talk to that guy.

"He's kind of a jerk," I tell my dad, deciding honesty really is the best policy.

He winces. "He's not had the best life."

Curiosity rises within me. "What do you mean?"

"I can't really discuss it with you." Reaching out, he sets his big hand on top of my head and messes up my hair. I dodge away from his touch and his hand drops. "Just give him a break. Okay?"

"Sure." I shrug. No way am I ever giving him a break.

Ever.

CHAPTER 3

*I*t's the first day of school, and I walk into my sixth period chemistry class, smiling over at Mr. Curtin, who's sitting behind his desk, already chatting with a couple of students. All of them girls. He's younger, in his late twenties, and I've heard more than once from girls who think he's hot or they have a crush on him.

Ew.

But anyway.

I realize quick I don't have any friends in this class. I sort of knew that already, since none of my closest friends have chem during sixth period, but I was hoping for a few acquaintances at least.

I know no one.

Making my way to the back of the classroom, I settle in at the last table in the left row, closest to the door. I pull my phone out of my backpack and check Snapchat—Dad finally gave in and let me have it—where I have a message from Kaya. She's my best friend, and we constantly talk. Even though we just saw each other at lunch, which ended not even ten minutes ago, we still snap each other. DM each other. Sometimes text each other.

I open her snap to see a blurry photo of the back of some guy's head. It's vaguely familiar, but I can't quite place it.

Ben Murray is in my history class!

Jealousy rises, but I tamp it down. I've had a minor crush on Ben for the last few months, and Kaya knows it.

I take a selfie and quickly tap out my response.

No one I know is in this class

She responds almost immediately.

You get to stare at Curtin for the next forty-five minutes.

Kaya included a heart eyes emoji and I send a rolling eyes emoji in response.

I'm not hot for teacher like everyone else in our grade, gross.

The girls surrounding Curtin's desk all scatter back to their tables and he rises to his feet, walking over to the open door and pushing it shut. Immediately the sounds from outside are gone, and the class becomes eerily silent. He goes to the board and picks up a pen, writing his name across the blank white expanse, then turns to face us.

He remains quiet for a moment, his gaze sweeping the room, before he finally speaks up.

"Please tell me I don't scare you," Mr. Curtin says with a chuckle, and we all smile in response.

Yes, even me. I can admit his easygoing personality will go a long way with this class, a subject I'm not particularly looking forward to. But I have to take it, especially if I want to go to a good college and get away from this boring little town my parents seem to love so much.

Curtin starts talking about chemistry and I immediately start spacing out, forgetting all about my good intentions. A syllabus is passed out. He mentions that we'll be partnering up with the person sitting next to us at our table for our lab projects, and I glance over at the empty seat beside me.

"With the exception of Miss Callahan, it seems," he says, making everyone turn to look at me and laugh.

My cheeks burn and I slump in my seat. I still have a problem with attention being focused on me. I took dance, I competed on stage for a couple of years, and that was no big deal. I'm now on the cheer team and while we haven't cheered at a game yet, I'm not worried about it. Yet a teacher calls me out for something minor and I want to disappear.

I need to get over it.

Suddenly the door bursts open and in strides the very last person I thought I'd see.

Ash Davis.

The smirk on his face is annoying, even though it's not aimed at me. His hair is dark as sin and a mess, flopping across his forehead in a clear indication that he needs a hair-cut. His eyes are so dark they look pitch black, and I swear if Satan had a son, it would be this boy.

Mom has said from the moment Dad started coaching the football team that Ash looks like trouble, but there was always an affectionate tone in her voice. As if for some reason, my mother actually likes him.

I don't understand why.

"Ah, Mr. Davis." The teacher smiles, but it doesn't quite reach his eyes. More like he appears super irritated, which I think is a consistent emotion among the teachers when it comes to dealing with Ash. "So kind of you to finally join us."

"Sorry I'm late, Curtin." Ash casts his smirk upon all of us in the classroom, as if he's performing on stage and we're all watching him from the audience. "What I'd miss?"

A few girls giggle, me not included.

I just stare straight ahead, not really looking at him, not really looking at anything. I've never had a class with Ash before. I figured we were on different tracks and our paths wouldn't cross, at least not during class time.

This is what I get for thinking I'd never have to deal with him again—more like I was in a major state of denial. I should've known. More than that, I should've remembered that we share a friend group, though he's more on the fringe of it. He's on the football team and I'm a cheerleader—though he's on JV so we don't cheer during his games. At lunch, or whenever our friends are sitting together, I try my best to avoid him.

And he knows it.

I don't know why I avoid him. Maybe I didn't like how he blunt he was when we first met. Maybe I don't like how he struts around campus like he owns the place. Maybe I don't like the way he looks at me, as if he can see right through me, right down to the very essence of my soul.

That sounds dramatic, but it's true. Ash Davis makes me uncomfortable. Most of the time in a bad way.

Sometimes, though I'd never tell anyone this, he makes me uncomfortable in...a good way.

Though I refuse to have a crush on him. Every other girl in the sophomore class does already. He doesn't need to add me to his list.

"Lucky you, Asher, you haven't missed much. Here's the syllabus." Curtin hands Ash the piece of paper he passed out only a few minutes ago and then flicks his head. "Go find your seat. It's next to Autumn Callahan, who'll be your lab partner this semester."

I sit up straighter, looking over at the empty seat next to me before I search the room, mentally counting...each... full...seat.

Oh my God. He's going to be *my* lab partner?

For the entire semester?

Kill me now.

Asher saunters toward my table and I watch him, our gazes connecting. Holding. His smirk disappears, his lips thinning the slightest bit, as if I might disgust him, and I swallow hard, curling my hands together on top of the table.

"Hey." He nods in my direction as he flops into the chair next to mine, tossing his backpack on top of the table, making a lot of noise and causing Mr. Curtin to pause for a second in his discussion. "It's been a while."

I look away, staring straight ahead once more. "Please don't talk to me," I say as quietly as possible. He knows I don't like him.

Well…it's not that I dislike him.

More like he completely unsettles me. Just having him this close, I feel something crackling between us. Electricity? Chemistry?

Oh, ha ha. That's funny, considering we're in a chemistry class.

I frown and dip my head, staring at the table. My thoughts are ridiculous. My reaction to Ash is ridiculous too. He's just a boy. A very good looking, confident boy, who leaves me on edge every time I so much as look at him.

Chuckling, Ash shakes his head as he unzips his backpack and pulls out a tattered notebook and a pen. Didn't even bother to buy school supplies for the new year, while I live for that kind of thing. The back-to-school section at Target in early August is my favorite place ever. "You're something else, Callahan."

I say nothing. I just lift my head and keep my eyes glued on the whiteboard as Mr. Curtin keeps talking. I reach for the brand-new binder that's already on the table in front of me and flip it open, finding the color-coded tab for chemistry and turning to that section so I can slip the syllabus into the folder. I can feel Ash watch me the entire time, that smirk returning when I glare at him, and he looks ready to laugh.

"You're one of those girls who gets off in office supply stores, huh." Somehow he makes that sentence sound dirty.

"I do not." I lift my chin, not daring to look in his direction.

He scoots his chair toward mine, closer and closer, until his breath causes strands of hair to fan across my face. "Liar." His breath is hot, his voice low as he speaks directly into my ear. "I bet you practically cream your panties every time you're in the planner section."

A gasp leaves me and I turn my head so fast, our noses practically touch. He rears back, though not far enough. Anger has my blood running hot, though it's not enough to drown out the weird, tingly feeling I'm experiencing.

I hate that weird, tingly feeling with everything I've got.

I also hate Asher Davis.

"You're disgusting," I practically spit at him.

He leans back in his chair, looking very pleased with himself. "You like it."

"No," I say vehemently. "No, I do not."

"Is there a problem here, Mr. Davis? Miss Callahan?" Mr. Curtin asks.

Ash says, "No."

At the same time, I say, "Yes."

Curtin rests his hands on his hips, staring us both down. The entire classroom has gone silent once more, a few people turning in their seats to watch us, and I wish I could disappear.

This is so not how I wanted to kick off my first day of sophomore year.

"Do I need to separate you two?" Mr. Curtin continues.

"Please," I say.

"No, we're good," Ash chimes in.

I glare at him again, but this time, he's the one who won't look at me. His clutched hands are resting on top of the table, the expression on his face is downright angelic, and that is not a word I would've ever associated with Asher Davis before.

"You two need to keep quiet," Curtin finally says before he resumes his lecture yet again.

Forty long minutes later, the bell rings and I gather up my things quickly, shoving everything into my backpack without care, which is totally unlike me. I have seventh period P.E. because of cheer, and I'm guessing Ash has P.E. too since the entire football team takes weight training the last period of the day. This means we're both headed to essentially the same place, and I don't want him to walk by me or even try to talk to me.

I don't want anything to do with him.

Ever.

I'm out the door before he can even get his lazy butt out of the chair, and I shoot down the hall, making my way toward the gym, where I can hide in the girls' locker room and never have to see him again.

Until tomorrow.

Ugh. I honestly don't know how I'm going to survive the next semester working with him.

Withholding the agonized groan that wants to escape, I turn left, running right into someone. We collide so hard I make a weird startled noise, and strong hands reach out to grab my arms, steadying me. When I look up, I see it's...

Asher?

He's grinning. "Can't get away from me that fast, Callahan."

How did he catch up to me so quickly? It's like he did it on purpose.

"Don't call me that," I tell him, which of course makes him squeeze my arms tighter. Not enough to hurt, but not enough to easily break away from him either.

"What do you want me to call you then? Autumn?" His voice pitches higher when he says my name and he makes a disgusted face, shaking his head. "That's, like, the stupidest name ever."

I'm totally offended, which is annoying. I'm also...hurt, which makes me mad. He shouldn't affect me whatsoever. He's nothing. And how I feel about him is nothing too. "Right, and Ash is *such* a great name," I throw back at him, sounding absolutely ridiculous.

He releases his hold on me so fast that I stumble a little, though I catch myself before I fall. I didn't realize how strong he is. Or how my skin is still tingling where he touched me. "It was my dad's name."

He sounds defensive, the expression on his face arrogant. Like I should bow at his feet and tell him how great he is.

Well screw that.

"So you both have a stupid name, huh? Ash? More like you're a total *ass*. Your dad is probably an ass too, just like you." My voice is taunting, and what I'm saying is stupid, I know it is.

But I can see the way his eyes darken—not sure how that's possible, they're so dark already—and I can tell he's angry.

Maybe even...

Hurt?

No. No way.

"Real nice, Callahan." His voice is flat, his expression devoid of any emotion. "I hope making fun of someone who's dead makes you feel better about yourself." And with those final words...

He walks away.

CHAPTER 4

"*M*om?" I stand in the doorway of my parents' bedroom, hoping she's alone. Dad's still at football practice and I always get home before he does. Mom might have Ava with her, or Beck. Or even Jake, though I'm pretty sure he's locked up in his room playing video games like he usually does after school. He has youth football practice at six, so Mom will take him over to the high school in a few minutes.

I really need to talk to her before she leaves.

Mom exits her closet, stopping short when she sees me. "Oh, Autumn. I thought I heard someone calling me. You okay?"

"Yeah," I lie as I enter their bedroom and glance around, my gaze snagging on the giant windows that line the wall facing the lake. It's a gorgeous view. Peaceful. My bedroom faces the front of the house, which isn't as pretty. "I just wanted to ask you a question."

"I hope I have an answer." Mom smiles and sits on the side of the bed, patting the spot beside her.

I go to where she's sitting and settle in, leaning my head

against her chest briefly when she wraps her arm around my shoulders and pulls me into her, squeezing me tight. It feels so good, so comforting, that I almost want to cry.

In fact, I sort of do, and she can tell, because I'm sniffing and suddenly wiping at my eyes.

"Aw, sweetie, what's wrong? Did something happen at school today?" Her voice is soft and I'm flooded with memories of my mom comforting me when I was little after I'd fall and hurt myself. Scraped-up knees and scratches on my arms are nothing compared to the pain in my chest I've been feeling this afternoon, though. I couldn't concentrate at practice today. I kept messing up and my coaches were getting annoyed with me.

"Yeah." I nod and close my eyes tightly, like that's going to stop the tears from flowing. Side note—it doesn't stop them at all. "Is it wrong to insult someone's dead father when you didn't know his father was dead in the first place?"

Mom's arm is around my shoulders again, her hand rubbing my arm. "What are you talking about?"

I'm almost afraid to tell her. I don't want her to yell or worse, tell me she's disappointed in me.

"There's a boy at school," I start, my voice shaky. I clear my throat, hating how nervous I sound. "He's awful."

"Awful in a bad way or awful in a good way?"

I frown as I pull out of her hold and sit up straight, meeting her gaze. "Is there such a thing as a good awful?"

"Yes. Definitely," Mom says firmly. "He could be annoying you and it makes you angry, yet you also like him a little bit, which makes the entire situation worse. Is that how he's making you feel?"

I don't know how to think of Ash. He's awful, but I don't think I could call it a good awful. He's not very nice to me. It always feels like he's mocking me, as if he thinks I'm a big

24

joke. But today I stooped just as low as him, and I said such a terrible thing.

I hate myself for it.

"I don't like him," I tell her. "He's not nice. And he made me so mad during class…we have chemistry together and Mr. Curtin said we have to be lab partners, honestly I don't know how I'm going to survive it. He wouldn't stop making fun of me, so I finally said something…not so nice in return."

Mom frowns, that defensive mother look crossing her face. She doesn't like it when anyone messes with her kids. Of course, what mother does? "Who is it?"

"Asher Davis," I say, my lips twisting around his name.

"Ahhh." Mom nods, her expression turning pensive. "You do know he's had some—trouble in his life."

"What sort of trouble?" I remember what Dad said, and how he couldn't reveal anything. "What did he do?"

Mom sighs. "It's not what he did. It's what's been done to him."

I drop my gaze to my lap, staring at my hands as I link my fingers together. "Was he abused?" Maybe by his dead father?

"It's not my story to tell." She pats my knee and I glance up to find she's already watching me. I see myself in her face. We share the same green eyes, our facial structure is similar, same mouth shape, same nose, though I have darker hair than her, which I got from Dad. I'm short and stacked, just like she is, which kind of sucks, if you ask me. I hate it when the boys stare at my chest, which they used to do a lot in middle school. I mean, they still do it, but it's not as bad as it used to be.

Or maybe they got better at hiding it.

"What exactly did he do that made you so angry?" Mom asks when I still haven't said anything.

"He made fun of my name, which hurt my feelings. So I tried to get back at him, and when he told me he was named after his father, I said their name wasn't Ash, it was more like ass." I shake my head. "And then he told me his dad was dead and made me feel terrible."

Mom actually…laughs? Not a full-blown laugh, more like a discreet chuckle. She even covers her mouth with her fingers. "Oh Autumn."

"I'm a horrible person," I tell her morosely, hating how my voices cracks. *I* feel ready to crack. Like my heart is going to split open and spill out all my misery everywhere, soaking me with it.

She slips her arm around my shoulders again and gives me a shake. "No, you're not. He was making fun of you, and you lashed out, which is normal. How were you supposed to know his father's dead? And honestly? That was kind of a good one, trading ash for ass."

A shocked laugh escapes me and I cover my mouth just like she did, trying to stop myself. "It was mean."

"But a funny play on words, not that I'm condoning you making fun of someone." She gives my shoulders another shake. "He's defensive, and I'm guessing when it comes to him, you are too. Just know, he's had a tough life, and he puts on a tough persona, but he's…vulnerable. Losing a parent, especially when you're so young, is hard. I know what that's like."

"Right, because of your mom." I can't imagine my mother having anything in common with Ash Davis, but I also know Mom had a rough childhood, not that she's told me much about it.

"My mom was a drunk who couldn't keep a job. She did drugs too. Slept around, had lots of boyfriends she'd bring home and try to get us accept as our new dad or whatever. It was—bad. She didn't care about me, and she didn't care about your Uncle Owen either." Mom stares off into space, lost in her memories. She told me she had to take care of her little brother before, but never offered up many details until now. "I had to grow up fast and take care of Owen and our apartment. I had to get a job to help pay the bills, and I barely graduated high school. I'm still not quite sure how I did it."

"What do you mean, you barely graduated?" I lean away, her arm slipping off my shoulders. I've never heard this story before, and I have to admit…

It's fascinating.

"I was never at school, especially the last couple of years. I missed a lot of class because I was working all the time. I got my diploma, but barely. I didn't even go to the ceremony; they mailed it to me. My grades were absolutely terrible." She turns to look at me, really look at me. "School is so important, Autumn. You need to get good grades so you can get into a good college."

I become defensive at her quick subject change, as I usually do when my parents start talking to me about college. That's so far away, I don't know why I have to worry about it now. "My grades are fine."

"I know." Mom smiles gently. "Your father and I, we push you all because no one pushed us. At least, not one of our parents pushed us in the right direction. We just want the best for you and your brothers, and your sister."

Ugh. That reminds me… "Ava won't stop going through my makeup."

"I'll tell her to stop," Mom promises, amusement tinging her voice, but it never seems to matter. Ava goes through my stuff all the time.

"What should I do about Ash?" I ask, my voice small.

Mom sighs. "Tell him you're sorry."

I make a face. "I can't do that."

"Why not?" Her brows rise, and she's got that total Mom face going on. "It's pretty simple, Autumn. Just approach him and say you're sorry for calling him an ass."

I think about what she said. I think about it for the rest of the night. While I'm doing homework, while I'm FaceTiming Kaya and she's encouraging me to go after Ben Murray, that she thinks we'd make a cute couple. I laugh and agree, but deep down, I'm still thinking about Ash and what I said to him, and that flash of pain in his eyes when I said it. It was there and gone, not even for a second.

But I saw it. I hurt him. And that made me hurt too.

I don't understand why.

CHAPTER 5

I've never told Asher Davis I was sorry. I couldn't work up the nerve. It's been a month since our conversation on the first day of school, and we never spoke about it again. We don't really talk ever at all, beyond about school stuff.

It's mid-September, and Ash and I have come to an unspoken truce. After I insulted his dead father, he stopped taunting me. Stopped smirking at me. I guess I should be glad he's leaving me alone, but I still feel bad about what I said. Was his dad nice, or was he mean? Is that why Ash is so mean to me? Mom said it doesn't matter how they treated you, we always love our parents.

Lucky for me, I have great parents. I love mine so much, and I know they love me. I have no idea what it's like for Asher. Dad mentioned that he didn't have an easy time of it, but I don't know what that means or what he's referring to. My father doesn't talk to me about it, and of course Ash isn't talking to me, so I don't know what's really going on.

Ash keeps his distance, and so do I, and when we work

together during lab hours, we're polite to each other. To the point that it's downright painful to witness, I'm sure.

But I'm not going to break. And neither is he. I don't like him. He doesn't like me. In chemistry, we don't have a choice, though. We *have* to work together.

It sucks.

I walk into chemistry class today, my stomach jittery, my mind racing. I didn't eat much at lunch, because I couldn't. I know it's dumb to worry about this kind of stuff, but I'm excited. Nervous. I'm not going to be able to focus in class, so thank God it's not a lab day.

No way do I want Ash to notice.

The reason I'm a wreck? Homecoming court announcements are happening. Three boys and three girls from each class—with the exception of the seniors, who nominates six boys and six girls—are chosen to be part of the homecoming finalists. During homecoming week, there are themed dress-up days, games at lunch, and the coronation is Wednesday night for the lowerclassmen. The king and queen are crowned at halftime during the football game Friday night, and everyone else who won will be presented as well.

It's kind of a big deal.

A bunch of my friends have already told me they nominated me, and I can't help but anticipate our vice principal Mrs. Adney announcing my name near the end of class. I know I shouldn't assume. I know I should tell myself to calm the hell down, no way is it going to happen, so I don't get my hopes up only to have them come crashing down. But something is telling me...

It's going to happen.

I'm so amped up I'm squirming in my chair, and when Ash walks into the room, he sends me a weird look as he settles into his chair beside mine. "You got ants in your pants or what?"

My mouth pops open, I'm so shocked he said something conversational to me beyond "Hey, pass me the test tube." My throat dries up and I'm somehow rendered speechless, which never happens.

He shakes his head once, tilting it to the side. "Hello? Can you not speak?"

"I'm—uh." I shrug and look away from him. "I'm anxious." I close my eyes briefly, silently cursing myself.

Why did I say that?

"About what?" The curiosity in his tone is unmistakable.

I shrug, still keeping my head averted. "Nothing." No way can I tell him. He'll just make fun of me.

"Uh huh." Clearly he doesn't believe me. And since when does he manage to come to class early? He usually runs in late, causing Curtin to scold him, not like Ash cares. He pretty much does what he wants, when he wants. Well, within reason.

Mostly he avoids spending time with me as much as possible.

"Benny boy finally gonna work up the nerve to ask you out?" Ash asks nonchalantly.

My jaw drops open again and I turn to look at him. How does he know I like Ben Murray? And wait a minute—does he know something I don't? Is he friends with Ben? Ha, doubtful. "What are you talking about?"

"It's pretty obvious. You two keep eye fucking each other at lunch." Ash shrugs and looks away. "He needs to make a move."

"You're so gross." The words leave me before I can check myself, and I wince, ready for him to say something worse. But I mean, really. Eye-fucking? Ben and I don't do that.

Do we?

"Why? Because I speak the truth?" He shifts closer to the table, propping his forearms on the edge. "He needs to put a

31

lockdown on that before someone else sneaks in and steals you from him."

I make a face. "Like that's going to happen."

Ash raises his brows, glancing over at me once more. "Wanna make a bet?"

I stare at him, confused by the tone of his voice. He made that question sound downright...suggestive. As if he knows someone who's interested in me.

As if that someone could be...

Him.

No. No, no, no.

We hate each other.

His eyes suddenly light up, and he snaps his fingers. "I know why you're excited."

I frown. He changes subjects so fast, I'm going to get whiplash. "Why?"

"You think you're gonna get nominated for homecoming."

Oh. I did *not* want him to figure that out. "No, I don't." I protest too quickly, and he knows it.

"Yes, you do." He shifts closer to me, and I turn and glare at him. "You think you're going to be a pretty little princess on the stage at the homecoming game?"

I snort and immediately regret it. That sounded disgusting. "No, not at all."

"Uh huh. Well, just so you know..." His voice drifts and he shakes his head, his lips forming a tight line. "Never mind."

Now I'm curious. "Just so I know what?"

He waves a hand. "It doesn't matter."

I hate when people do this sort of thing. It is truly the absolute worst. "No, tell me. What is it?"

His expression turns serious. Like, deadly serious. "You're going to think I'm stupid. Or worse, you won't believe me."

My mind is scrambling. What in the world is he talking about? "Tell me."

Those dark eyes stare into mine, and I can see the eternal struggle. Whatever it is, he's not sure if he should say it.

Meaning he's probably going to insult me.

He mutters something I can't make out and shifts closer, his head angled toward mine, and he cups his hand around my ear, rough fingers brushing my skin, causing me to shiver.

I hope he didn't notice. He's the type of boy who'd use my body's uncontrolled reaction against me. He'd turn it into something dirty, and I don't have those sorts of thoughts about him. No way.

Uh uh.

"Don't tell anyone," he whispers into my ear, pausing for a moment. His breath is hot, smells like cinnamon, and I swear he just licked his lips. Wait a minute, did he actually touch my ear with his *tongue?* "But I voted for you."

He pulls away right at the exact moment the bell rings and Curtin immediately launches into a lecture. I don't hear anything the teacher says. I don't notice if Asher is laughing at me or not. I feel like I'm in shock, frozen in place as the same questions keep running through my mind.

Asher Davis voted for me for homecoming princess? And did he really just lick my ear? What a perv!

What's worse?

I kind of liked it.

When the announcement comes seven minutes before class is over and Mrs. Adney reads my name just as I secretly predicted, I can't help it.

I'm beaming with pride.

My smile fades in an instant when I hear Ash's name announced too. My gaze flicks to where he's sitting and he appears shocked. My friend Kaya was nominated as well, along with her boyfriend. Another couple was nominated too. Tradition is everyone pairs up and runs together during homecoming week, participating in the games and dressing up together. Which means...

"Looks like it's you and me," Ash says when the announcements are over. He smiles, his dark eyes glittering. "Hope Ben doesn't mind."

I don't know how I'm going to survive this.

CHAPTER 6

"*H*ere." I pull a reusable shopping bag from my backpack and drop it on the table, pushing it toward Ash. "This is for you."

The wary expression on his face is new, one I've never seen before. It's like he doesn't trust me. "What is it?" He stares at the bag like there's a snake inside that's going to bite him.

"Clothes and costumes." It's Friday, and we've never talked about what we're going to do or wear for homecoming week. We were nominated two weeks ago, so this is kind of ridiculous.

But after asking around some, I found out this is fairly normal, especially for those who are running together but aren't *together* together. The girls usually arrange everything and the boys are clueless. They always just do what they're told and suffer through the dress-up days and games they have to play.

So unfair.

He frowns. "Clothes and costumes for what?"

I roll my eyes. "Homecoming. You know, it's next week?"

"I know that." He sounds defensive as he reaches for the bag and peeks inside. His lip curls as he reaches into the bag and pulls out a pair of navy-and-white checked fleece pajama pants. "What's up with these?"

"Monday is pajama day." I do my best to keep my tone even. Pleasant. "So we'll wear matching PJs and T-shirts."

"Aren't you cute? With the PJs?" He's mimicking me, his voice rising to a higher pitch. "I think you just want to think about the two of us in bed together, Callahan."

"Stop it." I yank the pants out of his hands and stuff them back into the bag. "Your stupid remarks are just that: stupid. If you want to win, we have to dress up together and match. Plus we have to play the games together and actually try to win. Participation counts."

"Maybe I don't want to play the games."

"Then we won't win."

"Maybe I don't want to do that either."

I roll my eyes, but deep down inside, I'm worried. I'm dying to win, not that I can ever admit it to him. But I won't win if I have to carry Ash through the entire week while he does nothing. "Come on. Winning won't be that bad."

"If I have to play a bunch of stupid games to win, then it's going to suck." He slumps in his chair and crosses his arms, reminding me of a big ol' baby.

Maybe I need to approach this in a way that will matter to him. "Won't winning homecoming prince, like, earn you status with girls or whatever? If you win, they'll all know who you are."

"The only girl I want to notice me hates me." He sends me a knowing look and I can't help but think—yet again—that he's talking about me. If I said that, he'd say the world doesn't revolve around me and I'd end up feeling stupid. So I keep my mouth shut. "She's not interested. She never will be."

"You don't know that for sure." My voice goes soft and I

lean toward him a little bit, like an idiot. "She might be interested."

Those brown eyes meet mine, and I lose myself for a second in their depths. He has the darkest eyes I've ever seen. They're beautiful.

They're also unnerving.

He sits up straighter, his arms dropping to his sides. "She's not my type. I'm wasting my time."

Mr. Curtin enters the class and I turn away from Ash, focusing my attention on what the teacher is writing on the board. Forcing myself to not think about what Ash said. Yet his words run through my head over and over, on a continuous loop. Who is he talking about? It can't be me. I'm reading too much into his words. He's not interested in me. He thinks I'm gross, just like I think he's gross. He's not my type. At all. I need to make a move on someone safe and sweet. Someone like Ben.

The problem with Ben? He's safe and sweet and also clueless. As in, I don't think he realizes that I like him so much. If he did, he'd ask me out, right? We'd at least be talking, like seriously.

I can't help but notice when Ash discreetly stuffs the bag I brought him into his backpack that's sitting on the floor, then zips it up. He glances up at me and catches me watching him, his hair flopping over his forehead and hanging in his eyes. I blink away, my stomach doing that weird twisty thing it does when I think about Ash for too long.

I need to stop thinking about him. So I do.

I do it so well, I don't even notice halfway through class that he's trying to get my attention. He taps the edge of the old table extra hard, causing Curtin to pause in his lecture for the briefest moment before he resumes, and I look at Ash to see he's now lightly tapping the edge of his notebook with his pen.

Glancing down, I see he's written something. A note.
For me.

What do I wear Monday?

Pressing my lips together, I flip to an empty page in my notebook and write him a response.

The pajamas. I left a note in the bag listing what to wear each day.

He reads my reply and pulls the notebook toward him before he hunches over and starts writing again, biting his lower lip in concentration.

Like a complete dork, I can't help but stare. He's extra attractive for some reason, and maybe that's because he's not saying rude things or taunting me. He's treating me...normal, and I like it.

I'm startled when he moves the notebook closer to me so I can read what he wrote.

I don't own a suit.

My heart falls. He needs to dress up a little bit for coronation night. I love the dress I found last weekend when Kaya, our friend Daphne, and I dragged my mom to the mall the next town over. We shopped for hours. Mom never complained once when Kaya and I tried on dress after dress, Daphne offering up her opinions, the both of us moaning and groaning we were never going to find anything.

Well, I eventually found what I wanted, and so did Kaya. Mom didn't say I told you so, but the smug smile on her face as we drove home told me that's what she was thinking. Daphne reassured us that we both chose gorgeous dresses, and we were glad we brought her. She's our most honest friend, and you need that type of friend when dress shopping for one of the most important nights of your life.

Realizing Ash is waiting for me to respond, I scribble something quick.

Do you have a button-down shirt?

His gaze meets mine and he slowly shakes his head.

How about a pair of black pants?

Reaching over, his arm presses against mine as he writes on my notebook this time.

Black jeans.

He doesn't remove his arm from where it rests next to mine, and I'm tingling. Literally tingling all over just from that simple contact. I don't move my arm either. His is warm and strong, and I know that's his throwing arm. Where all the power lies, as my father might say.

Okay, maybe he wouldn't say that. I think I've been reading too many love stories about football players on Wattpad lately. My secret addiction.

Are they faded? I write.

Ash frowns, his eyebrows crinkling. I write some more.

The jeans.

He shakes his head. Still doesn't remove his arm.

Then they should be fine. Just make sure they're clean!

Oh my God, I sound like a total mom. I sort of want to slap my forehead, but I restrain myself.

But he doesn't call me out on it. Instead, he scribbles across the paper:

I'll work on finding a shirt.

I'm about to write a response when the classroom phone rings and Mr. Curtin stops lecturing to go answer it. The entire class starts talking in a low murmur and I glance over at Ash to find he's already looking at me, his dark brown gaze unreadable.

"I'll look for a shirt this weekend," he tells me, finally removing his arm from where it rested against mine. His voice, his entire demeanor is nonchalant. Like this moment we just shared was no big deal. To him, it probably wasn't. I'm the one who's making something out of nothing. "I might be able to scrub one up, or borrow a shirt from somebody."

"Okay." My voice cracks and I clear my throat, feeling dumb. This was nothing.

Nothing.

And when he zooms out of class the moment the bell sounds, his actions confirm my thoughts.

Nothing at all.

CHAPTER 7

"*I* miss you."

I turn at the sound of the male voice behind me, shocked to discover it's Ben standing there with a forlorn expression on his cute face. And I really do mean it when I call Ben cute. He's got golden hair that curls at the ends, he's really tan and he has bright blue eyes. He had a total glow up over the summer, growing a few inches so now he's just under six feet, and he's not as scrawny as he was when we were freshmen. I liked him back then too, but he didn't really notice me.

At least, I don't think he did.

Smiling brightly, I tilt my head to the side. "What do you mean, you miss me?"

My heart is thundering in my chest as I wait for his reply. It's just before lunch, and I need to go meet Asher in the quad so we can play our homecoming-themed game. The nominees are supposed to participate every day. We won our round Monday playing a complicated ring-toss game that involved me sitting on Ash's shoulders.

Talk about awkward.

Yesterday, we came in second with the build-a-snowman game. It's not easy wrapping a dozen rolls of toilet paper around Ash in a quick manner. I kept having to touch him and it made me nervous.

Yay. More awkwardness.

Today is Wednesday, the last day of games and I'm glad.

I'm so over the game thing.

"I haven't really seen you or talked to you at lunch this whole week," Ben explains, offering me a shy smile. Ughhh, so adorable.

"It's only been two days," I remind him.

"Two days too long," he says in reply, his smile growing.

If Kaya were with us, she'd be digging her elbow in my ribs and practically bouncing with excitement. She's wanted something to happen between Ben and me since summer.

Looks like she might finally get her wish. And I'll get my wish too.

"One more day of games, and then it's over," I tell Ben before I glance over my shoulder. Most everyone is already gathered in the quad, and I spot Ash standing next to the student council teacher, watching us.

He looks away when I catch him.

"Good." Ben reaches out and tugs on the end of my braid. It's tourist day today, and I'm wearing a pair of khaki shorts that are probably *too* short, a Hawaiian print shirt that Daphne loaned me, and I did my hair in two French braids. Plus I'm rocking the black socks and Birkenstocks look, which turns my outfit from cute to dork. Ash is wearing a T-shirt that says *Stay HI in Hawaii*, which he borrowed from one of his teammates, and a pair of too-long denim shorts that should be ridiculous on him, yet somehow he still manages to look decent.

It's so irritating.

"Yo Callahan!" I wince, recognizing Ash's voice. I don't

bother looking back at him. "Get over here! You're holding up the game!"

Offering Ben a sympathetic smile, I decide to go for it and reach out, grabbing his hand and giving it a quick squeeze. "I'll see you later?"

He appears pleasantly shocked by my bold move. "I'll see you at coronation tonight."

My heart races. "You'll be there?"

Ben nods. "Wouldn't miss it."

"Callahan!" Ash screams.

"Sorry. Gotta go," I whisper to Ben before I take off into a run and head for the quad. I come to a stop next to the vice principal, who sends me a pointed look.

"Nice of you to finally show up, Miss Callahan," Mrs. Adney says before she launches into an explanation of today's game.

And oh God, I don't know if I want to do this.

"I'm fast," Ash tells me once they've handed out the sacks. His expression is full-on serious when he asks, "Are you fast?"

I shrug, nerves already eating at me. "I've never won a race before, if that's what you're asking."

He glances around as if he's making sure no one's listening, before he ducks his head and lowers his voice. "Listen, just hold on to me and let me do all the work."

"How am I supposed to do that?" We're competing in a sack race. The couples each have one leg in the sack and have to hobble together across the lawn that slopes toward the student parking lot. Whoever crosses the finishing line first wins.

I can tell Ash really wants to win this one.

"Follow my lead."

Once the freshman nominees compete—and it ends with one couple in a tangle on the ground and the other two practically tying, it's our turn. My palms are sweating and I curse my shoe choice as I slip my left leg into the sack after Ash has already inserted his right one.

"Birks?" Ash slowly shakes his head, his lips thinning. "We're fucked."

"You're wearing flip flops," I accuse, because he is.

"Kicked them off." He lifts the leg that's not in the sack to show me his bare foot. "You should take yours off too."

Somehow I manage to take off both Birks and Daphne appears out of nowhere, grabbing them from me and wishing us good luck. I gasp when Ash wraps his arm around my shoulders. "Put your arm around me," he commands, and I glare at him. "Do it before they blow the whistle."

I hate when people boss me around, but I do what he says, slipping my arm around his broad back just below his shoulders. The way we're positioned is both intimate and awkward, and now it's not just my palms that are sweating, and when that whistle blows I feel like I'm propelled forward by Ash.

He clutches me to him, his left hand holding one side of the sack, my right hand holding the other. Kaya and her boyfriend are next to us, and I glance over at her just as they both tumble to the ground.

"Focus!" Ash yells, and I stare straight ahead, my gaze zeroing in on that finish line that's just out of reach. I do my best to keep up with his strides, but I'm short and my boobs are jiggling extra because like a dummy I wore a bralette today instead of a regular bra.

Suddenly Ash's arm tightens around me and I swear to God, he lifts me off the ground and we really start moving, my fingers still grasping the edge of the sack. He's huffing and puffing, and I'm huffing and puffing, and everyone watching us is yelling and screaming and jumping up and down. All I can think about is how Ash is lifting me with just one arm.

He is so freaking strong.

We barely make it across the finish line before we collapse into a heap on the ground, me landing right on top of Ash with a loud *oof*. He rolls so I'm pinned beneath him, and I glare up at him, my chest rising and falling, his chest rising and falling, his hips nestled between mine.

It's all I can focus on, that spot where we're pressed up tight against each other. Liquid heat pools there and I part my lips, though I can't find any words.

"We fucking won. Good job, Callahan," he mutters before he leans in and brushes the quickest kiss to my cheek, startling me completely. Then he's kicking off the sack from our legs and someone pulls him into a standing position. I rise to my feet shakily and stand beside him, squealing with pure joy when Adney yanks my arm and Ash's arm up in a victory pose.

People are laughing and clapping, including my best friend, who appears genuinely happy I won despite the fact that we just beat them. Daphne wraps me up in a big hug, bouncing up and down with me, the both of us laughing. I revel in the moment, cracking up when Mrs. Adney pins a blue ribbon first on Ash's chest, then on mine. I'm beaming as someone from the yearbook staff takes our photo, and when I spot Ben smiling at me and giving me a thumbs-up, I can't help but smile back.

And think of Ash and the way he kissed me the entire time.

* * *

"Please, just—don't give them a stupid answer, okay?" I offer Ash a smile, but he just rolls his eyes, continuously running his fingers through his hair. I'm sure he thinks he's straightening it out, but he's only making a bigger mess of it.

It's Wednesday night. Coronation. We're backstage at the student theater, waiting for them to call us out. The freshmen are currently on stage, the girls pretty and the boys awkward, all of them making a mess of their answers when they're asked questions like *What does school spirit mean to you?*

I have no idea how I'd answer either, but I'm sure I'll do better than anyone on that stage right now.

The seniors are in a different area, not that I'm surprised. They don't want to deal with lower classmen. The juniors are in their own little world, talking amongst themselves, so it's just up to us sophomores to make the best of it.

"Nervous?" Kaya asks me.

I nod, swallowing hard. My mouth is so dry. I might end up a sputtering mess. My parents are out there, as well as my brothers and sister. God, I think Uncle Owen and his wife, my Aunt Chelsea are with them too, along with my cousins. Mom wanted to make sure I had solid family representation tonight and I didn't want her to make a big deal out of it, but I couldn't stop her. Neither could Dad.

"Me too." Kaya offers me a kind smile just before she leans in and whispers, "I think you're going to win."

"What? No way." She and Jaden have been together for seven months. They're the most popular couple in our class. They've got this.

"Want to make a bet?" Kaya raises a brow.

"I don't want to win. Then we'll have to be in the parade and I'll have to go out at halftime when Coach will want to keep me in the locker room to strategize," Jaden gripes. They may be popular, and Jaden plays football with Ash, but he's the most low-key guy I know.

"Don't worry about it." Kaya jabs Jaden in the ribs. She has the most pointiest elbows ever, I swear. She returns her attention to me, her expression shrewd. "I saw you and Ben talking earlier. What's going on between you two?"

"Not too much." I don't want to discuss Ben right now, not in front of Ash. He'll just make fun of us later in class.

"Uh huh." Kaya's eyes gleam, her mouth popping open to ask yet another question when a couple of leadership kids come over to where we're waiting, interrupting her.

Thank God.

We line up, watching as the freshmen exit the stage, including the newly crowned freshman prince and princess. My nerves ratchet up, my breaths coming faster, and Ash grabs hold of my hand, pulling my arm through his.

"Calm down, Callahan. You've got this," he reassures me in that arrogant way of his. He somehow found not only a white button-down shirt but also a black tie, and his jeans are in perfect condition. He looks dressed up without trying too hard.

Me? I look like I tried too hard, but I don't care. My dress is a dark silvery gray with a lace overlay and a short, flared skirt. The top covers me up so my boobs aren't spilling out, which they already want to do. Even if I don't win, I still feel like a princess, and I love it.

Not gonna lie, sure would be nice to win that crown, though.

We stand on the stage and they announce our names, reading off the short bios we all had to turn in a few weeks ago. The longer I stand there, the more wobbly my knees get, and I clutch Ash's arm tight, clinging to him. He shifts closer, as if he knows I need him to hold me up and keep my focus on the audience. My mom and dad are sitting in the front row, Ava and Jake and Beck sitting in between them, and I don't look at them for too long. I might start crying or something stupid like it.

When it's finally our turn to talk, we approach the host—

the junior class president—and I have to answer the question first.

"Who's the person who's influenced you the most?"

I gaze out at the audience, my smile firmly in place as I say, "I'd have to say it's my mom. She takes care of our family, my dad, my brothers and sisters and me. She always listens to me without judgment, and she makes time for all of us no matter what. Plus she's a lot of fun. I like spending time with her and I basically want to be her when I grow up."

The applause makes me stand up straighter, and I swear I hear a loud sniffle—probably got Mom right smack in the feels. I'm still smiling when they ask Ash his question.

"If you could have any superpower, what would it be?"

Ash makes a face like he's concentrating, and a few people in the audience—mostly girls—giggle. I'm sure he has a fan club that came in his support tonight. So many girls in our class—and a few freshman too—have major crushes on him.

"I'd want to be able to read minds. So I'd know exactly what everyone's thinking," Ash says.

"You sure about that?" the announcer says jokingly. "Some things you might not want to know."

"True. But then again, there are some things I *do* want to know." Ash looks over at me. Like he wants to read my mind.

That would be disastrous.

Within minutes, they're ready to announce the winners, and the anticipation is nearly killing me. I wait breathlessly, almost crumpling with relief when they announce my name.

And Ash's too.

The couples that run together don't always win together too, but it's happening for us, and honestly I couldn't be happier. We worked really hard for it this week. The costumes, the games, trying to show we have school spirit. Plus, I had cheer practice every day this week, getting our halftime routine perfected. It's been exhausting.

The moment they set that crown on my head and place the flowers in my arms, I know it's all been worth it.

Within minutes of us being hustled onto the stage, we're ushered backstage just as quick, and I'm bouncing up and down in my too-tight heels, my hand resting on my head, tracing the edge of the tiara. Ash is watching me, amusement lighting his eyes, his homecoming royalty sash hanging from his chest crookedly. Unable to help myself, I reach out and straighten it, my fingers brushing against his shirt, and I can feel the warmth emanating from his skin, even through the fabric.

"Are you actually helping me out, Callahan?" He sounds surprised yet pleased.

"It was crooked." I shrug. "And hey, we won!"

"I know." He leans back against the wall, his arms crossed, a satisfied smile on his face. "I knew I'd win."

"You did not." I shove at his shoulder, which is like pushing a brick wall. He might only be fifteen, but he's solid.

"I definitely knew you'd win." His voice goes serious. "Everyone loves you."

"Not true." I can think of at least five people who don't like me, but I don't want to list them. "But I guess just enough people do, because we got the votes."

"It was the sack race," he tells me, and we go back and forth like this for the rest of the time we're waiting backstage, until we're called out one last time when the coronation ends. I'm immediately swarmed by my family, my mom and aunt fighting to hug me first, my dad telling me he's proud of me like I won the big game, and my Uncle Owen giving me knuckles like he's always done since I was about three.

It feels good, to have everyone I love surrounding me, telling me how happy they are for me, taking photos with me. My friends gather around and we all pose for endless photos, including me and Kaya, then me and Daphne, then all three of us together. Kaya's mom gives me a big hug and tells me she misses me, and I reassure her I'm definitely coming over to stay over after the homecoming dance on Saturday night.

Eventually, they all start asking for photos of Ash and me together, and we pose for a few for my parents, for my friends, for the yearbook staff yet again. Our arms are around each other loosely, as if we're afraid to touch each other too close, and I prefer the distance. Especially when I spot Ben making his way toward us, clutching a single red rose in his hand.

"For you," Ben says once he's standing in front of us. Ash releases his hold on me, and I'm suddenly in Ben's arms as he pulls me in for a hug. He feels safe, he smells good too, and when I withdraw, he thrusts the rose in between us and I take it, sniffing the delicate flower. "Congratulations."

"Thank you," I murmur, smiling up at him. No boy has given me flowers before.

"I can't believe you won," Ben says. "You looked pretty up there." His cheeks turn pink with the admission, and I can't help but be charmed.

I swear I hear Ash mutter something rude under his breath.

"Thank you," I say again, because I don't know what else to say, especially with Ash standing behind us. Listening in, most likely.

"Honey," Mom calls to me from where she's standing, chatting with Kaya's mom. "You almost ready to go?"

"Yeah. Give me another minute," I tell her before I return my attention to Ben. He's not even looking at my dad, who's standing next to Mom, and that's a first for me too. Every boy I know at school stares at my father with reverence.

But Ben only has eyes for me.

"You're going to the dance Saturday, right?" he asks me.

I nod, barely able to contain my smile. "Are you?"

"Yeah." He's smiling too. "Save a dance for me, okay?"

"I will!" I say too eagerly, waving at him before he walks away. Yet I don't care if I looked like an idiot just now. I'm on too much of a high to bother with playing it cool. Though I wish he would've asked me to be his actual date for the dance.

Once Ben's gone, I turn to find Ash is standing there by himself, looking kind of lost. I glance around, curious to know what his mom might look like, but I'm starting to think...

"Is no one here for you?" I ask him.

He shrugs, shoving his hands in his front pockets and looking down at the ground. "My mom couldn't make it."

"Oh." And I already know his dad isn't here anymore. "How are you getting home?"

"I've got a ride." He flicks his head in the direction of a couple of guys I don't know personally, but I'm pretty sure they're seniors. They have that hardened look to them, the one that tells you they most likely do drugs and cause trouble. I don't know why I think that, but I do, and I wonder if that's what Ash is going to turn into someday.

Maybe.

But maybe I'm also being totally judgmental.

"Ben was right. You looked good up there tonight, Callahan," Ash says sincerely.

My heart tightens in my chest. "Thanks," I say, my voice squeaky. "You did too."

He glances down at himself. "I clean up okay, I guess."

"You do," I agree, happy to make him smile. My heart starts thumping and I realize Ash's compliment made me happier than Ben's.

And I don't know how to feel about that.

CHAPTER 8

"*H*ere's your ride." Of course it's Mr. Curtin who's showing Ash and I what car we're in for Friday's homecoming parade. The parade is short—it only lasts about thirty minutes and goes for a mile or two. But it's so much fun with the homecoming court riding in classic cars and the band playing, the cheer team marching—I'm not joining them this year—and the football team walking and shouting along the parade route, getting the crowd pumped up. Teachers and office staff decorate golf carts and throw candy at the spectators, plus each class decorates a float.

Ash and I, along with the rest of the homecoming royalty and remaining senior nominees, get to ride in each of their own cars. Meaning *we* get our own car. We're in the backseat. Just the two of us.

Alone.

Together.

Well, the driver is accompanying us, a nice older gentleman who offers us a kind smile as he opens the back door, introducing himself as Lou as we climb into the car.

I'm in my cheer uniform because we have to perform at the rally after the parade, plus I've got on my tiara and sash. My hair is a little out there, with braids and white ribbon that the entire cheer team is wearing too, and I have face paint on my cheeks. I'm sure I look silly, nothing like I did on Wednesday night, though Ash isn't dressed up either. He's wearing his football jersey and jeans, his dark hair a complete mess, and the royalty sash hangs from him as if it's going to drop off his body at any second.

"Ladies first," Ash says as he waves a hand at me to enter the car before him. I'm reluctant to go, since I'm wearing my uniform and the skirt is short, like it's supposed to be, and I don't want Ash to stare at my butt.

Can't prevent it, though, so I get into the car, keeping hold of my skirt the entire time so I don't flash him.

Ash climbs in after me, Lou shuts the door, and then we play the waiting game, all the cars and floats and everyone else lined up for the parade as they get ready for us to start moving at ten o'clock on the dot.

We remain quiet for so long, it becomes awkward. Lou ignores us, fiddling with the car radio until he finds an oldies station and turns up the volume. I'm assuming it's sixties music, and it's kind of awful, not what I like at all, but I remain quiet, glancing out the window and willing the time away.

This moment is supposed to be fun, a high school experience I'll never forget, and instead I'm wishing it was already over.

What's wrong with me?

Deciding I'm going to be the one who breaks first, I finally have to say something to Ash so we can make conversation. "Nervous about tonight's game?"

He shakes his head, keeping his face averted as he

continues to stare out his window. "Nah. We're on a streak right now."

The JV team is having a better season than the varsity team, and I've heard a lot of that is credited to Ash. He has a great arm, according to my father. And an accurate throw. Dad can't wait to get him on the varsity team next season. It's weird, knowing how impressed my father is with Ash, when I'm not that impressed with him myself.

Liar.

"Feeling pretty confident you'll win then?" I ask.

"I don't want to sound like an asshole, but…" He finally turns to look at me, his mouth stretched into that familiar cocky smile. "Yeah."

I smile in return, unable to help myself. "Wait until you play on the varsity team next year."

"I can't wait. A lot of us are excited to move up so we can work more with your dad," Ash says.

My smile fades. I wonder if that's why Ash is nice to me sometimes. Because of my dad. I've heard a lot of the boys in my class are actually afraid to talk to me because of him, and that kind of sucks. The only boy I really want talking to me is Ben, and he doesn't seemed fazed by my father whatsoever.

So that's kind of nice.

"Listen, I'm not looking to get a pussy shot like the rest of those assholes were last year," Ash says, earning a hard stare from Lou in the rearview mirror. Ash, as per usual, completely ignores him, while I'm slowly dying of mortification. "I'm not talking you up so I can get closer to your superstar pops."

No one has ever referred to Drew Callahan as my *superstar pops* before. "My dad would probably smack you upside the head for calling him that."

"Your dad *has* smacked me upside the head for saying something much worse," Ash says, making me laugh.

"I'm sure he has," I say.

He sobers up fast. "You know I'm not using you to get closer to your dad, if that's what you're worried about."

How did he know that was on my mind? I don't like how perceptive he is. "I didn't think that."

"Sure you didn't, Callahan," he says slowly.

"Seriously."

"Seriously." He mimics me, repeating the word with his voice high pitched, and I really hate that.

I reach out, ready to punch him, but he's quicker than me, grabbing my wrist and stopping me before my fist makes contact with his upper arm. "Let me go," I tell him through clenched teeth.

He only tightens his grip on my wrist. "None of this has to do with your dad."

"None of what?" I jerk against his hold, but he still doesn't let go.

"What's going on between us."

"Nothing's going on between us." I sound way too sure of myself.

He lets go of me, and I immediately miss his touch, which is so stupid, I want to slap myself. "You go ahead and keep telling yourself that."

I gape at him, trying to come up with something to say, and at that exact moment, Lou puts the car into gear and it lurches forward, my body toppling over as if I have no control over myself. Again with the quick reflexes, Ash grabs me before I face plant against the back of the bench seat, his hands gripping my upper arms as he carefully settles me onto our seat once more.

"Thanks," I mumble, annoyed that he just came to my rescue.

"Gotta be careful," he warns, but I ignore him. Instead, I turn toward the open window, smiling when I spot people I know from school standing on the side of the road. They see me too and start waving, and I wave back, laughing when they shout my name.

It's like this for the entire parade, both of us preoccupied with waving out our respective windows, our hands braced on the empty spot between us, our fingers brushing against each other's for the entire two-mile drive. Ash eventually curls his pinky finger around mine and I don't pull away. I hardly move for fear he'll shift his hand away from mine completely. It's the stupidest thing ever, but I don't want to lose the connection, no matter how minuscule it is.

Seems like he doesn't want to lose it either.

No one dresses up for our homecoming dance, thank God, so the pressure is off tonight. I show up at the dance with Kaya, Daphne, and a few other friends, since we all got ready at Kaya's house together. I'm tempted, but I end up telling no one about my encounter with Ash in the car, though I don't even know how I'd describe it. That we held pinky fingers like a couple of kindergarteners? That once we climbed out of the car, we never spoke again for the rest of the day or night? Even when we walked out onto the football field together with the rest of the homecoming court during halftime? It was weird, how we remained silent the entire time.

I don't understand what's happening between us, so I can't really tell anyone else about it either. It's my little secret.

Our little secret.

We're thirty minutes late to the dance, but that's okay since things really don't get started until the dance is about an hour in. Jaden's waiting for Kaya when we arrive, so he sweeps her away and I know I won't see her until we ride home together.

The rest of us go out on the dance floor and jump around to the beat of a popular song, singing along with the lyrics as loud as we can, making asses of ourselves. Daphne and I hold hands and dance around in a circle, laughing and screaming at the top of our lungs. The seniors send us withering stares and the freshmen jump right along with us, and while I'm excited to be a junior next year so I won't be treated like such a little kid any longer, I know I can let loose and be silly tonight and not really care about anyone judging me.

I am, after all, the homecoming princess of the sophomore class, right? I have to use that for as long as I can, because I'm thinking my expiration card is happening by the end of this dance.

Ben magically appears, and I'm so glad to see him. Within seconds he's dancing with our group, smiling at me as he shakes his hair out of his eyes. I let him monopolize me, because he's the reason I'm here tonight. He asked me to save a dance for him, and I want to save all of my dances for him. I've had a crush on him for so long, and finally, *finally* he seems to be just as into me as I'm into him.

It feels good, to have his attention. He grabs me a bottle of water and stays with me when we decide to sit out for a few songs. His friends come around and they join us, and soon we're all talking and laughing and having a good time. My friends are sitting with us too, and eventually so are Kaya and Jaden, which is a pleasant surprise. I feel good, sitting among my friends, laughing at someone's dumb joke, Kaya collapsing onto my side when Jaden says something that strikes her funny.

That's what I want, I think as I watch her and Jaden. I want a relationship like that, where they can joke and laugh and hug and sneak away so they can kiss for a while. They're like friends, but better. They sort of remind me of my parents, though I know they're probably nothing like them, considering we're only fifteen and I can already hear Mom saying you won't find your true love at such a young age.

But what does she know?

We're still all grouped together, the dancing long forgotten, when I finally spot Ash enter the building, sauntering in as if he owns the place. I know he doesn't see me, I'm so completely surrounded by people, which means I can totally spy on him without his noticing me.

He glances around, like he's looking for someone, and there's no way he's looking for me. That's just me being a complete egomaniac.

The moment he finds me, it's like I can feel his gaze. It settles over me, heavy and brooding, and when I glance up, he's got that exact look on his face.

Heavy and brooding.

He's not bright and sunny like Ben. He's dark and foreboding, like a stormy night.

Yet here I am. Drawn to the darkness when I should be seeking the light.

"Hey." I settle my hand on Ben's knee and he turns to look at me, seemingly shocked by my touching him so freely. "I'll be right back." I stand up and stretch my arms above my head, fighting the nervous tussling in my stomach.

He glances up at me with a frown. "Everything okay?"

"I'm good," I reassure him. Reassure myself. "Just want to go say hi to someone real quick."

Ben reaches out and squeezes my hand, and I study our linked fingers. I wait for the tingles, for the warm, fuzzy feeling to envelop me.

It doesn't happen.

I pull away from Ben and push my way out of the crowd, then walk across the room, heading straight for Ash. He's leaning against the wall, chatting with those same guys he rode home with on coronation night, and I walk right up to him, reminding myself I need to be bold.

Ask for what I want.

"Can I talk to you?"

That's how I approach him, and I know he's surprised. He looks me up and down slowly, as if he's undressing me with his eyes, which I always thought was a totally gross saying, but no. It's true. That's exactly how he's examining me, and my skin is growing warmer the more his gaze lingers on particular spots.

There's the warm and fuzzy feelings. The tingling. It only happens when I'm with Asher Davis.

"No *hey, how you doing*, huh, Callahan? You're just ready to get down to it?" His tone is amused, yet...

He manages to make what what's happening between us sound dirty, and maybe that's because I'm thinking vaguely dirty things, I don't know.

"Please?" I don't want to beg, but he needs to know I'm serious about this. I really, really need to talk to him. Or... whatever with him.

"Come on." He pushes away from the wall and I follow after him, my gaze drinking him in just like he did to me only moments ago. He's wearing a black T-shirt and a pair of jeans, nothing special about his outfit whatsoever, but he somehow makes it look extra good. The T-shirt is kind of tight, so it stretches across his chest and back, and the jeans mold to his legs and butt perfectly.

As in, he has a perfect butt.

Oh my God, I feel like a complete perv.

I follow him through an open door, down a short hallway, until we're tucked away into an alcove that I didn't even know existed. Of course Ash knows about this place. He probably brings girls here all the time so they can make out—

He pulls me into his arms and does just that. Kisses me. He pushes me against the wall, his body pressed tight against mine. His body is hard, hard, hard and his mouth his soft, soft, soft.

So soft.

When his tongue sneaks out to flicker against my lips, I gasp, allowing him entry. He deepens the kiss, his hand going up to cradle my cheek, his other hand gripping my waist as our tongues tangle and twist. This is my first real kiss and it's nothing like I thought it would be. All sweet, shy presses of lips and blushing cheeks, tentative touches and lots of awkward fumbling.

No, he's practically devouring me and I'm devouring him right back. Everything inside of me ratchets up, higher and higher. Hotter and hotter. My hands are in his hair and it's just as soft and silky as it looks. His hand slides down to cup my butt, tugging me even closer to him, and when his knee presses in between my legs, I gasp again. Louder this time.

He breaks the kiss, staring down at me, his chest rising and falling with his rapidly panting breaths. "Is that what you wanted to talk about?"

I blink up at him, sliding one hand down his neck to press against his chest. "Wh-what?"

One side of his mouth lifts in a smile. "That's what you said. You wanted to talk."

"I didn't—want to talk," I admit, sinking my teeth into my lower lip.

He groans, positively agonized, and the power that whips through me at the sound leaves me breathless. "Fuck, you make me crazy, Callahan."

Still calling me by my last name when I'm in his arms. It's so frustrating. I'm about to call him out on it when he kisses me again, making me forget what I wanted to say.

Making me forget everything.

We're like this for minutes. For what feels like hours, until I can feel my phone buzzing in the back pocket of my jeans and I know one of my friends—probably Kaya—is looking for me. I shove Ash away and pull my phone out to see I have about a bazillion texts from her.

Autumn.

Where are you?

Why aren't you answering your phone?

I'd accuse you of sneaking off with Ben but he's sitting right next to me.

Autumn?

AUTUMN!

Where the hell are you?????????

Hurriedly I type out a text, batting Ash's hands away from me when he tries to make a grab for my waist again. **Sorry, be there in a minute!**

The less I say, the better.

"I have to go," I tell him once I shove my phone into my pocket again.

He doesn't release his hold on me. Nope, he rests his hands on my waist and leans in, dropping delicate, damp kisses along my neck. Holy shit, that feels so good. "Not yet," he murmurs against my throat.

I shove at him, but that's like shoving at a steel wall. "Ash. Seriously."

"There you go again with the *seriously*." He lets me push him away, and he watches me, his swollen lips parted, his dark eyes hooded. His hair is a mess from my hands and he just had his tongue in my mouth only moments ago, and I can feel the warmth seep into me as I realize what just happened. I made out with Ash Davis. "When are you going to admit that you have a crush on me and not Ben?"

His question lures me out of my kiss-drunken state, and I

blink at him, hating how he's trying to make me confess I have a crush on him first. "What about you?"

"What about me?"

"Do you have a crush on me?" My heart is thumping so hard I swear it feels like it's climbing up my throat, ready to fly out of my mouth when I speak.

His hand rises, and he tugs on his bottom lip. "I don't know."

I.

Don't.

Know.

Frustration ripples through me, and I turn on my heel, making my way back into the gym where the dance is still going on. He follows after me, his fingers circling around my wrist, and I let him turn me around so I'm facing him.

"Why are you leaving?" He looks confused as hell.

Nice. I'm confused as hell too.

"Why can't you say how you feel?" The words blurt out of me as if I have no control, but I need to know. Why can't he tell me he likes me? What's the big deal?

Of course, I can barely confess my feelings to him. I don't understand my feelings for him either. I hate him.

I like him.

I'm drawn to him.

He repulses me.

Sometimes, I think I repulse him too.

"I don't really know how to feel…anything," he admits, and I know from the look on his face, his body language, that he means every word he says.

"Then neither do I," I lie before I run back into the gym.

Fighting back tears the rest of the night.

JUNIOR YEAR

CHAPTER 9

I'm a different person this year. I don't bother chasing after boys who don't know how to feel anymore. Talk about a waste of my time. Instead, I stick with the good ones, the solid ones who are there for you no matter what. Who don't push too hard and are easygoing to the point that sometimes I feel like the pushy one. The one who pokes and prods and makes too many demands.

But Ben Murray doesn't ever seem to mind. We've been together for six months. Since March, when I asked him to the Sadie's dance and he eagerly said yes. After the homecoming dance fiasco aka makeout session with Ash, I sort of withdrew from boys in general. I kept them all at a distance, figuring that none of them knew how to feel. I considered talking to Mom about it, but she'd only make excuses for Ash, so that wouldn't work. No way in hell could I talk to Dad. He had a thing for Ash I didn't quite understand, plus he doesn't want to hear me talking about kissing his future star quarterback.

Not that I *want* to tell Dad anything like that.

I fed Kaya bits and pieces but never told her exactly what

happened between Ash and me. How could I? I still don't quite understand it myself.

So I focused on school for the rest of my sophomore year, just as my parents wanted, and my report cards reflected that. I'm in student leadership this year, along with still being on the cheer team. I'm also taking advanced courses, so my homework load is major, but I'm making it happen. Ben's a big help. He's really smart and we actually go on study dates. I know my parents don't believe that's actually what we're doing, but guess what?

That's actually what we're doing.

Yeah, we kiss. Some nights we kiss a lot, and there are wandering hands involved too. I refuse to let him kiss me on campus. That's gross. We'll hug and hold hands. Everyone knows we're a couple, and we're at that age where a lot of us in my class have been in long-term relationships.

But I've never told Ben I love him. He's never said it to me either. I have friends who are in relationships where they say *I love you* within a week. That's moving way too fast for me. Almost like they say it only because they think they have to.

Love should be earned. And once earned, it should be considered precious. A gift. You give it away too freely, and it becomes meaningless.

Do I still see Ash at school? Of course I do. He's on the varsity football team this year, our quarterback, and I'm right there on the sidelines, cheering him—them—on. We've played four games so far this season and we've won all four of them. In fact, I'm walking to my car right now after a game, exhaustion making my steps slow. Fridays are the worst. The long day in class, the time after school where we're hanging out in the cheer room and getting ready before we finally go out and cheer at the game.

It's past ten, and my car is in the side lot at the high school where no one else really parks. My coach is still up in the cheer room, and I walked out to the parking lot with Kaya, who's also on the team with me this year. But she already took off with Jaden, who was waiting for her in his black Dodge Charger.

Meaning I'm all alone.

The school campus is sprawling, and this particular parking lot leads to the school bus and van parking area as well. No one's really out here at this time of night. The band room isn't too far from the cheer room, and I can hear some of the band members still calling to each other. See a few parents waiting in their parked cars for their kids to come out so they can leave. Normally I'm gone by now, but I helped our coaches put away some of our equipment, a duty those of us on the team trade off every time there's a home game.

Usually I leave with Ben. We go out for pizza with our friends, or sometimes we sit in his car at the park close to school, where we usually end up kissing for a while. But he's out of town this weekend. He's at some sort of bonding retreat for the basketball team and won't be back until Sunday night, so I won't see him at all. Which is probably a good thing. I need to clean my room. Catch up on laundry. All that boring stuff I usually push aside, which aggravates my parents to no end.

I hear a familiar voice call my name and I stop, glancing over my shoulder, but no one's there. Uneasiness sends a shiver down my spine and I look around, spotting a giant man sitting in an equally giant truck. I recognize him. A parent of one of the boys on the band's drum line. He doesn't know my name, so I know it's not him calling me, but it's reassuring to know someone is out here. I can scream bloody murder and he'll probably come running.

I've started walking again when I hear my name once more. Louder this time. Coming from my left. I turn, squinting into the darkness, and that's when I see a flame light up. A match. It illuminates his face, the sharp angle of his jaw. I recognize those dark eyes and the equally dark hair, and everything inside of me lights up like that match he's still holding.

Asher Davis, sitting in his vehicle.

"What do you want?" I call out to him, sounding completely put out. I don't want to talk to him.

I so want to talk to him.

He laughs and practically leans out the driver's side window. "Now that's a loaded question."

Rolling my eyes, I slowly approach his vehicle, a beat-up old truck that's probably seen better days, and those days were a long-ass time ago. I tell myself I shouldn't do this. Someone might see us—who, I'm not sure. All I'm doing is talking to him. Big deal. Is that such a crime?

Look at me mentally arguing with myself.

The passenger window is open and I lean into it, wrinkling my nose when the scent hits me. Ash is propped between the driver's seat and door, his gaze hooded, with what I think is a cigarette dangling from his mouth. Or maybe a joint, I don't know, so I decide to ask. "Are you smoking a joint on school property?"

"No." He plucks the cigarette from his mouth and shakes his head, laughing. "When did you turn into such a prim little maiden, Callahan?"

I can't even believe he called me a prim little maiden. Who says that? "Then what are you smoking?"

"Just a plain ol' cigarette. Looking for that nicotine rush," he says, as if that's the most logical answer ever. "I'm guessing since you can't distinguish between the two, you've never smoked a joint before?"

"No." No one I know smokes *actual* joints. They all use

wax pens, not that I ever have. Drugs scare me. Mom's preaching against them actually worked, at least with me.

"Have you ever vaped?"

"Ew, no." I shake my head. Thank God Ben isn't into vaping, though I know a few of his friends are. We've gone to parties together and drunk alcohol, but I'm always a little scared of losing control, so I keep it in check. "You?"

"No." He sucks on the cigarette and then blows the smoke out, filling the cab of his truck. "That shit will kill you."

Ah, the irony.

"And cigarettes won't." My voice is flat. I don't know why we're having this conversation. It's pointless.

It's like my feet are rooted to the spot, though. I haven't talked to him in almost a year. A *year*. That's insane.

"Not as fast as a fucking vape will. Don't you watch the news?" He doesn't give me time to answer. "Besides." He shrugs, leaning forward to stub out the cigarette in the ashtray that's near the gearshift. "I'll quit before I turn twenty."

"If you're still alive by then." The moment the words leave me, I feel bad. That was rude as hell to say to someone, even Ash.

But he's not offended. He's grinning at me like a big dope. "Nothing can kill me. I'm invincible. Didn't you see me out there?"

I'm guessing he's still feeling high from their win tonight. "You played a good game," I admit reluctantly.

"Took everything out of you to tell me that, didn't it?" His smile widens, if that's possible, and it's a sight to see. He's usually scowling when I see him on campus. Scowling on the football field right before he throws another amazing pass. Scowling whenever I pass him in the hallway or see him in the quad at lunch. Scowling in class—though we don't have any classes together this year, so I can't confirm if that's true or not.

Did I mention he transferred out of chemistry a week after our infamous makeout session? Yep, he sure did.

The coward.

When he's not scowling, he's got his tongue shoved down some other girl's throat. Usually during lunch. It's enough to make me want to lose my actual lunch, every time I see his possessive hands on a girl, their lips locked. It's so disgusting.

He's so disgusting.

He's all the rage, and I hate him for it.

"No. I can admit when you've played a good game," I tell him, hoping he sees that he has no effect on me whatsoever.

"Gee, thanks." He goes quiet, contemplating me. The way he watches me makes me want to squirm, and I wish I wasn't still in my cheer uniform. I feel super exposed right now. "Want to join me?"

"What? No." I stand up straight, my fingers still curled around the edge of the window. "I should go."

I *need* to go. I release my hold on the old glass, taking a step backward.

"What's the rush? Benny's not in town." The look in his eyes is a dare.

How the hell does he know this? Though we do go to a small school, so everyone knows everyone else's business. "I have to get home."

"Curfew?" He raises a brow, like a challenge.

"Not really." I shrug one shoulder. I'm lying. My parents want me home by midnight at the absolute latest, though there's a state curfew for new drivers like me and technically I shouldn't be driving after eleven.

"Then get in." He waves at the door. "Let's catch up."

I take one step closer as I contemplate him, my hand automatically going for the door handle. I shouldn't do this.

69

If I knew Ben was in a car with another girl, a girl he'd kissed before but never got around to telling me about it, I'd be mad.

Really mad.

"Come on." Ash's voice softens. "You know you want to."

Another dare.

Without thought I open the door and climb inside, falling onto the bench seat with a huff. I pull the creaky door shut, slamming it so hard the cab rattles from the force of it. Ash just studies me, seemingly surprised I'm actually inside his truck. My skirt rides up and I tug it back down as best I can, but my thighs are basically on full display and I feel totally exposed.

"You're a little rebel, aren't you?" He grabs the half-full pack of cigarettes from the dashboard and tugs one out, placing it in his mouth before a lighter magically appears. He holds it to the tip of the cigarette until it catches flame, then flicks off the lighter and tosses it onto the dash.

"I thought you had matches." I'm so lame for bringing this up, but I swore he lit a match when I first noticed him.

"I did. I do. I have matches, lighters—you name it, I light that shit on fire." He takes a drag from the cigarette, then averts his head, blowing the smoke out the window.

I think he did that for me, but I'm not going to look into it too much.

"I'm surprised you're not an arsonist." My tone is snotty, and I cross my arms, increasingly uncomfortable with how close we're sitting next to each other. I should leave. In fact, I'm reaching for the door handle, ready to make my escape, when he starts talking.

"I was an arsonist. When I was six." That's all he says. Just keeps taking drags on that cigarette, filling his lungs with smoke, blowing it out the window. Again and again. I can hear his lips making a sucking sound and the burn of the paper, and finally I can't stand it any longer.

I have to say something.

"What do you mean?"

Ash launches into his story right away. Makes me think he was just waiting for me to ask.

"I started a fire up by the lake. Not too far from your house, actually." He stares off into the distance, the memory coming back to him, I guess. "I liked fire. I always have. It fascinates me. I found my dad's lighter and I kept playing with it. Then I basically stole it. My parents were too busy arguing all the time to notice what I was doing, and I decided I wanted to make that silver lighter mine. So...one day we went to the lake to go fishing, my dad and me. And I brought my lighter with me. Kept it in my jeans pocket because it made me feel cool, you know? Right before we left, I lit a bush on fire and then ran for my dad's truck."

I'm gaping at him. I can feel my mouth opening and closing like a dying fish. "What happened after that?"

"The fucking brush caught everything around it on fire, that's what. Burned a couple hundred acres by the lake, even threatened a few houses at one point, but they were able to put it out pretty quickly." He shrugs again, but I see the way his eyes light up. Like the old story excites him. "They never did figure out who exactly started that fire."

"Who didn't? Your parents?"

"No, the arson investigators. I took the lighter with me, you see. Even back then, I guess I knew you can't leave evidence behind. Though it never happened again, because my dad sure as hell figured out it was me and he whooped my ass when he saw the fire reported on the news later that night. I loved seeing that news report, knowing I was the one who did it. Felt like a big secret that belonged to only me, but Dad knew. He always knew."

I don't know what to say. The fondness in Ash's voice is obvious. He loved his dad. And he lost him. I want to ask how, when, why, but I keep my mouth shut.

"He gave up smoking that very same day too. I never saw him light up a cigarette again. All books of matches and lighters vanished from our house. Poof." He snaps his fingers, the sound loud in the otherwise quiet. "Gone. Like magic."

Is he making this story up? I don't know. There are too many details...

"I could've ended up in jail," he continues.

I snort-laugh, unable to stop myself. "Please. You were six."

"Already a hardened criminal at six." He smiles, his teeth shining in the darkness. "I think you like bad boys, Callahan."

"Shut up." I shove at him, my hand making contact with his thigh, and I marvel at how lean and hard it is. All muscle.

"See? You did that so you could touch me." He laughs and somehow produces a pack of matches, pulling one off the tab and lighting it with a flick of his wrist. He holds the match up close to his face, the flicker and glow casting shadows across his sharp cheekbones. His equally sharp nose. His full lips. "I still like playing with matches."

"I know. I remember the first time I met you, that's what you were doing." How could I forget? The sullen boy sitting on the bench, talking about pussy shots and lighting matches.

"I remember that too." He stretches his arm out toward me, the lit match coming closer to my face, and I flinch when the flame flickers. "Don't worry. I won't burn you."

Such a pretty lie that falls from his lips. "You already have."

His smile falters and he brings the match up to his mouth, blowing out the flame. The interior of the truck goes dark, and it takes my eyes a few seconds to adjust to the dim light that's shining from one of the parking lot's lampposts. "You've burned me too."

How, I'm not sure, but I'm not in the mood to argue with him.

"The problem with fire is that it burns," he says when I haven't responded to him. "Hot and fast. Totally destructive."

He could be talking about himself.

"Destroying everything in its path."

Definitely talking about himself.

"Turning everything to ashes," I add, sending him a pointed look.

Yes, I'm talking about you, Ash. And your name.

"Makes sense, right? That they call me Ash. That I like fire. I'm a goddamned cliché." He stubs the forgotten cigarette out in the ashtray and then reaches for a pack of gum that's sitting on the dash. I look around, noticing there's a lot of miscellaneous crap on his dashboard. It's actually pretty huge. "Want one?" He offers the pack to me. "In case for later?"

"What's going to happen later?" I take a piece, glaring at him. "I'm not going to let you kiss me, if that's what you're thinking."

He laughs. "I like how you go straight to kissing. Makes me think you missed it."

"I kiss Ben," I say primly.

"Is it the same, though, Callahan? Really?"

"Definitely not," I say confidently. I enjoy kissing Ben.

Kissing Ash left me...unsettled. Restless.

Needy.

Sighing, he shakes his head. "I'm not the one who wants to kiss. More like you're gonna want to kiss *me.*" He unwraps the stick of gum and shoves it into his mouth, chewing obnoxiously. "I won't have to do a damn thing. You'll be slobbering all over me in minutes."

"Fuck you." I delicately set the piece of gum in my mouth and start chewing, keeping my lips closed.

"Jeez, Callahan, nice language." He's laughing again. Studying me like I'm some big joke. And I want to smack him. Hurt him.

"You bring out the worst in me," I tell him with a delicate sniff.

"Really? And here I thought I brought out the best in you." His gaze drops to my lips, and I know he's looking at them on purpose. Trying to get my imagination to go haywire so I'll uncontrollably jump him.

Or maybe that's my vivid imagination kicking into high gear. I'm not sure.

"It's best that we keep our distance." And that's exactly why we haven't spoke for the last year, I'm sure.

"Says who? Your faithful Ben?"

"Stop making fun of Ben."

"I'm not making fun of him. He is faithful, right? He cares about you? I'm sure he's told you he loves you. I bet he tells you that on the daily. The dumbshit probably means every word he says, too." Ash shakes his head, shaking the hair out of his eyes. The movement causes his scent to waft toward me. Clean. Soapy, and I'm guessing it's his shampoo. He smells like maybe he just got out of the shower. He most likely did. And I don't want to think about Ash in the shower. Naked. Warm water streaming over his body.

Briefly I close my eyes, banishing the mental image from my brain. I press my lips together, remaining silent. No way am I going to tell him we haven't said *I love you* to each other yet. He'd latch onto that and never let go.

"He's what you were looking for last year, and what I'll never be. You know that, right?" His voice is soft and I chance a look at him to find he's already watching me. His eyes glow in the darkness, and the sincerity etched all over his stupidly gorgeous face makes my heart soften a little bit.

"I wasn't looking for anything from you," I tell him.

"Sure you were. You all do." He pauses for a moment. "I made you mad."

"What girl wouldn't be mad when the boy who just kissed her said he couldn't feel anything?" The words escape me before I can stop them, but fortunately, I don't regret saying them. He should hear what I have to say. He should know how stupid he sounds.

"I still can't feel anything." His voice is deep. Low. I lean toward him to hear him better. "I think it's gone."

I'm frowning. "What's gone?"

He taps the center of his chest. "My heart. I don't have one. My chest is hollow."

I have a sudden memory of a movie Mom loves. I can't remember what it's called. A girl takes in this weird guy who claims to have a baboon's heart, and when I was young, I thought it was the stupidest movie ever. While Mom is sitting there crying over the end, saying how much she loved it.

Why would you love a movie that makes you cry?

And why does a sixteen-year-old boy say that he doesn't have a heart? Does he mean he actually doesn't have one? If that's the case, he'd be dead.

"What are you? Some kind of psycho?" I sound mean, but I'm still hurting over last year's interlude.

Not that I'd ever admit that to him.

His big brown eyes remind me of a puppy dog's, and the longer he stays quiet, the more I start to think he's putting one on me.

"You're so full of shit," I finally say with a shake my head.

He's grinning, the asshole. "Did you really think I meant that? That I literally have no heart? I mean, come on, Callahan. You'd have to be the stupidest person alive to believe that kind of shit."

"You definitely qualify for that," I mutter, reaching for the door handle.

He's on me in an instant. Hovering above me, I can feel his body heat, though we're not quite touching. "Don't leave."

"Why not?"

"Just—stay for a few minutes longer. It can be our little secret." He eases away from me when he must sense I'm not going to make a run for it. "It's nice, playing catch up."

It sort of is, but it's also incredibly annoying. I can't take him seriously, though I'm desperate to. I can't believe a word he says.

I also can't sit with a boy I used to like and pretend I have zero feelings for him. That would be...

A lie.

CHAPTER 10

"*S*o. Where is Ben anyway?"

Now we're making idle conversation? Okay, I can do this. "Don't you know? You're the one who told me he's gone for the weekend."

Ash makes a scoffing noise, focusing his attention on the windshield in front of us. He shifts his right leg up so his knee is resting on the edge of the steering wheel, and I stare at him unabashedly. I swear to God he's gotten even better looking over the last year. He's filled out some. More defined muscles, taller. His jaw is sharper, there's a shadow there, like he might need to shave, and I find that incredibly appealing.

"I don't give a shit about what he's doing," he says morosely.

I sit up a little straighter, contemplating him. He's lying. I can tell. I don't know why I know this, but my senses are tingling big time, like I'm Spider-Man and I just discovered the Green Goblin has been sitting next to me the entire time. "Right. That's why you keep bringing him up. Because you don't give a shit about him."

"I don't." It's like he refuses to look at me. "That guy sucks."

"That guy is my boyfriend."

"And don't the two of you make a lovely couple." His voice pitches higher and wobbles, as if he's trying to sound like a sweet old woman, and I want to laugh. "You probably have your baby names picked out along with your wedding colors."

No wedding colors. But I do keep a running list of favorite names on the Notes app on my phone. That has nothing to do with Ben. I'm just trying to keep a record of my favorites.

"I don't want to marry him," I say.

"Really?" Ash turns his head toward mine, our gazes meeting once more. "I figured you two had already sealed the deal."

He's not talking about promises of marriage. He's talking about sex. And I'm not admitting crap to him. "We're very close."

"That's very nice." He mimics my tone. "You two have my condolences."

I frown again. "Isn't that what you say to someone when they've lost their loved ones? Or they're at a funeral?"

"Exactly. So it's my condolences to you two for this ultra-amazing, soul-sucking relationship you're involved in. Enjoy it while you can. You two kids deserve each other." He's reaching for the cigarette packet when I stop him, my fingers barely touching the warm, smooth skin of the inside of his wrist.

He stops moving, his gaze flickering to mine, and I slowly shake my head. "You're just jealous."

Another scoff. This one louder. "My ass I'm jealous."

I part my lips, ready to let the accusations fly, when he's suddenly tugging me down, my butt sliding off the old bench seat, my entire body folded into the passenger floorboard beneath the dash. I glance up to find Ash lying down, stretched across the entire bench seat, a wild look in his eyes.

"What the hell is wrong with you?" I brush at the back of my legs, wondering exactly how many feet have rested against this floorboard over the years. And all the dirt and germs that might still linger.

Ash presses a finger against his mouth to silence me and I keep my lips tightly together, glaring at him for long, agonizing minutes, until he slowly raises his head before letting out a relieved breath.

"That was a close one."

I'm rolling my eyes. "What happened?"

"A bunch of people from the cheer team just walked by and got in their cars." At this very moment I hear the sounds of multiple engines starting.

"A bunch?" I know of a whopping two who were still in the cheer room, so I'm not sure what he's talking about.

"A couple of cheerleaders, your bitch-ass coach. That chick who runs the band and looks younger than me, for fuck's sake." Ash shakes his head. "They're the ones who walked by just now."

So glad my coach didn't see me with Ash. She might ask all sorts of questions. Questions I can't answer. "Can I sit back on the seat then?"

"Sure." He reaches for my hand and hauls me up, pulling with such force that I go toppling forward, landing right on top of him. Somehow, my knees end up on either side of hips, and I'm basically sitting on his lap. His hands automatically go to my waist, his fingers burning through the thick fabric of my uniform skirt, and I want to tell him to get his hands off me.

But I don't.

I also want to tell him to stop staring at my mouth.

I don't do that either.

It's like I melt against him. My entire body goes soft. Then hot. His hands slide around, until his hands are pressed against the lowest spot of my spine, and I tilt my head up, my eyes sliding close when his mouth finds mine.

It's wrong. So wrong. I'm with Ben. Ben is my boyfriend. He has been for six months, and like everyone says, we make a great couple.

Yet I can't deny the electric spark that flashes between our lips at first contact. I can't control the throbbing of my heart, the heat between my legs, the tingles that sweep over me in a slow, steady glide when Ash's tongue slowly circles around mine.

That last kiss. Our first kiss, was all heat and impatience and hunger.

This kiss, our second kiss, is just as hungry. But slower. More determined.

More delicious.

One of his hands comes up, cupping the side of my face. The other hand slides down, over my butt, slipping beneath my pleated skirt. I have on briefs and his hand is right there, covering practically my entire left butt cheek, and then...

And then.

I'm climbing him like a tree, trying to get closer. My lips, my hands, my body is filled with this strange urgency I've never felt before. I want to rub my body on his like I'm a cat. I want to wrap my legs around his hips and squeeze extra tight. I'm desperate to ease the ache that's growing inside of me. Growing, growing, growing until I'm panting against his lips.

He smiles, I can feel his lips stretching against mine, and he says, "See? I knew you'd be slobbering all over me."

His words are the icy-cold dump of water over my head that I need. I push away from him, disentangling myself, scrambling off his lap. Red-hot embarrassment burns like a river inside me, splitting me open, leaving me raw.

"I hate you." I fumble with the handle and somehow open the door, desperate to escape. To get away from Ash Davis once and for all.

He calls my name but I don't look back. I'm running to my car, stabbing the keyless remote with my fingers, eager to get into the car for fear he might catch up to me. Touch me again.

Make me weak again.

I collapse into the driver's seat and slam the door, starting the car and pulling out of the lot without thinking. I just do. My hands are on the steering wheel, I'm making my way home, turning onto all the right roads, and when I finally pull into our curved driveway, I realize I'm not sure how I made it here.

Dried tears leave my cheeks sticky, and my eyes burn. All because of him. That kiss, that moment was a mistake.

A big one.

CHAPTER 11

I spend the entirety of my Saturday in bed, holed up in my room. Mom and Dad left around two, taking my brothers and sister with them. They were going to a football game at the state university that's about an hour away from us. They got special box seats thanks to someone Dad knows, and Mom practically begged me to go, but I told them I didn't feel well and I'd rather stay home.

The last thing I wanted to do was go to the tailgate party and act like everything's fine. Mom said I could bring Kaya, but she's too perceptive. She'd know immediately something was up. I can't tell her what happened. She'd tell Jaden and he'd tell Ben and it would turn into a huge mess. One I'm not ready to face yet.

That's why I'm still in bed. Still weepy. The guilt is killing me, and it doesn't matter how much I try to justify it by thinking, *It was just a kiss. One little kiss. No big deal.*

I can't call it "just a kiss". It was more than that. It was a huge deal.

I cheated on Ben. I can't take that back. Anyone at school finds out, and our relationship is over. I'd bet a million bucks that Ash—the smug asshole—would totally tell Ben come Monday morning. I may as well prepare for it now. My first high school relationship is about to come to a spectacular end.

My phone starts ringing and I pick it up to see it's Kaya FaceTiming me. I wipe at my face, give up immediately and answer the call.

"Holy shit you look terrible," is how she greets me, Daphne appearing behind her with a frown.

"What happened to you?" Daphne asks.

I offer a weak smile. "Gee, thanks guys."

"Seriously, have you been crying?" Kaya looms closer in the screen, her eyebrows scrunched in concern. I know she has my best interests at heart, considering she's my best friend, and Daphne is my next closest friend, but I can't tell them this. I just...I can't. A secret isn't a secret any longer once another person knows.

Meaning my secret is already exposed, considering it's between me and Ash.

"No, I feel like shit." I sniff to emphasize what I just said, and decide I need to make it seem like I have a cold. Poor me, woe is me. Sick as a dog.

"It's been going around," Daphne says, sounding like a mom. She is sort of like a mother figure in our friend group, always taking care of everyone. "Don't tell me Ben gave it to you."

She'd die if she knew it was Ash who gave me my current illness. "He's not sick. He's not even here."

"Oh, that's right. I forgot he was gone for the weekend." Kaya's face brightens and she smiles at Daphne before turning to look at me. "You should come over and spend the night!"

That is the absolute last thing I should do. I'd rather wallow in my misery by myself, thank you very much. "I feel terrible, Kaya. Besides, you guys don't want to catch this."

"True." She wrinkles her nose. "You're probably contagious."

If misery is catching, then yes. I'm totally contagious. "Right, so you don't want to be around me."

"Have you done anything, gone anywhere?" Daphne asks. "Or just stay home?"

"I've been in bed all day. My family just left a while ago. They're going to a football game."

"And you didn't want to go?" Kaya's eyes are sparkling and she bursts out laughing. Daphne laughs too. "I'm already so over football and we're not even halfway through the season."

"We'll end up in playoffs too. You know we will."

"Right, and the season will go on that much longer. Over it." Kaya rolls her eyes, making me laugh. "Hey, so Jaden and I went to the movies earlier. And guess who we saw there?"

There's not much to do around the small town we live in, so the local movie theater is one of our only sources of entertainment. Whenever Ben and I go to the movies, we always see someone we know there.

"Who?"

"Mia Antonis and Ash Davis." Kaya shakes her head, her expression one of pure revulsion. "Why would he be with her? She's so gross. Do you think they're together?"

"Ash doesn't really date anyone exclusively," Daphne points out. "But maybe those two ho's would make a great couple."

My head starts pounding the moment the names left Kaya's lips. Mia and Ash. Mia and Ash.

He kissed me last night and this afternoon he's with another girl. A girl who's been with like every guy at our school. She's a senior, a year older than us, and she's gone through most of the boys at school. As in, she's given many of them blowjobs, hand jobs, had sex with them, whatever. At least, that's what I hear.

I can only guess what Ash is doing with her.

And just the thought makes me want to cry all over again.

"Wh-where did you see them?" I ask, hating how shaky my voice is.

"In front of the movie theater. They looked like they were about to go inside, and Mia was hanging all over him." Kaya rolls her eyes. "I really can't stand her."

"Me either," Daphne says.

Mom would say we're slut shaming, and that we don't know Mia's story. She's right. I don't know her story. It just seems she's always trying to seek attention, whether it's good or bad, and I hope I'm never like that.

"I've never really talked to her before," I admit, and both Kaya and Daphne pause.

"I never really have either," Kaya says.

"Maybe she's not so bad." I shrug.

"I've heard she's a total man stealer." This is from Daphne.

Feels like that at this very moment, I'll agree. Not that Ash was ever mine to steal in the first place. "Maybe she is, maybe she isn't. I honestly don't know."

Kaya changes the subject, and I feel bad for making them feel bad, but I'm telling myself I shouldn't be upset with Mia Antonis. It's Ash who's the asshole here.

I need to remember that.

Kaya, Daphne and I talk a little while longer and then they have to go, so we end the call. Secretly, I'm glad. I don't want to gossip about Ash or anyone else. I don't really want to think about anything. I send Ben a Snapchat, but he's not responding, which depresses me even further. Even though I know he's busy.

Though, really, how can I keep up the pretense that

nothing happened? That everything between me and Ben is fine? It's not fine. We're not fine. I'm a bad person, and he has no freaking clue what I've done.

It's past seven o'clock and I'm still in bed watching YouTube on my laptop when I get a text from an unfamiliar number.

Look out your window.

Fear slithers down my spine. I'm all alone. My family won't be back for hours.

This has to be a prank.

Kaya, knock it off.

The response is immediate.

Who's Kaya?

I shoot a quick text to her actual number.

Are you trying to trick me?

Kaya replies pretty quickly. **What are you talking about?**

I glance toward my window, dread hitting me when I realize the blinds are still open. Since my room faces the front of the house and my bedroom light is on, anyone outside can see inside my room.

Including the stalker who's currently texting me.

Don't make me break into your house, Callahan.

The dread is replaced with pure, white-hot anger. It's fucking Ash Davis who's texting me.

I go to my bedroom window and yank up the blinds, staring into the semi-darkness. The setting sun reflects on the lake in the near distance, casting the sky in an eerie orange glow, and I spot him standing in my driveway, his truck nowhere in sight.

What the actual hell?

He's wearing a white T-shirt and jeans, beat-up white Vans on his feet. His hands are shoved into his front pockets and he looks like a sweet little boy waiting for someone's approval.

Well, he's not going to get it from me.

Throwing open the window, I yell, "Go away!"

He grins up at me. "Found ya."

I slam the window shut. This is stupid. No way can I talk to him. Yell at him. We're watching each other through the glass and he eventually whips out his phone and starts tapping on it.

A text comes through seconds later, and I glance down at my phone.

Come out here.

Lifting my head up, I stare down at him as I slowly shake my head.

My phone dings.

I need to talk to you.

Without thought I throw the window back open. "Go talk to Mia! I'm sure she'll listen to what you have to say."

His eyes pop open wide. "How the hell did you—"

I shut the window before he can finish the sentence, cutting him off. This house clearly has stellar insulation.

My phone starts exploding with texts.

Come on.

Come outside.

Let me talk to you.

Callahan, don't act like this.

Come onnnnnnnnnnnnn.

Please?

It's the please that gets me. I'm such a sucker.

Glancing at myself in the mirror, I realize I look like straight hell, but you know what? I don't care. Nope, he can see me in all my wiped-out glory. I took a shower last night right before I went to bed and my hair is a frizzy mess. I'm wearing an old T-shirt that used to be my dad's and a pair of sleep shorts that have a tiny tear in the butt. I'm also wearing giant panties versus a thong because I thought I was going to start my period today, but it hasn't shown up yet.

I grab a blush-pink velvet scrunchie from my bedside table and throw my hair into a sloppy bun. Slip on my favorite flip-flops and skip down the stairs, clutching my phone in my right hand. If my parents knew Ash Davis was at our house, they would be furious. I'm not allowed to have a boy at the house alone. That rule goes without saying. I'm not even allowed to have my boyfriend in my room when the entire family is in the house.

My parents are super strict, but it never actually feels like they are. I've never been tempted to break the rules. Only when I first started high school did I go through a tiny rebellious streak. I was so mad over us moving, and losing all of my friends. I hated living in this stupid small town, in this stupid giant house.

Now, I'm happy. I like it here. I like school, I have lots of friends and I have a boyfriend who really cares about me. And I care about him too. So much, I'm going to tell this asshole waiting for me outside that he needs to leave. What happened last night was a huge mistake and while we can't take it back, we can move in and pretend it never happened.

Yep. That's exactly what I'm going to say to him.

I unlock and then throw open the front door to find Ash already standing on my porch, his expression serious.

Dead serious.

"How did you know about Mia?"

Blinking, I take a step back, clutching the door handle. "Word gets around."

"Tell me who told you. I don't remember seeing anyone there from school." He sounds angry, and isn't that a riot considering I'm the one who should be angry with him.

"It was—one of my friends. That's who."

One eyebrow arches. "That Kaya chick?"

"I thought you didn't know Kaya."

"Of course I know Kaya. She's your best friend, right? Goes out with Jaden?" When I nod, he snaps his fingers. "That's who saw me."

"It doesn't matter. Clearly you've moved on. Go be with Mia instead." I start to shut the door, but Ash inserts his foot, stopping me.

"Wait." I glare at him, but he doesn't remove his foot. "Hear me out."

I huff out an aggravated breath. "You've got five minutes."

"I ran into Mia in front of the movie theater. She started hanging on me like she does and I was trying to get away from her. That's probably when your little friend saw me," he explains.

"You don't need to tell me all this. I'm not your keeper. If you want to be with Mia, go be with her," I say, nudging at his foot with my own. But it still doesn't budge.

"I don't want to be with her." He hesitates, exhaling loudly, his shoulders sagging with the sound and my heart leaps to my throat. "I want…"

His voice drifts and this time I kick at his shoe. Which is stupid, because I'm in flip-flops and that hurt like a mother. "Just spit it out," I say through clenched teeth, my big toe throbbing.

"You."

I go completely still. My heart is beating so hard it's making my head throb. No way did I hear him correctly. "What?"

"You. I want you." Another hesitation and he glances down at the ground for a moment, his mouth kicking up on one side as he stares at my injured, wiggling big toe. "Mia doesn't mean shit to me."

"No one means shit to you," I remind him.

He looks up, the smile fading. "You do."

"Ash, you don't even know me," I start, but he interrupts me.

"I know you. I know you better than you think. I know you like to laugh, because you do it a lot. You have a lot of friends because you're nice to everybody."

"I thought they were nice to me because they want to get closer to my dad," I say sarcastically.

"You know that's not true."

We both remain quiet until I remind him, "You have two minutes."

"Your favorite food is pizza. You have a Starbucks addiction. You are the loudest person on the cheer team. Sometimes when I'm out on the field, I can hear your voice over everyone else's. When you're worried, you get this little crease between your eyebrows, and every time I see it, I want to smooth my fingers over that spot to help you relax."

My heart pangs when he says that.

"You take on a lot of projects, because you like to stay busy. When you're not busy, you think too much, or you get bored. You'd rather be on the go than alone with your thoughts," he continues.

My fingers curl around the door handle, so tight it hurts. His words are hitting too close. How does he know all this?

"You think you're happy with Ben Murray, but that guy is a wimp, Callahan. He just goes along with whatever you say, and you need someone who challenges you." He kicks at the door and I automatically open it a little wider. "Someone like me."

I do not need to be with someone like him. Someone like him would break me.

I know it.

"You're not allowed in the house," I say, my voice quiet. I'm purposely trying to change the subject. I don't want to talk about what he just confessed.

"Anyone home?" He peers into the open space, looking to the left, then the right.

Should I tell him the truth? Or lie?

"It's sure quiet in there," he observes, and I know he knows the truth.

"No one's home," I admit like the dumb girl I am.

"Ah." He nods, and I can see he's happy about this.

"I'm not allowed to have anyone over when my parents aren't here," I admit.

"Even Ben?"

"Especially Ben."

"Don't they know you'll figure out a place to do it no matter what? The back seat of a car, the bathroom by the biology building—"

"Gross!" He *would* say that.

Ash grins. "You know lots of people have had sex by the biology building."

"Not me."

"Oh really?" He shoves his hands in his pockets, tipping forward. "Where do you like to have sex then?"

"I am so not having this conversation." I make to shut the door on his foot and he pulls it out at the last minute, causing the door to slam so hard it rattles the house. "Go away!"

"I just poured my heart out to you and that's what you have to say to me?" He sounds incredulous.

"You don't have a heart, remember?"

"Yeah, because you stole it."

CHAPTER 12

*W*hat he said is so sappy, so unbelievable, I'm tempted to call bullshit.

There's another part of me, though, that wants to believe it. Believe him. His observations. Everything he said, his tone, the sincerity in his eyes…that dark sliver buried deep inside me is totally falling for it. Falling for *him*. I don't know when he noticed, or how closely he's been observing me, but he was right, pretty much with all of it.

Except for the part about Ben. Ben's too good for me. And I know it.

Especially now. After everything I've done.

"You gonna give it back to me or not?" Ash yells.

I slowly open the door. "Give you back what?"

"My heart." He shakes his head. "Wait. Never mind. You can keep it. I don't want it."

He is making absolutely no sense. "Why don't you want it?"

"It hurts too damn much. All the time." He rubs his chest, a slight grimace on his face. "This fucking sucks, Callahan."

"You're talking in circles. And your time is up." I mean it.

Yet again, I start to shut the door, and then he's pushing his way inside, standing in the foyer right in front of me. In my house. Something I thought I'd never see.

Asher Davis in my home. The two of us all alone.

"You need to go." My voice is firm, but my entire body is trembling. I'm afraid. Having him in my house is like an invitation to something I don't understand. Definitely something I'm not sure I want to happen.

"Just hear me out, okay? I—" He runs his hands through his hair, tugging on the ends. "You're all I think about."

I blink up at him. When did he get so tall? He's always been tall, everyone's tall compared to me, but I swear, he just keeps growing. Keeps getting broader too—

Wait a minute. Did he just admit I'm *all he thinks about?*

"I wake up and you're on my mind. I go to sleep thinking about you. Sometimes I even dream about you, and those are always a trip, because we're usually together, and I'm doing my best to fuck it up, yet you stick around. Like you're really into me or something."

His words are sort of breaking my heart.

"I try to see you at school, even if it's just in the hallway, and my day is automatically better when I spot your smile. Even when you're smiling at Ben, it doesn't matter, because you look so happy, and that's all I want for y—"

"You need to stop. Please, just…stop talking."

He blinks slowly, as if he's trying to absorb what I just said. "What do you mean? I'm telling you how I feel about you and it's like you don't care."

"You don't really feel that way about me. You just want what you can't have." I cross my arms, which reminds me I'm not wearing a bra. Thank God my T-shirt is oversized. Hopefully he can't tell. "That's all. I'm with someone else, and now you want me. You had your chance last year when I liked you, and you let it go. You let *me* go. That's on you."

We're quiet for a moment, and for some weird reason, it's not uncomfortable. It's as if we need the break, we need to absorb our words, our feelings.

"I really had a chance last year?" He lifts his brows.

Did he really believe he didn't?

"Yeah," I admit. "You did."

Ash shakes his head, running his hands through his hair once again, tugging the strands into a complete mess. "I don't know how to do this."

"Do what?"

"This." He waves a hand between us. "A relationship." He says that last word like a curse.

"We're not in a relationship. We can't be. I'm with Ben," I remind him yet again.

He squints, cocking his head to the side. "Are you happy with him, Callahan?"

I stand a little straighter. "Of course I am. At least he calls me by my first name."

"Is that all it takes to get you to jump ship and be with me? For me to call you by your first name?"

Pretty sure I haven't heard him call me by my first name since the first day of our sophomore year when I insulted his dead father. "No, of course not."

Ash glances around the foyer, tilting his head back to study the light that hangs on a chain all the way from the second floor. Whistling low, he shakes his head. "Your house is huge."

It is. I don't like a lot of people coming over to my house, since they tend to get dazzled by it. Mom and Dad are worth a lot of money. Dad came from money, and his NFL career gave him a big paycheck. So big, he's worth hundreds of millions. Plus he got endorsements, and neither of them ever have to work another day in their life ever again. My college is paid for, no problem. I have everything I could ever want.

Sort of.

Strangers seeing our wealth always ends up awkward. This is why I hang out at my friends' houses. Kaya will come over sometimes, and Ben has only been here once.

He looked as shell-shocked as Ash does now.

"You should probably go," I start, but Ash keeps talking.

"You got anything to drink in this house?"

Now he keeps walking. I chase after him. "Where are you going?"

"Looking for a kitchen." He stops at the hallway, turns to the left, and heads right for the very room he's looking for. "I'm thirsty."

"You're not supposed to be here, remember?"

"What they don't know won't hurt them."

"If my father finds out you're in this house uninvited, he'll hurt you."

Ash ignores what I say, striding right into our open-concept kitchen—that's what Mom calls it—like he owns the place. "Damn. This kitchen is niiiice." He looks around, then makes his way to the refrigerator. He opens the doors and peers inside. "You got beer."

"You can't have one of my dad's beers."

"I won't drink your dad's beer, chill." He pulls a can of Coke out of the fridge and hip checks the door, slamming it shut. "Thanks for the soda." He cracks the can open, then proceeds to drink at least half of it in a couple of swallows.

God, he's so irritating. He makes absolutely no sense. He claims he has feelings for me, then wanders off in search of a drink. He goes from one subject to the other so fast, I'm going to end up with whiplash.

Resigned with the fact that he's going to stick around for a while, I turn on the kitchen lights, illuminating the space to the point of it being almost too bright. "Kill the mood, why don't you," he mutters as he takes another swig from his Coke can.

"You're not even supposed to be here." I hop up on one of the barstools, resting my arms against the edge of the quartz countertop. "Seriously, Ash. My parents will be home soon, and if they find you in here, we're both dead."

"Then I'll at least die happy." He cracks a smile, but I just glare at him. "Don't you have a sense of humor?"

"No, I do not. Not when a boy I don't like is in my house, acting like he lives here." I tilt my chin up, hoping he thinks I'm acting like a snobby princess so he'll leave.

You don't want him to leave.

Yes, I do. I really, really do.

"A boy you don't like." Ash snorts with disbelief. "You're so full of shit, Callahan. You jumped my ass first in the truck last night. You were rubbing against me like you wanted to get off on my leg, and it was the hottest thing I've ever seen in my entire life. So don't tell me you're not into me. You are fucking dying for me to touch you right now, and you know it."

His little speech leaves me breathless. With anger. With— oh God—with lust. "You love rubbing my face in my mistakes, don't you?"

"What do you mean?" He truly appears confused.

"You always have to bring up my most humiliating moments so I end up feeling like an asshole. I hate it." I'm gripping the edge of the counter, afraid I might lunge toward him and beat him up. I'd love to pummel his pretty face with my fists and leave him bruised and battered.

His words leave me emotionally battered, and it sucks.

"Humiliating moments? What happened last night between us humiliated you?"

"You were so smug, hitting me with an *I told you so* right in the middle of us—of us—" I can't say it.

"Grinding on each other?" he finishes for me.

My cheeks go hot with embarrassment. "Yeah. That."

"I wasn't trying to hit you with an *I told you so*. More like I couldn't believe you were trying to get off on me like that. I mean, I know I said you would end up slobbering on me, but I didn't mean it. I thought you saved all that for Ben," he says, mentioning my boyfriend's name like he's purposely trying to annoy me.

"You want to know the truth?" *Don't do it. Don't say it.*

"Hell yeah, I do."

"Ben and I have never done it."

The second the words leave me, I'm covering my mouth with my hand, trying to stuff the words back inside. It's no use. They're out. I said them. I said them out loud. To Ash. He'll make fun of me now. He'll tell everyone we messed around behind Ben's back and I'll be the laughing stock of the school. Ben will publicly dump me and I'll turn into the enemy. Talk about humiliation.

Ash laughs. Shakes his head. "No way. You're lying."

I just stare at him, crossing my arms again. His gaze drops to my chest and I can feel him trying his best to burn a hole through my shirt with his eyes. My nipples harden, I lift my arms a little to cover them, but it's no use.

He's smirking.

I hate him.

"You're not lying."

I shake my head.

"You two have to at least be feeling each other up on the daily, right? I saw you at the back to school dance."

"You were at the back to school dance?" I don't remember him being there.

"Not that you'd notice. You were too busy dancing and grinding on Ben's junk." Ash makes a face. "He probably wouldn't know what to do with your perfect ass if you handed it to him on a platter."

How can someone make a compliment sound like an insult? It's Ash's particular skill. He's really good at it. "You are seriously so disgusting."

"Seriously. *Seriously.* You use that word all the damn time. Doesn't Ben get tired of that shit?"

"Will you please stop bringing him into this conversation?" My voice rises. If he keeps this up, I will soon be full-blown shouting.

"You're the one who told me you two haven't fucked yet." He shakes his head, collapsing onto the bar stool next to mine. "I can't believe it."

"Would you not call it that please?" I sound weary. I *am* weary. I've spent all day lounging in bed feeling sorry for myself and worrying, that I'm completely exhausted.

"What? Fucking? What do you want me to call it? *Making love?*" He draws the words out mockingly.

"I would never call it that." I can barely think the words making love without wanting to giggle.

"Boning. Banging. Doing it. Getting laid. Sex. Fucking. It's all the same, right?" He shrugs, angling his body toward mine. His gaze roams over me, as if he just realized I'm not wearing much, and my skin starts to burn.

"You're so crude."

"I'm sure your boyfriend is never crude." I open my mouth to chastise him and he points his finger at me, cutting me off. "I didn't say his name, did I?"

He's got me there. Sort of. "It would never work between us, you know."

"You really think so?" He sounds surprised.

"I know so." I don't, but it sounds good. "Maybe it's best if we're just friends."

Those dark brows shoot up practically to his hairline. "Really? You just want to be friends with me?"

"Yes." I nod, warming up to the idea. His earlier confession that I had his heart was nothing but a bunch of lies to try to worm himself into my house, and it worked. But he can only get so far, and he's hit his limit. "Friends are understanding of each other. When one friend tells the other that it's time to go home, they leave without arguing."

I stare straight ahead, trying my best not to look at him. I see the blue light of the oven clock glowing—the time says 8:22. My family won't be home for a while yet, but he doesn't know that.

"That's what you want me to do? You want me to go?" I can feel him watching me, yet I refuse to look at him.

"Yes. That's what I want." My voice is firm. It doesn't waver or shake, and I glance down at my hands to see they're clutched so tight around the edge of the counter, my knuckles are white.

"Okay. I'll leave." He smacks the edge of the counter and rises to his feet, exiting the kitchen with a few long strides.

I chase after him until we're both in the foyer and he's got his hand on the door handle, his back to me, when I ask him a question. "How'd you get up here anyway? To the lake?"

"What do you mean?" he says to the door.

"I didn't see your truck."

"I hid it. Parked it behind a bush just before you come to the circular drive." He glances over his shoulder at me, his barely there smile irritatingly adorable. "Didn't want you to spot it and call the cops on me."

"I would never call the cops on you." I really wouldn't. I'm not that mean. Unless he was threatening me with bodily harm or being really aggressive.

"That's what they all say." He faces forward, opening the

door, then turns toward me once again. "Do friends give each other hugs? The friends I have do. Sometimes."

"There is no way I'm hugging you." I roll my eyes.

"A truce hug then? Come on." He lets go of the door handle and faces me fully, stretching his arms out in invitation. "I'll leave you alone after this, okay? I promise."

I'm not sure if he's the type who keeps his promises. I'm guessing no.

This could be the last time I hug him. This entire encounter has been weird. Confusing. We're a mess. We would never work, and us going 'round and 'round in circles tonight just proves that.

So what's the harm in getting one last hug from Ash? It's just a hug. A brief moment of bodily contact and then I'll send him away. He won't bug me again. He'll get over his so-called feelings for me. He'll give his heart to someone else or even better, he'll discover he actually has one, and he'll forget all about me. He'll give it to someone else, and he'll finally leave me alone forever.

Why does that thought make me feel so empty inside?

Deciding it's do or die time, I walk right into his hug, my arms sliding around his waist, my head resting on his chest. I can feel the steady thump-thump of his heartbeat and I close my eyes when his arms come around me. Slowly. Enfolding me into his body so that we're snug tight.

He holds me with a desperation, almost as if he's afraid to let me go, and when I lift my head, tilting it back so I can stare into his eyes, I find he's already watching me.

"Friends don't make each other feel like this," he says, his voice a gravelly whisper.

The hairs on the back of my neck rise. "Feel like what?"

"Like you could be my everything."

My shoulders sag. "Ash—"

"Stop talking." He presses two fingers to my lips, silencing me. When he's seemingly assured I won't speak, he lightens the pressure, gently caressing my lips. Back and forth. Making me tingle.

Making me want him to do more than touch my mouth.

I want him to kiss me.

"You have the sexiest lips," he murmurs, and the blush returns, setting my face on fire. No one has referred to me as sexy before. "What we're doing is fucking crazy. You know this right, Callahan?"

I ignore his question. "How could I be your everything when you told me you don't know how to feel?"

"The only time I seem to feel is when..." He presses his fingers into the corner of my mouth, so gentle, I could almost think he never actually touched me. "I'm with you."

"What are you feeling right now?" I have to ask. I might never get this opportunity again.

"Sick to my stomach. Happy. Scared." He visibly swallows, as if all that honesty was tough to confess. "I want to kiss you."

Slowly I shake my head, even though everything inside of me is screaming, *yes! Please kiss me!* "Not a good idea."

"Nothing we ever do is a good idea," he says, heavy on the sarcasm.

So very true. "My parents will be home soon."

"No they won't. They're at a football game. And I can guarantee that game is still happening. I'd predict it's only in the third quarter," he says.

My mouth pops open. "How do you know?"

"Your dad was posting all over his social media earlier. The tailgate party. Entering the stadium and all his fans losing their shit. Showing off the view from the box seats. 'Check out this hot dog I'm eating'—he literally said that right before he shoved it in his mouth. Pretty sure I heard your mom laughing while she filmed it." Ash chuckles. "His Instagram story is popping tonight."

The joys of having a father who's also a public figure. Thanks, Dad, for letting Ash Davis know where you are at all times so he's able to keep tabs. No wonder he was so comfortable showing up here.

"But we're only being friends right now," I remind him. "And friends leave when they're asked, so…"

"You're the one who's still holding me," he points out, and when I glance down, I realize he's right. His arms are dangling by his sides almost awkwardly. And mine are still firmly wrapped around his waist.

I let go of him as if he's a poisonous snake. "That's your cue to leave."

He takes a few steps backward, his gaze never leaving mine. I rest my hands on my hips, trying to look tough, most likely failing miserably. He examines me with his eyes, my skin burning the longer he stares, and I don't know why he affects me this way. Leaves me feeling warm and squirmy and completely conflicted.

I shouldn't like him.

Yet I do.

I *think* I do.

"You really want me to leave, Callahan?" His voice is quiet. The entire house is quiet. My heart is thundering, and I wonder if he can hear it.

I wonder if I really affect him like he does me. Or if he just says all those sweet things to get in my pants or whatever.

"I'm with someone else," I remind him. "You shouldn't be here."

"And you shouldn't be with someone else." He pauses. Swallows hard. Looks down at the floor before he lifts his gaze to mine once again. "You should be with me."

"I know nothing about you," I whisper, hating how shaky my voice sounds. It's true. I don't know him. I only know of him. His background is a mystery. I've never really asked around about him, and no one volunteers any information. Does he have brothers or sisters? I don't know, I've never asked. And what's up with his mom? Where does he live?

"There's not much to know," he says with a shrug, glancing around the foyer once more. "I'm not rich like you, I can tell you that."

"I'm not—"

He interrupts me. "Don't bother denying it. You're definitely rich. Richer than I could ever hope to be."

I go quiet, because he's right. I did nothing to have my life. I was just lucky enough to be born to parents who make money.

"I don't care about money. If a person is rich or poor, I'm not going to judge them," I say, my voice level, my heart racing. I stare into his eyes. "So don't try to label me a snob when I'm not."

He actually grins, the asshole. "I like it when you get mad. It's cute."

"I'm not mad," I deny with a scowl.

"Sure. Whatever." He comes toward me, his strides quick. Purposeful. I back up, my butt hitting the door, and then his mouth his on mine. Quick and fleeting. The kiss over and done with before it had a chance to start. My lips are still tingling when he pulls away, and my hands itch with the need to grab him.

But I don't.

"See ya around, Callahan," he whispers as he reaches around me for the door handle.

I scoot out of his way, watching as he opens the door, then quietly closes it behind him, finally leaving me alone.

I'm lying in my bed hours later, unable to sleep. Replaying

every moment between us. Friday night, how I was drawn to him when I shouldn't have been. The kiss we shared. The slow, tortuous stroke of his tongue around mine, how he held me so tight, his fingers branding my skin. He was right. I was rubbing against him like I was desperate, and I thought I'd embarrassed myself, but he liked it.

He *liked* it.

He likes *me*.

Tonight's conversation was ridiculous. I find it difficult to believe a word he says. Most of it feels like shock value. He doesn't really care about me.

Does he?

The frustration, the joy, the anger. All three emotions rush over me, even more intense this time around, and I don't know what the hell I'm doing with Ash.

It needs to stop, I tell myself.

But I don't know if it can.

CHAPTER 13

Surprisingly, Ash keeps his mouth shut at school. He doesn't breathe a word about our interactions over the weekend. Ben texted me late Sunday afternoon to let me know he was back home, and I was so relieved to see his text, to know he's close and doesn't hate me, that I almost started to cry.

Or maybe that's the guilt trying to strangle me alive. I'm not sure.

The week goes by without any issues. Everything is normal. I have cheer practice. I get a B- on my math test. In leadership we're planning homecoming week, and even though it's a month away, everyone's already stressed out. Ben and I go to Starbucks after school on Wednesday and hang out with our friends. He kisses me deep as we're leaning against his car before we each head home, and I have to admit, I felt that little tingle, stirring deep in my stomach.

Maybe that's also because I thought of Ash when Ben kissed me, which means I'm most likely going to hell.

I don't see Ash at all. Not once. We don't have the same classes, we're not even on the same track, so that means we don't really bump into each other in the halls. Our freshman year we hung in the same social circle, even part of our sophomore year, but now we don't really have the same friends at all. He's always with his football bros at lunch. Or sneaking off campus to go out to lunch with his senior friends.

At cheer practice on Thursday, our coach Brandy hits us with an announcement. "We've been invited last minute to eat dinner tonight with the football team."

Some of the girls groan, a few of them get excited, but the rest of us remain quiet. That is the absolute last thing I want to do.

"I know, I know, it's a pain in the ass." Brandy always keeps it real with us. "But I said yes, because it's hard to say no to that sweet woman who runs the football boosters club."

That's true. Ann Gibson is a first-grade teacher at the local elementary school and no one can refuse her when she makes a request. It doesn't matter who you are, she speaks in this high-pitched, slow voice like she's talking to a six-year-old, and the next thing you know, you're agreeing to whatever she asks you do.

"Some of you probably have plans or can't get a ride home that late, and I totally understand. This isn't mandatory. Who can go tonight?" More than half the team raises their hands, including me. Dad will be there, so I sort of have to go. He'd expect me there. "Okay, good. We'll head over after we're done."

It's all I can think about throughout practice. We're out on the field, working on our halftime dance routine for tomorrow night, and I'm going through the motions like a zombie. I think about the smug look on Ash's face when he first sees me walk through the door. He'll probably say something rude about me to impress his friends and they'll all laugh at him at my expense.

Now I have mad regret. I should've told Brandy I couldn't make it.

We're stunting, and I'm a base. Even though I'm short, I'm heavier than the freshmen girls who are flyers, plus I have strong legs. I'm so distracted when we throw our flyer into a basket toss, I almost drop her, which sends Brandy into a complete tizzy. She's been sitting on the bleachers, making sure we're lined up okay, and now she's running down the steps, headed straight for us. "Holy crap Autumn, you almost dropped Emma! What's wrong with you?"

"Sorry, sorry." I rise to my feet and brush myself off, little bits of dry grass fluttering to the ground. I was the one who took the brunt of the fall, collapsing under Emma so she never touched the ground. My side hurts, as does my shoulder, and I try to suck it up. "Actually, I don't feel so great."

Kaya's in the other stunt group and she sends me a look, one that clearly asks, *are you all right?* I give a shrug as my answer.

"Emma, are you hurt?" Brandy asks as she approaches our stunt group.

"No, Autumn dive bombed under me." Emma pats me on the arm. She's funny and sweet. I really like her. "Thanks for saving me."

"No problem." I say nothing else, but I can feel my coach's assessing gaze. I never drop anyone. Being a base is one thing I'm really good at, so I know Brandy's wondering what's wrong with me.

Not like I can tell her either.

I force myself to focus and we stunt for another twenty minutes. Once I push Ash out of my brain, I'm back to normal. To the point that when we're finished, Brandy approaches me with a compliment.

"Good job just now. I think you guys threw Emma up in the air higher than you ever have before." She pats me on the back. "Whatever was bothering you earlier, you must've gotten over it."

Not particularly, though I'm not going to admit that to her. If I told her I had a problem, she'd ask all the right questions and next thing I'd know, I'd be confessing all to my cheer coach. I adore Brandy, but I do *not* want to tell her about my troubles with Ash.

The less people who know, the better.

We go back to the cheer room to get ready after practice is over. The girls who can't go to the dinner leave, and the rest of us change back into the clothes we wore to school. I'm thankful I had on my favorite pair of jeans, and I consider re-curling my hair, but that would look like I'm trying too hard. And there's supposedly no one on the team I'm trying to impress.

"I'm so glad we're eating with them tonight," Kaya tells me as she removes her mascara with a makeup wipe and then immediately reapplies it.

We're both sitting in front of one of the full-length mirrors that's propped against the wall in the cheer room. I'm brushing my hair, pleasantly surprised at how well the curl in my hair held. "Of course you're glad. You get to see your boyfriend," I tease her.

"Hey, I forgot to tell you." She turns to look at me. "Ash told Jaden that he's not with Mia."

My head immediately starts to ache. "What are you talking about?"

"He was telling Jaden at practice that he knew we saw him with Mia on Saturday, and he just wanted to reassure both of us that he's not with her. As in, Ash specifically mentioned my name." Kaya frowns. "Isn't that weird?"

"Totally weird."

"Like, why does he care what I think?" She frowns even

harder. "Maybe he didn't want us to tell everyone we saw them together?"

"Did you tell everyone you saw them together?"

"I don't know about Jaden, but he doesn't usually gossip about stuff like that. He doesn't really care who's dating who, you know? And the only person I told was you," Kaya says.

He told them so it would get back to me. I'm sure of it. Yes, I sound like I believe the world revolves around me, but I don't. Not usually. But this situation is definitely about me. He told Jaden because he knew he would tell Kaya and Kaya would tell me.

Now Ash looks like a good guy trying to squash rumors. What the hell ever.

I decide to curl my hair after all, because I'm bored and we still have twenty minutes before we have to go. As time draws closer to us heading over to the dinner, I get more nervous. To the point my stomach is twisted in knots and I feel like I'm going to puke.

This. Sucks.

Eventually we drive over to the church across the street from the high school, where the team dinner is held every Thursday night. The parents' booster club puts on the dinner for the JV and varsity teams, and sometimes they have a speaker who gets them pumped up for the game. We went to a couple of dinners last year, but this is our first one for this season.

I'm literally shaking as I walk into the room where the dinner is held, thankful Kaya has already ditched me for Jaden so she won't notice my over-the-top nerves. I'm surrounded by my oblivious team, me being the oldest one with the group since our two seniors both couldn't make this dinner. The younger girls are acting like they're about to lose their minds at the prospect of eating dinner with the football team.

"You know none of them pay attention to us," I say, just to burst their bubble. Though it is actually true. Maybe they'll come around when the dinner is over and flirt with us for a few minutes. But for the most part, they're too wrapped up in their own heads, focused on tomorrow's game.

"That's not true," Emma says. "One of them is looking at us right now."

"It's Asher Davis," one of the other girls—I'm not sure who—squeals.

Dread socks me in the stomach, and as discreetly as possible, I glance over my shoulder to find Ash standing a few feet away from us, surrounded by his friends who are all talking animatedly. His gaze is zeroed in on me.

I turn away, hoping he didn't notice me looking at him.

"Why doesn't Ben play football?" Emma asks me.

I return my attention to her, pushing Ash out of my mind. "He used to, but he kind of hated it, so he quit after sophomore year. Says he prefers playing basketball."

"I bet you're excited to cheer for him." Emma grins and starts doing this weird little dance like the goof she is.

We're a two-season sport, as in we cheer for both football and basketball. Sometimes we even cheer for the girls' volleyball team. By the time February rolls around, we are all so over cheer, it's not even funny.

"Yeah, it's fun cheering for basketball," I tell her absently. I can still feel Ash's gaze on me, and I want to turn around so I can glare at him, maybe even yell at him, but of course, I don't.

No way do I need to cause a scene.

My father approaches the wooden podium that's at the head of the room, and the boys immediately go quiet. The respect they have for him is pretty awesome. It makes me proud to see him command the room, and how they all look at him with reverence.

He makes a few announcements, then thanks the cheer team for joining them for dinner tonight. "…and since we're all about doing the polite thing, we'd like the ladies to go grab their dinner first," he says, looking right at me with a big smile on his face.

I smile in return, unable to stop myself. I may hate the fact that I'm in the same room with Ash Davis, but I love my daddy, and he loves me. So I'll bask in that for a few minutes.

We all line up at the buffet, which is being served by some of the parents. A local Mexican restaurant sponsored the dinner, so we have enchiladas and beans and rice to eat, as well as a small make-your-own taco bar. I wish I were hungrier, because it smells delicious, and I pile the food on anyway, hoping my appetite returns.

As I make my way back to my table, I spot Ash sitting two tables away from mine. He's watching me, as usual, his intense dark gaze trailing my every move, his expression serious, and I look away, hating how agitated he makes me feel.

What's weird is that Ben *never* makes me feel this way. Edgy and nervous and full of restless energy. Spending time with Ben is like hanging out with a good friend who I can also kiss for like twenty minutes. It's easy. Fun.

There is nothing easy or fun about Ash.

The more I listen to the girls at the table talk and gossip as we eat dinner, the better I feel. Their energy is endless, and I get swept up in their giggles and gossiping until I'm giggling and gossiping too. I've noticed something clicks in your brain at the end of sophomore year, when you realize you need to get serious and focus on your grades and your future. In the last few months, I sort of forgot what it felt like, to be silly and laugh and joke and gossip about boys.

The conversation helps me forget that Ash is even in the same room with us. To the point that when I make my way over to the dessert table all by myself, I find Ash standing next to me not even a minute after I got there.

"Glad you came tonight," he murmurs, standing way too close to me. "I've missed you, *friend.*"

I grab a small paper plate and set a cupcake on it. Then I take a chocolate chip cookie. I keep thinking my period is going to happen and it doesn't. I'm in full-on PMS mode. "You haven't missed me."

"I totally have. I even dreamed about you last night." He shifts even closer and bends his head, his mouth right at my ear. "You didn't kick me out of your house. In my dream, you took me to your bedroom and let me fuck you all night long."

I really hate his sweet and gross ways.

Oh, I dreamed about you!

Sweet.

I dreamed I was fucking you.

Gross.

He is such a contradiction. I never know what I'm going to get.

"If you're trying to be romantic, it's not working." I grab another cookie. No way am I going to eat all of this.

"I'm not going for romance. We're friends, right? I'm just keeping it real." He moves away from me, grinning. "In my dream, you kept saying my name."

"And I'm sure in your dream, you kept calling me Callahan," I return dryly.

"How'd you know?" He reaches out, giving me a gentle sock on the upper arm with his fist, and the seemingly innocent touch is like a caress to my Ash-starved soul. "I think you like it that I only call you Callahan."

"Not really."

"You'd rather I call you by your first name?"

I long to hear him say my name, not that I'd ever admit it. "I don't care what you call me."

"So I can call you fuck buddy and you'd be good with it?" His expression is one of pure innocence.

"Only if I can call you major asshole," I say sweetly.

And with that, I turn on my heel and make my way back to my table. I hear a few guys laughing, telling Ash that I got him good, and pride suffuses me. I know I shouldn't be happy that I insulted him so well, but I have to take my victories where I can. Most of the time, he has me so confused, I can barely speak.

A local former Division One college football player starts giving an inspirational speech once everyone has grabbed dessert, and I try my best to focus on what he's saying, but I can feel the vibration of my phone blowing up. At first, I think it might be Ben, but when I see that now familiar number that has no name attached to it on my screen, I know exactly who it is.

My friends think you're funny, Callahan.

And they're not just saying that because you're the coach's daughter either.

They have mad respect for you.

That you stood up to me.

You're kind of a badass.

His texts shouldn't make me feel better, but they do.

But then I start to panic, and worry over what exactly he might've shared with them about what happened between us.

You haven't told them anything, have you?

He responds quickly. **Told them anything about what?**

About us.

That we're friends? Yeah, they know we're friends.

Do they know anything else? I ask.

Like what? You talking about the night you were grinding on my dick? Yeah, they definitely DON'T know about that.

I hate him so, so much.

If you mention that to anyone, I'll...

What would I do?

You'll what? Send big, bad Ben after me?

Huh. I don't know who'd win in that fight. They're both pretty equally sized.

I would never send my boyfriend after you.

Yeah cuz he'd dump your ass if he ever found out what we did.

Glancing up from my phone, I spot Ash staring right at me. His expression is completely neutral, but I see the glimmer in his eyes. He's enjoying this.

Far too much.

Frustrated, I whisper to my coach that I need to use the restroom and I bail out of there, unable to take it any longer. The droning voice of the speaker, the watchful eye of my father. The even more watchful eye of stupid Ash Davis. I'm tempted to leave. Send Brandy a text that I'm not feeling well and I went home. She wouldn't be mad. She'd probably be jealous.

I stand in the lobby of the church where the team dinner's held, debating what I should do next, when I hear the door behind me quietly click shut. I turn to find Ash standing there, all by himself, a smug look on his handsome face.

"You need to leave me alone," I whisper hiss at him.

The innocent look on his face is pure bullshit. "What are you talking about?"

"You're following me."

He rests a hand on his chest. "I would never follow you."

"Liar." I spin on my heel and march right for the double doors, pushing my way outside. Ash is right behind me, so I keep talking to him. "I'm sick of you harassing me, Ash."

"I'm sick of you pretending you're hot for your boyfriend when we both know who you're really hot for," he retorts, his eyes flaring.

I gape at him, my surprise rendering me silent. "Why do you always have to make everything sound so dirty?"

"It's a particular skill I have." A strong breeze comes up, making all the leaves in the trees surrounding us rattle, and I wrap my arms around myself. The wind isn't that cold, but I'm chilled just the same.

By the look in Ash's eyes.

By the harsh tone of his voice.

"Isn't it exhausting, pretending all the time?" he asks when I still haven't said anything. "Pretending that you're someone you're not?"

I lift my chin. "I don't know what you're talking about."

"You act like you're better than me. You act like you and Ben are the perfect couple, when we know it's bullshit. And when I say we, I mean you and me." His lips thin as he contemplates me. "I could go back inside right now and tell everyone what we did. That would totally ruin the illusion you've so carefully built."

Panic rises in my throat, nearly choking me. "You wouldn't."

"I'm tempted."

"You can't." I take a step toward him. Then another. Glancing around, I make sure nobody is around before I whisper, "My father is in there."

"Yeah, and he'll probably shit his pants when I tell him his little princess isn't quite as perfect as he thinks."

Tears sting the corner of my eyes and I shake my head, fighting them off. Willing them to stop. I refuse to cry in front of this asshole. "Why are you like this?"

"Like what?"

"You act like you're obsessed with me and then you turn around and insult me." It's so true. He's mean. He's nice. He's mean.

I hate it.

"I don't know why," he says, looking down at the ground and kicking at a rock. He sends it skittering across the sidewalk just as the leaves start rattling again from the wind. "You make me crazy."

"You make me crazy too." And not in a good way. "You need to leave me alone."

"We can't be friends?" He sounds genuinely sad, and I know that has to be complete bullshit.

"There is no way we can be friends," I tell him, my voice firm. "This would never work. Right?"

He's quiet, shoving his hands in his front pockets, watching me like he does. A minute ticks by, or maybe it's only thirty seconds, I don't know. When he finally nods, I exhale shakily. I didn't even realize I was holding my breath.

"I'll leave you alone if you leave me alone," he says.

Relief floods me. "Deal."

"Shake on it?" Ash extends his hand toward me.

I take it, trying my best to ignore the currents of electricity that travel through my veins when our palms make contact.

CHAPTER 14

ASH

I open the door of our apartment and walk inside, holding my breath when the smell hits me. Stale air, tinged with a hint of cigarette smoke and rotting food.

Guess someone forgot to take out the trash.

The only light in the tiny living room comes from the TV on the wall, flickering and blue. It may be a flat screen, but it's old. And I'm pretty sure Don stole it from someone.

Don. My mom's boyfriend. The asshole who tries to tell me what to do, like he's my dad or something. I hate that guy.

I miss my dad.

"You bring me anything to eat?" Mom's scratchy voice startles me, and my backpack slips from my fingers, falling with a loud thud onto the floor. "Shh, you'll wake him up!" she whisper-screeches at me. I can only assume she's talking about Don.

"I didn't bring you anything," I tell her as I grab my backpack and sling it over my shoulder. "It was team dinner night."

Sometimes if I'm feeling generous or guilty, I'll bring Mom home half my Subway sandwich or nuggets from

McDonald's. I can't remember the last time she cooked a meal. She doesn't take care of herself. She doesn't take care of me either. There's never any food in the kitchen, and Mom doesn't have a consistent job, so there's never any money either. I used to work odd jobs here and there, helping people in the neighborhood, mowing lawns or cleaning out garages, but the money wasn't good enough.

Now, at least a couple of times a month, I sell Mom's prescription pills to my friends at school. I make good money doing it, even though it's a risk. If I get caught, they'll kick me out. My life will be fucked.

It's fucked already, so most of the time it's worth the risk. Besides, Mom doesn't even miss them. She has so many painkiller prescriptions, I don't think she notices when I swipe a few pills here and there.

"You don't care about me." Her words are slurred, and I wonder how much she's had to drink tonight. How many pills did she pop? "None of you care about me."

I stare at her, squinting into the darkness. She's lying on the couch, an old, threadbare blanket covering her thin body, her dark hair piled on top of her head in a sloppy bun. When I was younger, I remember thinking she was beautiful. Don't all boys believe their mama is the most beautiful woman in the world? I loved her, even when she pushed me away, griping that I wrinkled her clothes or messed up her makeup when I gave her a kiss on the cheek. All I wanted was her approval. Her love. I had Dad's love, but hers was always just out of my grasp.

She pushed me away so many times over the years, both literally and figuratively, that I eventually stopped trying.

Stopped caring.

I love her, but it's not the same. It's a guilty love. An obligation. She's my mother.

But she's not a good one. I realized that a long time ago.

"You didn't even bring me a sandwich?" she whines.

Without a word I exit the living room and head for my bedroom. She's complaining, her voice rising, following me down the hall, and I want to remind her that she doesn't want to wake Don up, but I keep my mouth shut. Just as carefully as I open my bedroom door, I close it, then grab the chair that sits at my old desk and slip it beneath the doorknob.

I don't want Don busting in here, or Mom. It's the only way I feel safe.

Setting my backpack on the desk, I unzip it and pull out the binder that holds all my classwork. It's big and already a mess, though we've been in school not even two months. I have homework I need to finish, and a test to study for. I may be a fuck-up who sells prescription pills on the side and sometimes drinks too much, who messes around with too many girls and acts like an asshole, but I care about my grades.

Maybe, if I'm lucky, my football skills and my grade point average will be my ticket out of the hellhole that's my life.

I collapse on top of my bed with my homework, determined to focus, but my mind drifts. I think about Autumn.

When do I not think about Autumn?

She is gorgeous. Sexy as fuck. A little mean. A lot sweet. She hates me, and I antagonize her whenever I'm near her, which only makes it worse. I don't know why she can't admit that she likes me. I lay it all on the line for her, and she turns me away every single time.

I'm also the one who says something stupid when I've got her in my arms, making her run away. Am I afraid when we get too close? Is that my problem? She's on a whole different level compared to me. She's rich and beautiful. She can have anything she wants.

No way would she want me. I'm broke. Broken, really.

Bad. Her dad is a good coach. He's worked with me one on one, given me plenty of attention and pointers and lectures, and all of it seems to come from a good place. I don't feel like he wants something more from me. He just wants to help.

It's weird, someone giving you something and not expecting anything in return. I'm used to takers. Mom's a taker. So is her asshole boyfriend. So are all my stupid friends. I tried to make nice with coach's son Jake, but that guy just glares at me like I'm his worst enemy and he wishes I'd go drown myself in the lake.

So I leave him alone.

I should leave his sister alone too. There's something between us, but it would never last long. It would definitely burn bright and hot, but then I'd say or do something and ruin it all. Autumn Callahan is not for me.

I need to remember that.

We were a perfect match,
    But sadly, matches burn.
    (unknown)

SENIOR YEAR

CHAPTER 15

AUTUMN

"For once in my life, I feel so grown up, you know? Like I'm an actual, real-life adult." I turn to look at my best friend, who's frowning at me like I've lost my mind. Kaya and I are walking through the senior parking lot, heading toward my car. We've been back at school for around a month, and now that we're seniors, we can go off campus for lunch. Which we do on an almost daily basis. This newfound freedom is exhilarating.

I can't wait until I leave for college. Talk about freedom.

"You feel grown up because you broke Ben's heart?" Kaya asks incredulously.

I restrain myself from rolling my eyes or worse, saying something I might regret. She's still Team Ben, and while I appreciate her feelings about Ben and that she likes him so much, I would love it if she were actually more loyal to me. "We can't all have perfect relationships like you and Jaden."

She scoffs. "Please. Jaden and I aren't perfect."

"You two are the epitome of the ideal high school relationship."

124

"Ugh, that's so obnoxious, right?" Kaya sends me a look. "I feel obnoxious, at least. I know we annoy people."

"When you've been the it couple your entire high school life, yeah, it's a little obnoxious," I say teasingly. I hit the keyless remote and my Jeep doors unlock. I didn't want to be that girl at school with the rich parents who buy her whatever car she wants, but I can't help it that my parents surprised me with my dream car over the summer. Before they gave me the Jeep Wrangler, I'd been driving my mom's old Lexus. And when I say old, I mean it was like a 2017, so it was practically brand new.

It was such a mom car, though. They traded it in for the Jeep, and I about screamed my head off when they surprised me with it right after the Fourth of July. I treat the Jeep like it's my baby and my friends make fun of me, but I don't care.

I know I'm spoiled. My brothers and sister are too. But our parents also make us work for our privileges. And I'm not talking about an actual job either. They want us to concentrate on school. Our grades slip, and phones are taken away. Or cars. Jake turns sixteen next year and then they'll have two drivers. Jake is so reckless, I don't know if they want him behind the wheel.

Jake is also super popular. More popular than I am, that's for sure. He's the star of the junior varsity football team. Everyone seems to like him—teachers and students alike. Even some of my more casual girlfriends want to be friends with Jake—or they want to be *with* him.

That's just weird.

Kaya and I climb into my Jeep, and I start the engine, carefully pulling out of the parking lot. There are eyes everywhere, and I'm talking about school administration. They make sure we don't speed out of the parking lot or drive over curbs. People in the community will call the school and report teenage drivers whenever they see someone speeding or driving like a total ass.

Sometimes, it feels like you can't get away with anything in a small town.

"I kept talking about me and Jaden when I didn't mean to," Kaya says as I pull onto the street. We're headed for our favorite sandwich shop in town, and we're going to meet Daphne there. "Tell me why you feel like such a grown up."

"Well." I clutch the steering wheel, keeping my eyes on the road. "It's because I made the very grown-up decision of breaking up with Ben before things got too deep."

"What do you mean? I thought you guys were in pretty deep with each other, if you know what I mean." Kaya waggles her brows.

Honestly? It wasn't that deep. Our relationship bored me. Don't get me wrong, he's a decent guy, he was a good boyfriend, he never did anything wrong. But there was no real spark between us. No fire, no passion. I always thought of Ben as a great friend who I could make out with, and I realized over the summer, that's not enough.

I want more. Maybe I can't find that here, so hopefully I'll find it in college.

"We never had sex," I confess to Kaya.

"Say what? Are you kidding me?" She's squealing, so loudly she's making me wince. "I thought you two already had!"

"Nope." I shake my head. Oh, we touched each other when we kissed, but all of it was hands-over-clothes type touching. Nothing too scandalous. "He never really tried to— pursue it."

"Pursue what?"

"Sex, Kaya." This time I do roll my eyes as I make a right on the street the sandwich shop is on. "He never really tried to take it to the next level."

"Really? Huh." Kaya seems surprised.

I don't know why. I've given her plenty of information about my relationship with Ben. The writing's been on the wall for a long time—we're not meant to be. We're better off as friends. I know that sounds like a total cliché and a line of bullshit, but it's true. And though Ben was disappointed and made a halfhearted attempt at asking me if we could try to make it work, we ended up both agreeing we're better off as friends.

Which is cool, you know? I'd rather be his friend than have him be a mortal enemy. I do care about him. A lot. I just know that we didn't work as boyfriend and girlfriend.

Hopefully he feels the same way.

I've been free since late June, when we split, and I haven't really tried to get with anyone else. It's been kind of nice, not having to deal with a boyfriend. Kaya has no idea what that's like, since she and Jaden have been together for years.

Years.

That's just crazy.

I park my Jeep and we enter the crowded restaurant, spotting Daphne who's already waiting in line. There's a few other seniors but it's mostly filled with business people, since it's prime lunch hour. Daphne, Kaya and I order our sandwiches and then find a tiny table to wait for our numbers to be called.

"Why didn't you try to pursue it?" she asks.

I frown. "What are you talking about?"

Daphne's frowning as well, since she's walking into this mid-conversation. "Yeah, what are you talking about?"

Kaya glances over at Daphne. "Ben and Autumn never had sex."

Daphne's eyes practically bug out of her head. "Are you serious right now?"

"Why is this such a big deal?" I shrug. "So we didn't have sex. So what?"

"You guys were together a long time," Daphne points out.

"And why didn't *you* try to pursue having sex with Ben? You can make the first move too, you know."

"Maybe I didn't want to?" I wince. "Is that bad?"

"I mean, kind of. Daphne's right. You two were together for like a year. Did you not like him that way?" Kaya seems genuinely perplexed.

"I don't know." I shrug. "It's hard to explain. He was like my—cuddly friend. The guy I could kiss and hang out with and who was always there for me, but did I want to jump his bones and fuck around at all hours of the day and night with him? No. He never made me feel that way," I explain.

It feels good to admit that. I wondered if something was wrong with me. Ben really is a great guy. He's nice, he gets along with everyone, he's cute, he's smart. I should be totally in to him, but I'm not.

I could blame it on a certain someone, but that's like using the certain someone as an excuse, and I don't want to do that.

"There's nothing wrong with having a cuddly friend," Daphne says brightly, and I know she's trying to make me feel better.

Kaya sends her a look. "It's kind of weird."

"I don't think I was really in love with him," I confess, making both of them turn and gape at me.

"I can't believe you never told us that before," Kaya says just as they call her order number.

"There are a lot of things I've never confessed to you before," I say under my breath as all three of us get up and approach the pickup counter. My number is called immediately after hers, with Daphne's called after mine.

"What do you mean, there are lots of things you've never

confessed before?" Kaya asks once we've resumed our spots at the table.

Oops. I didn't think she heard me. "I was kidding." I start eating my sandwich, but Kaya just stares at me, as does Daphne. "What?"

"You're keeping secrets." Kaya's eyes dance and she starts wiggling in her chair. "Come on, tell us."

"I just said that to be funny." I take another bite of my sandwich. Maybe if I keep my mouth full, I won't confess my sins.

"Bullshit." Daphne takes a sip of her drink, Kaya laughing. "Spill it. You know you want to tell us."

Should I tell them about Ash? They'll probably freak. We kept the promise we made to each other last year. He didn't talk to me, and I didn't talk to him. For the remainder of our junior year, we were able to avoid each other completely. Just like we did the year before that, after homecoming. It was easy, for the most part, since we didn't have many opportunities on campus to run into each other.

But sometimes after school we'd pass by each other in the parking lot, one of us always looking the other way real quick.

Usually me.

At prom, I was headed for the bathroom just as he exited the men's room. He stopped short when he first spotted me, his gaze sweeping over me, lingering on my dress, leaving me warm. I can admit I looked damn good that night, and while Ben said all the right things, telling me how beautiful I was, his words didn't come close to what Ash made me feel.

Just with a look.

Looking back, it was that night when I knew it could never work between me and Ben. It took me a little while to work up the courage to end things, and while I missed him at first, I can truly say I'm glad we aren't together anymore. I'd rather be alone than in a relationship that isn't that great.

So far I haven't seen much of Ash this school year. I don't run into him in the parking lot at all, since he's at football practice four days a week plus the games on Friday. I see him out on the field on Friday nights, but he's just a guy with a helmet on. Not like I can actually *see him*, see him. He's still the star quarterback, and my brother is thrilled he's graduating this year so he can take Ash's place next year. Dad talks about him over the dinner table sometimes, though I'm able to mostly tune it out. I don't need to hear about Ash's amazing arm or how he has no fear and will actually run the ball when he can't find someone to throw it to.

Well, maybe I *am* absorbing what Dad is saying, though I'm trying my best to forget about it. Forget about Ash.

"You are being way too quiet for way too long," Daphne says, interrupting my thoughts. "This has to be huge. You're crushing on someone else?"

I shake my head. "Not really."

"You did it with another guy and Ben has no clue," Kaya guesses.

"Kaya!" My cheeks burn hot and Kaya's eyes widen before she starts elbowing Daphne in the ribs.

"Oh my God! You did! You so did!" She's pointing at me, her voice rising, and I shush her, sending her a severe look.

"Be quiet." I lean across the table. "I don't want the entire restaurant to hear you."

Daphne glances around the room before turning to look at us once more. "I don't think they're paying any attention to us."

"Sorry, sorry." Kaya takes a bite of her sandwich and so do I, though my nervous stomach is sending me major signals that is a big mistake. "So what exactly happened?"

Hesitantly, I launch into the entire Ash and me saga. What

happened our sophomore year during the homecoming fiasco, and how I thought we had a chance, only for him to reject me. Last year when we kissed in his truck, and then he came to my house, the weekend Ben was gone. How rude Ash was to me that night at the team dinner and that's when we decided we needed to avoid each other. How we shook on it.

"And you've never talked to him again?" Kaya asks when I finish.

"Nope." I shake my head. "We leave each other alone."

"How did you keep this a secret from us?" Kaya shakes her head. "I can't believe you never told us."

"Are you mad?" I don't want them upset with me, but how could I explain my feelings for Ash when I didn't understand them myself?

"Not really," Kaya says. "I guess I understand."

"I'm not mad," Daphne says. "But you should know Ash is going out with Rylie Altman now."

My stomach drops, like I'm on a twisty roller coaster. "He is?"

Daphne nods. "They just made it official like a few weeks ago."

Rylie Altman is a star volleyball player. She's a year younger than us, tall and lean and super cute, with great style. Blonde hair and golden eyes, nice to everyone. She's popular. I've never heard anyone say a bad thing about her.

I don't personally know her, but she's always been polite to me, and I've been polite to her in return. Now, I sort of want to pull her hair out. Which makes me a petty human being.

"You and Ash never did anything else beyond kissing, did you?" Kaya raises her eyebrows.

"No." I shake my head. Though if he would've pushed, I probably would've caved in. Actually, I'm sure I would've.

Every time we were together, he made me burn. "Just kissing. Nothing else. And that's bad enough, considering the last time we kissed, I was still with Ben."

"And we had no idea." Daphne reaches over and swats my arm, making me yelp. "You're a big ol' sneak."

"I was embarrassed." More than anything, I didn't want it to get out. I didn't want them to judge me. I didn't want the entire school to judge me, really. Not that I think Kaya and Daphne would've blabbed and spread my secret, but you just…

You never know.

Sometimes it's best to keep things to yourself is my motto.

"You big ho." Kaya acts like she's going to hit me and I dodge away from her, making her laugh. "Was he a good kisser?"

I press my lips together, thinking about it. Honestly, I don't have to think for long. "Yeah."

"Better than Ben?" Daphne asks.

"Yes." I don't even hesitate with my answer.

They both laugh. "Oooh, this is so juicy," Kaya says.

"You can't tell anyone. I'm serious. If this gets out, and Ben finds out?" I shake my head, unable to comprehend what could happen. "That would be awful."

"My lips are sealed." Kaya motions zipping her mouth shut. "I swear."

"Same." Daphne nods vigorously.

I change the subject to cheer stuff. We're already over it and the season has barely begun, and I'm blaming that on senioritis. It is real and I feel sort of bad that I feel this way, especially when Mom's always telling me to enjoy my senior year, it's my last year of school where I can truly be a kid, and blah blah blah. She means well and I know what she's saying, but seriously.

Get me out of here.

CHAPTER 16

*I*t's late. I'm sitting on my bed, binders and textbooks open and spread all around me, along with my laptop. I'm watching my favorite YouTubers while trying to do homework and I can't necessarily concentrate on both, which means homework is suffering. Leaning over, I slam my laptop shut, and immediately hear loud voices.

At—I glance at my phone—9:37 at night.

Sliding off my bed, I make my way to my closed bedroom door and slowly open it to find my sister is already lurking outside her room in the hall, her expression full of concern. When she spots me, she raises her fingers to her lips, and I nod to let her know I get it.

What's going on? I mouth to her.

Ava drops her finger from her lips and shrugs, then waves a hand for me to follow her, so I do. Beck should already be asleep and Jake's in his room, meaning it's just the two of us out here.

Raised voices is not a common thing in our household. My parents don't fight much. Oh, they squabble a little bit here and there, but if they ever full-blown argue, they never let us catch them doing it.

We creep down the hall to the stairwell, standing at the top of it. Ava looks at me and it's like we can read each other's minds—we both sit at the top of the stairs, listening. We can hear everything said, yet no one can actually see us unless they're standing right in front of the stairs.

It's a risk we're both willing to take.

"...I don't know if he should be here, Drew. You know how I feel about bringing problems home. We vowed to each other a long time ago we wouldn't do that," Mom says.

I'm frowning. Bringing trouble home? What is she even talking about?

"He's sitting outside right now because he's too damn embarrassed to face you. You need to see him. Talk to him. What his mother's boyfriend did to him is..." Dad's voice drifts and he makes an angry sound. "If that asshole ever came near me, I'd tear him apart."

Who in the world are they talking about?

"I just want to protect our babies. You know that's all I've ever wanted," Mom admits, and she sounds so sad, it's almost heartbreaking.

"I know. You also always want to help those who are in bad situations, and this boy...he needs our help, babe. He's in the worst possible situation ever."

Unease sweeps over me. I'm pretty sure I know who they're talking about.

Mom sighs. "Is it a good idea that he stays with us, though? He's troubled. Beyond troubled, really. Do you want him constantly around our children? Our son, who'll take his place next year on the team? And our daughter, who's the same age? I think Autumn's had a few run-ins with him over the years, though I'm not exactly sure," Mom says.

Oh God. I was right. They're talking about Ash. Something bad happened to Ash. And Dad wants him to…

Stay at *our* house?

No freaking way.

Uh uh.

"I thought they were friends." Ah, clueless Dad.

"Not exactly friends, no."

"Maybe friendly then? They did run for homecoming together, right? I thought they might've become a thing at one point."

Me too, Dad. Me too.

"No, they're definitely not a thing. They've never been a thing. But I don't know how she'll feel about him living in our house. I don't know how *I'll* feel having him live in our house." Mom sounds upset, and it makes my heart hurt.

Ava nudges me in the ribs, and when I glare at her, she makes an exaggerated pouty face before she whispers, "Are they talking about Asher Davis?"

"Shh." I don't want to miss a word they say.

"He has nowhere else to go, Fable. The kid desperately needs a stable environment, and we can provide him with that. We have plenty of rooms in this place. He'd probably get lost. Hell, we'll probably never see him," Dad says, using his most persuasive voice. I've heard him use it on Mom before, and it usually works.

They're quiet for a moment before she finally speaks.

"We'll have to set down rules." Look, she's cracking already.

"Let's go outside and talk to him," Dad says.

"Why can't he come into the house?" Mom sounds confused.

"I already told you: he's embarrassed. He doesn't even want to be here. I pretty much forced him to come home with me."

"Drew! That's probably against the law or something!"

"Where's he going to go? And who's going to report me? His bitch mom who had her boyfriend beat the shit out of him? Like CPS is going to be on her side," Dad mutters. I hear the creak of the back door opening. "He's sitting by the pool. Come on."

The door shuts, and then there's no more talking.

"We should go find Jake. He'll know what happened." Ava rises to her feet and runs down the hall, knocking on our brother's door. She tries the handle, but it's locked. "Jake! Let me in."

"Go away!" Jake yells in response.

Ava sends me a look, and now I'm the one shrugging. "If the door's locked, you don't want to go in there. If you get what I mean."

Ava makes a face, then knocks on Jake's door again. "Come on! Autumn and I have questions!"

"Ava, quit screaming. You'll wake up Beck." Though that kid sleeps like the dead.

We hear stomping, the door unlocks and then Jake's standing there, his tall, lanky body filling the space. "What the hell do you want?" he growls, glaring at Ava.

"Hey, leave her alone." I jump to my feet and go over to where Ava's standing. I'm very rarely on her side. Ava is annoying as crap. But we need information, and Jake's probably the only one who's got it.

Jake clamps his lips shut, frustration pouring off him. He reminds me so much of Dad. The dark hair, the piercing blue eyes, the same body shape. They walk the same, they talk the same, and girls at school trip over themselves to gain his attention. "What do you two want?"

"What happened at practice today?" Ava asks.

He glances over at Ava, then me. "She shouldn't hear it."

"Too late. We were both spying on Mom and Dad just now. She's heard plenty," I tell him.

With a sigh, Jake runs a hand through his hair. "Where are they?"

"Outside."

"With Ash?"

"I'm assuming so," I say as Ava nods.

"He didn't show up for practice, and all the coaches were mad. Dad looked ready to rip someone's face off, he was so angry. People kept calling and texting Ash, but he wouldn't answer. After a while, Dad wasn't so much pissed as concerned. Ash never, ever misses practice. He may be an arrogant motherfucker, but he always shows up for the team," Jake explains.

"Jacob," I hiss, flicking my head in Ava's direction. "Don't cuss in front of her."

"I hear worse at school," Ava says matter-of-factly, making me roll my eyes. I mean, she *is* a freshman in high school, so I know what she's saying is true.

"Continue," I tell Jake.

"So with about an hour left in practice, Dad leaves. He goes to Ash's house, and he lives in this shitty place on the other side of town, near the elementary school. You know those old apartments behind the school?" When we nod, he does too. "Yeah, he lives there. Dad rolls up, just as Ash is practically thrown out the door of his apartment, and he's just beat the hell up. Bruises and cuts on his face, a black eye. The works. Guess his stepdad or his mom's boyfriend, whatever the hell you call him, kicked his ass because he stole a pack of smokes from him."

My heart clenches at hearing Jake's story. "Did you see him?"

"Dad came back to pick me up after practice with Ash in the backseat, so yeah. Swore me to secrecy on the drive home. Well, Ash did. He doesn't want anyone knowing what happened," Jake says.

"So Ash actually came home with you?"

"Like I said, he was sitting in the back of the car holding an ice pack to his eye when Dad came to pick me up. It was hard to look at Ash. His mouth was all swollen. He looked like hell." Jake shakes his head. "Dad dropped me off here first, then they took off. I think he was trying to take Ash to a doctor? But he was already telling Dad there was no way he could go to emergency or whatever. He was afraid he'd get picked up. Like from the cops? I don't know. I guess he threw punches too. Sounds like a freaking nightmare if you ask me…"

My brother keeps talking, but I tune him out. I want to go find Ash. Make sure he's okay. But would he let me see him? Would he even talk to me? Probably not. He'd most likely tell me to go fuck myself.

Once there's nothing more to say from any of us, I make my way back to my bedroom and try to resume finishing my homework. But I can't concentrate.

All I can think about is Ash.

Deciding I can't do this, I shut my notebooks, my binders, my textbooks. I pile them all on top of my desk and then I leave my bedroom. Sneak down the stairs, making my way through the mostly darkened house until I'm in my mom's office, which overlooks the backyard and the pool.

Where I spot Ash sitting on the edge of one of our lounge chairs, his hand over his eye, his head tilted back as Mom stands there, talking to him. Dad stands just behind Mom, his hands on his hips, his face full of concern—and barely contained anger. My heart lurches, seeing all three of them outside. Together.

Having Ash at our house will change everything.

And I don't know if I want anything to change.

CHAPTER 17

FABLE

*D*rew takes my hand and leads me toward the pool. The water is lit, a gentle blue that casts our backyard in an almost ethereal glow, and I see the boy. Sitting with his back to us, hunched over as if he wishes he could make himself disappear. Our steps slow, and when I glance over at my husband, he sends me a look, one that says *go easy.*

As if I'd come hard at this poor child who's just been beaten by his mother's piece-of-shit boyfriend. Please. I totally feel his pain. I dealt with enough of my dead mother's piece-of-shit boyfriends to last me three lifetimes.

"Hey Ash. You've met my wife before, right? You remember?" Drew's voice is soft, like he's speaking to a skittish animal, and I have a flash of memory of him talking to me the same exact way. In those early days of our relationship, when I was always this close to running.

Though the real runner in those early days was Drew. Can't remind him, though. He hates that.

"Yeah. Hey." The boy's voice is a raspy croak, and I wonder if the man also choked him. "Mrs. Callahan. Sorry to show up like this."

We're standing right in front of him now, and I'm over-whelmed with the need to reach out and touch his shoulder. Offer him comfort. I'm sure he'd flinch, whether he was injured there or if I spooked him, so I keep my hands to myself. "Don't apologize. And please, call me Fable."

He lifts his head, flicking dark hair out of his eyes, and it takes everything I have not to gasp out loud. It physically pains me to see how badly he's been beaten, to know that someone pummeled this poor child's face, all over a pack of cigarettes. His left eye is swollen and there's a cut above it that looks painful. He rests his hand over it, as if he knows it's horrible to look at, the poor thing.

"Maybe he should see a doctor." I turn to Drew, who has a helpless expression on his face.

"Fuck that," Asher Davis spits out, then immediately looks contrite. "I don't want to go to the hospital, ma'am. If I do that, they'll report what happened to me. And then they'll put me in foster care, or worse: jail." He grimaces, then immedi-ately evens out his face as best he can, as if that might've hurt him. "Sorry for cursing, but I do not want that to happen."

"Then you'll have to let me take care of your wounds and clean you up," I tell him. "The cut above your eye looks serious."

"I cleaned him up a little," Drew starts, but I whirl on him, sending him a look, and he goes quiet.

Drew has been there for this boy from the start. It was Asher Davis's raw talent that had convinced my husband he needed to volunteer as a coach for the team, besides preparing our son to eventually be on the football team. Now Drew is the offensive coordinator for the varsity team, and I still can't believe how lucky our little local high school is to have this former Super Bowl *champion* as their coach, yet here we are. Living our best life with Drew the Do-Gooder.

I love my husband more than words can say, but sometimes he does so much for others that I feel selfish. I want him for me, for us, for our family, and no one else. He's mine. Ours. No one else gets him.

But all sorts of people get him, including this poor child who's currently dripping blood on my thousand-dollar chaise lounge cushion because his mom doesn't give a shit about him. And that makes me furious.

"I'm fine. The cut's no big deal. Might give me a cool scar," Ash assures me, tilting his head back farther, and that's when I see them. The fingerprint bruises on his neck. I raise a hand to my mouth, stifling the cry that spills, and he immediately hangs his head, knowing I spotted them. "It's nothing," he mumbles to the ground.

Without thought, I kneel in front of him, resting my hands on his knees gently, so I don't hurt him if he's injured there. He doesn't flinch, he doesn't move at all. Just keeps his head bent, his dark hair just long enough to fall forward and obscure his face. He's like an injured puppy. An animal who's been kicked and beaten again and again. I bet if I got him to take off his shirt, I could find some old scars. Others might not recognize them, but I could. I've seen that sort of thing. On myself.

On my brother, Owen.

The scars eventually fade to nothing, but the wounds remain. And seeing Ash like this opens up all those old wounds, filling me with pain. Pain for him. Pain for myself.

"Asher." He doesn't so much as twitch when I say his name. "Ash. Will you let me take you inside and check your injuries? Then you can take a shower and once you've cleaned up, I can apply some bandages if needed."

Oh so slowly, he lifts his head, until his black-as-night eyes meet mine. He's scared. His entire body is trembling, and his face is covered with a thin sheen of sweat. It's colder up here, close to the lake, and maybe that's why he's shivering, but I don't think so.

I think he's terrified. And the shock of what's happened to him is starting to wear off, leaving him a mess.

If I knew he'd go willingly, I'd probably pull him into my arms and clutch him tight. Tell him everything's going to be okay, even though I don't know if that's the case. I don't want to lie, but who knows what's going to happen to him?

Drew and I will just have to take care of him as best we can.

"I don't want to go to school tomorrow," he whispers, his voice still raspy, as if it hurts to speak. "I don't want anyone to see me."

"You don't have to go to school for a few days, but eventually you need to get back there. You don't want to get behind in your classes." I glance over my shoulder to see Drew nodding in agreement, his hands on his hips. The frustration is coming off him in waves, and I know he feels helpless.

I do too.

"Whatever. Everyone will know by tomorrow morning anyway. They'll probably say I'm dead." His mouth quirks into a half smile that doesn't reveal any teeth, but then he groans in pain. "Fuck, my lips hurt." He sends me a look. "Sorry."

"I've said worse," I reassure him, making his eyes go wide. Reaching out, I gently place my hand on his head, ruffling his hair. He ducks away from my touch, like it's a habit, and I'm afraid this boy is going to steal a part of my heart. I thought my heart was full enough with my four children and my husband.

But I have a feeling I could end up loving this one as my own too.

CHAPTER 18

AUTUMN

*M*om is with Ash until past midnight. I scramble back upstairs by the time the back door opens and they all come inside the house. Mom sends Dad upstairs, and I hide in my room with the door wide open while he fetches extra clothes from Jake, who's close in size to Ash.

Meaning Ash has to be spending the night. In our house.

I can't believe it.

Once I hear Dad running back down the stairs, I came out of my room to find Jake's door open. He spots me and frowns. "He's staying here."

"Ash?" I whisper, needing one hundred percent confirmation.

"Yeah. He's in the guest bathroom shower now. Dad asked if I could loan him a couple sets of clothes to see him through the next few days until he can get back to his place and pick up the rest of his stuff." Jake shakes his head. "What the hell is going on? Are they going to let him move in here?"

Jake doesn't seem too happy about this. "Maybe? I'm guessing he has nowhere else to go."

"Yeah, but why do they have to bring him here? So he can be our new family charity case?"

"That's mean, Jake."

"It's true, and you know it. Dad likes to have projects. Now Ash can be his." Jake punches the doorframe, curses under his breath, and then slams his bedroom door.

Well. That was interesting.

I argue with myself over going downstairs and then finally decide screw it. I live here. I can go in the kitchen and get myself a glass of water if I want. So I go running down the stairs, my steps extra heavy as a warning that I'm coming.

When I enter the kitchen I find Dad already standing there, a neutral expression on his face. "Hey princess. You're up late."

I grimace. "Don't call me that."

He raises his brows. "Sorry. How's, hey Autumn?"

Smiling, I make my way to the refrigerator. "That's much better."

"I don't know how much you heard earlier..." His voice drifts and I shut the fridge door, turning to look at him with complete innocence.

"What are you talking about?" I don't want him to know Ava and I were spying. I want to see exactly what he'll tell me, and if he'll be one-hundred percent truthful.

He blows out a harsh breath before bracing his hands on the edge of the counter. "Ash was—abused today. By his mother's boyfriend. He didn't show up to practice and after no one could get a hold of him, I went over to his place to find him tumbling out the front door of his apartment, kicked by that asshole who beat the hell out of him. Sorry."

I smile gently, touched he'd want to apologize to me for cursing. "It's okay, Daddy. You're mad."

"I'm mad as hell," he agrees with a ferociousness I've never heard from him before. "If I could, I'd go personally kick that animal's ass myself. But I don't want to go to jail, so there's that."

"We don't want you to go to jail either." I take a deep breath, exhaling slowly. "Where's Ash?"

"In the shower. Your mom is making up the bed in the guest room for him. I got some clothes from Jake that Ash can borrow. I think." Dad hesitates, uneasiness appearing in his gaze. "I think he's going to stay with us for—a while."

"Oh." I go still, standing on the opposite side of the kitchen island from my dad. "How long?"

"I don't know. Does that—bother you? Having Ash here?"

"We're not really friends." And that isn't necessarily a lie.

"You get along with him okay, though? Right? At least you can try to? Poor kid has been through hell today. He's hurt." Dad shakes his head, his expression grim. "He's probably been through hell for some time now."

"Should he see a doctor?"

"He refuses, but I think we'll take him to one in the morning. Right now, we all need to go to bed and start the day fresh tomorrow. You included." He approaches me, smiling as he reaches out and gently squeezes my shoulder. "You finish your homework?"

"Yes," I lie. I can finish it during lunch tomorrow. Or during other classes. "I'm going to go to bed. Good night, Daddy."

"Night, princess. Ooops, Autumn." He chuckles and the sound does something to me. Twists my heart and makes me sad. I run to him, run *into* him really, my arms wrapped tight around his waist as I bury my face against his chest. His scent is familiar, comforting.

"I love you," I tell him, my voice muffled.

He runs his hand over my hair, and I swear I hear a hitch in his voice when he says, "I love you, too."

* * *

It's past one in the morning and I'm walking through my house like some sort of creeper, coming to steal whatever I can find. I'm downstairs, on the opposite side of the house, the side not many people see. I rarely come over here. Mom's office is here, along with an exercise room she and Dad use on occasion, but not really. Beck is currently requesting they turn it into a theater room, and knowing how things work out for him, he'll probably get his wish.

The guest bedroom and bath, which is like a second master suite, is on this side of the house. I remember that when we first moved here, I wanted this room for my own so bad. I begged and pleaded, but they weren't having it.

Now I can see why. I'd be isolated. I could slip in and out of the house easily. In fact, I still can, but I'm not wanting to leave the house.

I'm trying to seek out the newest person who's staying here.

When I spot the guest bedroom door, I'm surprised to see it's partially open. I figured he'd keep that door tightly closed and possibly locked. But it's not.

And then I see a camera flash. Ash is awake. He's most likely on Snapchat. But would he really take a selfie when he looks as bad as he does? I mean, I don't know how bad that is, since I haven't seen him yet, but still…

"Callahan." His voice is low, but I can still hear it. "Is that you?"

I'm shocked. What did he do, sense my presence? That's just weird. I go to the doorway, stopping just outside of it. "Can I come in?"

"Hell no. I don't want you to see me." The mattress moves, and I assume he's shifting into a more comfortable position. A grunt escapes him, then a little groan. "Go away."

Now it's finally his turn to tell me to go away. "Are you okay?"

"No. No, I'm pretty fucked up, but thanks to your parents, I'm hoping I'll be okay in a little while," he answers.

I bet that is the most truthful Ash has ever been with me. And I can appreciate that. "Do you need anything?"

"Just your tender loving care," he says, and I know he's teasing me.

"You won't even let me come in the room." I'm now standing in the doorway, and there's no light on, but the shine of the moon through the bare window that faces the backyard illuminates the space with a silvery glow.

"Trust me. You don't want to. I look fucking awful." He chuckles under his breath. "Feel pretty damn bad too."

"What happened?"

"I don't want to talk about it." He says those words quickly, and I respect his wishes.

"I guess I should go."

"Yeah, you should. Let me get some sleep."

"You weren't sleeping when I showed up here."

He sighs. "Caught me."

"Who were you talking to?" I squint, trying to make out his features, but there's a shadow across his face. His mouth appears swollen, and I see there's a white bandage above his eye. He's holding himself stiffly, as if it hurts to move, and I feel bad. Despite everything we've gone through, how terrible he's been to me, how awful I've been to him, I want to tell him sorry. I want to comfort him.

But I can't, because he has a girlfriend.

"I wasn't talking to anyone," he says, knocking me from my thoughts.

"I saw the flash of your camera."

"I was taking a photo of myself to document this shit. So I don't ever forget it."

I believe him.

Taking a deep breath, I say, "Well, good night."

I'm turning to leave when his voice stops me. "You going to try to follow me around all the time now, Callahan?" He just experienced the worst thing ever, and now he's teasing me. He could've suffered worse injuries, he could've *died.*

And he's acting like it's no big deal.

"Of course not," I retort, determined not to make it a big deal either.

"Good," he returns just as fast. "Guess we're going to have to try real hard to avoid each other then."

"Guess so," I say, leaving before I say something more.

Something stupid.

Something untrue.

I ENTER the kitchen the next morning to find Ash sitting at the counter, eating scrambled eggs and bacon with toast. Mom never makes us breakfast during the weekdays. That's a weekend thing, and since we've moved here, it's become Dad's weekend thing.

I'm not in the best mood in the mornings, so seeing Ash get better treatment annoys me. This also means I'm a heartless bitch and I need to get over it.

"Morning," I say in general, though I'm really talking to Mom, who's plating more food, I'm assuming for me. I don't look at Ash. It's like I'm afraid to see his face, though I need to turn and see it eventually.

"Good morning." Mom is extra cheerful—also unusual. Pretty sure I inherited my cloudy morning moods from her. She smiles at me and indicates the plate before her with the spatula in her hand. "You want breakfast?"

"Sure." I take my breakfast and turn, fully facing Ash for

the first time. I stare at his face, our gazes meeting, and the plate slips from my fingers, falling onto the wood floor with a loud clatter, eggs and toast and bacon everywhere.

He grins at me, and he reminds me of a pirate with only one eye open. All he needs is a patch. His mouth looks like he received Kylie Jenner-style lip injections, they're so swollen. His cheek is bruised, along with a few scratches, and there are finger-sized bruises on his neck. "Mornin', sunshine," he says, his voice raspier than usual.

I press trembling fingers to my lips as I take him in, and my heart literally aches for him. How can he act like this is no big deal? "Oh Ash."

His smile fades, replaced by a scowl. "Don't feel sorry for me."

He's mad. Mad because I feel bad over what happened to him. Mad because I had the indecency to show sympathy. I don't understand him. I will probably never understand him. And I wish I could.

I wish I could go to him and hug him close. Tell him everything's going to be okay. But that would be a lie, because I don't know if his life will be okay. He's a mystery, and so are his circumstances. I doubt he'll ever tell me what's really going on.

And I'm not sure if I want to know.

At a loss of what to say, I kneel and start picking up the mess I made, grabbing the food with shaky hands and throwing it on the thankfully still-intact plate. Mom helps me, sending me a look as we're both bent over the floor.

"Act normal," she whispers, and I just stare at her incredulously. How can I act normal when the very boy I've dreamed about my entire high school existence is now staying in my house? And who appears to have been beat within an inch of his life?

We both rise, Mom dumping the food in the trash before

she grabs another plate. "Sit down," she tells me. "I'll bring you your breakfast."

I go to the counter and sit on a stool, not right next to Ash, though. I leave an empty seat between us, because I can't be that close. I don't want to see the damage that closely yet. I'd rather stare at it from a distance.

But I'm not distant enough. I study him unabashedly as Mom engages him in tentative conversation. The bruises around his neck break my heart. Did his mom's boyfriend actually try to *kill* him? The bruises that ring his eye go from black to purple to red, and his actual eye is swollen into a slit, while the cut above it is held together with a butterfly bandage. I wonder if that wound actually needs stitches. Dad mentioned they'd probably take him to the doctor this morning, and I really hope they do. Ash looks like he needs serious care.

Ava is next to enter the kitchen, and before she can even catch a glimpse of Ash, he's gone. He doesn't bother catching my eye or saying anything. Just slips off the barstool and makes his way toward the opposite end of the house, where the guest room is.

I'm wondering if we're going to start calling it Ash's room now.

Mom turns away from the stove with a plate in her hand, stopping short when she sees the empty barstool occupied by Ash only seconds ago. "Where did he go?"

I shrug. "He just—left."

Ava settles onto the stool, smiling at Mom. "What did we do to deserve a big breakfast?"

Mom parts her lips, ready to answer but I interrupt her. "She did it for Asher Davis. We just benefited."

"That's not true." Mom presses her lips together.

I send her a look. "Come on."

With a sigh, Mom deposits the plate in front of Ava. "Fine, you got me."

I munch on my last bit of bacon and stand, grabbing my plate to take it to the sink. "Hurry up, Ava. We have to leave in ten minutes." I drive my brother and sister to school every morning, since we all go to the same one now, which is kind of weird. It's been a long time since I've been in school with Ava, though this is our last year together.

I'm leaving the kitchen as Beck comes barreling in. "I smell bacon!"

Mom laughs. "Good morning to you, too. I guess you want some breakfast? Autumn!"

I pause in my tracks, glancing over my shoulder at her. "What?"

"Tell Jake to come down here and eat real quick before you guys leave."

"I'm not going upstairs." My backpack is in the laundry room/mudroom that leads into the garage. "Text him."

Mom rolls her eyes. "Fine." She whips her phone out of her pocket and starts tapping on the screen, ignoring me.

Which is good. Because I have other plans.

I hurry down the hall toward the guest bedroom, pausing in the open doorway just in time to see Ash, naked from the waist up, his back to me. He bends over slowly, as if it pains him, and snatches a T-shirt from the bed, then tugs it on.

Deciding I'm a total creeper who needs to make herself noticed, I clear my throat and knock on the door lightly. "Can I come in?"

He keeps his back to me. "As long as you don't fling a plate of food at me, Callahan, we're good."

"I didn't fling the plate—" I clamp my lips shut, annoyed with myself. I don't need to defend what happened earlier. I was seriously so shocked by his condition, I couldn't help but react. And now, as usual, he's trying to play it off as one big joke.

"I almost wore eggs and bacon this morning." He turns to face me, and I hold everything in. The words, the pain, the surprise at yet again seeing him like this. His beautiful face, marred. Almost unrecognizable. "All thanks to you."

"I'm sorry," I whisper. "It was just so…"

"Don't apologize." He starts pacing briskly, then immediately slows his steps, and I know he has to hurt. "And don't— don't tell anyone what I look like, okay?"

"I won't talk about you at all," I promise.

He stops in front of me. "Really? You won't?"

I shake my head.

"They're all gonna talk anyway." He's not wrong. Our school is one big gossip fest. "I texted with Rylie a little last night before I went to bed, but I didn't tell her where I was," he says.

"You didn't?" Why not?

"I don't want to bring her into this."

"Speaking as a someone who's been a guy's girlfriend, and depending on how serious you two are, I think she deserves to know. She'll only worry about you."

"We're not really together." He shrugs, and his admission makes me happy, which means I'm a terrible human. "Why would she give a shit? Why does *anyone* give a shit?"

Oh. I've been around a variety of Ashes, but never a poor, pitiful Ash. "I'm guessing Rylie gives a shit about you. She's a nice person."

He squints at me with one eye, since the other is pretty much swollen shut. "You friends with her?"

"Sort of?" My answer is like a question. We're not close. We have mutual friends.

Ash nods once, then reaches up, tentatively running a

hand through is unruly hair. "Rylie won't like this. This might be too messy for her."

I'm frowning. "Too messy?"

"She likes things to look a certain way. Sort of like you, Callahan, and your pretend life." He smiles, but it fades fast.

I'm guessing he saw the hurt flicker in my eyes. I have no idea what he's talking about, or if that's an insult. I think it was.

"I have to go." I smile brightly. Falsely. "See ya later."

I exit the room before he can say anything else, which he doesn't.

He doesn't stop me from leaving either.

CHAPTER 19

The high school is humming with gossip about Ash all morning long, to the point that by lunch I hear a rumor he's hooked up to machines in a hospital and near death. I remain quiet, though it downright kills me not to correct anyone. All the stories about what happened between Ash and his mother's boyfriend have a hint of truth wrapped up in a bundle of lies.

I'm in the quad as usual, eating with Kaya, Daphne and our group of friends, when Rylie Altman approaches our table.

Of course she does.

"Hey Autumn." She smiles, and it immediately wavers. There's so much emotion swirling in her eyes, I'm afraid she might burst into tears at any moment. "Can I talk to you for a minute?"

"Sure." I set my sandwich down on its wrapper, ignoring the curious looks Kaya is shooting me. I haven't even said anything to her, and she's my best friend. I told her my parents said I couldn't talk about it, because she knew Ash was with my father yesterday, thanks to Jaden, who was at practice when it happened.

But that's all she knows. I'll reveal all when I can, what I can, but right now, I have to stay true to my word.

Stay true to Ash.

I follow Rylie to a little alcove behind the library building, and we both sit on the empty bench with plenty of space between us. I refuse to speak first. She's the one who wanted to talk to me, and I don't want to slip and say something I shouldn't.

She's the only person on this entire campus who I believe deserves to know what really happened. Even if it's just glossed-over details, she still should know that Ash has been hurt, but he's safe. Even though he said they're not together, they have some sort of connection. Why else would she want to talk to me?

It's when I hear sniffles that I realize Rylie is crying. I glance over to find she's sitting with her head bowed, clutched hands resting in her lap. She's wringing her fingers, the tears falling onto her hands, and I scoot closer to her, slipping my arm around her shoulders and giving her a squeeze.

We've barely said more than twenty words to each other in the years we've gone to school together, but I hate seeing her pain.

"He won't talk to me," she finally says, her voice trembling. "I keep texting him and he won't respond. I don't know where he's at, or how badly he's been injured. All the rumors are scaring me so bad, and everyone keeps coming up to me since we're together and I look like an idiot, because I. Don't. Know!"

The last three words explode out of her and then she starts sobbing in earnest. I think about what she said, that they're together, when he claimed last night that they're not. Who's telling the truth here?

I don't know.

All I can do is hold Rylie as she cries, pat her back, make sympathetic sounds. I let her get it all out, glaring at anyone who dares to check on us, but there are very few. When she finally quiets, her crying minimalized to a few hiccups and lots of sniffles, I say something.

"He's safe. He stayed at my house last night."

Rylie pushes away from me, her tear-filled eyes wide. She's really pretty, even when she cries—blonde and pink-cheeked, with golden eyes. No wonder Ash is drawn to her. "He's safe? He stayed at your house?" She rests a hand over her chest. "Your dad is a hero."

He is *my* hero, and I don't like hearing anyone talk about him like that. Makes me feel possessive. "He did the right thing. They were supposed to take Ash to a doctor this morning. Maybe that's why he hasn't responded to your texts yet."

Relief makes Rylie sag a little, and she exhales raggedly. "So he was never in the hospital. Or jail."

"No. He's moving slower, and he's definitely been beat up, but it's not as bad as everyone is making it out to be," I reassure her. "And he definitely isn't in jail."

"Thank you for letting me know." Her gaze meets mine, direct and so grateful. This girl is an open book. "Thank you for..." Her voice drifts and she slowly shakes her head. "For letting me cry on your shoulder. Literally."

We both laugh a little. "You're welcome. You're the only person I thought who should know, since you two are—together."

It took me a second to get that last word out, like the lameass I am. I need to get over my weird feelings for Ash, once and for all. We're nothing. We've never really been anything. All that crap he said to me last year was just that—crap. He didn't mean a word of it. Plus, he has Rylie now, even if he denies it.

She appears to be totally into him.

"You know, I always thought you two got together when I was a freshman and you were sophomores." Rylie tilts her head, contemplating me. "During homecoming."

I sit up straighter, my spine rigid. Not something I want to talk about. No one really paid attention to us during that time.

At least, that's what I thought.

"I've liked Ash for years, since the beginning of my freshman year. So I couldn't help but notice you two together during homecoming week and I was soooo jealous." Rylie laughs and laughs, but what she said wasn't that funny. "Dumb."

"We weren't together," I say, my voice low.

"Ash said the same exact thing when I asked him about it." She giggles, her gaze meeting mine. "I confronted him about you."

She *confronted* him about me? That seems like a strong choice of words.

"He said he's never liked you like that," she continues, her lips tilted upward in a closed-mouth smile. " He reassured me I was just seeing things."

Her words are like a direct stab to the heart. Did he actually say that and mean it? I'm sure he did.

The asshole.

"I was surprised when you broke up with Ben," Rylie continues, one delicate eyebrow arching.

Not wanting to ruminate over my past relationships, I rise to my feet and change the subject. "Are you going to be okay?"

"Oh. Yes. Of course." Rylie stands as well, then spontaneously pulls me into a hug. She clings tight, leaving me no choice but to hug her back before I pull myself out of her sticky grip. "Thank you again, Autumn. It means so much, that you told me he's okay. I've been worried sick."

I forget about what Ash said. I forget everything but this poor girl, and I squeeze her again before releasing her. "You're welcome. I'm sure he'll text you soon."

"I hope so. Maybe I could even..." Her voice drifts and her eyes light up. "Come over to your house sometime soon? So I can see him? I need to see him." She sounds almost...

Desperate.

And besides, that is the absolute last thing I want to happen. Seeing them together, her fussing over him while he's hurt, will make their relationship one hundred percent real.

And maybe I don't want to witness that. Not yet.

"We'll see," I tell her, because I can't answer for Ash, or my parents. "Bye Rylie."

"Bye."

* * *

LATER THAT NIGHT, I'm in my room watching some boring-ass movie on Netflix when I receive a text from Ash.

We should talk.

My heart starts to race. I only got home not even an hour ago because of practice, and then Kaya and I went to dinner. I know she wanted to pick my brain over Ash, though she never brought him up. Meaning I didn't either. She's probably mad at me, or at the very least irritated that I won't talk about it.

Too bad. She'll find out when I can actually tell the story.

Since I've only been home for a little while, I haven't seen Ash. Or Dad, for that matter. Mom told me they were together in his office when I got home, and I wasn't about to disturb them.

Deciding I need to answer Ash, I send him a reply. **Why?**

He immediately starts typing, the gray bubble appearing.

Meet me outside? By the pool?

Sighing out loud, I answer. **Sure.**

I run a brush through my hair and make sure I look presentable. I don't even want to talk to him. We have nothing to say to each other. Talking to Rylie, seeing how upset she was over what happened to Ash and how he was ignoring her, confirmed that I needed to leave him alone. Let the past stay in the past. We never amounted to much back then, and we're certainly not going to amount to much now.

He even said so. He never liked me that way. Rylie was just seeing things.

I hate that her words bothered me, but they did. They still do. It's almost worse that *she* said it versus hearing it come from Ash's mouth. All this time I thought he felt the same way I did about us. That our timing was never right. That's what I always believed.

But no. He doesn't like me that way. He never did. Proving that everything he said to me was a lie. He's still an unfeeling asshole. Considering his circumstances, I shouldn't be surprised. He's trouble.

Or troubled, as Mom puts it. And who needs that?

Not me.

Realizing I don't really care what I look like when I go talk to Ash, I toss the brush onto my vanity and leave my room, making my way down the stairs and to the door that leads from the kitchen to the backyard. The pathway lights are on—they always are, they're powered by solar—and I can see Ash stretched out on one of the lounge chairs, looking very comfortable. As if he belongs here.

Well, he doesn't. I need to talk to my parents and find out

when he's going to leave. I already know Jake doesn't like having him here. He said as much on our drive to school this morning. He's afraid Dad's going to forget all about him and focus on Ash. I can't imagine our father doing that, but who knows? Stranger things have happened.

"Took you long enough," Ash calls when he spots me.

I remain quiet until I'm standing at the foot of his lounge chair. I rest my hands on my hips, glaring at him. "You can't yell like that. You might wake someone up."

He raises his brows. "Like who? Your parents' bedroom is in the front of the house. I'm sure they can't hear us. And I doubt your sister or brother care."

Ava would totally care, the little sneak. Jake would just be pissed. For some reason, he views Ash as the enemy. I think he's just jealous of him. "My little brother is sleeping."

Beck can sleep through anything. Not that Ash needs to know that.

"Oh. He won't hear us." He waves a hand at the lounge chair next to me. "You should sit down."

"Why?" I cross my arms "I have homework to finish."

"Fine, let's get right to it." He leans back, giving me a chance to really check him out, and I swear he looks worse than he did this morning. All the bruises have become darker, and the cut above his eye is now stitched versus bandaged. "You promised you wouldn't tell anyone what happened to me, or where I was."

"I didn't," I start, but he cuts me off.

"You told Rylie."

I clamp my lips shut, staring at him. He looks...pissed. "She's your girlfriend, Ash. She came to me crying, she was so worried about you. I thought you would want her to know."

"I wanted *no one* to know. What part of that did you not understand?" His voice is cold. Like ice. His expression is like stone. "You promised. I thought I could trust you. And you blab your mouth to the first person who asks."

"I didn't *blab my mouth,* you asshole. I told your sobbing girlfriend, who was going out of her mind with worry over where you were by the way, so she would calm down. All she wanted was to know you were all right, and you didn't have the decency to answer her texts. Which is some straight-up bullshit, if you ask me," I tell him, swallowing hard. Blood is pounding in my head, in my ears, I'm so pissed. I can't believe he's calling me out for this when he's the dick who couldn't bother to tell his poor girlfriend he's alive.

"A promise is a promise," he says solemnly. "And you broke it."

I gape at him, my mind scrambling to come up with something to say. He's being ridiculous. Can he not see I did the right thing?

"I guess I shouldn't be surprised," he goes on, looking away from me. "Everyone breaks their promises eventually, right?"

"I thought..." I start, but he whirls around to face me, rising to his feet, positioning himself so he looms over me, making me feel smaller than I already am.

"You made a fucking promise, Callahan. You said you wouldn't tell anyone, yet you told Rylie, who now won't stop texting me. She wants to see me, she wants to take care of me, she wants to come over, and honestly? I don't need her shit right now. I don't need *anyone's* shit. I'm trying to figure this out, and I'm in fucking hiding. Did you know my mom's asshole boyfriend claims he wants to press charges against me? Isn't that funny? If Don finds out I'm here, the cops will show up and cart me away to *jail.* He already turned in the drugs he found in my room to the police. I'm fucked."

Drugs? What sort of drugs? I can't ask that right now.

"Rylie would never tell him..."

"No, but she could tell someone, and then they tell someone, and it goes on until they find my ass. Now I'll have to go somewhere else. And I've got nowhere else. This is it." He reaches out, poking the center of my chest with his index finger. And that one little jab freaking hurts. "You. Fucked. This. Up."

He has a lot of nerve, blaming all of his problems on me. I guess he's right that I shouldn't have told Rylie anything. I should probably feel bad, but I also can't help but think he's acting like a complete asshole.

"The police will probably come here anyway, since everyone on the team saw you with my dad," I point out, but he doesn't even flinch. God, I hate him. "I was trying to help you."

"You're never a help. *Ever.* More like you're a giant pain in my ass."

"Fuck you!" I shove at him, and he goes stumbling backward, teetering on the edge of the pool deck. He's about to fall, I know he is and I reach out, taking one of his hands, and instead of keeping him upright, he tugs me right along with him.

Straight into the water.

Oh, and it's cold. Shockingly so. Once Labor Day passes, we usually stop using the pool for the year, with the exception of Beck, who'll jump in when one of his little friends dare him to, which is basically every other weekend.

I pop up out of the water first, gasping, the water streaming down my face. Ash appears only a few seconds later, making these snorting sounds that concern me at first, until I realize...

He's laughing.

"What the fuck, Callahan? You pushed me in the pool!" He sounds shocked. Maybe even a little...

Impressed?

"And you pulled me in right along with you," I mutter, reaching up to push my hair out of my face. I never look good in a pool. Some girls can pull off the slicked hair, strutting around in a bikini look, but I'm not one of them. I'm short and a little pudgy in the middle, and my boobs are so damn big. My hair always goes everywhere, usually streaking across my face in a knotted mess, and I swear, I really do wear waterproof mascara, but I always end up looking like a raccoon with thick black rings under my eyes.

But I'm not in a bikini, and I scrubbed off what little makeup I wear to school right when I first got home, before I hopped in the shower. I'm wearing an old cheer team T-shirt that just so happens to be white, and a pair of sleep shorts with no freaking undies beneath them, meaning I am pretty much naked. The shirt will cling to me, as will the shorts, and while I keep myself mostly trim down there, I'm not shaved or waxed bare, so he'll probably see my nipples and my freaking bush if I climb out of the pool right now.

No. Nope. Not going to happen.

"Get me a towel," I demand, and he starts laughing even harder, shaking his head as he stares at me.

"Hell no. You're the one who pushed me in the pool. Get your own damn towel." He splashes me with water and I shift away from him.

He's right. I should be glad he's laughing now, considering only moments ago he was super pissed at me.

With an outraged growl I make my way toward the shallow end and hurriedly climb out of the pool, keeping my back to him as I stomp my way toward the deck box where we keep the towels. I fling the lid open and rummage around for my favorite one, pulling it out and wrapping it around my shoulders. The towel's big enough that I'm pretty much covered except my legs, so I don't feel as exposed.

I hear water splash, and I turn to watch Ash climb out of

the pool, his soaked clothes clinging to his long, rangy body. He tears off his T-shirt, letting it fall to the ground with a wet plop, and my gaze greedily roams over his broad chest. Then he reaches for the waistband of his navy athletic shorts, shoving those off too, until he's standing before me in nothing but his black boxer briefs.

My still greedy gaze drops to his front, and my cheeks grow warm. Not like he's sporting a boner or anything, but I can tell it's…

Impressive.

"Quit checking out my junk and get me a towel," he demands.

"Get your own fucking towel," I tell him, slamming the deck box lid closed with extra force.

"You're not going to help me? Even after everything you did?" He raises his brows.

"I did nothing!" I throw my hands up as best I can, refusing to apologize for telling his girlfriend he's, you know, *alive*. "So no, I'm not going to help you."

"You leave me no choice then." His hands rest on his hips, and then with one quick jerk, he sheds the briefs and kicks them off.

Oh I look. For a solid five seconds, which isn't very long at all, before I turn away from him. I saw everything. *Everything!* I can't believe he freaking did that!

I open the deck box once more and grab a towel, the biggest one we own, the one my dad always likes to use, and hold out my arm behind me, the towel dangling from my fingers. "Take it."

Nothing happens for long, agonizing seconds, and I clutch my towel around me even tighter, waving my other hand so the fresh towel flips this way and that, like a giant flag dragging on the ground. "Take it!" I repeat a little louder.

Wet footsteps draw closer and then he's tugging the towel

from my grip, his fingers trailing across mine. That didn't have to happen, it's like he did it on purpose, and I bite back the curse that wants to escape when tingles erupt from the simple brush of our fingers.

I react to him no matter what. He's yelling at me, I'm disgusted with him, we're arguing, yet I still feel the spark.

I hate that stupid spark with everything I've got.

"Thanks," he drawls, his confident voice grating on my nerves. "You can look now. Nothing to see."

"You sure?"

"I don't lie like you do," he retorts, and my head whips toward him to find he's smiling at me. Though his eyes are dark. Serious. "You act like you've never seen a dick before."

"I'm looking at one right now," I respond with a serene smile, making him chuckle under his breath.

"Good one, Callahan. You're always good for a fight."

"I'm sure that's all I'm good for with you. Since, you know, you never liked me like that and your girlfriend was only seeing things."

The second the words are out, I want them back. I want to stuff them down my throat and swallow them so they disappear.

Too late. Ash is studying me with seeming confusion, his head cocked, water dripping from his hair. He has the towel wrapped around his waist so his entire torso is on display, rivulets of water dripping across the stretch of muscles and taut skin, and I look away, hating how breathless I suddenly feel.

"What are you talking about?" he finally asks.

"Nothing," I say too quickly, keeping my head averted. "I need to go inside."

I start to walk away, but he grabs my hand, halting me. I turn to find him watching me, his gaze questioning. "What did Rylie say to you?"

"Nothing," I repeat. "Let me go."

He tugs me closer, until I almost collide with his chest. "I guess we're alike after all."

Now he's just flat out confusing me. "What do you mean?"

"I'm a liar, just like you."

CHAPTER 20

"What did you lie about?" I ask, my voice barely above a whisper. His fingers curl around my trembling fingers, entwining them, and he slowly presses his palm to mine, his thumb sweeping along the side of my hand. It's a simple touch, really, yet I feel it all the way down to my toes—and in some other areas too.

When Ben touched me even more intimately than this, I didn't feel even a tenth of what I'm experiencing now. My pulse is going haywire, my entire body trembling, and I know it's not from the cold.

It's from Ash.

"I lied to Rylie." He hesitates, shaking his wet hair out of his eyes, and little droplets hit my face, making me wince. "About you. More like how I felt about you."

"Felt?"

"Felt. Feel. Same difference." He shrugs one bare shoulder and my gaze settles there, marveling at how muscular yet lean he is, and how tall. How attracted I am to him. It's frustrating. He's frustrating.

I should run. I don't need to hear any of this. He has a

girlfriend. One who must really care for him, considering her earlier behavior at school. Would I be that hysterical if I knew something terrible had happened to the boy I loved, but I couldn't find him and he wouldn't respond to me?

Yes. Probably.

"We're friends," I remind him gently, and he laughs. Just full-blown laughs like I told him the funniest joke ever.

And then he releases his grip on me, doubling over with pain, arms wrapped around his ribs. "Fuck, that hurts."

"Are you okay?" I reach for him, my hands fluttering around him but never actually making contact. The towel slips from my shoulders and I grab for it, not wanting to expose myself to him. "What hurts?"

"My ribs. They're—bruised." He shifts away from me, like he's afraid I'm going to make it worse, and he turns so his back to me, his arms still around his middle as he struggles to take in deep, shuddering breaths.

"Do you need anything?" I ask once his breathing has calmed some.

He turns his neck so he's watching me from over his shoulder. "Your mom suggested I sit in the hot tub. She said the hot water will help with my sore muscles." He cracks a smile. "Want to join me?"

"No," I say too quickly, and his smile fades.

"You're no fun."

"You called me a liar."

"Yeah, well, I was pissed."

"I was just trying to help her—"

"You were supposed to be protecting *me*, Callahan. Not helping Rylie," he reminds me, and I go quiet.

He's right. I'm wrong.

"I'm sorry," I tell him.

Slowly he turns to face me once more, and it looks like

the towel has loosened around his waist. Not good. "Did you just apologize to me?"

I nod, swallowing hard. There's nothing else for me to say.

"I accept your apology." He sounds serious and he stands up straight, the towel loosening even more. I blink up at him, trying my best to not look at his waist and the towel, but I don't think he realizes what I'm doing, or what's happening. He's wagging his finger at me like someone scolding their naughty child or pet. "You promise to keep your lips shut? For real this time?"

I nod, my lips clamped tightly together.

"Good." He reaches for the haphazard knot on his side, undoing it with a quick flick of his fingers and flapping the towel open for the briefest second. I catch a glimpse of his hipbone, the smooth skin there, the very top of his hair-covered thigh. *God.* "I can see your nipples."

A gasp escapes me and I look down at myself to see that the towel has come loose around my shoulders, my wet T-shirt exposed and clinging to my chest. I tuck the towel back into place, covering my very cold, very embarrassed nipples, and I want to die.

Just…

Die.

"They're nice, by the way," he continues, like we're having a normal conversation. "I've always been more of a tit man."

"I hate you," I whisper miserably.

"No you don't," he says with a grin. Then he does the oddest thing.

Ash leans in and presses his cheek next to mine, his lips right at my ear. "Get inside before I do something stupid like kiss you."

I run back into the house, his laughter chasing after me.

* * *

THE NEXT DAY AT SCHOOL, the rumors aren't as rampant. Now they're more along the lines of *the cops are looking for Ash, he's going to get arrested!* Which I guess is maybe true? Three sheriff deputy patrol cars were spotted in the admin parking lot around third period, and one of the student office assistants overheard the conversation between the deputies and Mrs. Adney, our vice principal.

They were questioning her about Ash.

That particular detail scares me. Are we hiding a criminal at our house? Could my parents get in trouble? Could I get in trouble? I'm less than six months away from eighteen, so I'm practically an adult. No way do I want to go to jail for harboring a known criminal or whatever.

My imagination is clearly getting away from me, and I mentally tell myself to calm down. At lunch, Rylie actually joins us, which sucks since I planned on telling Kaya and Daphne a little bit of what was going on.

But maybe that turns out to be a good thing because then I keep my mouth shut and we talk about other things. Normal things. Like the fact that my brother's going to play in Ash's place at Friday night's game. I didn't even know that was happening, it's Kaya's boyfriend who tells me, not my own brother or father, and I think that surprises Jaden.

It surprises me too.

"They didn't mention it?" he asks.

We're sitting across from each other, Daphne next to me and Rylie on the other side of her, Kaya pressed against his right side, her arm through his and her head on his shoulder. They are the epitome of the perfect high school relationship. They'll probably get married within the next few years too. I wouldn't doubt it.

Ash and I are the epitome of the toxic high school relationship. The back and forth, the getting with other people when we really want to be with each other—God, I don't even know if that last part is true—and how we constantly argue. It's not normal.

I really, really want normal.

"They've been busy," I tell Jaden, and he nods, accepting my answer.

Rylie keeps trying to talk with me about Ash, and I don't say a word. In fact, I'm constantly trying to change the subject, as does Daphne, who I know is doing it for my benefit. But it's almost like Rylie trying to force me to admit Ash is still at my house, and she mentions more than once that he's barely texted her since everything happened.

That's not my fault, and that's not my story to tell, so I remain quiet.

In class, I can't concentrate. My mind drifts to what Ash said last night. What he did. What I saw. How he affects me. How I try my hardest to deny it. He's frustrating, everything about our situation is frustrating, and deep down, there's a secret part of me that wishes he would just break up with Rylie so I could have him all to myself.

Our timing is never right.

Wednesdays we don't have cheer practice, so I'm home early. Right after school. Dad brings Jake home from football practice, and Ava is at dance class, so she'll also ride home with Dad and Jake. When I pull into the driveway, the garage doors are closed, which usually means no one is home, and my thoughts are confirmed when I enter the silent house.

I realize quick it's not actually silent at all. I can hear someone talking, very, very faintly. And I think it's Ash.

Carefully I set my backpack at the base of the stairwell so I can grab it later before I head up to my room, and make my way toward the other side of the house. It's all bare floors throughout our home, and footsteps can sometimes echo, so

I'm creeping carefully like a stalker, praying he doesn't hear me.

So I can spy on him.

I'm at my lowest point, I realize. Spying on this boy who makes me so angry, yet also fills me with this uncontrollable lust I've never experienced before. But I'm not stopping myself. I'm going to listen in on this conversation he's having, and I sort of don't care if I'm crossing any boundaries.

He constantly crosses my boundaries, so it's only fair, right?

I'm in the hallway, dangerously close to his bedroom door, which is partially open, when I can hear him talking. "Ry. Baby. Stop crying. I can't take it."

My heart feels like it's shriveling inside my chest. He just called her *baby*.

So gross.

Now I sound like I'm mentally reverting to a thirteen-year-old.

He remains quiet, and I swear I can hear her muffled voice, which sounds very upset. Like she might be crying/raging at him over something.

"I already told you, I can't have you come over here," he finally says, his voice lower than usual. It's not as raspy today, and I'm hoping that means whatever damage that asshole who choked him did is healing. "It's not my place to just invite you. I don't live here. Besides, I'm trying to lay low."

My parents would probably let her come over. I'm thinking this has more to do with Ash than with him imposing on our family.

"Yeah, I miss you too." He almost sounds bored when he says it.

Maybe that's wishful thinking on my part.

I also wish I could hear what she's saying.

Then again, I don't.

"What do you mean, you don't believe me?" He pauses, and I assume she's talking. "Give me a break, Ry. I got beat the hell up and you don't think I sound like I miss you enough? What do you want, to hear me crying like you are? Like crying somehow proves that I care?"

Now she's yelling. I can actually make out a few words. Like, *mean* and *I don't matter* and *need you*.

"We've only been hanging out for a few weeks," he says, and I get this sense that he's feeling what I'm feeling. She is moving way too fast. "And what just happened to me is… serious. Like, I can't give you all the details type serious."

More screaming. The bed creaks and I take a few steps back, afraid he might start walking around. Maybe even exit the bedroom outright, only to discover me in the hall.

I'd have to play it off. Pretend I was coming to see him, though I have no reason to. I'm supposed to be mad at him still, right?

"She doesn't know everything, I swear. I'm not even spending that much time with her. She's always—" Rylie must interrupt him, and I realize…

She's talking about me.

"Ry. I'm telling you the truth. She doesn't know anything more than you do." That's a lie. "And no, I'm not spending any time with her." Another lie. "Come on. Stop acting like a jealous bitch."

And…

The call's over.

If my boyfriend ever called me a jealous bitch, I'd dump him. End of story.

I take a few steps back, then start walking down the hall like I've just arrived, even rapping my knuckles along the wall in warning, like my dad does to Jake, so he doesn't interrupt him doing something my dad or mom never, ever want to see.

"Hey." I stop in the doorway, oddly exhilarated at seeing a sullen Ash sitting on the edge of the unmade bed, his legs and arms sprawled out, hands braced behind him on the mattress, his dark gaze meeting mine. His jaw is tight, as are his lips, and ooh man, he looks furious. Especially with the bruises and scrapes.

He also looks deliciously, dangerously attractive.

"How are you?" I ask brightly when he still hasn't said anything. "Just so you know, the rumors at school are a little quieter today."

"I thought you promised you would never lie to me?" He lifts one brow in challenge.

"Well, that part is true. They weren't talking about you as much." I wince. "Also, the cops were at school, asking about you."

"There's the truth I was looking for. But thanks, I already heard about it."

I'm frowning. "Who told you?"

"Rylie. God, she was acting like *such* a bitch just now. I don't have time for her whining, not with everything else that's going on." He shakes his head and sits up straighter. "I should block her number."

Hope lights me up from within and I tell myself to stop it. "She's just worried about you."

"Stop defending her. She was saying all sorts of bullshit about you," he mutters.

"Like what?"

"She's just jealous." He waves a hand, dismissing what he said. "You still mad at me, Callahan?"

"Why am I mad at you?" Just being in his presence makes me forget things, like holding onto any anger toward him.

"For dragging you into the pool. For flashing you my

dick. For complimenting your nipples." He holds up his hand and ticks off each reason with his fingers. "That's three things. I'm sure I can come up with a few more."

"I'm over it." I step into the room and glance around. It's a very bland room, with a small dresser, a desk and a bed. Of course, it's a guest room, and they're supposed to be bland, so…no surprise. "What did you do today?"

"Hid out in here. Your dad and I had a talk. He told me your brother is taking my place at Friday's game." The grim expression on Ash's face tells me he's not happy about it. "Fucking sucks."

"You can't play. You're still hurt," I start, but Ash cuts me off with a look.

"If that motherfucker ruins my football career, I will kill him."

"Are you talking about my brother?" I start to back out of the room.

"No, of course not!" I stop in my tracks, relief flooding me. "I'm talking about that asshat boyfriend of my mom's. Don." Ash curls his hand into a fist and smacks his thigh. "I have to play next week. Keep up my stats. Your mom says colleges could be watching me, and I need more film to upload."

"Upload where?" I have no idea what he's talking about.

"There's a website where you can upload game film for college scouts. Not like I'm going to be picked up by one, but your mom is filling my head with unicorns and sunshine every time we talk, so you never know." He rises to his feet and starts heading in my direction. "Hey, whatcha doing right now?"

I back up as he keeps coming. "I was going to do homework."

"Wrong answer." He smiles, and I realize his eye is not as

swollen today. It almost looks normal. "How about we go for a drive?"

No. Don't do it. It's like he's playing with fire and I'm dying to get burned. He has a girlfriend-friend-I don't know what to call her who's jealous of me. If she found out we went for a "drive," she'd be so upset.

"I can't," I say weakly, and he shakes his head.

"Wrong answer again, Callahan. I need your help." He stops directly in front of me, reaches out, and slips his fingers beneath my chin to tilt my face up so I have to look at him. "And you won't turn me down when I ask for help, will you?"

The sigh that escapes me is louder than I meant it to be. "What do you want?"

"Take me to my house so I can get my shit?" he asks hopefully.

"That sounds dangerous."

"Mom's at work and the asshole is too. Not dangerous at all," he says swiftly.

If my parents found out, they would be so angry. At me, and Ash. "You know my parents won't approve."

"When has that ever stopped you?" He raises his brows. "Come on, live a little. Walk on the wild side with me. It'll take me all of five minutes to grab what I need, 'cause I don't have much. Not like you do."

His words make me feel guilty, and it's the guilt that has me agreeing to this stupid plan.

I hope I don't regret it.

CHAPTER 21

When I drive into his neighborhood, I notice immediately it's pretty run down. The houses are older and small, and the yards aren't as well kept. Ash makes me park down the street from where he lives, which I think is a bad idea, but then he casually mentions that people's cars get broken into at his apartment complex's parking lot all the time, so I decide his decision isn't so bad.

We dart down the sidewalk and approach the building from the opposite side than he normally does, or so he tells me. We're acting like we're spies in a teen thriller and it's almost kind of funny, if it also wasn't so scary.

It's still sunny outside, considering it's close to five on a September day, and the complex seems fairly quiet. There are a few kids running around on scooters or bikes. An older woman is sitting out on her tiny front porch, talking loudly on a cell phone while simultaneously screaming at one of the kids, who must belong to her. Ash is clinging to the edge of the building, watching everything play out in the courtyard of the apartment building, and I'm standing right behind him, waiting for his word to go.

"I wish Mrs. Conrad wasn't sitting outside." He shakes his head, glancing back at me. "She's got a big mouth."

Everyone has a big mouth in this town, I want to tell him. Someone could spot my car and recognize it. Tell my parents that they saw it parked on this road and bam, Ash and I would be totally busted. "Where's your apartment?"

He points to the door that's on the opposite end of the building from where Mrs. Conrad is sitting. The blinds covering the single window that overlooks the courtyard are bent and tangled, and I wonder if they've been like that for a while, or if they got damaged from the fight Ash got in with this Don guy.

"Why don't we sneak in by going this way?" I gesture with my hand that we should go right instead of straight. "Go around this building and come out the other side."

He smiles, his eyes lighting up, and in this moment he looks so young, despite all the fresh damage on his face. "Brilliant idea, Callahan. I knew there was a reason I brought you with me."

The only reason he brought me was to use my car, but I don't mention that. I may as well bask in his kind words while I can.

We sneak around the apartment building closest to us and come out the other side, right in front of his door. He holds me back with one arm braced across my stomach, and his casual touch sends butterflies fluttering in my belly. "Stay here," he whispers, and I do as he says, remaining as still as he is until finally, with a single nod, he gives us the signal we can go. "Run."

I follow after him, impressed with his speed, though I shouldn't be surprised. I've seen him run on the football field; when there's no one to throw to, he just runs the ball in himself. He's already got the key in the lock when I stop just behind him, and then we're inside, my eyes adjusting to the darkness, my nose wrinkling as the smell hits me.

It looks like a bomb went off inside the living room. There's a stack of empty pizza boxes on the battered coffee table, accompanied by various beer cans, some of them toppled over. It smelled like rotten food and dirty laundry in here, like it hasn't been cleaned in God knows how long, and I chance a look at Ash, but he's not even paying attention to me.

He heads down the short hall and opens a door, muttering something under his breath as he pushes his way inside. "Fucker went through my stuff!" he yells.

Looking for the drugs Ash mentioned to me? Probably.

I follow after him, stopping in the doorway of his bedroom. It's a mess, there's stuff everywhere, and it looks like every drawer of his dresser was pulled out and dumped. All of his clothes are on the floor, and there's a small stack of shirts still on the hangers thrown on top of his unmade bed. It doesn't smell as bad in here. In fact, I can smell traces of his soap or cologne lingering in the air.

"Do you need any help?"

He grabs a duffel bag from the top shelf of his closet and tosses it onto the bed, unzipping it. "Just watch for anyone approaching the front door while I get my stuff."

I freeze, fear slipping down my spine with icy-cold fingers. "I don't know what your mom or her boyfriend look like."

"That doesn't matter. Just keep watch for anyone coming to the front door, okay?" He sends me a look, one that says *don't argue with me,* so I do as he says and go back out into the living room.

I stand at the very window I stared at only a few minutes ago, peeking through the bent blinds every few minutes.

Mostly I take in the damage that's been done in both this room and the kitchen, which is where the worst smell of all is coming from. The sink is piled with dirty dishes, most of them covered with dried, crusted food. The small counters are covered with more beer cans, to-go coffee cups and lots and lots of crumbs. It's like the people who live here just don't care.

And that makes me sad. Sadder than I've ever felt for Ash, and that's saying a lot, considering how bad I felt for him when I first saw his face.

This is the environment he lives in. Has grown up in. His father died, I don't know when, and his mother doesn't seem to care much about anything, if her house is an indication.

Ash emerges from his bedroom to walk into the bathroom directly across the hall. "Give me a few more minutes. Almost ready."

I glance out the window again but see no one. Just the kids playing in the courtyard. The old woman is still sitting in front of her place. The buildings are rundown, and they look like they could use a fresh coat of paint. This is the poorer section of town, a section I don't visit much, if ever, and I realize why.

This place is depressing. Almost...scary. Our town is small, but we have our fair share of crime and homelessness. Ava did a report on the local homeless problem last year for one of her final eighth grade projects, and she even sent it in to the county supervisors' office, but she never heard back from them. She had some decent solutions too.

"Okay." Ash approaches me, and I can tell he's actually thrown on more clothes too. He's layered up, wearing a thick school hoodie and a pair of fleece joggers. He's going to be hot when he gets outside. "You ready?"

I nod. "No one's out there except for your one neighbor still."

He brushes past me and peeks through the blinds, staring

at her for a while. "She probably saw us sneak in here already."

"You think so?" What if she called Ash's mom and her boyfriend? What if one of them is on their way over right now?

Or worse, what if she called the cops?

"She might tell Mom. Or Don. For all I know, she already has." He turns to look at me, and I know I must seem totally freaked out. "Fuck it. Let's go."

We leave, Ash not bothering to lock the door behind him. We run behind the building, toward the street, and when we're sliding into my car only a few minutes later, both of us are breathless, Ash clutching his side and chuckling. "You did good, Callahan."

I warm under his compliment, even though it's the stupidest one ever. "I did nothing, if we're being honest."

"You helped. You got me here, remember?" He tosses his stuffed duffel bag into the backseat of my car, then tugs the hoodie off, wincing when he pulls it over his head. "Thanks for bringing me."

His tone has gone terribly serious. I glance over at him to find he's already watching me, his dark eyes fixed on my face. "You're welcome."

"Means a lot." He swallows hard. "That you helped."

"It's fine."

Ash reaches for his hips and starts shoving the fleece joggers off, practically taking his shorts with them. I catch a glimpse of flat stomach, a dark trail of hair from beneath his navel that leads into the waistband of his gray boxer briefs, and I know I'm openly staring.

I also don't really care.

"Like what you see?" The amusement in his raspy voice is unmistakable.

Glancing up, I catch him smiling at me. My cheeks are

red, I can feel how hot they are, but I'm so tired of denying my attraction to him. "Yes," I admit, surprised at my bold admission.

He parts his lips, ready to say something else, and I lean toward him in anticipation. But then a car on the road catches his attention and his eyes go wide. "Oh shit. Duck!"

Ash tugs my arm and we both go down, hovering below the dash, our breathing harsh. A car goes driving by—I can hear its overly loud motor—and then it's gone.

"You get up first. He won't know you." Ash actually sounds…

Scared.

I lift my head and peek around, but there's no cars on the road, no asshole coming for my car, shaking his fist. I push the button and start the engine, then pull away from the curb, desperate to create as much distance as possible from this place.

Ash settles into the seat and tugs the seatbelt on, which surprises me, even though I watched him put it on earlier when we drove over here. He seems the sort to ride without one defiantly, saying, *"When my time comes, God will take me no matter what. What's the point of wearing one of these?"*

"Safety first," he says when he catches me staring. He clicks the belt into place and smiles at me. "That was a close one."

"Who was it?" His attitude is baffling. I can't help but wonder if this is all some big game to him.

"Don. The asshole who beat me up." He shakes his head. "I bet old Mrs. Conrad told him I was here."

Then it definitely was a close one. Fear ripples in the pit of my stomach and I clutch the steering wheel, the reality of what just happened starting to dawn. "What we just did was so dangerous."

"Yeah." He shrugs. "But we didn't get caught, so…"

"I don't do dangerous things," I tell him, my voice even, my thoughts in chaos. "Like...ever."

"Hang around with me and you'll find yourself doing something dangerous every single day," he says with a grin.

There's innuendo there. I'm not stupid. He's referring to himself. I should tell him that won't work, considering Rylie's still in the picture. I might've kissed him when I was still with Ben, but I still haven't forgiven myself for that. No way can anything happen between us while he's with Rylie. I can't do that to her.

I won't do that to anyone ever again.

"I'm serious, Ash. That was freaking scary. What if he caught us? What if he caught me? And did something to me?" My hands are trembling, and I clutch the steering wheel as tight as I can.

"Your dad would've had my ass, and Don's too," he says conversationally, like no big deal. "He would've been so pissed."

"I could've been hurt. Can't you see that?" I sound near hysterics, and maybe I am. Maybe I shouldn't be driving. I pull over to the side of the road so I can catch my breath, calm my pounding heart, still my racing mind.

"You weren't, okay? Everything's cool. We're good. We're safe," he reassures me, his brows furrowed.

Like the wimp that I've suddenly become, I start to cry. And I feel so stupid, especially after hearing him tell Rylie earlier to stop crying. He must not like it when a girl cries, and I want him to like me. Despite everything, despite how mean and rude he's been to me over the years, and how fucked up his life is, I like him. I care about him. I want him to feel the same way about me, but he probably won't because I'm a crying, lame-ass wimp.

"Aw, Callahan, don't cry. You're breaking my fucking

183

heart." He rests a hand over his chest, rubbing it absently as I sit there and just bawl like a baby.

"You don't like it when a girl cries, I get it." I sniff, wipe at my eyes, but the tears keep coming.

And then he does the craziest thing.

He unbuckles his seatbelt and scoots closer, unbuckling mine as well. He hits the starter button, turning off the car but not the radio, and he leans over the center console, pulling me into an awkward embrace.

"I'm sorry," he murmurs into my ear as he gently strokes my back. "I didn't mean to scare you."

I press my face into his shoulder and breathe deep, desperate to get myself under control. He smells so good. Nothing like that disgusting apartment he lives in. He's wearing an old football T-shirt, and it's so soft. He feels so solid and warm. And he's most likely still in pain from the beating he took only a couple of days ago.

Yet here he is, comforting me. Telling me it's going to be okay. Apologizing.

"I'm sorry." I pull away from him, our faces still so close. Kissing close. His breath wafts across my face, and it smells like mint. "I didn't mean to fall apart."

"Hey." He curls his fingers around my chin and lifts so I have no choice but to gaze up at him. I must look a mess. "I would've protected you. If Don had showed up, I would've thrown myself in front of you before he could even look at you. No way would I let that asshole lay a hand on you."

I blink, trying to push away the tears still clinging to my eyelashes. "Really?"

"You think I'm going to just stand there and watch that asshole put even a single finger on you? Hell no. I would've killed him."

He says it with such conviction, I almost believe him.

"I scare you," Ash says when I remain silent. He tucks a

piece of hair behind my ear, his fingers lingering, playing with my earlobe, and I close my eyes, savoring the sweet touch. "I'm not good enough for you. I know that."

My eyes pop open and I part my lips, ready to protest when he rests a single finger over my mouth, silencing me. "It's true. You saw where I live. You know what I am." He skims his finger across the seam of my lips, then traces my cheek, his touch featherlight, making me shiver. "If you just gave me a chance, I'd give you anything you want."

My heart catches, along with my breath. What is he saying? What does he mean?

"Are you k-kidding?" My voice is so shaky I can barely get the words out.

He laughs, the sound dying as fast as it started. "Never. Not with you. I mean it. One hundred percent."

This is it. Do or die time. I can tell him to stay away from me or I can give in.

"What can I do to make you believe me?" he asks.

"I can't be with you if you're with Rylie," I tell him.

"I was never actually with her in the first place, so that's not a problem. I'll tell her we can't hang out anymore," he says without hesitation. He makes it sound so easy, but I don't know...

My tears have all dried up now, and I can't help the hope that's rising in my chest, making me feel as light as air. Like I could possibly walk on clouds. "Really?"

"Really," he says firmly.

I stare at him, shocked by how agreeable he's being.

Shocked yet pleased.

"Meet me at the hot tub tonight. Eleven o'clock. I'll prove it to you that we're done," he says, his voice, his eyes, his everything so utterly sincere.

"Ash..."

"Don't say another word, Callahan. You know you want

this." His mouth rests on mine, but he doesn't kiss me. His lips are parted, and so are mine, and it's as if we're breathing each other's breath. Filling each other with strength.

With courage.

"Say it. Say you'll meet me later." When he speaks, his lips tickle mine, and I can't help but smile.

"I'll meet you," I whisper, and he kisses me. A simple, sweet kiss that makes me burn for more.

"Now let's get the hell out of here," he says as he slowly pulls away, settling once more in the passenger seat.

It takes everything I have to not speed home. Ash strikes up conversation, talking about miscellaneous stuff, and I can't believe how casual we are. How normal this feels. Everything is always so high intensity when Ash and I are together, that it's nice, just driving home and gossiping about people at school. Laughing over something that happened at last week's football game. Getting annoyed with him but not really when he starts making fun of some of our dumber cheers.

Yes, we have a few dumb cheers. Yes, sometimes we're embarrassed to do them in front of the crowds, but our cheer coaches make us, and honestly, a lot of the people in the stands seem to appreciate them. So we do them. And grin and bear it every single time.

"I like knowing you're cheering me on, Callahan," he says right when I turn onto my street.

My whole body grows warm. "Really? Or are you just saying that?"

"I've told you before, I always can make out your voice above everyone else's when you guys are cheering. Even when I'm out on the field and my head is buzzing, trying to make the next play. Knowing that you're yelling for me, encouraging me..." He rests his hand over his heart. "It does something to me inside."

Laughing, I reach out and push on his rock-hard bicep, shaking my head. "You're so full of it."

"I'm being real with you right now." He is dead serious when he says it too.

"Oh."

"Yeah, oh." Now he's laughing as I pull into my driveway. "There's something about you. You turn me into a sappy motherfucker."

"I do?"

He nods, grabbing my arm when I make to open my door. I turn to look at him, hoping like hell my little brother doesn't come running out, or worse, my mom. She's home now. Her car is in the garage and here we are, staring at each other a little too closely.

"Once I'm inside, I'm going to talk to Rylie. I'm a shit person for not doing it face to face, but fuck it. I'll at least call her. Maybe even FaceTime her."

"Um, all right." I mean, what am I supposed to say to that?

"So I might be in my room for a little while, because Rylie is pretty damn persistent," he says. "She might not go easy."

I nod once. "O-okay."

"And we're still on for eleven at the hot tub?"

I nod again.

He smiles, and the sight of it makes my heart sing. "Good. See you later." He grabs his duffel bag from the backseat...

And then he's gone.

CHAPTER 22

I am an unfocused mess for the rest of the evening. At the dinner table, I ignore pretty much everyone. I'm so inside my head I keep staring off into space. The entire family is sitting at the table tonight, including Ash. Jake glares whenever Dad speaks to him, and I send Jake looks of my own, trying to kick him to make him knock it off, but I can't reach across the table to make contact with his leg, damn it.

There's no need for him to be jealous of Ash. Jake will have his glory moments for the next two years as our varsity quarterback. He needs to relax.

Mom keeps sending me strange looks and asks me twice if I'm feeling all right, and I tell her I'm just tired.

Ash snickers under his breath, the jerk.

Ava goes on and on about some girl in her class who let a boy touch her butt if he gave her some candy, and she's beyond irritated. Ava is a bigger feminist than Mom and I put together, and we tell her to complain to the principal about it. But then she says she doesn't want to be known as a snitch, so she isn't sure what to do.

Just another fun day at our high school.

Every few minutes, I catch Ash watching me, his mouth curved into the faintest smile. I think he likes my annoying family, though I'm not sure how he can. When we're all together, it's always a little chaotic. Beck brought a Spider-Man action figure to the dinner table, and while he's not as much into action figures as he once was, he's feeling it tonight. Trying to feed Spidey dinner with his fork, or trying to get him to drink, or hooking the toy's curved hands onto the edge of the salad bowl.

Beck is also irritating the shit out of our mother, who keeps telling him to knock it off and put the toy away. Beck pouts, Mom eventually relents, and then it's the same thing, again and again.

Jake is sullen over football bullshit. Dad tells Ava to stay off her phone. Ash is keeping his conversation to a minimum, with the exception when Mom asks him about college.

"I doubt I can get in to any colleges," he tells her, wiping his mouth with a napkin. I'm staring at him like some sort of freak, and when he catches me, he offers up a quick wink in my direction. That should be cheesy, but my heart flutters.

Mom looks downright offended. "Why not? How are your grades?"

"They're not terrible, but they're not straight As either," he answers.

"What are they then?" Mom asks.

"Mostly Bs. I always manage a few As in the easy classes. Freshman year I got a C in math because that shit is hard." He sends Mom a remorseful look. "Sorry."

"Don't apologize. Look, Ash, I think you should try to apply to some colleges. With your sports ability and grades, you could probably get accepted to a few state colleges. Maybe you could even get a scholarship," Mom says.

"I don't know about that," he starts, but Mom shakes her head, silencing him.

"Go to the office tomorrow and meet with a counselor. Get your transcripts and bring them home so we can go over them. My gut is telling me you could get in somewhere. You still have time to apply."

He smiles when Mom said bring them home. I'm sure he liked that.

I sort of like it too. That my parents have so readily accepted him. If you'd told me Asher Davis would be staying with us a few days ago, I would've laughed. I also would've freaked.

But having him here has drawn us closer together. It's also helped us be honest with each other. For once.

"I'd love to get out of here, that's for sure," he mutters.

My heart aches for him. Now that I've seen where he comes from, I understand somewhat why he acts the way he does. Why he's so self-destructive. He needs someone to believe in him. Like my mom. Like me.

I want to be that person.

If he'll let me.

We're all roped into helping Mom clean the kitchen, and somehow I got put on dishwashing duty with Ash. He rinses the dishes and I set them in the dishwasher, and we wash the remaining pots and pans Mom prefers to be cleaned by hand. I don't understand the point of a dishwasher if it can't wash *all* your dishes, but whatever.

"I ended it," Ash says conversationally as he hands me a plate.

It nearly slips from my fingers when I hear what he said. "With Rylie?"

He nods as he goes to rinse another plate. "I told her we couldn't hang out anymore, and she took it fairly well. When I say fairly well, I mean she cried and begged me to give her another chance, over and over. I finally had to end the call."

We're all alone in the kitchen, which means we can talk about this freely.

I set the plate he hands me into the dishwasher. "That's awful." I didn't want her to be hurt over it, but what did I expect? She cares about him. I get it.

But I think he cares about me more.

"It's done, and I'm glad. I only hung out with her because no one else interested me, and she was there. Eager and willing."

My stomach sinks. Eager and willing to do what, exactly?

I don't want to know.

Yes, I do.

"But she wasn't you." His voice is so quiet, I almost didn't hear him. "None of them were you."

"How many of them were there?" Oh, I am wanting to feel pain right now, aren't I? Asking a question like that?

"Not many. None you need to worry about."

Those poor girls, used by Asher Davis.

Is he going to do the same to me?

"You're thinking too much," he teases, and I sigh, unsure of what to say.

Ash leans over and turns off the water, then scoots closer to me, so close I can feel his body heat radiating toward me. "You doubt everything I say."

"We've always had this weird back-and-forth relationship," I remind him.

"You're the one who always pushes me away," he reminds me back.

He's got me there.

"You going to wear a skimpy bikini for me tonight, Callahan?" He briefly touches my cheek, and I want more, just like that. I'm like a parched traveler in an endless desert.

191

"You going to skinny dip for me, Davis?" I return. I might own two-piece swimsuits, but I never feel totally comfortable in them.

"I can make that happen." He's grinning and nodding, and he looks like a dork. A cute, injured dork. "Definitely."

"Hey." I rest my hand on his chest, and he goes completely still. As if the center of the universe is where we're connected. "Please be—gentle with me. I'm a little slower paced than you, I think."

"Slower paced? What are you—*ohhhh.*" He draws the word out and rests his hand over mine, squeezing it. "I'm not going to push you into anything you don't want to do."

"Promise?"

"I swear."

"What are you guys talking about?"

We both turn to find Beck standing in the kitchen, watching us, his Spider-Man dangling from his fingers and about ready to fall to the floor.

I disentangle myself from Ash's grip and face Beck. "Why aren't you with Mom?" I ask my little brother. After dinner is when they usually hang out on the couch and watch TV so Beck gets his daily snuggle time. Really it's snuggle time for Mom, since none of us do that with her anymore, and I know it makes her sad, that she's down to her last one. So she squeezes on him as much as she can.

"She's too busy hugging on Daddy." Beck makes a face, like he's disgusted. "Like you're hugging on him." He waves Spider-Man at Ash.

"We're not hugging on each other," I tell Beck, smiling at him. The last thing I want is my brother to say something like that to our parents. "We're just friends."

"Uh huh. I need to go find Mom. Mom!" Beck takes off, leaving the kitchen as fast as he came in.

"Your brother is cute," Ash says when I turn to face him once more.

"He's a pain. They all are," I tell him, and he slowly shakes his head, his expression…raw.

"You don't know how lucky you got it, Callahan. The big family. Parents who love you, who love each other. It doesn't matter if your dad has money or not, or that he's some big-time football player. None of that matters—he loves his family, and he loves his wife. Knowing that, you're so secure in it, you're downright smug."

My mouth pops open. "I don't think I'm smug."

"You're so smug you don't even see it, and that's the best part of it all. You're so fucking lucky. My dad loved me more than anything else, and then he died. And once he was gone, my mom didn't give a shit anymore. Not about anything. Definitely not about me." Ash reaches out and trails his fingers down the length of my arm, making me shiver. "I'm not insulting you, Callahan. I'm reminding you that you have a pretty kick-ass family, and they love you. Don't ever forget it."

We're standing in my dimly light kitchen having one of the most serious conversations ever, and I know I will never forget this moment. This night. This entire day. And I'm not even including what's going to happen later.

That'll just be the icing on the cake.

* * *

"You and Ash seem to be getting along well."

I turn to find Mom leaning against the doorframe of my bedroom. I'm sitting at my desk, working on homework, desperate to finish so I can take a quick shower, put on light makeup, throw on my favorite two-piece swimsuit beneath my usual sleep clothes and meet Ash out under the stars at eleven.

I'll have to suck in my stomach and stick out my chest to distract him from that extra roll I've got going on, but he'll probably be too entranced by my boobs to notice.

Hopefully.

"It's—better between us," I tell her.

Soooo much better.

She walks in my bedroom, and I hope she doesn't stay long. I love her, and I appreciate our close relationship, but right now, I don't want to chat with her. I already feel like I've been sneaking around these last few days since Ash arrived. Guilt is something I don't quite know how to deal with, and I'm feeling plenty of it at the moment.

"I know you took him to his place this afternoon." She settles on the edge of my bed and I turn to face her, trying to come up with ways to deny what she just said. "Don't bother trying to give me some lame excuse. I wasn't born yesterday."

"Mom," I start, but words fail me.

"I'm not mad. Well, I am a little. That could've been so unsafe. What if that asshole was still at Ash's apartment? Or his mom? She would've called the police and then what do you think would've happened?"

I remain mute and just let her talk.

"It would've been a nightmare, that's what." Mom shakes her head. "Next time ask me, okay?"

"Okay." I'm so relieved I'm not in trouble, I have to ask the next question. "How did you find out?"

"Ash. He told me he went and picked up his stuff earlier. When I asked him how he got there, he panicked and made up some outrageous story about a couple of friends coming to pick him up here and taking him to his apartment. This is the boy who didn't want anyone to know where he was, by the way. I put two and two together, and figured out it had to be you," Mom says, that familiar, knowing look crossing her face.

None of us are able to pull anything over on my mom, for the most part. She is all knowing. I'm thinking I can pull one over her tonight, though. My parents are in bed usually by ten. By eleven, they're sleeping.

By eleven-fifteen, I should be in the hot tub with a mostly naked Ash.

I can't wait.

"Just...be careful with him," Mom says. "Troubled souls are hard to fix."

There are so many things I want to say. But I can't. To say those things would reveal my true feelings, and I'm not ready to examine them yet. Let alone have someone like my mother examine them.

"Troubled souls also just need someone to love them sometimes. Someone to believe in them when they already feel so defeated." Mom's gaze grows distant and a tiny smile curls her lips. "Your father was like that."

My father has always seemed perfect in every single way. It's Mom who went through the rough childhood, or so I thought. "He was a troubled soul?"

"Very much so," Mom says with a nod. "A big ol' mess, truthfully. But I stuck it out. I told him how I felt, and even though he ran away from me for a while, he eventually came back to me, and I took him back, because I knew he was worth it. I wasn't complete without him. We've been together ever since."

"Someday you'll have to tell me the entire story."

"Someday, when you're older, I will. I'll share every excruciating detail with you, including the time your Uncle Owen punched your dad in the mouth and knocked him to the ground." Mom laughs. "Oh, that was a surprise."

"Uncle Owen punched Dad?" I'm in shock.

Mom nods, still laughing. "He deserved it."

There is so much more to my parents than I even know.

Maybe I *don't* want to know.

Her words stick with me, though. How she wasn't complete without him. Is that what it's like, when you love someone, when you find your forever? That you don't feel whole unless they're with you?

It sort of feels like that with Ash. Maybe that's why I've been drawn to him for so long. I can't say that I'm in love with him, because I still don't feel like I know him that well, but I can say without a doubt that we definitely have a connection, and it's not one sided.

He feels it too.

We feel it together.

CHAPTER 23

*T*he cool mountain air makes me shiver as I dart across the expanse of green lawn toward the opposite side of the pool, where the in-ground hot tub is. The pool is dark, but the moon is mostly full, casting its silver-white glow upon the backyard. I can hear the water bubbling and swirling in the Jacuzzi, and as I draw closer, I see Ash sitting there.

Waiting for me.

Watching me.

I stop just at the edge of the tub, kicking off my flip-flops, tugging on the hem of my T-shirt. How am I supposed to do this? Just whip off the shirt and toss it on the ground, then step into the hot tub with confidence? I mean, that's what I *want* to do, that's what I envision. But I'm not sure if I can pull that off…

"Callahan, what are you doing?"

I blink Ash into focus to see he's watching me with confusion. "I don't know. You make me nervous."

He flicks water in my direction, wetting my feet. "You

make me nervous too. Especially when you stand there and stare off into space. Now come on. Get in here."

Deciding I have nothing to lose, I tear off my T-shirt just as I envisioned only a moment ago and daintily step into the hot tub, gasping when the steamy water laps around my ankles, then my knees when I take another step. I stand on the bench seat, trying to work up the courage to submerge myself neck-deep in the water when I catch Ash whistling low, his gaze sliding over me.

"Damn, girl, you are hot as fuck."

I burst out laughing and duck myself fully into the water, more gasps escaping me as the steamy water licks at my skin. "More like the water is hot as fuck."

He laughs and shakes his head. "I'm trying to give you sexy compliments and you're making jokes."

"How can I take you seriously when you say things like *sexy compliments?*"

He's grinning. He looks so cute, despite the wounds. Maybe the wounds add a certain appeal, which means I'm weird, but I don't care. I think Ash is pretty weird too. "You are definitely unexpected."

"What do you mean by that?"

"You keep me on my toes, Callahan." He somehow finds my hand under the water and pulls me closer, so we're pressed next to each other, side by side. "I never know what you're going to say or do."

"I feel the same exact way about you." I turn so I can really look at him, our thighs pressed together. He stretches an arm along the rock edge that surrounds the Jacuzzi, and I lean into him, my shoulder pressing gently against his chest. "This water is so hot."

"Give it a few minutes. You'll get used to it." He squirms a little, making the water slosh around us. "I think it feels good."

"Is it helping ease your pain?"

Smiling, he taps the tip of my nose with his finger. "You're helping ease my pain, I know that."

I lean my head back against his arm and stare up at the starry night sky. When I was younger and we lived near San Francisco, I don't remember ever seeing the stars. The sky was obliterated by city lights.

But out here, in the middle of nowhere, the sky is a black velvet background studded by twinkling lights. The occasional plane. A racing satellite or two. Even with the shining moon, which typically drowns out the stars, I can still see them tonight.

"The sky is so beautiful," I say on a sigh, letting the water keep me buoyant. My butt rises off the seat and I stretch my legs out in front of me, kicking my feet a little.

"You're so beautiful," Ash whispers close to my temple before he drops a kiss there. My heart squeezes at the sweet gesture. "And it's like you're trying to tease me right now."

"I'm not trying to tease you." I kick my feet again, harder this time, water splashing everywhere.

"With these you are." He reaches around me to touch my chest, which is above the water. He lightly traces his index finger up the length of my cleavage, leaving me breathless.

"I didn't mean to," I say softly.

"Hmmmmmmm." He runs his finger back and forth, back and forth, drawing closer to the right edge of my bikini top. Just the tip of his finger slips beneath the damp fabric, and I bite back the moan that suddenly wants to escape.

No boy has ever made me moan before. Like, ever.

"Maybe you should take this off," he whispers.

I use my weight to settle my butt back on the bench seat, my feet firmly planted on the bottom of the Jacuzzi. Turning, I face him once more. Our gazes meet, our mouths so close it would only take a fraction of an inch for us to make contact.

"You're moving so fast," I tell him, nerves eating at my insides.

He frowns. "Too fast?" He touches my cheek, shifting close to drop a kiss on my lips. "I'll stop if you want me to."

"I don't want to stop. Just…" I smile and shake my head. "I'm being silly."

"You're never silly." He kisses me again, though he doesn't touch me with his hands, and something churns deep within me, making me want more.

He always makes me want more.

"Maybe I should take it off," I say once he breaks away from my lips. "You don't think my parents will catch us, do you?"

"Nah, didn't you say they're in bed by ten? It's gotta be past eleven-thirty now," Ash says reassuringly. "You sure you wanna take that off?"

Leave it to Ash to bring us back to the task at hand. "It's only fair," I say with a shrug.

"You're right. I'm topless." He waves at his bare chest and I stare at it, transfixed by the water bubbling against his skin. "You should be topless too."

Swallowing hard, I reach behind my neck and undo the tie with a few gentle tugs, then remove my bikini top completely. His eyes never leave mine as I drop the top onto the hot tub's edge, and then his hands are right there, cupping the sides of my breasts, his gaze sliding to my mouth.

"So beautiful," he whispers just before his lips capture mine once more. I kiss him back eagerly, a hum sounding low in my throat when his hands start moving, caressing my skin, his thumbs drifting across my nipples. Our tongues meet and twist, and then I'm climbing on top of him like I always do, my knees resting on the bench seat on either side of his hips, my arms circled around his neck, my bare breasts flush against his chest. The skin-on-skin contact does something to me, and I rub against him without restraint, going on pure instinct.

"Fuck, I love it when you do that," he mutters against my throat as he kisses me there. His hands are wandering, fingers gliding over my butt, slipping beneath my bikini bottoms. I can feel him between my legs—he's so hard—and angle myself so I can hit that particular spot again and again.

"You feel so good," I tell him just before he devours my mouth once more. Fleetingly I remember we were supposed to talk about Rylie. About us.

But I don't want to talk. All I want to do is feel and give in to this madness that he creates every time I'm with him. I grind my pelvis against his, a whimper escaping me when I feel his erection twitch, and I reach for him, reach between us, my fingers circling around him.

"Ah Jesus, be careful," he says on a gulp when I awkwardly stroke him.

"Am I hurting you?" I release my grasp on him.

He laughs, though it sounds pained. "Fuck no. I just—I might come too quick, you know?"

Oh. The power that surges through me at his words is a wondrous thing. I'm affecting him just as badly as he's affecting me, and I love it.

"You said you were going to skinny dip," I remind him, my voice teasing. "So what happened?"

"I can still make that happen." His eagerness makes me laugh, and I shift away to watch as he takes off his swim trunks underneath the water and tosses them onto the edge next to my swim top. "Now it's your turn."

Slowly I reach beneath the water, Ash's eyes never leaving me as I pull my bikini bottoms off. Over my hips, down my thighs, over my knees, until I'm stepping out of them and tossing them onto the ground behind me. I move even farther away from him, my breathing accelerated as I savor the sensation of the hot water swirling all around my naked skin. Ash still stares at me, his gaze heavy, his beautiful lips parted, and I rise a little, flashing him my chest, my hard nipples peeking through the bubbling water.

"You're definitely a tease," he says with a hungry smile.

"Do you like it?" I tilt my head to the side, wondering what in the world has come over me.

Feminine power, maybe? It's a heady thing, knowing that Ash wants me. Wants my mouth and my body.

"I fucking love it," he says without hesitation. He starts to drift closer and I move a little faster, darting out of his reach when he tries to grab me. "You want to play?"

Nodding, I sink my teeth into my lower lip, surprised by the laughter that's rising in my chest.

"You're gonna lose, Callahan," he promises. "You know I'm fast."

I do know he's fast. Fast out on that football field. Fast with the words, with the lies, with the truth. Fast with the kisses and the touches and the promises. I put up a little fight, because I think that's what he wants from me, and it's fun to swim away from him, even though the hot tub isn't very big.

He's got me. He knows he does. He's just teasing me too.

When he pulls me into his arms, I go willingly, our mouths connecting like the final pieces in a puzzle. We just fit. Our tongues circle and slide, our hands search and wander, and when he slips his fingers between my thighs to touch me where I want him so badly, I spread my legs wider, giving him better access.

"So wet," he murmurs, and I laugh.

"Everything is wet in a hot tub," I remind him, dropping a light kiss on the already fading bruise on his cheek. He strokes me gently, pressing an important spot that causes a jolt to run straight through me, and I swear my toes just curled. "Oh God."

"Wet and slippery," he says as he keeps touching me. "Different than the water. It's all you."

"Ash." I close my eyes as he continues to stroke me, and then he ducks his head, his mouth on my nipple, tongue licking, lips sucking. The tug of his lips pulls on another part of me deep inside, and I curl my arms around his broad shoulders, clutching him tighter.

I've been waiting for this, wanting this for so long, and now it's finally happening. His magical hands are doing things to my body I've never really experienced, even though I've touched myself before. Given myself an orgasm before too. I used to try to do it while thinking about Ben, but that never worked.

I'd think about Ash and his wicked mouth and dark eyes. His muscular body and tanned skin, imagining him completely naked and all mine, and I'd come.

Every single time.

My breath increases as his fingers move faster, and then he slips one inside before stretching me with two. I cling to him, my eyes tightly closed, everything I have focused on his fingers moving inside of me, his thumb pressing against a certain spot that feels extra good.

"You're so damn tight," he marvels.

"I've never done this before," I confess, shifting my hips and sending his fingers deeper. I feel so full. Imagine when he actually enters my body. Will I be able to handle it?

"Really? Not even with Ben?"

I pull away so I can look into his eyes, my fingers going to his lips to shut him up. "Don't ever bring up his name again."

Ash blinks at me, and I notice there's little drops of water clinging to his thick, black eyelashes. He looks adorably confused. "So never?"

"Never." I shake my head before I press my lips to his. "Only with you," I murmur against his mouth, and he kisses me hungrily, his tongue moving in rhythm with his fingers, and within seconds my hips are keeping the rhythm as well. His thumb circles and presses, and then I fall completely apart.

The orgasm comes quicker than I thought it would. Though I guess we've been toying with each other like one big foreplay-type moment for years. I shudder against his fingers, a moan falling from my lips, and I clamp my thighs tight around his hand as the shivers course through my body again and again.

When it's finally over, he slowly removes his hand from between my legs and presses a gentle kiss to my lips before he slips his fingers into his mouth. I watch him, my own mouth falling open, a little bit disgusted and a lot turned on by what he's doing.

"You taste good," he says when he's done licking his fingers. "Though you also kind of taste like chlorine."

I shove at his shoulder and start to laugh, which is another surprise. I figured Ash and I would angrily hate-fuck each other, what with our turbulent past. "You're kind of disgusting sometimes."

"Hmm, and you're kind of hot." He kisses me once. Then again. "Watching you come was actually really hot."

I'm embarrassed, but then again not really. "It's your turn," I remind him, but he's already shaking his head.

"I bet it's late," he tells me. "You should go back to your room. Get some sleep."

Say what? I don't think so. "Ash. Come here."

He slides away from me. "Nope. It's all about you tonight."

"It doesn't have to be." I move toward him, my body rippling through the water, and Mr.-I'm-so-Fast isn't as fast as he thought. I catch him, circling my arm around the back of his neck, my other hand going for his front, and I feel the tip of his erection brush against my palm.

I swear his eyes cross just from that brief contact. "I don't know if I can handle this," he says.

"Handle what?"

"Your hands on my dick." He releases a shuddery breath. "I'm gonna end up coming all over your fingers."

His words conjure up an image I want to make happen. "That sounds nice."

He laughs and shakes his head. "That's not how I want this to go down."

"Are you serious right now?" I reach for him again, tickling my fingers along his length. He's big. Though really, I have no one else to compare him to, so I have no idea.

"Callahan." His voice is a warning.

"I bet I'll have you saying my first name within the next five minutes," I croon, my fingers curling around the base.

His entire body jolts and he sends me an uneasy look. "I'll make that wager."

"You're going to lose." I start to stroke in earnest, just before I glide through the water and press my body completely against his.

"What the fuck are you doing?"

"Just teasing." I reach for his erection and put it between my legs. I won't let him inside, but oh my God, it feels so good to have him right there, pressing against me. Flesh on flesh, hot and hard and wet.

"I'm not wearing a condom," he chokes out.

"And I'm not on the pill." I am literally riding his dick, as they say. It's between my legs, and I am sliding across it like it's a pole made just for my pleasure. Which it sort of is, if you think about it.

"So what we're doing is fucking risky as hell." He gently

pushes me away so I fall off his lap, leaving me floating in the water. "One thrust and I'd be inside you."

I want that.

"And then I'd probably lose all control because that's what you do to me, Autumn. You make me lose control and then I'd come inside you, and next thing we know, you're pregnant." He slowly shakes his head. "No way. Uh-uh. We'd be fucked."

I know he's right, but my heart pangs at the idea of us having a baby together. Which is insane, considering I'm only seventeen.

"Do you have condoms in your room?" I ask.

"What the hell, Autumn?" He runs his hands through his hair, slicking it back. "No, I don't have condoms in your family's guest room. I didn't think I'd be having sex with anyone at the Callahan house while I'm recovering."

"Yet here you are, naked in a hot tub with me." I point at him. "And you called me Autumn. Twice."

He grins, like he can't stay mad at me. Not that I think he was angry in the first place. "You're right, I did. You win."

"I knew I would," I say arrogantly.

"What do you want your prize to be?"

"Watching your face when I make you come for the first time," I say sweetly.

From the look on Ash's face, I can tell he's surprised by my bold request. "I think I created a monster."

"You so did." I settle in on his lap once more but keep some distance between us, my fingers curling around him, and I start to stroke him in earnest. "We need to get condoms," I say just before I kiss him.

"I'll add it to the shopping list, honey," he whispers against my lips, but then all thoughts of condoms and shopping lists and jokes disappear, replaced by needy groans and harshly whispered curse words while I work him into a frenzy.

I stroke and tease, rub my thumb against the tip, let him guide me when I'm not fast enough or rough enough. I'm pleasantly surprised at just how rough he wants it, and I finally slap his hand away, doing exactly as he shows me.

When he comes with a long, loud moan, I swallow it with my mouth, feel the spurt of his semen on my hand, and I smile in triumph against his lips.

Ash is right.

He did create a monster.

CHAPTER 24

*I*t's the day after the hot tub incident and I'm walking down the hall toward my fourth-period class when I hear a familiar girl's voice mutter, "Slut," beneath her breath.

Pretty sure she's talking about me.

Coming to a stop, I turn to find Rylie standing there. Glaring at me. "Did you just call me a slut?"

She nods and lifts her chin, her expression defiant. "You *stole* him from me."

Unease trickles down my spine. I'm not used to confrontation. I avoid it as much as possible. "What are you talking about?"

"Don't play dumb, Ash moves in with your family and now you two are together! I know it!" Rylie yells.

I glance around, hoping no one is listening, but let's be real. They're *all* listening. Everyone's down for a girl fight. "Keep your voice down."

"Why? Because you don't want people to know you're fucking Asher Davis?"

How could she even know what happened between us

208

last night? "We're not together." And that's not a lie. We might be on our way to being a couple, but nothing's official yet.

"Please." Rylie rolls her eyes. "You may as well be. I know you two have had a thing for each other for *years.* I don't care what Ash says, and I don't care what you say either. The minute your famous daddy brought him home, you treat Ash like he's your own personal toy to play with whenever you want."

Now I'm getting mad. "You have no idea what you're talking about."

"Sure I do. You're a man-stealing slut, that's all I need to know." Rylie shoves at my shoulder, propelling me backward into a couple of people walking by. One of them catches me before I fall on my ass, and I scramble to right myself, anger and fear sending me straight toward Rylie.

"He wasn't yours to steal," I tell her and the rage that fills Rylie's eyes is enough to make me take one step back.

"You're such a bitch," she screeches, rearing her arm back, fingers clutched into a fist.

Like she's going to hit me.

"Stop!" My cheer coach Brandy appears out of nowhere, coming in between Rylie and me. Brandy's facing me, her expression full of fury, and I take another step back, my entire body shaking. "What the hell are you doing, Autumn?"

I gape at her. "I'm not doing anything. She started it!" I point at Rylie, who's slowly backing away.

Brandy turns to look at Rylie. "Go to the office."

"But—"

"Now." Brandy's voice is firm. When she's like this, I know I never want to mess with her.

Rylie gives me the finger from behind Brandy's back and then takes off.

"What are you two fighting over? Please don't tell me it's

it something stupid, like a boy." Brandy lifts her brows, sending me a knowing look.

With a sigh, I glance around before I grab her hand and pull her over to the side of the hallway so not as many people can overhear us. "Ash Davis broke up with her last night and now she's accusing me of having sex with him."

"And now what? You're causing drama between them? Is that what's going on?"

My cheeks go hot and I try my best to keep my expression neutral. "Of course not."

"Why does she suspect you two did it?" Brandy asks.

I shrug. "I don't know."

"Autumn..."

With a sigh, I lean in close so I can murmur in her ear. "He's staying with me, okay? No one really knows, but my dad brought him to our house the night he got beat up and he's been there ever since."

When I pull away, I see Brandy is slowly shaking her head. "Your father better watch it or he's going to get in trouble."

I frown. "What do you mean?"

"Ash Davis is a minor. And I'm thinking his mom reported him as a runaway. Not that you heard that from me." Brandy sends me a pointed look, and I'm guessing she's telling me without telling me that his mother *did* report him as a runaway.

Will she give me other information too? "He's afraid if he goes home, they'll have him arrested," I tell her.

"That could happen," she says with a nod.

Fear makes my heart knock against my chest and I rub at the spot between my boobs absently. "He wants to come back to school."

"He should probably get in contact with his mother first."

"That is the absolute last thing he wants to do."

"I advise before he returns to this campus that he do exactly that." She makes a tsking noise and shakes her head. "The longer he's gone, the more behind he's going to get with his schoolwork."

"Can I get his homework for him?"

"I can help make that happen." Brandy's in good with the vice principal. As in—that's her mom.

I breathe a sigh of relief. "That would be so great. Thank you."

"I'm serious, though. Ash needs to get into contact with his mother. The longer he stays away, the worse it's going to get." Brandy pats my shoulder just as the bell rings. "Now get to class."

"You're not going to make me go to the office like Rylie?" I ask incredulously.

"Did you call her a slut first?"

"No."

"Then you're fine. For now. If Mrs. Adney calls you up, just tell her what happened," Brandy says, and I take off, hustling into my classroom before I can be marked late.

* * *

THE MOMENT I get home from cheer practice, I go in search of Ash. Mom is in the kitchen making dinner for us, and I call out a greeting to her as I pass through the room, but otherwise I don't stop.

I need to find him. I need to talk to him.

At lunch, Rylie sent me death stares from across the quad but otherwise left me alone. I had to explain to Kaya what happened between Rylie and me in the hallway, while leaving out the pertinent detail that Ash and I actually *did* mess around last night, which proved difficult. And the only reason I explained myself is because the rumors about our confrontation had already spread like wildfire and everyone knew about it by the start of lunch, though the details were, of course, exaggerated.

"I always thought she was such a sweet girl," Kaya said sadly when I was done with my story.

"A sweet girl who called me a slut," I reminded her.

It was awkward. The entire afternoon was awkward, thanks to Rylie. Mrs. Adney ended up calling me to her office during seventh period, just like Brandy predicted, and I explained exactly what happened. Even gave her a few names of people I knew were in that hallway with us who could be witnesses.

"I don't think that'll be necessary," Adney said when I was finished. "I would suggest you avoid Rylie Altman as much as possible for the rest of the week. Getting into a physical altercation on campus is grounds for suspension."

I didn't bother explaining myself. What was the point? I'm sure Adney would've just brushed me off and told me to get back to class.

Music comes from the guest bedroom, and I stop in the doorway to find Ash lying on the unmade bed in only a pair of navy blue sweatpants, tapping a pencil against the edge of a white binder that's next to him. I don't know what inspired him to attempt schoolwork when I have his latest homework assignments in my backpack, but I sort of don't care about that at the moment.

All I can do is stare at his rippling abs with longing. He has the best body I've ever seen, and it's hard for me to grasp that I had my hands all over it last night.

If Rylie hadn't confronted me, I would've been a daydreaming mess all day long, thinking about what happened between Ash and me last night. But his stupid ex had to ruin it all with her jealous outburst.

"Callahan." He smiles when he sees me, and it's like a ray of sunshine being shot straight at me. "I didn't hear you."

"Your music is loud." It's some rap song that's vaguely familiar. A few years ago Mom tried to stop all of us from listening to *that kind of music* because she hated the foul language, but after a while, she gave up, admitting that when she was our age, she liked that music too.

He hits pause on his phone and the music shuts off. He must have it hooked up to a speaker—where did he get it? And where is it?

I'm so concerned with a stupid speaker I don't realize he's slid off the bed and made his way to me until his arms are around my waist, pulling me in close so I make contact with all that gloriously warm, hard skin that's on display.

"Missed you," he murmurs just before he kisses me.

I try to wiggle myself out of his arms. "I'm all sweaty from practice."

"I don't mind." His hands slide over my butt and tug me in nice and close. I can already feel his erection beneath his loose sweatpants, and this time I do manage to get myself out of his hold.

"My mom is in the kitchen," I whisper-hiss. "Ava and Beck are home too."

"So." Ash shrugs. "No one comes back here."

He's not wrong, but I don't feel right messing around with him when my mother is *right there*, making dinner and chatting with Beck. I can hear them. They're really not that far.

"Something happened today," I start, but Ash interrupts me.

"I heard."

I'm gaping at him for a long, confused couple of seconds before I snap my lips shut. "What do you mean, you heard?"

"Rylie tried to start a fight with you and called you a slut.

I heard." He shrugs again, and I'm starting to hate those shrugs. He's so nonchalant, like it's no big deal, yet his psycho ex-girlfriend or whatever he calls her tried to *fight me* and she called me a *slut.*

That's kind of major. I don't deal with that sort of thing. It's not the norm.

"I've never had that happen to me before," I tell him slowly, overly pronouncing each word like he's a little kid and can't understand.

"Welcome to my world, baby," he says with a grin, trying to grab me yet again, but I dodge away from his hands.

"No, that's bullshit. I had to go to Adney's office. She told me if Rylie and I get into a physical fight, I could get suspended." I stare at him incredulously while he chews on a hangnail. "That kind of thing *never* happens to me, Ash."

"You said that already." He studies his hands, doesn't even bother looking at me. "Happens to me all the time."

"And you're okay with it?" My voice is shrill, and I tell myself to calm down.

"I'm used to it." He pauses. "Clearly you're not okay with it."

"I'm not. Not at all. Rylie scared me. She *pushed* me. If my coach hadn't shown up when she did, I think Rylie would've started fighting me."

"She's a complete bitch. Fuck that chick." He waves a dismissive hand. "What did you tell her anyway?"

"I didn't tell her anything. She talked like she knew what happened between us last night. She accused me of fucking her boyfriend." I narrow my eyes, studying him. "*You* didn't talk to her, did you?"

"Hell no. Why would you even ask that question? Are you accusing me of telling her about us? Why the hell would I do that?" His voice starts to rise, and I can tell I'm making him angry.

This is getting out of control quick. I'm not used to this sort of thing. Ben and I rarely, if ever, fought. I haven't really had any other boyfriends besides Ben. My parents don't argue. I don't even argue with my friends. The only person I fight with is…

The boy standing in front of me.

"I'm not accusing you of anything," I say slowly, again like I'm talking to a child. "I just don't know how she knew about us."

"She's just guessing, and she guessed right. That's all. No need to be paranoid." He goes to the closet and pulls a T-shirt off a hanger, tugging it on. "Ignore her. She's just pissed because I told her I didn't like her like that anymore. She's the one who's making a bigger deal over it, and we weren't even officially together."

"Try telling her that," I say.

"She'll get over it. They always do."

The question pops out of my mouth before I even have a chance to think about it. "Did you have sex with her?"

He goes still, then turns to face me. "What?"

"You know what I said." I cross my arms, waiting for him to answer.

He at least has the decency to look embarrassed. His cheeks turn a ruddy color and he rubs the back of his neck, his gaze downcast. "Maybe."

A big sigh escapes me as my shoulders slump. "Really, Ash? You two were only together a few weeks!"

"We messed around a little bit, that's it. It was never anything serious. I don't know how many times I need to say that." When I glare at him, he glares right back. "What did you expect? Me to act like a monk while you're off with Ben for a fucking year?"

"Ben and I never did anything!"

"How was I supposed to know that?"

"Oh, I don't know, maybe because I told you?" My chest hurts, and I feel like I could start crying. Which is so stupid because it's no big deal, right? So Ash had sex with Rylie Altman. So what. He's probably had sex with lots of girls at our school. But I'm special. I'm the one he's always wanted. I'm the one he really cared about.

Even in my head it sounds like a giant load of shit.

"I didn't believe you, okay? I figured you were just saying that to make me feel better." He's rubbing the back of his neck so hard he's making the skin red. "It meant nothing."

"What meant nothing?"

"Sex with Rylie. Sex with any girl I've been with before." He blows out a frustrated breath and runs his hands through his hair, making a mess of it. "I'm not perfect. I never said I was."

"I'm not perfect either," I say, my voice small.

"Yeah, well, you damn well act like it. Autumn Callahan, the pretty little princess. Adored by her daddy, loved by her mama. Captain of the cheer team, vice president of the senior class. Gets good grades and never let the dirty boy touch her until last night. Now look at you, you're gonna cry all because I had sex with some dumb chick who's now pissed off and ready to fight you. So what!" And with that, Ash storms out of the room.

The tears come the second he leaves and I collapse on the edge of the bed, burying my face in my hands. I feel so stupid. So, so stupid. I thought I mattered. I thought he cared about me.

I guess not.

CHAPTER 25

*W*e don't talk for the rest of the night. He doesn't come to the table when Mom calls that dinner's ready, and I know he gets away with it because Dad is at the team dinner along with Jake. I'd bet money Ash would never disrespect my father.

Yet he'll disrespect me. No surprise.

During dinner, Beck never shuts up, as usual, and Ava constantly argues with him, which has Mom coming down on her. I don't say a word. Just push the food on my plate around with a fork before I ask to be excused.

The sad look Mom sends me tells me she knows I'm upset, and she nods her answer. I'm out of the chair and upstairs within seconds, vomiting what little food I had in my stomach into the toilet, crying and gasping the whole time.

God, I really hate throwing up.

I really hate boys too.

I brush my teeth and then take a shower and cry. I blowdry my hair and cry a little more. It's not even nine o'clock and I'm in bed, the lights off, my phone plugged in and sitting on my bedside table, forgotten. I don't want to talk to anyone or scroll Instagram or watch people's stories. And I sure as hell don't want to watch TikTok videos to try to put me in a good mood.

Forget that. I want to wallow in my sadness and curse Asher Davis's existence under my breath.

I finally drift off to sleep and my dreams are terrible. Rylie punching me in the face and there's nothing I can do to stop her. She keeps hitting me until my eye is a slit and I can't really see. Then it switches to me at a football game, but I'm not cheering. I'm sitting in the stands as I watch Rylie run out onto the football field after a game, hugging Ash close while he stares at me the entire time. He mouths the words *it could've been you*, and that's enough to jolt me wide awake.

Only to find Ash sitting on the side of my bed, his hand curled around my shoulder, trying to wake me up.

"What are you doing in my room?" I scoot away from him and his hand falls from my shoulder. I try my best to breathe evenly to calm my racing heart, but it's so difficult when he's right there, especially after my shitty dream.

I don't want him in my room, on my bed. I'm still mad at him.

Yet my skin prickles with awareness when he touches the side of my face, his roughened fingertips skimming my cheek. "I'm sorry," he whispers. "So damn sorry, Autumn. I didn't mean to fuck this up."

That is the first time I've ever heard him say those words, and I hate this, but I don't know if I can believe him. "You're sorry for what?" I ask warily.

For lying to me?

For being mean to me?

For kissing me?

For fingering me?

There are all sorts of things he could be sorry about.

"For yelling at you earlier. For not understanding where you're coming from." He shakes his head, his hand curling into a fist. "I'm fucked up, Callahan. You know this."

"No you're not—" I start to say, but he pounds the mattress with his fist, startling me, and I go quiet.

"Yes, I am. I'm a complete piece of shit and you know it." His breathing is ragged, like he's just run five miles, and I realize he's extremely upset. More upset than I thought he was. "I'm not worthy of you, and I know it. You know it too. I don't know what the fuck you see in me, or why you like me so much. We shouldn't work together."

I sit up, pushing my hair away from my face. "You don't want us to work?"

He stares at me incredulously. Even in the darkness, I can make out his features. And he looks positively tormented. "What the fuck are you saying? Of course I want us to work. I've been chasing after you since freshman year."

My heart pangs at his confession. "I probably overreacted. About you having—sex with Rylie."

"She doesn't matter," he says, his words quick. Fast, fast, like he always is. "She's never mattered. I only got with her because I didn't think I could ever be with you. I waited, you know."

"Waited for what?"

"Waited for you. I knew you and Ben broke up at the beginning of the summer. That *you* broke up with *him*. I thought you'd come to me eventually. But you never did. You kept doing you, and I kept doing me, and I thought, well, she's free, and I'm free, and she knows where I'm at. But you never came for me. And then Rylie started sniffing around right when school started, and I was like, fuck it. I'll get with her. She was a distraction." He pauses, sending me a rueful smile. "A part of me wanted to make you jealous."

"It worked," I say without hesitation. I'm still a little upset, but it doesn't pay to lie. I've learned that. "Kaya and Daphne told me you two were together, and I was devastated."

"Why didn't you talk to me?"

"Why didn't you talk to me?" I throw back at him.

"You're the one who always pushed me away. You're the one who always told me no." He shakes his head. "I thought it was your turn to come to me."

"I can't read your mind, Ash," I tell him, my voice dry.

"Too bad. Well, wait a minute. Maybe that's a good thing. Then you won't know about all the dirty things I want to do to you right now." He grins, his teeth shining white in the semi-darkness, and I smack him lightly, realizing too late my hand makes contact with the bare skin of his chest.

He grabs hold of my wrist before I can remove my hand, pressing my palm against the center of his chest. "You feel that?"

His heart is pounding rapidly, like he just ran across a football field at hyper speed. "Yes," I say softly.

"That's all for you. My heart only beats for you, Autumn." He brings my hand to his mouth and presses a soft kiss upon my skin. "No one else. You own it. You own me."

I melt at his words, at the touch his lips on my hand. He loosens his hold on my wrist and I cup his cheek, leaning in so I can press my mouth to his, and then we're kissing.

This is a mistake.

The words pound through my mind as I open my mouth to Ash, my tongue darting out to meet his. He's still just in those loose sweatpants, and I'm only in a tank top and a pair of panties. The moment our bodies brush against each other, it's electric, sparks crackling between us, and I eagerly reach for him, my hands sliding down his back, fingers slipping beneath the waistband of his sweats to find him bare-assed beneath.

How can it be a mistake when it feels so good? When we

know just how to touch each other? Maybe it's not a mistake. Maybe this can work after all.

Ash groans against my lips, and within seconds I'm lying in the middle of my bed, his hips nestled between my legs, his entire body aligned with mine, our lips locked, tongues tangling. His hands slip beneath my tank and I help him get rid of it. I shove at his sweatpants and he kicks them off. His fingers slip beneath the front of my panties and then I'm batting his hand away, pushing *him* away, sitting up so I can catch my breath.

"What's wrong?" He leans in and drops tiny kisses down my neck, his fingers brushing back and forth across my left nipple, making me tingle.

Making me squirm.

"Stop," I tell him, my voice firm. "I can't think."

His mouth is gone in an instant, his fingers falling away from my breasts. He backs up until he's standing naked by the side of my bed, and I stare up at him. "You say stop, I'll stop." He holds his hands up in front of him like the cops have their guns drawn and he's about to get arrested.

"I'm guessing you still don't have a condom," I say, and he shakes his head.

"We don't need condoms. Not tonight. Just…let me touch you." The pleading look on his face is my downfall.

I hold my hand out to him and he takes it, rejoining me on the bed. "Lie back," he whispers, and I do as I'm told, whimpering when he kisses me, drugs me with his tongue and lips.

It's too much and it's not enough, all at once. He moves down my body, kissing me everywhere. My neck, my shoulders, my chest, the skin between my breasts. He cups them, his thumbs rubbing my nipples before he sucks one, then the other in his mouth. I watch him, then close my eyes, embarrassed. Overwhelmed. It's so weird, to do this, to be so intimate with someone.

Yet it's not weird at all, not with Ash. It's like we were meant to do this, and that's why I couldn't do it with anyone else. I was saving myself.

For Ash.

He kisses me across my stomach, licking at my bellybutton and making me yelp. He drops a kiss on my left hipbone, and then my right. And then he spreads my legs, his mouth landing on the inside of my thigh, and I almost jump out of my skin.

"Sshh," he whispers. I didn't realize I made a noise, but I must've. "Be quiet."

I clamp my lips shut and close my eyes tight, a little moan falling from my lips when he kisses and nibbles my sensitive skin, drawing closer and closer to where I want him. My hand falls on top of his head and I curl my fingers in his thick, soft hair, tugging hard, making him grunt.

He goes still, he's not doing anything, and I crack my eyes open to find he's staring at me, his face between my legs, his eyes wide and unblinking.

"What are you doing?" I ask softly.

"Looking at you," he answers.

"Why?"

"I can't believe we're doing this. That I'm in your bed." He drops a kiss just above my pubic hair, making me jump. "That you're letting me do this."

"Do what?" For some twisted reason I want to hear him say what he plans on doing to me.

"Eat you out." He says this with a grin just before he plants both hands on the inside of my thighs and nuzzles me with his nose. Then licks me with his wicked tongue.

It's like this for long, torturous minutes. Anytime I make a noise, he shushes me. He licks me everywhere, and I mean *everywhere,* and I almost want to die from embarrassment, but it feels too good so I just savor it. I close my eyes sometimes because it's too much, and then I have to open them so I can watch his dark head between my thighs, his tongue licking, his lips sucking, and then it becomes too much again.

And when he slips his fingers inside of me, it's way too much, and I'm coming. Shivering and shaking, my legs bowed, my toes curled, my entire body going stiff just before I collapse in a boneless heap.

He kisses his way back up my body, his mouth landing on mine, and the kiss turns dirty in an instant. All tongue and teeth and sucking lips. I can taste myself, like tangy salt, and when he breaks the kiss he smiles down at me, looking very pleased with himself.

"You're a dirty girl, Callahan."

I wrap my legs around his hips, anchoring myself to him. "You like it."

"I fucking love it." He kisses me again, and it goes on for minutes. Long, delicious minutes until I start to feel his insistent erection poking against my thigh.

It's his turn, but this time I'm not going to announce that out loud. Instead, I break the kiss and gently shove at his shoulder, sending him onto his back. He watches me, his lips curved into a closed-mouth smile, his dark eyes dancing with excitement, and then I'm the one who's raining kisses all over his beautiful body. I explore every inch that I can, flicking my tongue against his tiny nipples, licking at his navel, my tongue blazing a path along the line of dark hair that leads from the base of his navel all the way to his erection.

He's big, just as I thought. Being face to dick makes me realize that real quick. Taking a deep breath, I grasp the base of him and start licking the sides, and he practically bends in half toward me.

"What are you doing?" he chokes out.

"Really, Ash? What do you think I'm doing?" I lick him like a popsicle, trailing my tongue up one side and down the other.

"You—don't—have—to." Every time my tongue meets his sensitive skin, he pauses, and I sort of want to laugh, but I don't.

"I want to," I whisper just before I slip the head of his erection between my lips. He tastes like tangy salt too, and I test his width, nerves making me hesitant.

"If you think you're doing it wrong, trust me. You're not," he says, panting. Like he's a mind reader.

His words give me the confidence I need to keep going. I suck and lick, drawing him deeper into my mouth, until I can't take him any farther. I don't really know what I'm doing, so I just copy from the few porn clips I've seen on the internet, using my tongue and lips and hand, squeezing him extra tight like he taught me to last night. It must work, because he's a writhing, groaning mess within minutes, and he even gives me a warning.

"I'm gonna come," he says, his eyes pitch black and filled with desperation.

"Good." I slip my mouth over just the head again and suck extra hard, wanting him to come in my mouth. Just so I can see what it's like.

It's a blast of salty liquid is what it's like, hitting me right in the back of the throat within seconds of that warning. His entire body jerks and shivers, and I pull away from him, my hand still curled around the base as I give him a couple more strokes, swallowing his come with a slight grimace.

Of course Ash notices my face once it's all over. And he starts laughing, the jerk. "Didn't like it?"

I release my hold on him and wipe my sticky hand on my discarded tank top. "It wasn't my favorite."

He starts laughing even harder and I crawl up the length

of his body, resting my hand across his mouth. "You're going to wake everyone up," I warn him.

When he calms down and I move my hand away from his mouth, he says, "No one is as loud as you, Callahan. All that moaning when I licked your pussy."

I clamp my hand over his mouth again. "You can't say that."

"Say what?" he asks, his voice muffled.

"You know." He can't get me to say it.

He licks my hand and I drop it away from his mouth. "Lick your pussy? You don't like it when I say that?"

I shake my head, laughing when he rolls to his side and pulls me with him. "No, it's gross."

"Gross? So you're saying your pussy is gross? I don't think so. Maybe you want me to stop licking and touching it then." His hand starts to wander. Across my stomach. Down lower. Until his fingers are between my legs. "Huh. It's all wet and pink and glistening…"

"Stop." His hand stills and I give him a look. "Well, you don't have to stop that."

"You can't have your cake and eat it too, sweetheart." He kisses me once, whispering, "I like talking about your pussy. It's my new favorite thing."

I slip my hand between our faces and settle it over his mouth. "I don't know if I want to hear you talk about it all the time."

"Too bad. You're gonna." He wraps his lips around my finger and bites it, but not too hard. Just enough to sting. At the exact moment his teeth sink into my flesh, he starts to stroke, softly. Lightly. Making me tingle. Making me wetter.

He releases my finger from his teeth. "See? Damn, that pussy of yours is amazing. Look at how I barely touch it and you get so wet for me."

"Ash..." My voice drifts and I close my eyes when he starts playing with my clit.

"Yeah, baby? What do you want? You want me to make you come again?"

I never, ever thought I'd be so responsive to someone who talks to me while we're having sex. I figured it would make me uncomfortable. But for some reason, Ash's deep voice saying dirty things is only making me more aroused.

"Yes please," I whisper and he cracks a smile, kissing me while he increases the pressure of his fingers.

"I could lick this pussy all night long," he practically croons, and a full-body shiver washes over me at his words, the tone of his voice. "You want me to keep touching it?"

I nod, biting my lip.

"So pretty." I can actually hear his fingers as he strokes me, I'm so wet. "So juicy. Can't wait to fuck it."

Oh, that's it. Yep, I'm coming, all because he said he wants to fuck my pussy.

Clearly, I'm a total pervert.

And I love it.

CHAPTER 26

$\mathcal{I}$t was weird not seeing Ash out on the field Friday night during the game. No mention of his name, no one calling out his jersey number. Despite my missing him, I gave it my all, cheering on my brother, who I have to admit played the best game of his life. We won, and afterward a local news photographer took a photo of our entire family, and I realized that was probably the only time I will cheer on the sidelines for Jake while he plays for the varsity team. When he moves up next year, I'll be gone.

Unless for some reason Ash won't be able to play anymore and Jake ends up taking his place for the rest of the season.

I can barely stand the thought.

When I arrived at the house after the game, I noticed Dad's car was already in the garage. How did he and Jake beat me home? Usually they stay long after the game's finished, talking with everyone, but they must've left when I was still in the cheer room. I had plans on seeing Ash, possibly sneaking into his room once everyone was asleep, but all three of them were in my dad's office with the door closed. Probably talking about football and going over the game.

I felt so completely left out, I stomped upstairs like a baby and took a long, hot shower. I shaved my legs, I shaved between my legs and afterward, I lotioned up my entire body in anticipation of Ash and me getting together later.

And then promptly fell asleep, only to wake up the next morning past eight o'clock.

It's the scent of bacon that lures me awake. I throw a sweatshirt on and head down the stairs, finger-combing my hair so I don't look like a total nightmare when I enter the kitchen. I'm guessing Ash will be there, waiting for me with one of those wicked smiles curving his perfect lips.

I guess wrong. He's nowhere to be found, and neither is Dad. It's Mom who's making breakfast, this time bacon and French toast. My absolute favorite, though we rarely have it because both Dad and Jake don't really like it.

That's when I notice they're not in the kitchen either.

"Good morning!" Mom says cheerily, her long blonde hair pulled into a perfect messy bun. She makes things look so effortless sometimes, I find it almost annoying. But in a good way. In a *I have lots of aspirations to be just like my mom* way.

"Hey," I say. Ava and Beck are sitting at the counter, both of them quiet because they're too busy shoveling food into their mouths. "Where's Dad and Jake?"

"They left about an hour ago with Ash." I wait to see if she'll say anything else, but that's all she gives me. "I'm assuming you want breakfast."

"Sure." Frustrated, I go to the coffeemaker and pour myself a cup, then dump in a bunch of creamer before I take my mug over to the counter. On weekends Mom makes a giant pot of coffee versus us using the Keurig or stopping at Starbucks, which is what I usually do before school starts.

Mom flips the piece of French toast that's in the pan, slowly cooking it to that perfect golden brown. "You're grumpy."

You know what a grumpy person hates? When someone calls them out for being grumpy. "I'm fine."

"Uh huh." Mom piles a couple of pieces of French toast onto a plate, adds a few slices of bacon and deposits the plate directly in front of me, then pushes the maple syrup my way. "Any of this have to do with Ash not being around this morning?"

I pause, the bacon hovering in front of my parted lips. She's got her back to me once more as she prepares a couple more pieces of French toast, I'm assuming for herself. My brain scrambles, trying to come up with an answer.

"I guess his mother reached out to him last night, wanting to meet with him this morning, and so he asked your dad and your brother to go with him," Mom explains, her back still to me as she stands in front of the stove.

I drop the bacon on my plate, my appetite leaving me just like that. "What do you mean, he's meeting with his mother?"

"I mean exactly what I say." Mom places two pieces of French toast on her plate, switches off the stove burner, and then turns to face me. "They're meeting for breakfast at Pop's."

"All four of them?" I can only imagine Jake sitting there watching it unfold, bored out of his mind. Dad I can definitely see wanting to help, maybe even acting as a mediator, but my brother? That's a big ol' nope.

"Your father and brother planned on sitting at another table nearby. They discussed it beforehand and decided Ash wouldn't mention to his mother that they were there, just so he had backup. He was supposed to meet with her alone, but that made him nervous. He thought she might bring Don, so your dad and Jake offered to go," Mom says, sounding perfectly logical.

But what she just said sounds perfectly terrible. I can't believe Ash agreed to meet with his mom. Worse, I can't believe he didn't tell me. I'm sort of hurt. Not even a text to let me know where he's at? I'm not his keeper or anything, but after everything we've shared this week, I at least deserve a message, right?

Or maybe I'm just being unreasonable.

"Jake went for a free breakfast," I mumble as I start munching on my bacon. It turns out I'm starving, and this is the most delicious bacon I've had in a long time. And Mom's French toast is to die for.

"I'm sure he did. He loves Pop's." They're a local place known for their homecooked breakfasts, which everyone loves, both locals and tourists. "But don't complain. You're getting your favorite breakfast since they're not here." She smiles at me as she settles onto the stool next to mine, and I can't help but smile in return.

We talk about last night's game. Ava admits she wishes she tried out for cheer and I gave her a *told you so* look, but keep my mouth shut. It's Mom who hits her with the I told you so.

"I'm gonna play football like Jakey and Daddy," Beck announces, pounding the quartz counter with his fist. If Jake heard Beck call him *Jakey* he'd probably threaten bodily harm.

"You already do," Ava points out, but Beck shakes his head.

"Not peewee stuff. I wanna play high school. And college. Then one day, the pros!" he yells.

"I'm sure you will," Mom says in agreement as we all start cleaning up the kitchen, even Beck, who's tossing all the napkins in the trash. "You're a tank on the field."

Beck will never be a quarterback like Dad and Jake. When he gets on the field, he just wants to mow down everyone in his path. He's the perfect lineman.

I'm a ball of nervous energy as I help Mom wash the pans. I wish Ash were back already. I don't like thinking of him alone with his mother, even though I know Dad and Jake are both there. Nothing bad will happen, but what if she did something terrible like…call the police?

What if they come to the restaurant and arrest him? What if they haul him off to jail? It's Saturday, so he'd probably have to stay there the entire weekend. He's so young. He's only seventeen, but I bet they wouldn't put him in juvenile hall. Nope, they'd put him in actual jail with the real criminals and he'd probably freak out and—

"Autumn, are you all right?" Mom rests a hand on my back, and I realize I'm just staring at the soapy water in the sink, my hands gripping the edge, not doing really anything.

"I'm fine." I reach deeper into the sink and undo the plug, watching as the water slowly drains out. "Just still a little tired, I guess."

Mom rubs my back soothingly, and I lean into her a little bit, needing the reassurance. I appreciate that she's not making a big deal over what she said earlier, about me being grumpy because Ash isn't around. I figured she'd start questioning me, but she hasn't really said much of anything. "You don't think she'll pull something on him, do you? Like call the cops?"

"Who? Ash's mother? She's a terrible human, but I don't think she's *that* terrible," Mom says. "Plus, I'm sure she has her own secrets to hide."

Curiosity fills me. "What do you mean by that?"

"That's not my story to tell."

Ooh, I hate it when she says stuff like that.

"I've noticed you two have gotten closer," Mom continues.

Uh oh, I thought too soon. Here come the comments and questions.

My cheeks grow warm and I hate how I blush so easily. I give all my feelings away, I swear. "We—have."

Mom slips her arm around my shoulders and gives me a squeeze. "I'm surprised it took you two this long."

"Why would you say that?" I duck away from her arm and grab a damp rag, then start wiping the counter.

"You two were awfully cozy during homecoming week your sophomore year. I thought for sure something would happen then, but it didn't." Mom smiles. "And by the way, Ava already cleaned the kitchen counters."

"Oh." I toss the rag back into the sink and cross my arms, feeling dumb. I also feel like I'm about to burst with my feelings for Ash. I can't tell her everything since I don't want to freak her out with all the sex stuff, but I can share a *few* things. "I really like him."

"I think he really likes you too." She tilts her head, studying me. "I just hope he treats you with respect."

"He does," I tell her, standing up straighter. "He's a little rough around the edges, but that doesn't bother me."

"I'm the one who used to be a little rough around the edges," Mom says with a faint smile. "He reminds me of myself when I was that age. With the terrible parents and the bleak outlook on life. The devil-may-care attitude and the self-destructive behavior. He could graduate, get out of here and do something with his life if he continues to focus and made the right choices."

He so could. Not that I want him to leave me, but I plan on leaving this town too. Maybe we could go somewhere together. A college not too far away, but just far enough, where he could play football and I could watch him and we could eventually move in together…

Whoops. I'm moving way too fast.

"Just—Autumn." I turn to look at her, noting the serious tone of her voice, her equally serious expression. "Be careful with Ash. I know you're a smart girl and you've always made good choices, but…I know how young love is. Don't do anything reckless."

Too late, I want to tell her, but I don't. Instead, I smile and go to her, wrapping her up in a big hug. "I'm always careful, Mom," I say, but deep down, I know that's a lie.

When it comes to Ash, I *am* reckless. And if I don't watch it…

I might get burned.

* * *

I'M in my room sorting my laundry, my least favorite chore in the entire world, when I finally hear my dad, Jake and Ash enter the house through the kitchen. I practically run out of my room and sprint down the stairs, slowing down as I approach the living room where all three of them are, along with Mom.

"…so it went all right?" Mom asks.

"As well as can be expected," Ash answers, annoyance bleeding into his voice. "She wants me to come home. She wanted to take me back with her from the restaurant, but I told her I had to think about it first."

"Oh dear." Mom sounds like a total…mom right now. "Do you want to go home?"

I stand just on the other side of the wall, waiting for his answer.

"I don't know. If I go back there, it'll be the same old shit, you know? Sorry, I don't mean to keep cursing," Ash says.

"But I know she won't change. Once we lost my dad, it's like I lost her too."

His words make me so sad. He may have his mother physically, but she's not really there for him. I can't imagine dealing with something like that.

"Stop apologizing. We all curse in this house. Sometimes even Beck," Mom says wryly, which is the truth. When Beck was younger, he was a total parrot, mimicking all of us, usually only the bad words. "If you don't want to go back and live with your mom yet, you don't have to."

"I told him the same thing," Dad chimes in.

"I'm going up to my room," Jake says, sounding totally bored. He exits the living room, stopping short when he notices me lurking, and sends me a quizzical look. "What are you doing?"

"Sshh." I rest my finger over my lip, but too late. Everyone heard Jake call me out.

Ash leans around the edge of the doorway to see both Jake and me standing there. "Callahan, whatcha doing? Why you lurking around out here like a stalker?"

The amusement in his voice, the smile on his face and the sparkle in his gaze fills me with infinite relief. It seems like forever since I saw him last, even if it's only been around twenty-four hours, and I wish I could run up to him and grab him like I want to.

But I don't. Instead I smile at him in return and duck my head, a little embarrassed I got caught spying. "I thought you might want to talk to my parents alone. I didn't want to interrupt."

"I think we're done." He leaves the living room without saying another word to either of my parents and comes toward me. His dark gaze is all for me, and I tilt my head back as he draws even closer. Probably too close, especially if

Dad's watching. "Let's go outside and talk," Ash says, his voice low. Intimate. "I'll tell you everything that happened."

I send him a look, trying to communicate with my eyes that maybe that's not a good idea, but he's not getting it. Of course he's not. He's too focused on me, and while I appreciate that, we have to watch what we're doing. I don't want to make my mom worry, or my dad suspicious.

"Come on," Ash says when I still haven't spoken and I follow after him, going through the kitchen, pleasantly surprised when he opens the back door for me.

All I know is I was an antsy mess while he was gone, and I'm so glad to have him back. To know he's safe and in my house. With me.

I don't know if I ever want him to leave.

CHAPTER 27

DREW

"Why are they going outside together?" I watch my baby girl, my firstborn, follow after Asher Davis, toward the pool. They disappear from view for only a moment only to reappear, and I watch in disbelief as Ash settles himself on a lounge chair and pats the spot in between his now spread legs, a shit-eating grin on his face.

Just like that, Autumn plops in between his legs, snuggling up close, her back to his front as Ash wraps his arms around my daughter and gives her a squeeze, dropping a kiss on the side of her neck.

What the ever-loving fuck?

"I think you know why they're going outside together. They want to be alone," Fable murmurs as she stops to stand next to me. She's staring out the window as well, slowly shaking her head, though she's not scowling. I know I'm scowling. I can't believe that little shit is touching my daughter like he owns her. "I knew this was going to happen," she adds, like the all-knowing mother figure she is.

"What was going to happen?" I tear my gaze away from Ash and Autumn, my heart twisting in my chest. My baby girl isn't a baby any longer. I know this. I've known it for a while, but it's hard for a father to look at his daughter, and not see a precious little toddler screaming *Daddy! Daddy!* every single time she caught sight of me.

Now she's a seventeen-year-old, in her senior year, about to graduate and leave our home to go to college, and she's sitting way too close to one of the horniest players I've got on my football team.

I fucking hate this.

"I think they're together. As in, they're in a relationship," Fable says, like it's no big deal.

But it's a huge deal. "We've got to break them up."

"What?" I turn to see Fable is staring at me, her green eyes narrowed, her cheeks turning pink like they do when she's upset. "Why in the world would you want to break them up?"

"He's not good enough for our daughter," I say with a fierce shake of my head.

"Andrew Callahan, I can't even believe you would say something like that." The disappointment in my wife's voice is undeniable. I just thoroughly pissed her off. "I thought you liked Ash."

"I did. I do. But come on. Let's be real, no one is good enough for our daughter. None of these kids are. Hell, I couldn't stand that little Ben Murray wimp," I say, not bothering to hide the disgust in my voice.

Fable rolls her eyes. I must frustrate her on a daily basis. "Ben was the sweetest boy. I adored him."

"I never liked him." I shake my head, glance through the window one more time to see Ash and Autumn's heads bent close together as if they're kissing, and I can't take it any longer. I leave the living room completely, heading into the kitchen with Fable hot on my heels.

"Don't you dare go outside and cause a scene," she says.

I turn to face my wife. "Like I'd do that." That wasn't my plan. Not really.

Fine. I was going to head out there, make a lot of noise to get them to jump apart, and then I would've asked Ash to help me with…something. A made-up project, maybe.

She stops short and makes a funny little face. "Hey, I don't know. Just seconds ago you're saying he's not good enough for her and now you're making your way to the back door like you're going to barge outside and tell him to keep his hands off your daughter."

That's a good idea too. But I'm guessing Fable's joking. "You're really okay with the two of them together?"

Fable stands quiet for a moment, and I know she's mulling it over. I trust my wife's judgment completely. She doesn't make rash decisions—not anymore—and we've been together for so long, we can usually read each other's thoughts.

But I'm shocked when she finally gives me her answer.

"I'm okay with the two of them together. I like Ash. He reminds me so much of myself when I was a teenager. My mom was a nightmare, you know this, and I don't think Ash's mom is much better," Fable explains.

"His mother is piece of garbage, and that's me being polite," I say tightly. I watched how that woman talked to her son over breakfast. I made sure I was facing their table. I even heard a few of the things she said to him. She tried her best to manipulate him, even crying while she said she missed him so much and wished they could be a family again. She kept saying she wanted him to come back to their apartment.

Her behavior made me suspicious, and I could see the guilt written all over Ash's face as she kept talking. And talking. I'm not sure why she wants him back so badly. When he's home, which isn't much, she yells at him all the time, even smacks him around a little when she's completely wasted. Ash never fights back, because he's not about to hit a woman, especially his own mother. That's what he confessed to me a few days ago.

Just hearing that story broke my heart, yet it also infuriated me. Yes, I like Ash. I think he's a fucking amazing quarterback, he's a decent kid, but he follows trouble. He also causes trouble. He's reckless and does stupid shit, but hell, he's seventeen. Of course he does.

If he keeps his head on straight, he could possibly go on to do amazing things. He's talented. Smart. His grades are decent. He has tremendous potential. I could help him with his future if he'll let me. Guide him. Just like I plan on doing with my son.

But if I'm being real with myself, I don't want him with my daughter. She doesn't need someone with so much baggage. Asher Davis comes with an entire set of baggage, and it's loaded with a bunch of bullshit.

"I think these two have circled around each other for years," Fable says, her voice soft. "He's just looking for someone to love him. To believe in him. You remember what that's like, right?"

She's getting to me, and she knows it. When I was seventeen, I was a fucked-up mess. That was a full four years before I even met Fable, and my life was in the absolute toilet. Any girl who tried to approach me at school with a pretty smile and a raging crush on me, I denied them. It didn't matter how nice or how pushy they were, or how attracted I was to them. I didn't want any of them to get too close.

I didn't want them to find out my secrets.

But Fable showed me that she really cared. That she wanted to help me. That my secrets didn't matter. She healed me. She changed my entire life.

For the better.

"Drew." Fable is now standing directly in front of me, and she's such a shrimp. She's looking up at me with all her love for me shining in her eyes, an imploring expression on her face, and I can feel myself start to weaken. I'd do anything she asked me to, and she knows it. "Let Autumn work her magic on him. She's such a strong-willed, smart girl. She can help him. Just like I helped you, and you helped me. Give him —give *them* a chance."

I exhale harshly and hang my head, slipping my arms around my wife's waist when she stands on tiptoe and wraps her arms around my neck. Pressing my forehead to hers, I mutter, "If I catch him in her room in the middle of the night, I'll cut his balls off."

Fable laughs, the sound light and full of happiness. "And I'll cut his dick off, so we're in agreement there. I don't think they're at that stage yet."

"Fable." I pull away a little so I can stare into her eyes. "Be real. She's seventeen. He's seventeen…"

She sighs. "Maybe I need to talk to her about getting on the pill."

I cover her mouth before she says anything else that'll burn my ears right off my head. "Please God, don't make any more references to the possibility that my daughter will be having sex. I don't think I can take it."

"Now it's your turn to be real, Mr. Callahan." She presses her hands against my chest, her voice lowering to a seductive murmur. "We should go to our room."

I frown, confused by her suggestion. "Why? Where are the kids?"

"Well, we know Autumn's outside with Ash. Jake's probably already asleep. He likes to nap on Saturdays after a game. Ava went to a friend's house right before you got here, and so did Beck," she explains.

Now I'm smiling. "Really?"

Fable smiles in return. "Really."

"Well, let's go have some alone time then," I say, chasing after Fable as she heads for our bedroom, reaching out to give her perfect ass a slap. She laughs, glancing over her shoulder to smile at me, and I know I'm the luckiest man in the world.

Can't shake the worry that hangs over me about the Ash situation, though. We'll get that figured out eventually.

Together.

CHAPTER 28

AUTUMN

"What if my parents can see us sitting like this?" My protest is half-hearted at best. I haven't seen Ash in what feels like forever, but really was only about a day, and I love how he immediately pulled me into his arms.

I'm snuggled up so close to him. We're sitting out by the pool on one of the oversized lounge chairs, me between his spread legs, my back leaning against his chest. He's warm, I can feel his heart beating, and his arms are strong and firm as they wrap around me.

I don't want him to ever let me go.

"Who cares if they can see us? We have to tell them what's going on between us eventually." Ash kisses my temple, his mouth lingering, and I shiver from the touch of his damp lips on my skin. "I missed you."

"I missed you too." My heart fills so much, it's like it's going to crack open and spill my overwhelming emotions all over the place. It feels so good to have him admit something like that first.

Of course, he's always been better revealing his feelings than me. I used to think he was lying all the time, trying to trick me to get in my pants or whatever, and that's why I held back.

Now I know better.

"My mom is a complete bitch. I hate her." His voice is strangely flat, emotionless, and I pull away from him so I can stare up at his face. His expression is equally lacking emotion.

"What happened? What did she say?"

"She tried to tell me the fight between Don and me was all *my* fault. Can you believe that?" Ash shakes his head, his jaw going tight. "That's what *she* wants to believe, even though she witnessed the entire damn thing and knows the truth, deep down."

"She was there?" I'm in shock. I don't know many details about what happened. I've heard a lot of rumors, and Ash has given me bits and pieces, as well as my dad, but that's about it.

"Yeah, she'll deny it to her last breath, but she totally egged Don on. Told him to, and I quote, 'beat the shit out of him'. She'll win Mom of the Year for that one, I'm sure," Ash says sarcastically.

His words make my heart heavy. "I had no idea."

"I didn't want tell you." He squirms a little, and I can tell he's uncomfortable with his confession. I wish I could make him feel better. "It sucks, when you realize just how awful your mom is. I've known it for a long time. I just didn't want to face it. I'd blame it on the alcohol, or the pills she's always popping, but no. She really is an awful person who doesn't give a shit about me."

"She said she wanted you to come back and live with her," I point out, because I don't want to believe Ash's mother

243

doesn't really love him. That has to be one of the worst feelings in the world, when your parents don't love you. I can't imagine.

"She can't stand the fact that I don't want to be with her anymore, though I've been giving her signs for years. I was rarely home, always trying to stay at a friend's house or whatever." It's the whatever that makes me uncomfortable. Staying with a girl, maybe? I can't hold his past against him, but it's difficult. I don't like hearing about the other girls.

"When I told her no, I wasn't coming home with her, she started cursing me out, though never loud enough for your dad or brother to hear." Ash sighs, and I hear so much pain in that one sound. "Then she called me a fucking piece of shit, told me I'd never amount to anything, and that I'd be nothing but a drain on whoever I was staying with. She thinks I'm at a friend's house, like usual."

"Well, you sort of are." I smile at him, wishing I could lighten the mood.

"True." He chuckles, his arms tightening around me. "She's so stupid. She had no clue that a Super Bowl-winning NFL player was sitting in the restaurant three tables over."

She might be awful, but I don't like hearing Ash insult his mother. "I guess she's not into football."

"Nope. She never has been. That was a thing between me and my dad." He pauses, his gaze growing distant. "Everyone at the restaurant left your dad alone, and I thought that was pretty cool. I think he appreciates it when that happens."

"We've lived here long enough that when he goes to a local restaurant, no one's fazed by him anymore. When we first moved to the area, everyone would approach him no matter where we were. They were always asking for his autograph, wanting to take photos with him. Beck didn't get it. He wanted to know what was so special about Daddy." I laugh, running my fingers up and down Ash's arm, which is draped over me. "Now when people approach my dad, they usually want to talk about the high school football team."

I hear the rumble of a laugh in Ash's chest. "That's funny."

"I know."

We grow quiet for a while, and he plays with my hair while I stroke his arm. It's warm outside, with a breeze that cools us off every couple of minutes, and I think I can sit out here forever if he'd let me.

"Did the argument really start because of a pack of cigarettes?" I ask a few minutes later, my voice soft.

Ash sighs, and it's a ragged sound. "As stupid as that sounds...yes. That's exactly how it started."

Realization dawns and I sit up in a flash, turning so I'm facing him. "I haven't seen you smoke once since you've been here."

"Gave it up." He shrugs one shoulder. "When you get the shit beat out of you for a couple of cigarettes, you realize they aren't worth the risk."

Huh. Maybe that's why he's been so touchy.

A sympathetic sound leaves me and I reach out to cradle his cheeks in my hands. His stubble prickles against my palms, and I study his face, examining his wounds. The swelling in his lips has gone down and they look normal, which is good because we've been kissing each other a lot. The cut above his eye doesn't look as angry as it did, the redness faded. The bruises have faded too, especially his black eye, though it's still visible, and gives him a dangerous air.

Ash doesn't say a word as I quietly drink him in. It's like he knows exactly what I'm doing, and that I need to do it, so he lets me look my fill in silence.

"I hate that he hurt you," I whisper, unable to even say the jerk's name. "He should rot in hell for what he did to you."

His mother isn't much better, but now is not the time for me to say that.

"So should my mother for encouraging him," Ash says for me. He turns his head and presses a soft kiss to the palm of my hand, making it tingle. "Don't waste your time hating them. They're not worth it."

He's so right. And even though this conversation was hard to have, I'm glad we had it. We need to be real with each other. It's the only way we can move forward. And that's what I want more than anything. To move forward.

With Ash.

"I'm going back to school Monday," he admits.

I lightly stroke his cheeks, my hands dropping away from his face completely. "Are you ready for that?"

"I have a shit ton of homework to catch up on, but yeah. I'm ready. I need to get back to normal." He hesitates, and I notice that he swallows hard, as if the next words might be difficult to say. "Your dad is going to take me in with him and we're meeting with Adney on Monday too. See what we need to do to get me out of my mom's house for good and into the temporary care of your parents."

I'm shocked. My parents want to take him in completely? If they knew about us, they might try to put a stop to it. "Why would Adney know anything about that?"

"She deals with kids from shitty families all the time. She actually called your dad Thursday afternoon and told him if he needed to talk, she had plenty of advice to give him about my situation," Ash explains.

Oh. That probably happened because of my confrontation with Rylie and the subsequent conversation with Brandy. Which I never did mention to Ash. "I hope she can help my parents—and you."

"I hope to hell she can too." He shifts, his head moving

closer, his mouth hovering just above mine. "I wish we were really alone."

"Ash," I chastise him, but a shiver moves through me because I wish we were really alone too.

"You know you want it." He grins, that familiar, arrogant smile, and I'm desperate to kiss him.

But I'm also afraid my parents are watching us, so I can't risk it.

Not yet.

"Found any condoms yet?" I tease.

He chuckles. "Nope. Know where I can get some?"

"Maybe we should go shopping later," I suggest.

He raises his brows. "For condoms?"

"And other stuff," I say with a little shrug. Though I really don't want to go into the local CVS and pick up condoms. People I go to school with work there on the weekends. They don't need to know our business.

"I can buy some," he says. "Or I can go to my apartment and grab some out of my room. Pretty sure I have a few in there somewhere."

I frown. No way do I ever want to go back there. "That's too risky."

"I thought you like it risky." He pulls me in tight and drops a kiss on my lips. So quick, it's almost like it didn't happen.

Curling my fingers into his shirt, I pull him in for another kiss, this one deeper, longer. He breaks away first, breathing heavily, his gaze hooded as he studies me. "How's that for risky?" I ask him.

His lips curve. "I'm guessing your parents will shit if they knew we were doing this."

"With you living under our roof? Definitely." My dad would kill him if he knew what Ash and I have been up to. In the hot tub. In my room.

My entire body prickles with awareness just thinking about it.

"Let's meet tonight," he whispers, his gaze lifting to scan the yard before he kisses me again. "Come to my room."

"We probably shouldn't go shopping together," I say with a little frown, though I want to. "It's probably best if we lay low."

"You sure it's not because you're embarrassed to be seen with me, Callahan?" He's joking, I can tell by the tone of his voice, but when I look into his eyes, I see the vulnerability there. The unease.

Does he really believe that?

"I would be proud to tell the whole world that we're together," I say, my voice firm, my hands holding his face again. Such a pretty face. And it's all mine. "But with my parents, and your mom, and Rylie, I think we're better off keeping it quiet. Just for a little while."

"Yeah. Okay. You're right." He nods, then kisses me yet again. "Meet tonight at eleven?"

"Make it midnight," I suggest, and when he frowns, I continue. "The entire household stays up later on Saturday. It's safer."

Ash licks his lips. "Hope I can wait that long." He grabs hold of my hand and settles it right on his lap, where I can feel his burgeoning erection. "I want you already. All the time."

My cheeks go hot and I give him a squeeze, then snatch my hand away. "You'll have to wait."

"You're a tease."

"You've already called me that."

"Yeah, well, I'm calling you a tease again." More kissing. More hugging, until I finally disentangle myself from him and stand. "Leaving already?"

"I'll see you later. I have laundry to finish," I tell him as I start to walk away.

"Your rich-ass parents make you do your laundry? Why don't you have a maid?" Ash calls after me.

"My parents want to instill good habits in their children," I yell back, laughing, as I start to run toward the back door. I feel so good, so light, so happy. It's all going to work out between Ash and me.

It has to.

CHAPTER 29

*O*ur midnight meeting wasn't going to happen after all. Kaya had a moment of crisis—she and Jaden were arguing—and she texted me when I was up in my room finishing sorting my laundry. Without thought, I invited her over to hang out so we could talk about it. She's my best friend, I had to be there for her, and I know she'd do the same for me. When she asked if she could spend the night, I couldn't tell her no.

When I tell Mom that Kaya's coming over to stay the night, she gives me a stern look. "Will she be able to keep it quiet that Ash is here?"

I found her in her room, making the bed, which is weird because she usually does that first thing in the morning. I think it's funny how Ash believes we should have a maid. We are normal people with a lot of money. Why wouldn't we make our own beds and do our own laundry? But Mom does have a housekeeper come in once a month and do a thorough clean, which she says is worth every penny.

"Autumn?" Mom says when I haven't answered her. "Will she?"

My mood deflates like a busted balloon. "Are we still keeping that a secret?" I hate all the secrets. They're starting to get to me.

"Only until Monday. Once we get everything squared away, it won't really matter if people know Ash is staying here or not," she explains.

"She'll keep it quiet. Kaya's a good secret keeper." So why haven't I told her about me and Ash yet?

Maybe I should.

I go in search of Ash once I'm done talking to Mom and find him hanging out in his room, sprawled across the unmade bed. I lean against the doorway and watch him as he messes around on his phone, sending one text message after the other in rapid fire succession.

"Who are you talking to?" I ask, startling him so bad, his phone drops out of his hands.

"Shit, Autumn!" I swear he only says my actual name when he's upset with me. "Why you gotta sneak up on me like that?"

"I'm sorry." I push away from the doorframe and enter the bedroom, lifting my leg to nudge his bare foot hanging over the mattress with my own. "You didn't answer my question."

"My mom." He grabs his phone and sets it face down on the bed on the other side of him, closest to the wall. Like he doesn't want me to see it. "She really wants me to come back."

"Tell her no."

"It's not that easy." He crawls off the bed and comes to me, slipping his arms around my waist. "Couldn't wait any longer, huh? It's a long ways to midnight."

"I wanted to talk to you about that." I pull out of his grip and wander around his room, having a difficult time facing him when I'm about to deliver this news. "Kaya's coming over right now."

"Yeah?"

"She's going to spend the night." I glance over my shoulder to see Ash's thunderous expression. "She's having problems with Jaden and needs my support."

"Okay. Cool." He nods once, and I can tell by the tightness in his jaw that he's mad. "Hope you girls have fun."

I go to him, my heart racing. "Are you angry?"

"I thought we had plans."

"I'm sorry." And I really am. I was so looking forward to those plans. "Kaya was crying when she FaceTimed me, and she never cries. I couldn't say no. She'll be here in a few." I grab hold of his hands and intertwine our fingers. "We can get together tomorrow night."

"Sure." He won't look at me, and a muscle flexes in his jaw. "Tomorrow night. Let's do it."

"Ash. Come on." I squeeze his hands. "Don't be like this."

"I was really hoping for some alone time with you tonight," he says, his voice dropping to a gravelly whisper. "I need you."

My heart pangs. He's been through a lot. I know this. "Maybe after Kaya falls asleep I'll come see you," I suggest.

"You will?" he asks hopefully.

"I'll try."

"Okay. Try real hard." He kisses me. Yanks me closer, and I go willingly. He feels so good. I can't get enough of him, and clearly he can't get enough of me either.

"I have to go. She'll be here soon."

"Go. Go see your friend." He releases me so fast I practically stumble out of his arms. "See you later."

His dismissive tone hurts. More than I want to admit. I slink out of his room, but he doesn't even notice.

He's too busy typing away on his phone.

* * *

"...I think we're going to be okay. In fact, I know we're going to be okay. I'm just overreacting as usual," Kaya says, and I nod. Offer her a wan smile. She frowns in return, tilting her head to the side, studying me. "Are you okay?"

I just sat with Kaya on my bed for the last fifteen minutes and listened to her drone on and on about Jaden. I care about her, I really do, but her problems with Jaden seem almost... trivial. And I know it's mean of me to think like that, but I can't help it. He didn't want to get together with her this weekend, that's what the problem is. He told her he'd rather lie in bed and watch Netflix. Claimed he was tired after last night's game, which I get, but Kaya wasn't having it.

"I'm fine." I offer up another one of those wan smiles and Kaya shakes her head, pointing her finger at me.

"You're a liar. What's going on?"

I warned her earlier that Ash was staying at my house and she claimed she already knew about it, so I was worried about nothing I guess. I thought Ash might even come out and greet Kaya when she arrived, but he remained in his room when I knew he could hear me and Kaya talking.

It's like our conversation earlier meant nothing to him. All because I couldn't meet up with him tonight? Is he jealous of my friendship with Kaya? If that's the case, we're never going to work because my friends are important to me. I refuse to ditch them all over a guy.

"There's nothing going on." Kaya and I are sitting on my bed, and she's wrapped up in my comforter because she's always cold. I have my favorite blanket draped over my lap, and I pluck the fuzzies off of it, keeping my head bent. "Okay, fine, there's something going on, but you have to swear on your life you won't breathe a word of it to anyone."

"I swear," Kaya says quickly.

I glance up at her, heave a big sigh, and decide to go into it. "Ash and I...we're kind of together."

Kaya purses her lips, looking ready to burst. "I knew it! After you told me what happened between you two in the past, I was waiting for this."

"Shush, keep your voice down." I know my room door is shut, but I swear, sometimes the walls are thin. Or there are spies lingering outside my door. Though Ava is at a friend's house right now, so maybe that won't be a problem. "I think he was mad that you were coming over. We were supposed to…meet later tonight."

Kaya's eyes go wide as her mouth drops open. "Oooh, what are you two up to already?"

"Nothing much." I shrug, trying to be nonchalant, but my hot cheeks give me away as usual. "We've messed around a little."

"And?"

"And what?"

"How was it?" Kaya's expression is curious, and she's shared details with me about her sex life with Jaden, so it's only fair I share a few details with her.

"It was—good." My entire face now feels like it's on fire. "We haven't had actual sex yet. We've just messed around, like I said."

"Messing around can be a lot of fun." Kaya's smiling and I can't help but smile too.

"It *is* fun. He—really knows what he's doing." I yank the blanket in my lap up over my face, making her laugh. "It's not funny! I feel weird, talking about this stuff."

"It's weird when we start doing that stuff too, but it's fun, right? I mean, it always makes me and Jaden feel closer after. Plus, it's really meaningful when you're doing it with someone you love," Kaya says, and I peek over the edge of the blanket to see the dreamy look on her face, her earlier anger and sadness over Jaden completely forgotten.

I drop the blanket. "I wonder if I'm in love with Ash."

"You haven't been with him long enough," Kaya points out.

"But we've been connected for *years*. Circling around each other, saying things, doing things, practically daring each other. I don't know how to describe it, but there was a lot of push and pull between us. We kissed our sophomore year. We kissed our junior year. This was bound to happen," I say, like it's perfectly logical, even though really, I know it's not. "It's like we're meant to be together."

"Star-crossed lovers?" Kaya asks, teasing me. "Like Romeo and Juliet?"

"God, I hope not. They both die at the end." We start laughing.

"I guess you two could be halfway in love with each other," Kaya says once our laughter dies. "But you still need to get to know him, right? It's not like you guys have talked a lot over the years."

"No, we really haven't. We were either too busy arguing or too busy kissing." Sighing, I stare off into space, bunching the blanket up in my hands. "He went and met his mom for breakfast today. She sounds awful."

"Is it true, what they say at school? That his stepdad beat him up?" Kaya asks softly.

"Don's not his stepdad, he's just his mom's boyfriend, but yeah, it's true. And it was all over a pack of cigarettes. I guess his mom was encouraging her boyfriend to hit Ash." I shake my head, my stomach churning. "I can't even imagine."

"He's had a rough life, I think," Kaya says.

"There's no thinking about it. He's had it tough these last few years, after his father died." I frown, hating that I don't know exactly *when* his father died.

Kaya's right. I don't know anything about Ash. Not really. Oh, I know a few things, and our earlier conversation was a good one. But we need a lot more of those conversations, where we share bits and pieces about our lives. I want him to know more about me too.

What if this is just a sexual relationship? What if my original fears are actually coming true? He's only interested in getting in my pants, and once he does, he'll dump me. Or maybe he only wants to be close to me because he really wants to be close to my father. I know if given the chance, Dad would assist in any way he could with Ash's future in football, and he would be a tremendous help. My father is a respected man in the NFL. He could help Ash get places.

If that's all Ash really wants, then...

I'll be devastated.

"Hey." Kaya grabs my bent knee and gives it a shake. "You're getting too caught up in the shitty details. I didn't mean to make you feel bad."

"You didn't." I offer her a weak smile, lying through my teeth. She totally made me feel bad, though I'm not blaming her for it.

I'm completely at fault. Ash and I moved too fast. I need to figure out exactly what he wants from me. It doesn't help, how upset he got earlier when I told him about Kaya coming over. Or how he was texting someone on his phone—and I don't know if that was really his mom, which means maybe I can't trust him. Should I? And will he always have a jealous streak? I don't know if I can deal with that. Does this mean our relationship is doomed to fail before it even started?

"I'm starving." Kaya hops off the bed with a bright smile. "Let's go dig up some snacks and watch a movie or something."

"Okay," I say weakly, feeling dumb. I wish I could forget about my troubles with Ash for a while and just focus on hanging out with Kaya.

Kind of hard when the boy who's so troubling is actually living at my house.

CHAPTER 30

*I*t's closer to one a.m. when I find myself sneaking down to Ash's room. As I make my way through the house, I feel like this all I've been up to for the past week. Sneaking here, sneaking there. If my parents caught me, I'd be in big trouble.

Despite all my troubling thoughts earlier, I still believe Ash is worth the risk.

Within minutes, I'm in his room, only to find him sleeping, sprawled across the bed, the sheets and comforter caught around his waist. He's on his stomach without a shirt on, his arms spread wide, his head turned to the side, and I stare at him unabashedly, thankful for the night light that's shining in the hallway, just bright enough to cast light into the room through the cracked open door. Mom must have plugged that in for Ash for some reason—so he could find his way to the bathroom? Or maybe so I could find my way to Ash's room, and then spy on him like I'm doing at this very moment?

Yeah, I'm sure that's a firm *no* to my last mental question.

The longer I stare at him, the more my heart aches. I can

see the remnants of the physical wounds that mark his body, but what about the emotional ones? What has he been through that he hasn't told me about? He looks so vulnerable in his sleep, reminding me of a little boy. It baffles me, how someone can be so cruel to their own child. I hate what his mother did to him. I hate that he's been put into such a terrible situation through no fault of his own. I wish I could change his circumstances. If he stays here, my family will help him.

Yet if my parents find out I'm doing this, they'll kick him out with zero hesitation. Dad might want to murder him for touching me. Maybe it's not worth the risk. Maybe me risking it all just so I can feel close to him would be detrimental for Ash's future.

Deciding I need to go back to my room and go to bed, I start to tiptoe out of Ash's room when he stirs, rolling over onto his side so that he's facing me.

"Where you goin'?" he mumbles, squinting in the semi-darkness.

I come to a stop, then go to the bed, where I bend over and drop a kiss to the top of his head. "I was just checking on you. Go back to sleep."

"C'mere." He snags my hand and pulls me down onto him, with only the sheet between us. "This is a nice surprise."

"Kaya's waiting for me," I tell him, hating the lie. But I have to do this to keep him safe. "I told her I was going to the bathroom."

He studies me for a moment, our faces close, his gaze searching. "Really, Callahan? You're going to start lying to me now?"

Sighing, I drop my head so my forehead nudges against his chin. I wish I could confront him about his earlier lie, but I don't the courage to do it. Not yet. "I shouldn't be in here."

"Why not? I thought that was the plan." He plays with my

hair, making me want to melt into him. "You don't want to be with me?"

"Of course I do. It's just…" My voice drifts and I lift my head so I can look into his eyes when I say this. "I don't want you to get in trouble with my parents."

Frowning, he reaches for me, pushing my hair away from my forehead. "They won't come looking for you right now."

"We don't know that for sure. And I don't want to risk it," I whisper, resting my cheek against his chest.

He holds me like this for a long, quiet moment, the only sound the steady beating of his heart. When we're like this, together, alone, it feels like we can do anything. Like we can conquer the world as long as we have each other.

I know that's not the truth. We just feel protected in our little bubble. The real world is still out there, waiting for us, and it doesn't go easy, especially on Ash.

"Is the door still open?" he asks.

I nod, my hair rubbing against his chest. "Yeah."

"You should go shut it."

"I should leave."

"I don't want you to go." His hands slide down my back, resting lightly on my butt. "Where's your friend?"

"Sleeping in my bed."

"Does she know where you're at?" When I lift my head to frown at him with confusion, he explains himself further. "Will she freak out if you're not in the bed if she happens to wake up?"

"Oh. No. I doubt it." She'd probably figure out exactly where I'm at.

"Then go shut the door, Callahan. And lock it, too."

I shouldn't. If I leave, everything will stay the same. But if I stay, if I get up and lock that door and come back to bed with Ash, everything could change.

Everything.

"Please stay," he whispers in my ear just before he kisses it, his big hands smoothing over my backside, making me tingle.

Again, it's the *please* that does it. How can I resist?

I pull out of his arms and make my way over to the door, closing it carefully. Softly. I turn the lock as slow as possible so it doesn't make any noise, and then I go back to the bed. Ash scoots over and tosses the covers back, patting the now empty space invitingly. I crawl in with him and snuggle close to his warm, hard body, sighing when he pulls the covers over both of us. I rest my hand on his belly and figure out quick that he is totally naked.

"Ash." My hand springs away from his stomach, and he chuckles, grabbing my hand and placing it right back where it was. "You don't have any clothes on."

"I know." His voice is dark, devilish. As if he enjoys shocking me, which he probably does. "Thought I might surprise you if you did happen to come by tonight."

"Well, it worked. You've completely taken me by surprise." I raise my hand higher, not ready to touch him in that area just yet. I don't want to move too fast, though that seems to be the way we operate lately.

Well. We either move too fast or not nearly fast enough. It's like we can't make up our minds.

"I have another surprise for you too." He lifts my chin and kisses me, his lips insistent, stealing my thoughts, my breath. When he breaks the kiss, he reaches over to the bedside table and pulls the drawer open, rummaging around before he finds what he wants. "Look what I've got."

He waves a condom packet in my face.

"Where did you get this?" I try to snatch it from his fingers, but he moves too fast, raising his arm out of my reach.

"Your brother's room." His voice and his face are smug.

"You stole it from Jake?" And why the hell does my brother have condoms?

Oh God.

I don't want to know.

"Yeah. I snuck into his room earlier, when you were all still downstairs in the kitchen." Ash nods with satisfaction. "They were in his bedside table. He has a giant box of them."

I need bleach to scrub my ears with after hearing this.

"So I figured he wouldn't care if I snagged a couple," Ash finishes.

The idea doesn't settle well, that he went into my brother's room uninvited and stole the condoms from his bedside table. What a violation of privacy. What if he snuck in there again and stole other things? Things of actual value? "You probably shouldn't have done that," I tell him.

"What do you mean? Not like he cares. Besides, your family is loaded. He can go buy another economy-sized box of condoms like it's no big deal. He doesn't have to worry about money. Nothing but the best for the Callahans, right?" The mocking tone in Ash's voice rings clear.

And it pisses me off.

I pull away from him and sit up. "You're being really rude right now."

"And you're being really sensitive right now," Ash throws right back at me.

"You shouldn't have stolen those condoms from my brother. This is the same exact thing that got you in trouble before, with your mom and her boyfriend," I remind him. "You stole a pack of cigarettes from Don, and he beat you up for it."

"He just used the stolen smokes as an excuse," Ash starts, but I interrupt him.

"You did steal them, though, right?"

He looks away from me. "Yeah." His voice is scratchy.

"Okay, well, you just stole from my brother now too. Yeah, you took condoms, big deal. But you can't keep doing that, Ash."

"You really think your brother is going to rat me out that I stole his rubbers? Give me a break," he mutters.

"No, but it doesn't look good to me." I rest my hand on my chest. "*Me,* Ash. You're stealing, and it's not cool. You *keep* stealing. And you're going to end up getting in real trouble if you don't stop."

He sits up as well, running a hand through his hair as he contemplates me. His lips are parted, his eyes narrowed, and he looks thoroughly irritated.

Fine. I'm thoroughly irritated too.

"You'd rather sit here and argue with me about stealing some stupid condoms than use one of them." I think he's asking me a question, but it sounds more like a statement.

And no, I'm definitely not using that condom with him tonight. The mood has been ruined.

"It's the point that you stole, Ash. You think after what happened to you, you wouldn't do that," I say softly.

"What the hell do you know about what happened to me?" Ash glares at me, then stretches his arm out, pointing at the door. "You should go."

My mouth drops open. "What?"

"If I'm such a disappointment to you, then you better leave, Callahan. You're only proving my point."

I scramble out of the bed, angry. Sad. A swirl of emotions moves through me, settling heavy on my chest. "What point are you talking about?"

"That I'm not good enough for you." He waves his hand at the door. "Leave. Hurry, before I touch you with my dirty, stealing hands."

I run to the door and fumble with the lock, the tears

streaming down my cheeks before I even realize I'm crying. I'm finally able to open the door and I run out of his room, fully expecting to hear him laughing as I go, but I hear nothing.

Just silence.

I'm hustling through the kitchen when the light comes on, momentarily blinding me. I blink against the brightness, rubbing at my still tear filled eyes and dread socks me right in the gut when I hear my mother's voice.

"Autumn! Are you okay?"

Thank God it wasn't Dad.

Sniffing, I turn my back to her. "I'm fine. Just grabbing something to drink real quick."

"Really? Where is it?"

I stand up straighter, praying she doesn't want to look at me. I don't want her to see my face, or the tears running down my cheeks. "What do you mean?"

"Your drink?"

"Oh. I just drank water out of the tap. With a cup." I hunch my shoulders, hoping she doesn't look in the sink for that nonexistent cup I'm talking about.

"Autumn." Mom approaches, and then her hand settles heavily on my shoulder. "You weren't trying to sneak out, were you?"

"N-no." I shake my head, my back still to her, the tears coming anew.

"Where's Kaya?"

"Sleeping."

"Where's Ash?"

I hang my head. "I don't know. Probably in his room."

"You wouldn't lie to me, would you?"

It's killing me that she's asking that. I don't want to lie to her, but nothing happened. I may be angry at Ash, but I'm not going to get him kicked out of this house. Even if I have to avoid him until we graduate high school, I'll do what's best for him.

I'm either that kind, or that stupid.

"I'm not lying, Mom. Do you mind if I go back to bed now?" I quickly glance back at her, guilt swamping me when I see the concerned look on her face. I look away, fighting fresh tears yet again.

She gives my shoulder a squeeze. "Good night. Love you."

"Love you too."

I suck my tears up and head back to my room, where I slip quietly into my bed. Kaya is sleeping on the other side of the mattress, and when I pull the comforter over me, she doesn't even move. She's dead to the world.

I wish I could be so lucky. I'd rather sleep and forget my earlier argument with Ash ever happened. Maybe it was all a dream—or a nightmare—and I'll wake up in the morning realizing that I never snuck out to meet Ash. We didn't get mad at each other. And Mom didn't catch me crying in the kitchen.

But I know the truth. It happened, and we're going to have to face each other tomorrow, whether we like it or not.

You're Playing with Matches
And I Have a Paper Heart
(The Mayfair)

CHAPTER 31

ASH

I toss and turn all night, unable to think of anything else but me telling Autumn to leave my room and the look of total devastation on her pretty face before she ran out.

I am an undisputed asshole. I always have been, and I always will be. What happened last night just confirmed it. Didn't help that Mom kept texting me throughout the day, along with Rylie, irritating me more and more with each notification. Neither of them would leave me alone, and I took my frustration out on Autumn.

Meaning yep, I'm definitely an asshole.

Giving up on sleep completely at around five in the morning, I grab my phone and check my notifications. I've got all kinds of Snaps from various people wondering if I'm dead or alive—valid question. I'm in a group chat via direct messages on Instagram with most of the players from the varsity football team and they're all talking about how great Jake played, and whether I'm going to bother showing up to practice or not come Monday after school.

Well, well, well. Aren't they in for a fucking surprise?

Mom texted me, a bunch of whiny *please come back* type messages, but I ignore every single one of them. She doesn't mean it.

She never does.

Rylie texted me yet again too. Angry shit that only seems to get worse when I ignore her. I don't know how to handle her, and I feel like I've handled some crazy girls in my lifetime. But this one? She's fucking unhinged.

Deciding I'm safe to send a text since it's five in the damn morning, I type out a response and send it.

Rylie. Get it through your head. We're through. I don't want to be with you. Stop texting me all day and night. I'm over it. I'm over YOU. Keep this shit up and I'm fucking blocking you.

I hope she leaves me alone. If not, I will block her everywhere.

I'm scrolling through Instagram, bored out of my mind, pissed at myself for hurting the one good thing in my life, when I get a text notification from Rylie the psycho.

You can't just ignore me! I told you I needed to talk to you, but since you won't meet me anywhere or answer my calls, I guess I'll just tell you now.

I'm just about to block her number, as in my finger is literally hovering over the button that says *Block this Caller* when I get the next message.

I'M PREGNANT AND IT'S YOURS.

The phone slips out of my fingers, falling onto the mattress with a soft thud. What the hell? She's gotta be fucking with me. I grab my phone and start typing.

I don't believe you.

Her response is quick.

I have proof.

Proof of what?

That I'm pregnant.

My heart thunders in my chest as I wait for her so-called proof. She sends a photo, and at first I can't tell what the hell it is, until I realize it's one of those ultrasound things.

That's our baby.

Squinting, I study the photo. It doesn't look anything like a baby. It looks like a bean.

I count back in my head, thinking to when we first hooked up. The very beginning of August, maybe? Nah, more like mid-August, right before school started. It was a hot night, and I was feeling lonely, hanging out at the lake with a bunch of people from school, watching as they all coupled up and I had no one. She appeared out of nowhere, all alone and wearing a crop top that showed off her tits and flat stomach, and the shortest denim shorts that gave me a flash of her ass cheeks every time she turned around. Next thing I knew she was sucking my dick out behind a grove of pine trees and we ended up having sex.

Pretty sure I used a condom too.

Well???? Do you have anything to say???

What am I supposed to say? *Gee, yay can't wait! Let's get married!*

I don't think so.

Instead, I tell her, **I don't believe you.**

It's yours, Asher. I know it.

We had sex for the first time not even a month ago, I reply, anger making me see red. I feel like she's trying to trick me. I don't understand why.

One time is all it takes is her response.

Then she sends a baby face emoji.

This time I toss my phone and it hits the floor with a loud thunk. I run my hands through my hair, tugging on it until it starts to hurt, and I appreciate the pain. At least it makes me feel something.

Why is everyone piling up on me, trying to tear me

down? I don't fucking get it. What did I do to deserve this? I just want to live my life in peace. Get through my senior year and get the fuck out of this town. I might even leave now, if everything with the Callahan family goes to shit.

That thought alone almost breaks my hard-as-steel heart.

I ignore my phone, though I can hear all the text notifications coming through as Rylie continuously sends me messages. I throw myself down on the bed and turn on my side, facing the wall, my back to my phone. Fuck this. I don't need anyone.

Anyone.

Somehow I fall asleep, and have disturbing dreams. Rylie showing up at school with a stroller, not just one but *two* babies crying uncontrollably inside it. Autumn running away when she spots me and Rylie with the babies, and me chasing after her all while Rylie is screaming NO! in a voice that reminds me of a monster.

Don't need a professional analysis to understand what that's all about.

I wake up around nine and hear a bunch of voices coming from the kitchen. I lie there and listen to them, their joyful chatter and laughter making my heart clench. This house is nothing like mine. It's big and airy and filled with happiness. There's no TV blaring all the time, always on to the point that you don't even notice it anymore. Not a bunch of yelling either, or dirty dishes in the sink, the smell of cigarettes lingering in the hazy air. This family actually gets along, they talk things out, they respect each other. Normally this sort of thing would irritate the crap out of me. I'd think it was a bunch of Mickey Mouse horseshit.

But being here, living with this family, seeing how they treat each other, makes me yearn for this kind of life. Yearn for something I know deep down will never be mine. I lost that when my dad died, and even before, when he was alive, things weren't that great. They fought a lot. Mom was drinking even back then, and Dad gave up trying to help her.

She didn't want help. She still doesn't.

I stay in bed all morning, drifting in and out of sleep, when there's a rapid knocking on my door and it's pushed open to reveal Fable Callahan standing there with a giant smile on her pretty face. She's wearing jeans and a T-shirt, no makeup, her long blonde hair pulled into a ponytail, and I swear she could pass for someone my age. I don't know how old she is, but I've seen stuff on the internet and back in the day, Fable was hot AF. She's still pretty hot. A total MILF if I'm being real, but I can't think like that because this is Autumn's mom and she's the girl I care about.

Fucked that up, though. Yet again. So that's done.

"Are you going to hide out in here all day or what?" Fable asks way too cheerfully.

"I don't feel so good." I run a hand through my hair and tug the comforter up so it covers me to my chin. The careful way Fable's watching me makes me feel exposed. "Didn't sleep good last night."

"Oh really." Fable raises a brow, her gaze sweeping the room before it settles on the floor. "I think you dropped your phone."

"You can leave it there," I start, but too late, the phone is in Fable's hands and the screen lights up when she touches it.

Revealing the long list of texts from Rylie.

"Looks like someone is desperate to talk to you." Fable hands me my phone and I take it from her, tucking it under the comforter where I don't have to see it.

"She's no one."

"Girlfriend?"

Hell no. "I don't have one."

"Not even Autumn?"

I meet her gaze, her expression dangerously neutral. I wonder if she's trying to trap me. That's all my mom ever does. Drops hints and tries to play nice, and when I open up or tell her something, *bam!* She comes at me, yelling and screaming and carrying on. Calling me a piece of shit like my dad.

Sucks.

"Not even Autumn," I tell her truthfully. "She's mad at me."

Damn. Didn't mean to be *that* truthful.

"Oh? What did you do?" Fable doesn't even bother asking if Autumn did something to me. I guess that's only natural, that she's defending her daughter.

Or she knows that all of us guys are stupid and we mess things up all the time.

"Something dumb." No way am I going to admit what happened. I'd get myself, Autumn *and* Jake in trouble.

"You don't want to tell me?"

"Not really." I swallow hard, embarrassment hitting me hard. And shame. I'm ashamed of my actions last night. How I talked to Autumn, what I did. She was right. I shouldn't have gone into Jake's room uninvited and stolen his condoms. It sounds stupid because it is, but I bet I could've asked him, *hey buddy, got any condoms I can use?* And he would've given me some, no hesitation.

But I didn't. No way I can give them back either.

"No problem." She grabs the back of the chair that sits in front of the desk and flips it around, plopping her butt right in it. "What else is going on?"

"I don't know." I sit up a little, scratching the back of my neck. "I'm going to school tomorrow."

"Drew told me. Are you ready?" Her gaze drops to where my discarded backpack sits. "You've worked on your homework? I'm sure you're behind."

"I'll work on it this afternoon." Lies. I won't work on shit. How can I concentrate when nothing's going right in my life?

"Don't let yourself get behind, Ash. That's the worst thing I ever did. I barely graduated high school. I was too busy working a full-time job and trying to take care of my little brother," she says.

At least I don't have a little brother or sister to worry about, though that would mean I wasn't in this alone, which might be kind of nice. But then again, maybe it wouldn't. "Where were your parents?"

"The truth? I don't really know who my dad was. Some loser who knocked up my mother and then abandoned her when she told him she was pregnant. Not that I can blame him." She laughs a little, but there's no humor there. "By the time I was your age, my mom was too busy drinking or off with one of her many boyfriends for days on end. No calls, no *hey, I'm over here*, so we'd at least know she was alive. She never worried about me and Owen."

Owen. That's right. Her brother is Owen Maguire, another retired NFL football player. This family is full of legends. Jake is one lucky fucker. He keeps it up and his dad will help get him a spot on a professional team. At least get him a chance. And that's all we need, the opportunity to show we've got potential. Without that chance, you're just another talented football player with no one looking at you.

That's me. That'll always be me.

"My mom was an absolute nightmare, but I didn't let her or her actions define me. I realized when I was around fifteen I had to take care of my brother and myself, or else I was going to end up just like her. And my brother would most likely end up in jail because of the kids he was hanging around with. I could already see it, and he was only ten, eleven." She shakes her head. "It was hard, you know? Reminding myself that I was better than that. That I could get away from it if I worked hard enough. Most of the time, that sounded like a pipe dream. When you're surrounded by drunks and losers all the time, you start to think that's your destiny. You'll never amount to anything else," Fable explains.

I nod, understanding her perfectly.

"Sometimes I'd find myself tempted to go down that path. Not even sometimes." She laughs. "More like *all* the time. It felt like no one paid attention to me. Teachers didn't care. Girls didn't like me, and when boys started to notice me, I chased after them. Did you know I was considered a total slut in high school?"

My eyes nearly bug out of my head at her confession, but she doesn't even notice. She's too caught up in her story.

"The rumor followed me after I graduated too. I grew up in a small college town, and when I was nineteen and working at a bar downtown, the rumor around campus was that I had sex with every player on the football team," she explains, like she's discussing the weather.

What the hell? I really don't understand why she's telling me this. This isn't something you share with a kid you barely know. "Was it—was the rumor *true?*"

She throws her head back and laughs, like I just cracked the funniest joke. "No," she says once she sobers up. "I'm going to be real with you right now. I've never really confessed this to anyone before. Yes, I messed around with a few of the guys, but not *all* of them. Not that anyone cared to know the truth. Then one of those football players, one I didn't mess around with, came to me with an offer I couldn't refuse. You want to know what his name was?"

"Who?"

"Drew Callahan." Fable smiles. "He saved me, though he's always the first to say that I saved him. But he got me out of that world, and he helped get my brother out of that world as well. Drew was rich, and smart, and talented on the football field. And he was damaged goods too. More damaged than me. But we fixed each other. We just—fit."

I digest what she's telling me, wondering if Autumn knows her parents' backstory. They're living the dream, anybody would want their life, but Fable's saying that when they were younger, their lives were a mess.

Kind of like mine.

"I'm telling you this because I don't want you to give up hope. Just like Drew was my ticket out of the hellhole that was my life, you need to know that Drew and I are willing to help you. We'll be your ticket out of the hellhole that is *your* life if you let us. We'll help you with school, with what's happening between you and your mom and her boyfriend, and if you want, we'll help you apply for college. We'll also give you somewhere safe to stay until you graduate," Fable says, leaning forward so she can pin me with her green eyes. Beautiful eyes that are just like Autumn's.

"Why?" I ask, my voice raspy, and I clear my throat. "Why do you want to help me? I'm nobody to you."

"You remind me so much of myself and my brother. I was nobody to everyone back then too, and I wished someone would've reached out to me when I was still in school." She smiles, and her eyes are extra shiny. Like she might almost start crying? Shit, I hope not. "You deserve more, Asher. And we want to help you get what you deserve."

Right now, I'm thinking I deserve a kick in the head for what I've done to Autumn. And what I've supposedly done to Rylie, but I'll go along with what this woman is saying.

"Okay." I say the word slowly as I'm still trying to digest what she said.

"You won't want to hear this, but you're going to need to keep a little distance between you and Autumn." When I open my mouth to protest, she holds up a single finger, silencing me. "I'm not saying you can't see her. I know you two like each other." Like. Such a small word to describe what I feel for Autumn. "Her father and I both saw you two together by the pool yesterday."

Busted. I thought for sure they weren't looking out the window.

"You two were awfully close. And I don't have a problem with that, but you're going to have to take it slow." She is now wagging that finger at me. "No sneaking around at night when we're all sleeping."

My face is hot. It's like Fable knows *exactly* what we're doing.

"There are cameras outside, all over the property. We have some of the best security money can buy. But we don't keep cameras in the house, because we don't want our children to feel like they're in jail. Don't do something where I have to make my children feel like they're living in prison," she says, her voice stern.

Swallowing hard, I nod my agreement, praying there isn't a camera that's aimed at the hot tub. "Yes, ma'am."

She smiles. "Aw, isn't that sweet? You just called me ma'am. I'm impressed, Asher Davis. I knew there was a sliver of politeness buried deep inside you somewhere."

I can't help but smile in return. I feel comfortable with this woman. Maybe like really does seek out like. "I try."

"Keep trying." She leans over and grabs my backpack, then hefts it up—that bitch is heavy—and tosses it so it lands on the edge of the bed. "I'd suggest you start your homework now. I'll let you know when the laundry room opens up so you can wash your clothes. You'll want to look fresh and clean for your meeting with Mrs. Adney tomorrow, won't you?"

"Are you going with us?" I ask hopefully. I know my coach is behind me, though maybe not as much since he witnessed me with my hands all over his daughter. Shit, I really do need to be more careful.

"I am." Fable stands, resting her hands on her hips, her gaze on me. "You have a lot of potential, Ash. Don't mess it up."

"I won't," I say earnestly, watching as she leaves the room. The moment she's gone, I lie flat on my back, staring at the ceiling and wondering at my complete turnaround. Before this woman walked into the room, I was ready to say fuck it to this entire family and get the hell out of here. Where I'd go, I don't know, but I figured anywhere would be better than this Mary Sunshine bunch of bullshit.

But hearing what Fable said has helped me see that she's been through this too. I bet she has some wild stories. Sounds like her husband might as well. No wonder they do their best to ensure their kids are healthy and happy.

I wish I had parents like that. My dad meant well, but he was limited by finances and his wife—my mother. And she doesn't give a damn about anyone.

Maybe, just maybe, if I can do what they say and keep my head on straight, I can make my life work. I'll graduate high school, get accepted to a D-1 college...

And get the girl.

But then I'm reminded of Rylie and what she told me, and my house of cards comes tumbling down, one after the other, until it doesn't exist any longer. I need to figure that out first. If she's really pregnant with my baby—I find that shit hard to believe. We had sex maybe twice? Wait, three times. And with a condom every time. Like I told Autumn, I have condoms at home, sitting in my bedside table, just like Jake. That's what I used when I was with Rylie, plus she swore she was on the pill.

Looks like she lied. Or she's lying right now.

Shoving all thoughts of Rylie out of my head, I unzip my

backpack and pull out my giant black binder and a couple of textbooks, along with the packet of worksheets Autumn brought to me late last week with the assignments I've missed while I've been gone. I started working on a few things when she first handed it to me, but eventually gave up when I got bored.

I can't give up. I need to remember that.

I need to live by those words.

Don't give up. Don't give up.

Don't.

Give.

Up.

CHAPTER 32

AUTUMN

Sunday was torture. Kaya had to get home so she left early, leaving me adrift. Ash stayed in his room for the entire day. The *entire* day. Who does that? When I caught Mom coming from his room, I couldn't help myself. I asked her what was going on, and she said he was working on homework and shouldn't be disturbed.

Ash was actually doing homework and he shouldn't be disturbed? What a bunch of crap! I figured he was lying to her.

But no, he sent me a text at one point, asking me a question about one of the assignments. He was perfectly polite, he didn't talk to me about anything else once I gave him the answer, and I didn't mention anything else either. Though I was dying to. I wanted to say things like:

I miss you.

Why were you so mean to me last night?

I want to help you.

Let me help you.

I don't want to fight anymore.

I want to be with you.

And on and on and on.

Are we just too toxic together? Are we complete opposites and it would never work? That's what I'm starting to believe, though of course I don't want it to be true. Yet what am I supposed to think? He runs hot, he runs cold. I can't figure him out. Yet I also do the same thing to him.

I basically accused him of being a thief, but I had to. He needed to see that what he was doing to Jake, he also did to his mom's boyfriend. Don had absolutely no right punching him in the face repeatedly, but Ash shouldn't have taken something that didn't belong to him. Like cigarettes.

And condoms.

Deciding I need to come clean for Ash's sake, I exit my bedroom and jog down the hall, knocking on my brother's door and entering his room when he says I could come in.

"What do you want?" He's sitting in his game chair, playing Madden. Of course.

I study the giant TV on his wall for a few seconds before I turn to Jake. "Don't you get enough of football already?"

"Are you just going to nag me or do you actually want something?" He never tears his gaze away from the TV, his fingers flying furiously over the controller clutched in his hands.

"I wanted to talk to you." I stop in the middle of the room, looking around. It's kind of dirty in here. Smelly too. I see the pile of laundry on the floor and wonder if that's clean or dirty. God, boys—brothers—are really disgusting.

"What did you want to tell me?"

"Um, Ash snuck into your room yesterday."

Jake throws the controller onto the floor with such violence I jump back, shocked. He rises to his feet, his hands clenched into fists. "What the hell did you just say?"

"Calm down, it's no big deal." I start to walk toward him, but the look on his face freezes me in my tracks.

"It's a big fucking deal if he's stealing my shit. Don't try to protect his ass either, Autumn. I know you two are fucking on the low."

My mouth drops open and it takes me a couple of tries before I'm able to form words. "We aren't *fucking on the low,* as you so sweetly put it."

"Messing around, whatever. I don't care what you want to call it. But don't protect that piece of shit if he's a thief. Tell me what he took."

"C-condoms," I stutter nervously. Holy crap, I have never seen my brother act like this. Ever!

"Condoms?" Jake's eyebrows shoot up, and the look on his face reminds me of Dad right now. Well, Dad if he was enraged and ready to pound his fist into a wall, which I've never seen our father do ever in my life.

"Yeah." I just proved to Jake that we are most definitely fucking on the low, and now I feel like a complete idiot.

He starts laughing, shaking his head. "That's it? He stole a couple of condoms so you two could bang? Big deal."

I want to correct him, tell him that we didn't actually bang, but he either a) won't believe me or b) doesn't really care.

I'm sure both options apply.

"I just wanted you to know, in case—" Oh, this is so awkward. "—in case you realized you were, uh, missing some, and wondered where they were."

"I probably wouldn't have noticed," he says, his laughter dying. He goes to pick up the controller off the floor and settles back in his chair, his attention once more on the TV. Like his outburst was no big deal. "Tell your boyfriend to stay out of my room. He does it again and I'll kick his ass."

"He's not my boyfriend," I protest, but Jake sneers.

"May as well be. I see the way you two look at each other. You're lucky Mom and Dad hasn't noticed or they'd boot his ass out of the house." Jake smiles, his gaze meeting mine once more. "Hey, that's not a bad idea, me telling them what you two are up to. They'd kick him out and then Dad can focus on me instead."

"Are you that jealous of Ash?"

"I don't think he deserves Dad's help. He's a low-life drug-gie," Jake spits out.

"Druggie?"

Jake sets the controller in his lap so he can focus fully on me. "Come on, Autumn. You can't be that naïve. You're two years older than me, you're in the same class as him. Don't you hear the stories about Ash that circulate around the school?"

I slowly shake my head. I mean, I've heard a few stories, but nothing involving drugs beyond a wax vape pin or what-ever. "I have no idea what you're talking about."

He blows out a harsh breath. "That's right. I forgot. You're such a goodie-goodie now, you don't know what the bad kids are up to."

His comments get under my skin. He's such an ass some-times. "Tell me what they're up to then."

"Word has it that Ash used to sell prescription pills. Never on campus because he's not a complete idiot, but supposedly he has a client list, and they all come from the high school." Jake sends me an evil smile. "What do you think about your boyfriend now?"

I'm tempted to remind Jake he's not my boyfriend, but I don't bother. Besides, I'm too overwhelmed by Jake's confes-sion. Is it true? Is Ash a…

Drug dealer?

"Part of the reason Ash got beat up is because Don stole from Ash's pill stash, and Ash called him out for it. You see, Ash gets them from his mom. She has a major Oxy addiction, and so she has this huge prescription that gets her so many damn pills every month, she'd probably die if she took them all. But she's not taking them all, she's giving half of them to Ash so he can sell them to his friends and whoever else, and they split the profits."

I'm in absolute shock. I had no freaking idea.

"Everyone's asking around at school when Ash is going to be back. Not that any of them care about him, though a lot of the guys on the team want him back, but everyone else? They just want their pills. They're running out, and a bunch of them are getting pissed." Jake shakes his head. "Wonder if he's managed to dig up some pills to sell yet. They'll be coming for him if he shows up to school tomorrow."

"This is a serious accusation, what you're saying," I remind Jake, my mind whirling with all this new and devastating information. "Calling Ash a drug dealer, saying he works with his mother and sells her pain pills. Like, is this really true?"

"Yes, my sweet, naïve sister. The boy you're chasing after, the same one you let shove his tongue down your throat, is selling prescription pills to minors after school. Most of the time in the Starbucks parking lot." Jake laughs. "I just blew your mind, didn't I?"

"You suck." It's the only thing I can come up with as I flounce out of his room, his annoying laughing following me. I storm into my room and slam the door, and now I'm the one banging my fist against the wall one time. Then again. Then again, until my wall rattles and my fist hurts and I wish I hadn't done it.

This is all a bigger mess than I thought. A much bigger mess. One I'm not sure I can get Ash out of.

* * *

IT'S EARLY EVENING, just before dinner, and I'm in my room still folding and putting away my laundry when there's a light knock on my door. I glance up to find Ash standing there, his expression contrite. "Can I talk to you?"

"Right now?"

"Your mom knows I'm up here."

"Oh." I nod once. "Yeah, sure."

He comes inside and scans the room, taking everything in. The last time he was here, it was the middle of the night and I don't think he bothered looking around much. "Can I sit down?"

"Sure." I point to the pink velvet chair that's at my desk.

Making a face, he pulls it out and settles in, his mouth curving upward. "This is soft."

"It's velvet," I tell him.

"And it's comfortable. I was gonna make fun of your pink chair, but it's pretty cool, Callahan."

I'm not in the mood for his jokes, or the way he avoids our problems. Ignoring them doesn't mean they don't exist. They're still there, and he was an asshole toward me last night. He needs to apologize.

"What do you want, Ash?" I sound short, full of impatience, because I am.

"I wanted to say I'm sorry for how I talked to you." He leans forward, resting his elbows on his knees, his gaze intense as it locks with mine. "I was a jerk, and I shouldn't have taken the condoms from Jake."

"I told him. That you snuck into his room and took them," I say, wanting him to know I'm not hiding anything. Unlike him.

He seems to hide everything.

"You told him?" Ash shakes his head, then rests his face in his hands for a moment, before he looks at me once more. "Was he pissed?"

"Furious. But then he thought it was lame, that you took the condoms. He also said if you ever sneak into his room again, he's going to kick your ass." I hesitate, wondering if I should tell him about the other stuff Jake said.

"I don't blame him," Ash says, heaving a big sigh. "I need to go apologize to him too."

Huh. This new Ash is certainly a surprise. A good one.

"That would probably go a long way." Or maybe not. Jake is jealous of Ash, and I don't understand why. "He mentioned some—other stuff to me."

"Like what?" Ash looks genuinely confused.

"Like how you sell prescription pills to people at school." I just blurt it out, and I can tell by the look on his face that I shocked him. "Why, Ash? Why would you *do* that? It's so risky. You could end up in jail if you get caught."

He jumps to his feet and starts pacing my room, running his fingers through his hair again and again. "I was trying to stop." He doesn't bother denying, and deep down, I'm relieved. "That night, when I got into the fight with my mom and Don, I was so tired of doing it. At first, I started stealing them from her and selling them to my friends for a little extra money. Then Mom caught me, and realized I had a good thing going. So she used me. She said it was less risky if I was the one selling the pills, considering I'm a juvenile and I'd get less time if I got caught. They'd throw me in juvie or whatever, and it would be over. Not on my permanent record."

I cannot believe this woman. Seriously, she is the worst mother ever.

"But I'm only a couple of months away from eighteen. Football is important to me. And I know no one really believes it, but I get decent grades. The last thing I need is to get caught selling pills to my friends. I'd lose all chances of getting into a D-1 school," he says, pausing in his pacing to look at me. "Not like I have a chance to get in one, but I have dreams, you know? So I told her I wanted to stop. I couldn't do it anymore. She said I didn't have a choice. I had to keep selling. We needed that money to live, and she made me feel guilty for giving up on it. For giving up on her."

God, I want to go to him so badly, but I remain seated on my bed, waiting for him to finish. He needs to get this story out first. And once he does, we need to figure out what to do next. My parents should know this.

They can help him.

"I left school early that day because I forgot my bag with my gear at home. I walk inside the apartment to find both Don and Mom bagging up pills for me to sell. I was pissed, because now the asshole is in on it too, you know? They were both telling me I needed to drop off a few orders before practice, and I said I didn't have the time, which was the truth. I can't be late. I needed to get to practice and they told me no. I didn't have a choice. I had a job to do. We start yelling back and forth, one thing led to another and..." His voice drifts and he points at his healing face. "This is what happened."

"So it had nothing to do with a stolen pack of cigarettes."

"Nope." He grimaces. "Sorry I lied. I'm always giving you shit for lying to me, Callahan, and here I am, keeping the biggest secret around."

"Why didn't you tell me the truth?" I ask, my voice soft, my heart breaking for him. I'm not even mad about the lie. I get it.

"Because you would've freaked the fuck out. I know you. I know you better than you think. You're a good girl. You follow the rules, you have your friends, you're a freaking cheerleader and in student council, you get good grades. Your parents love you. Everything's clean and good in your world, and I'm not. I'm the furthest thing from that. I'm a drug-dealing piece of shit who won't amount to anything," he explains.

"Don't say that." I slide off the bed and go where he is, so I'm standing right in front of him. "You're not a piece of shit. You just need someone to show you that you don't have to live like that."

He smiles, though there's nothing warm or sweet about it. It's almost like a baring of teeth. "You going to be the one who shows me how to live?"

"I want to be, if you'll let me." I lean toward him, wishing I could touch him, but I'm waiting for him to make the first move.

"You sound like your mom."

I frown. "What do you mean?"

"She's all gung ho, ready to help me, eager with her offers. And I want her help. I need her and your dad, but they don't know about this. The drug thing." His expression falters, and he blinks. Hard. Like he might be fighting away tears. "They won't help me once they find out. I know they won't."

"They will." Unable to resist, I grab hold of his hands and clutch them in mine. His fingers are icy cold, and I swear they're shaking. "If you tell them what you just told me, I know they will help you. You want to change, Ash, and that's half the battle."

"Yeah," he croaks, squeezing my hands in return. "Okay. Will you go with me when I tell them?"

"Of course."

"Can we go now? I want to get this off my chest, before we go see Adney tomorrow," he admits, his voice low. He hangs his head, studying our connected hands, and a shuddering breath leaves me. He lets go, reaching to cup my cheek, and when he lifts my face, I part my lips, waiting for his kiss.

It's gentle. Sweet. No passion, no tongue, just pure

emotion pouring from his lips to mine. "I don't deserve you," he whispers. "I don't deserve any of this."

"You do," I reaffirm, my free hand sliding into the hair at his nape. "I'll help you. We'll all help you."

"It could get ugly." He pulls away a little. "My mom will say whatever makes herself look good. She's a liar."

"Just stand by your truth." I release my hold on his hair and take a step backward, letting go of his other hand. "You are telling me the truth, right?"

His pitch-dark gaze never leaves mine as he nods slowly. "Yeah. I am."

"Then that's all that matters." I take his hand once more. "Let's go talk to my parents."

CHAPTER 33

ASH

*A*utumn sat beside me when I told my sordid tale to her parents. Her dad, my coach, my idol, appeared completely blown away when I talked about dealing pills, his eyes wide and unblinking, his lips parted in shock. Her mom's gaze was full of sympathy, but also understanding. That woman just gets me, which is sort of scary.

We were in Drew's office for little over an hour as we tried to strategize my next move. We still plan on meeting with Adney, but that's not scheduled until nine tomorrow morning. Before that, we're going to the county deputy's office.

That's going to suck. But I have to come clean and tell them the truth. I have proof. Shit, I have a prescription bottle of Oxycontin with my mom's name on it in my backpack because yes, I'm that idiot who's still wandering around with pills. At least they aren't in baggies—that would get me an automatic arrest.

"We'll get you through this," Drew says, Fable nodding in agreement. "As long as you tell the truth, you should be okay."

I want to believe them. But what I'm doing is illegal. I could end up in big trouble.

Huge.

Once the meeting is over, we all exit his office, Drew and Fable heading to the kitchen so they can start dinner together like it's just another normal night for the Callahan family. I guess Drew's going to grill hamburgers and Fable's going to make a salad and frozen french fries. Nothing fancy, but at least it's a semi-homecooked meal. More than my mom's ever given me these last few years since Dad died.

"Let's go talk outside," Autumn tells me as she takes my hand and leads me through the back door on the other side of the house, the one closest to my room. I've never snuck out of this house, though it would be so easy with that door nearby.

But I don't want to. I want to stay here. I like it here.

I don't want to fuck things up.

Autumn takes me to an area that's on the far side of the house, close to the front yard. There's a giant tree providing plenty of shade, with various flowers planted along the pathway, their heads bobbing and weaving with the gentle breeze. There's a bench beneath the tree and Autumn sits on it, pulling me down beside her, and I stare at her in wonderment for a while, until she laughs uncomfortably.

"Is there something on my face?" She touches her nose, her cheek.

"No," I murmur, wishing I could kiss her, but I'm going to use restraint. "Why are you so nice to me?"

Autumn frowns, her delicate brows furrowing. "What are you talking about?"

"I've been a complete asshole to you since the first day we met." I think back to that day. Me lighting matches, telling her that jackass only wanted to get a pussy shot from her. I rocked her world by talking so bluntly, I saw it in the way her eyes widened, her perfect pink lips parting in surprise when I said those words. I bet no one had ever talked to precious Autumn Callahan like that before.

Felt kind of good, shocking her. Made me want to do it again. Made me addicted to her. The fact that she's beautiful didn't hurt. Only made it worse, really. I like how short she is, all cute and compact while I tower over her. Her body is amazing. Her tits look great in just about everything she wears, though I could tell those first couple of years in high school she always tried to hide them. She came into herself by junior year. She was a lot stronger, a lot braver. Even more beautiful.

And she belonged to someone else. A wimp who had no idea what to do with her. I always knew what to do with her, knew just what to do to make her feel. I said all the right words, told her how I felt, and she still rejected me.

Repeatedly.

I did the same thing to her, I suppose. When I was younger, I wasn't serious. Not about Autumn, not about anything. I just wanted to toy with her. Kiss her, fuck her, be done with her. That had been my plan the night of the home-coming dance, and I thought I had her there for a minute.

As usual, she ran away.

Proving she's smarter than I first gave her credit for.

"You were a complete asshole," she agrees, her sweet voice pulling me from my thoughts. "I think I'm attracted to assholes."

"What about Ben?" I torture myself when I ask about him. I hate thinking of him with his hands on her. Kissing her. I didn't believe her when she told me they never did it, because come on. Why wouldn't Ben Murray fuck her as fast as possible?

But she was telling me the truth. I still can't believe that she is all mine. Completely mine. If I have my way, I'll be inside her at least once by the end of next week. I know I shouldn't be plotting and planning ways to sneak into her room, when my entire life could go up in flames tomorrow morning, but threats never really worked on me. Meaning I'm the stupid one who's willing to risk it all for a piece of ass.

But it's not just a piece of ass when it comes to Autumn. She's so much more than that.

I think I'm falling in love with her. If I even know what love actually is…

"Ben was who I thought I should be with. He's kind, he's polite. He was a good boyfriend to me. Supportive. Comes from a good family." She turns to look at me, her green eyes glittering. "He bored me. There was no spark."

Reaching out, I play with a strand of her hair, twisting it around my finger again and again. "We got spark."

"We have lots of spark," she agrees with a faint smile.

"I wish we could spark it up right now," I say, trying to lighten the mood. It's been nothing but heavy bullshit for the entire weekend. I'm over it.

"I wish we could too." I start to say something, but she presses her fingers against my mouth, silencing me. "But not yet. We need to get through the next few days first."

She's right, and I hate that. I'd drag her back to my room right now if she'd let me. Strip her naked and kiss her every-where. Use one of those condoms I stole from her brother—who the hell is he fucking anyway? God, who knows? Who really cares?

Not me.

I think back to the last time I had Autumn naked, when I licked her pussy and drove her wild. Her thighs clamped so tight around my head when she was coming, it was like getting squeezed by a vise.

It was hot as fuck.

I kiss her fingers and she smiles. Doesn't pull away when I lightly grab hold of her wrist and continue to kiss her there. Her eyes darken when I flick my tongue out and lick her index finger, then her middle finger. By the time I get to her ring finger, she's squirming and I'm pulling her in closer so I can drop a kiss on her puffy mouth. I know there are cameras out here, so I need to watch myself, but damn I can't get enough of her taste. The way her tongue tangles with mine, the little moans and whimpers that sound in her throat. She gets off on me so easily. I bet if I slipped my hand beneath her shorts, under her panties, I'd find her soaking wet.

All for me.

"Okay." She tears her lips away from mine, both of us breathing heavily. "We need to stop."

I pull her in for one last kiss, on her neck, just behind her ear. She shivers. "I never want to stop when I'm with you."

She clutches my shoulders, tilting her head back so I can kiss her there again, forgetting all about my one last kiss promise. "I don't either. But we have to."

She shoves at my shoulders, proving she's stronger than she looks, and I go scooting backward across the bench. "Damn, woman."

"I throw girls into the air on an almost daily basis," she reminds me. "I'm stronger than I look."

In so many ways, I want to tell her, but I keep my lips shut. I sound like a sentimental ass, saying stuff like that.

"You ready to go back to school tomorrow?" she asks, her eyes wide, her lips swollen from my kisses. I know she's trying to change the subject, to steer me away from thinking about getting her naked, but her question only reminds me of the one thing I'm trying to forget.

Fucking Rylie and her pregnancy story.

If that shit is true, I'm doomed. Fucked beyond measure.

Can't think about it now. Not while I'm sitting here with the girl I care about more than anything else in this world. Forget Rylie, forget all the bullshit. I need to focus on Autumn.

Autumn. I need to call her by her name more. But it's kind of fun, how I never do it. I think it drives her nuts.

"I'm ready to go to practice tomorrow," I say, and that's the truth. I miss football. I don't want Jake to permanently take my place either, so I need to get back to it.

Autumn rolls her eyes. "Of course you are."

"Hey, that's what I'm known for. And that's the only thing that's going to get me out of here," I remind her.

"I know. You're right. And you're a pretty great football player." She leans in and drops a quick kiss on my cheek.

"You want to wear my jersey on Friday?" I ask. This is serious stuff. I have never let anyone wear my jersey on game day before. Not even Rylie, though I know she was dying to. Still, it didn't feel quite right, letting her wear my number. Six. My favorite number since I was assigned it for my soccer jersey when I was six. Made sense to my first grader brain that I got that number, and it stuck as my favorite.

Autumn's face brightens, her eyes dancing as she nods enthusiastically. "I would love to."

"Consider it yours. I'll bring one of my spares home. I leave it in my locker." So it doesn't end up stinking like cigarettes or old, musty food. God, I hated living with my mom so damn much. If I never have to go back there again, I'll be satisfied.

She's grinning now. To the point that I can almost see her back teeth. "You just called it home."

Reaching out, I play with her hair again. It's dark. Silky soft. Everything about her is perfect. Perfect for me. "That's because it's like my home now."

"I'm so glad you're here," she says, her voice lowering to

whisper. "Despite the circumstances that you brought you to me, I'm glad it happened."

"I'm glad it did too," I whisper back.

Her smile fades. "Do you think we're moving too fast?"

I slowly shake my head. "We've been circling around each other for almost four years. I say it's about damn time this is happening."

She laughs, and it's this great, big sound that hits me right in the chest. Smack in the middle of my heart. Damn, this girl.

She will be my undoing.

CHAPTER 34

AUTUMN

*I*t's surprising how normal everything feels when Ash returns to school. My parents go with him to the sheriff substation first thing Monday morning, and though I normally take Ava and Jake with me every day, I also take Beck to school, so Mom doesn't have to worry about it. After meeting with the deputy and Ash telling them about his mom's illegal business, they meet with Mrs. Adney, who is able to help them start the ball rolling to get Ash in my family's temporary care.

Turns out the deputy helped with that too, offering up some suggestions. Within a couple of days, my parents are granted temporary guardianship of Asher Davis, and the county drug enforcement team performed a raid on Ash's mom's apartment. They found lots and lots of pills, along with all the paraphernalia that comes with dealing, and pressed charges against both his mother and Don, including distribution.

They're still in jail, and this makes Ash inordinately happy.

He's not off the hook, though. He confessed to what he

did, what his mother made him do for the past two years, and he agreed to a community service sentence. He'll be given an assignment within the next month or so, and once he completes his hours, the minor charges they pressed against him will be dropped, and forever sealed in his juvenile record.

Ash got off easy, and he knows it.

The entire week, he's his usual overly confident self at school. Strutting down the hall, smiling at everyone. He throws himself into practice, working to the point of exhaustion every afternoon. Once word spread that Ash wasn't dealing anymore and his mom got busted, all those people who were a part of his clientele list leave him alone. Or ask for recommendations on where they can get some Oxy.

Thankfully, he doesn't have any recs to give them.

By Friday night, the school is in a frenzy, ready to win our last home game before the team goes on the road for the next three weeks. They're undefeated so far for the season, and Ash is ready to prove to his coaches, to the entire school that he still has what it takes. I'm on the sidelines as usual, even more pumped up for this game than normal, and I'm talking with my coach when Mom approaches, a giant smile on her face. When she gestures for me to come closer, I walk over to where she's standing on the other side of the fence.

"An offensive coach from Fresno State is here tonight to watch Ash play," she whispers in my ear.

I pull away to stare at her incredulously. "Aren't they a D-1 school?"

Mom nods, looking very pleased. "Your dad called in a few favors."

"Did he tell Ash?"

"No way!" Mom laughs. "That kid would be a bundle of nerves if he did that. He has no clue."

And I won't have a chance to tell him. We never speak during games. He's too busy, I'm too busy.

The game starts, and the opposing team immediately puts points on the board, which riles up our crowd. The stands are full tonight, the student section at near capacity, and the rest of the bleachers are filled up as well. The town is small and there's not a lot to do on a Friday night so plenty of locals come to watch the game. Plus, many people who live here once went to this high school, so there are a lot of alumni filling the stands.

Looks like they all came out tonight. I'm sure part of it has to do with Ash. It was all over social media and the local news that his mom was arrested in the drug bust, though no mention of Ash's involvement was included. He's a bit of a celebrity right now thanks to his mom's transgressions, but he seems to be taking everything in stride.

Our team scores within two minutes and now the game is tied. It goes like this for the entire first half. Back and forth, back and forth, until we're 21 to 17 at the half, with the visiting team in the lead.

"Crap, you think we're going to lose?" Kaya's eyes are wide as the entire cheer team hooks arms and gets ready to meet the opposing cheer team in the middle of the field, as is our tradition. We'll invite them to sit on our side to watch us perform our halftime routine.

"No way. Ash won't let it happen," I say firmly. "They always have some huge inspirational speech during halftime that makes them come back ten times stronger and ready to tear the other team apart."

Kaya laughs. "So true. We witnessed that at a game a couple of weeks ago."

We gripe about how we hate football and are so over it, but truly, I love it. It's been a part of my life since I was born.

I always believed I wanted to avoid football players at all costs, figuring they only wanted to use me for my dad.

Yet here I am, halfway in love with the quarterback of our football team, and I'm a cheerleader. My dad's the coach. Ash and I are a total cliché.

Not that I mind.

The start of the third quarter we score immediately, and we take the lead for the rest of the game. I cheer loud and proud for my boy, for his team, for my father's team, and when it's all over and I can go out on the field to hug Ash, he sweeps me into his arms, holding me close despite all the equipment he's still wearing.

"You were amazing," I say, smiling up at him.

"I could hear you cheering, Callahan." He drops a kiss on the tip of my nose. "Loud as usual."

"Shush. You know you love it." I smack him on the chest, wrinkling my nose when he rubs his damp face against my neck. He's all sweaty and kind of smelly, but I don't care. It's so nice to actually be out in public with our relationship. People know we're together, and they don't really care. My parents seem cool with it, but they've also kept us extra busy so we never get a chance to be alone. No one at school seems bothered by it either. I thought Rylie would be a problem, but I really haven't seen her at all this week.

I let Ash go talk to other people, and I grab my cheer bag, which is sitting by the fence where my coach still is, cleaning everything up. Since the season's started, I've been helping Brandy put away our equipment every week after the game, so I'm not surprised when she smiles and says, "Go be with your non-boyfriend, Autumn. See you Monday at practice."

"My non-boyfriend?" I laugh, and so does she.

"You're the one who denied you had anything going on with him," she says.

"That was sort of true."

"Whatever."

Laughing, I turn and almost run into someone.

Rylie. And she looks totally different from the last time I saw her. Her hair is this jarring greenish blue color that isn't very flattering with her pale skin and she's wearing heavy eye makeup. She's a pretty girl, I've always thought so, but this new look isn't a good one.

"Oh, sorry. Didn't mean to run into you." She flashes me a smile, her eyes wide as she takes me in. Her smile fades and her lip curls in disgust. "I honestly don't know what he sees in you."

I take a step away from her, my heart pounding. No way do I want to deal with another confrontation. "Come on, Rylie. I don't want any trouble."

"Neither do I. Not with you. I do have a problem with Ash, though." She glances around, her gaze snagging on where he's standing out on the field, talking with a couple of football dads. "I have a *serious* problem with him."

I have no idea what she's talking about. The fact that he cut her off? She needs to take a cue from that one Disney movie and let it go. "Leave him alone."

"What, are you his keeper now? Oh, that's right, you are. So sweet. The big happy family all living together under one roof. If I didn't hate you so much, I'd be envious."

Why does she have to be such a bitch about it?

I'm about to say something, but she turns and walks away, heading in the opposite direction of Ash.

Thank God.

Since Ash has been riding with all of us in the morning to school—his truck isn't in the greatest shape and is still sitting in the parking lot of his apartment complex—we're going to ride home together. This is the first time we've been actually alone in what feels like forever.

I can't wait. In fact, I'm a nervous, jittery mess, and when

Ash asks if he can drive my Jeep home, I gladly hand over the keys.

"Fuck yeah," he says as he climbs into the driver's seat, smiling over at me as he starts the car. "Think we can go for a ride?"

"My parents will probably be waiting for us." I bite my lip, trying not to squirm in my seat. He shed all his equipment and tossed it in the back of the Jeep before we got in the car, and he looks so cute sitting in my car, still wearing the tight uniform pants and his jersey.

"Indulge me for a little while, Callahan. I've been dreaming of getting my hands up your cheer skirt for years," he drawls, his gaze dropping to my exposed thighs.

"Oh my God, stop," I tell him, blushing furiously. I do love the idea of him slipping his hands beneath my skirt, though.

"Let's go park by the lake. Just for a few minutes," he says, and I give in, because how can I resist him?

Besides, I want it too.

Fifteen minutes later, Ash is pulling into a day camp parking lot right on the edge of the lake. No one else is here, it's just us and the water and the moon reflecting its light on the rippling waves. Ash puts the car in park and rolls down the windows before he shuts off the engine. He turns off the radio and it goes silent, save for the outside noises. The rustle of grass from the breeze that always starts up just before sundown. An owl hoots close by, most likely perched in one of the towering pines above us. Another bird squawks, and in the near distance, I hear the insistent howling of coyotes.

"The coyotes scared me when we first moved here," I tell Ash.

"Really? Afraid they were going to cart you away and eat you alive?" He sounds amused.

"So gross." I laugh. Shake my head. "No, I was never afraid of them taking me away or anything like that. They just sound scary. Those howls in the middle of the night are eerie." I still hear them a lot, especially up where we live. We used to always have cats, and they preferred being indoors and outdoors, but we lost so many to coyotes or bobcats that Mom finally gave up. She couldn't stand losing them in such a terrible way. Neither could any of us kids, especially Ava. She'd cry and cry for days.

"Big city girl not used to living in the woods?" He lifts his brows.

"Not at all. I hated it here at first. I was a complete city girl. You didn't help matters either," I say, scowling at him.

He looks faintly embarrassed. "I was kind of a jerk."

"You were a total jerk," I agree.

"I was just warning you off. The entire team made a bet on who would get your nudes first," he says.

"So awful." I shake my head. "Just so you know, I will never send you nude photos. I got a big speech from my mom when I turned thirteen, warning me off. She pulled out the big guns."

"What did she say?"

"'What if the pics got out, Autumn? What if they were splashed all over social media? It could happen, considering how famous your dad is.' That was enough to convince me. She said the same thing to Ava," I explain.

"Damn, guess I'll just have to see it live and in person then." He tugs on his lower lip with his thumb and index finger as his gaze drops to my lap, something I haven't seen him do in a while.

I forgot how much I liked it.

"You've already seen it live and in person," I remind him, teasing.

"Yeah, but I want to see it again. And again and again and again." He settles his big hand on my thigh, then slides it up, beneath my skirt. "Your skin is so smooth."

My breath hitches in my throat. Ben and I may have made out in his car or mine pretty much every weekend, but we never went very far. I always figured he took it slow out of respect for me. But maybe he didn't feel the spark either.

Right now, with Ash's hand on my thigh, it feels like he could set my skin on fire.

"Come here," he says, his voice deep. Seductive. "Come sit on my lap."

He pushes the seat back to give us more room, and then I'm climbing on top of him, my arms around his neck, fingers buried in his soft hair. My knees are resting on the seat on either side of his hips, and when I lower my torso so our bodies are pressed close together, Ash closes his eyes on a moan.

"I've missed you so damn bad," he murmurs.

I watch him, mesmerized by the way his eyebrows crinkle, his eyes tightly shut. Most of the wounds on his face have faded completely, and I sort of miss the dangerous air they gave him. The stitches were taken out just yesterday, leaving him with an angry scar the doctor swore would fade with time.

I run my finger over the scar, dropping my hand when he flinches. "I like your scars," I tell him when his eyes slowly open.

"You're the only one who does," he says with a faint smile.

"I like everything about you." My voice is somber, as are my emotions. This feels like a serious moment. One I don't ever want to forget.

"Yeah?" He runs his hand over my hair, tugging on the end of my ponytail. His full lips curve upward, and his eyes never leave mine when he says, "Pretty sure I'm falling in love with you, Callahan."

My lips part as I stare down at him, and then we're kissing. I can't not kiss him after he says something like that.

Something so monumental. My heart is soaring. I have everything I could ever want, right here, right now…

"I'm falling in love with you too," I whisper against his lips, just before he kisses me again, his tongue teasing my lips. "It's probably too fast to say that."

"Nah. We've been playing around at this relationship thing for long enough." He deepens the kiss, his tongue stroking mine, his hands everywhere at once, until we finally break for air minutes later, both of us breathless. "Wanna go to the backseat?"

"Let's fold down the seats completely. I have a couple of blankets." I bite my lip, wondering if he brought one of those condoms he stole from my brother.

He glances over his shoulder at the backseat before returning his gaze to me. "I don't know."

My heart drops.

"If we start messing around back there, I won't want to stop. And we'll end up taking way too long and your parents will get suspicious and then we'll get in trouble. Maybe we should go back home," he says.

I stare at him, surprised by his suggestion. He sounds so… grownup. And rational. "Okay," I say with a nod. "But I really, really wanted to be with you in the back of my car. Just so you know."

He groans, the sound full of agony. "Why you gotta go and say something like that?"

"You should come to my room later." Ash opens his mouth, I'm sure to tell me no, but I cut him off. "They won't know. We'll be quiet. Come on. Please?"

We remain silent for a moment, studying each other, and I try my best to convey with my eyes just how badly I want him to meet me later tonight.

"Okay," he finally agrees, just before he kisses me. Hard.

"But you're going to have to be extra quiet. You know how loud you are when I make you come, Callahan."

Laughing, I climb off his lap and settle my butt into the passenger seat, watching as he starts the Jeep up and backs out of the spot with ease. "I can't believe you just said that."

"I can't believe you laughed when I said that. You're changing."

"So are you."

And I love it.

CHAPTER 35

ASH

*I*t's late. Past midnight, maybe closer to one. I've discovered the entire house stays up late after a football game. It's like everyone's hype and they have a hard time coming down. When Autumn and I enter the kitchen, the entire Callahan family is in there, even Beck, eating pizza and talking so loud, they don't notice us when we first come in.

They aren't mad we took so long, though in all reality we only took about a fifteen-minute detour, thanks to my speeding back to her house. Autumn squealed the entire drive home, especially when I took the curves too fast, and her road is extra curvy.

Kind of like her.

We settle at the kitchen counter with the rest of the family and I stuff my face full of pizza. Fable mentioned she picked it up on the way home and I tell her she's a goddess, I'm that hungry and grateful. She laughs and ruffles my hair, and I catch Autumn watching us with so much emotion in her eyes, just seeing her look at me like that makes my chest tight. This girl makes me feel way too much. It's almost scary, how she affects me.

When I admitted earlier I was falling in love with her, I lied. I'm full-blown in love with her. I just didn't want to say it too quick, afraid I might scare her. She's a take-it-slow kind of girl, and I'm a let's-go-fast-faster type of guy. We've been moving at warp speed the last few weeks, so capping it off with a "I'm in love with you" declaration might've been too much.

I'll probably spill my guts within the week. I'm not one to keep shit in.

Once everyone goes to their rooms, I go to mine and take a shower. Put on a pair of black boxer briefs and a T-shirt, mess around with my hair a bit before I give up on it. Shave my face and brush my teeth so I'll have minty-fresh breath. Then when I'm fairly sure everyone's tucked into bed, I grab one of those condoms I snagged from Jake and sneak through the house, creep up the stairs, and let myself into Autumn's room.

She's awake, sitting up in bed. There's a tiny lamp on her bedside table that's shaped like a flower, and it casts its pink glow throughout the room, just enough so I can see her. She's sitting on top of the covers, wearing a loose tank, and I can tell there's no bra underneath. Her nipples poke against the thin fabric, her hair is loose and wavy all around her face, and as I draw closer to the bed, I can smell her floral scented lotion.

"Hi," she whispers, her big green eyes glowing.

"Hi." I sit on the edge of her bed and reach out, skimming my fingers up her smooth calf. "You smell good."

"I think I used half the bottle of lotion on my legs." She smiles, and I can tell she's nervous. Her lips twitch and she keeps blinking.

"If you don't want to do this, we don't have to," I tell her, wanting to establish that from the start. I won't push her into anything that would make her feel uncomfortable. Even a couple of weeks ago I might've pushed her for more, not fully caring about her feelings. I was that much of a jackass.

Spending time with her and her family has helped me see that there's more to life than my own selfish needs.

"I want to do this," she says, her voice firm. Giving me permission.

"Here." I hand her the condom. "Put that on the table."

She does as I ask and then I'm crawling up the length of her body, stopping when I'm directly in front of her, our faces, our chests aligned. Tilting my head, I lean in and press my mouth to hers, drinking from her sweet, sweet lips. She opens for me easily, like she always does, and I slide my tongue in, circling hers, searching her mouth. I don't touch her anywhere else, and she doesn't touch me either. Yet my dick is already hard, just from her lips on mine, and I remind myself to slow down. Make it last.

Make it good for her.

But she makes me eager. Nervous. Fumbling. I skim my fingers across her shoulders, drift them down the front of her tank, catching on the neckline. It falls forward, and I dip my head, dropping a kiss on top of her exposed chest.

"Take it off," she whispers, and I do, whipping the tank off to find she's only wearing a pair of sheer, skimpy panties. I'm momentarily stunned, taking her in, and she scoots down the bed, lying flat on her back beneath me.

I kiss her everywhere, and like she promised, she tries her best to be quiet. I kiss her shoulders, her collarbone, her breasts. I lick her nipples. Suck them. She clutches my hair in her fists, breathing heavily, using just enough pressure to try to guide me down her body.

I know what my girl wants. And I'm going to give it to her.

My lips drift across her stomach, tease her bellybutton with my tongue. She gives a little jerk, a giggle escaping her, replaced by a low moan when I tug her panties down her hips. She kicks them off her legs, and then she's completely naked, her skin glowing.

I rise up on my knees and tear off my T-shirt, then kneel between her legs, my hands braced on the inside of her thighs as I spread her wide. She's pink and pretty and glistening, and when I swipe my tongue through her folds, she about jolts off the bed.

"Sshh," I murmur against her pussy, just before I give it a thorough lick. She tastes so damn good. Watching her writhe around while I drive her crazy with my tongue and fingers is my new favorite thing.

Within minutes she's coming, those strong thighs of hers clamping around my head again while she rides out her orgasm. It's hot as fuck. I can't believe this girl is mine.

All mine.

CHAPTER 36

AUTUMN

"*A*sh. Please." I'm desperate. I claw at him, my hands reaching, seeking, and all I think about is having him inside me. I'm needy, I want it, but I'm also scared.

What if it hurts?

What if he can't fit?

What if he comes before he gets inside me?

That would be…disappointing. But I can deal with it.

Hopefully.

I already had an orgasm, thanks to his magical tongue. God, I don't know if I can ever get enough of that. I remember when I first heard about oral sex, and I always thought it sounded so disgusting.

Of course, that's when I was twelve or thirteen and a complete idiot. Now that I've actually experienced it, I'm going to want him to do that to me just about every day. He makes me greedy like that.

"I'll give you what you want, baby." He finishes kicking off his boxer briefs before he reaches across me, his fingers grasping for the packet on the bedside table, and then he's rising onto his knees, tearing the wrapper open and rolling the condom onto his erection. I watch in complete fascination, marveling at how large it is. Wondering for about the fiftieth time if it's going to fit.

Is it? Will it?

God, it better.

"Try to relax," he says as he gets into position. He plumps the pillows beneath my head, as if he wants to make sure I'm comfortable, and my heart just cracks wide open from all the love I feel for him in this moment.

In all of our moments.

He touches my hip and shifts me to the right, and I follow his lead, my gaze drifting down to the spot where we're about to connect. His other hand grips the base of his erection. He gives it a firm stroke and then he guides it toward the spot between my legs. I spread them wider, feel the head nudge at my entry, and I swallow hard, trying my best to relax my muscles so I can accept him easier.

"Goddamn, you're so wet," he mumbles, sounding agonized. Slowly he inches himself inside me, and I bite my lip when I feel that first sharp pinch.

He goes still, gazing down at me, his hands propped on either side of my head. "You okay?"

I nod, pressing my lips together. It doesn't hurt so much anymore. I just feel really, really full.

With a few flexes of his hips, he's embedded fully inside me, and he pauses there, not moving, I suppose letting me get used to him. He presses his forehead against mine, his breathing harsh, his chest flush next to mine so I can feel his rapidly beating heart.

"Am I hurting you?" His voice is a harsh rasp, but there's tenderness there. Caring. He cares about me.

He loves me.

"No," I say with a shake of my head.

He shifts, sending himself even deeper, and a whimper escapes me. "You feel so good, Autumn. I'm going to have to take this slow."

"That's okay." I'd rather take it slow. So we can make this last.

We start to move, hesitantly at first, and then with more purpose. It's a little awkward, and I feel like a fumbling fool, but he's fumbling too, and I realize he's just as nervous as I am. I run my hands down the sleek, muscular skin of his back, and he shudders from my touch. I love that, the power I have over him, and I let my hands drift down farther. Farther. Until I'm touching his perfect butt, pressing down hard, so he has no choice but to sink deeper into me.

And then we start moving in earnest. Faster. Harder. I can feel the tingle start, and it's right there, just out of reach when he drops his face into my pillow, groaning as his hips jerk, and I realize he's coming.

Oh. Wow. That was fast.

"Shit, Autumn. I knew that would happen." He's speaking into the pillow, his voice muffled, and I sort of want to laugh.

"It's okay." I stroke his damp-with-sweat back, trying to sooth him. "It felt good."

"You didn't come."

"No, but you did." This time I do laugh and he lifts his head, smiling down at me. "We'll do this again. You can make it up to me. Plenty of times."

"I'm sure," he says, dropping a kiss on my nose. "I just wanted to make it good for you."

"You made it good for me," I tell him truthfully. It was so good. Better than in the back of my Jeep, that's for sure. "I promise."

He stares at me like I'm the most beautiful thing he's ever seen, and it feels so good, so right lying with him like this. Our bodies still connected, our hearts pounding. I will never,

ever forget this night. The game, kissing by the lake, laughing and eating with my family, having sex for the first time. All with Ash.

The boy who has my heart.

Completely.

We lie together for a little while longer, but then he reluctantly pulls away, grabbing a tissue from the box on my bedside table and peeling off the condom, wrapping it up in the Kleenex. "I'll find a place to toss this," he tells me, clutching it in his hand, and I'm thankful he thought of it. We have to get rid of the evidence. If my parents found out…

I don't want to think about that. Not now.

He throws his clothes back on and I watch him, regret filling me. I wish he could stay in my bed for a little while longer, but that would just be weird, right? And if my parents caught us, that would be the end of our relationship. I can't risk that.

We've already risked enough.

"I'm going back to my room." He leans over me and kisses me slowly. Deeply. With languid sweeps of his tongue that leaves my body tingling and wanting more. "Good night."

I catch his hand, stopping him from leaving. "You really have to go?"

"Autumn." My heart expands when he calls me by my name. He never says it enough. "I wish I could stay, but you know I can't."

"I know. I'll miss you."

"You'll see me tomorrow."

"It can't come soon enough."

"You're being kind of ridiculous," he teases.

"This is what you do to me. You leave me in a ridiculous state." I grin up at him and he kisses me yet again, like he can't help it.

"Good night," he murmurs against my lips, and I smile.

"Night."

"Love you," he whispers, and my skin goes tight.

"I love you too." Oh God, if I don't watch it I could cry from pure happiness.

This is the best night of my life.

CHAPTER 37

ASH

I smell the smoke before I see it, hazy yet visible, thin black strips of it drifting in the hallway that leads to the guest room. Right at the moment I notice it, a smoke alarm starts to go off, the incessant blaring making me cover my ears. I run toward my room, the tissue-wrapped condom falling out of my hand and onto the floor, forgotten.

I come to a stop at the doorway, flickering orange flames preventing me for going inside.

"Holy shit," I mutter under my breath, looking left, then right, wondering if they have a fire extinguisher in the house, and where it might be. I decide to look in the laundry room, which is closer than the kitchen.

And that's where I find it, tucked into a cabinet above the washer. I pull it out and run back toward the room, fumbling with the valve so I can hit the trigger. Footsteps sound behind me, and I glance over my shoulder to see Drew running toward me, clad in only a pair of black sweatpants, his forehead creased in concern.

314

"What the hell is going on?" he yells, and I point at the flames.

"Fire!" My fingers curl around the trigger and I spray as hard as I can, desperate to put out the fire, panic racing through me. All I can think is how this is going to ruin everything. They're going to think I did something stupid and possibly blame me for the fire, since pretty much every bad thing that happens to me is somehow my own damn fault. Then they'll kick me out. I'll be on my own, in the streets, left adrift.

I fucked everything up, and I didn't even do this.

Drew leaves me for what feels like five minutes but was probably no longer than thirty seconds, returning with another extinguisher clutched in his hands. He pulls the tab and starts spraying along with me, the both of us focusing on the bed. The flames are the worst there, and I wonder if that's where it started.

I also wonder how it started. I haven't smoked since I got here, so I know a discarded cigarette didn't start this. That was always my fear when I was younger. Mom always fell asleep on the couch, a cigarette dangling from her fingers, from her mouth…

I hear sirens in the distance and realize a fire engine has arrived, thank God. What we're doing isn't going to put this out.

"Hey!" Drew nods toward the door that leads outside. "Go out there and tell them what's going on."

He trusts me enough to do that? "O-okay." I do as he says, running outside to tell the firefighters, who are hopping off the engine, where the fire is, but someone is already there. Talking to them.

Squinting into the darkness, I can see it's a girl. She's tall and thin with long legs, and she has long hair that's dyed bluish green. She turns to look at the house, our gazes catching, and my heart stops.

Is that…

Rylie?

What the hell?

I run over to the firefighters, ignoring Rylie completely as I tell them where the fire is. I can't think about why she's here right now, or why. We've got other shit to handle, like preventing the house from burning to the ground.

They hook their hoses to the side of the fire engine and then they're following me to the door that leads to the guest room, one of them sending me a warning look as I was about to go inside with them.

"Stay here," he says, his voice firm. "We've got it."

I watch as Drew waves them over and takes over, and I try to catch his eye, get his attention so he'll come talk to me, but he's too busy talking to the guy who told me to wait outside.

Turning, I watch the house, my gaze scanning frantically, making sure it's not on fire anywhere else. I'm breathing heavily, my chest aches, and when I try to clear my throat, that sends me into a coughing fit, most likely caused by the smoke I inhaled earlier.

"You all right?" A feminine voice asks me.

Nodding, I keep coughing, unable to answer her with words. Thank God the fire hasn't spread. I think of Autumn, how I just left her room, and I'm so damn grateful she's okay.

But where is she? No way can they all still be in the house.

"Looks like it's contained to just the one room," one of the firefighters says after she finishes speaking on the radio that's hooked to her belt. She's standing with Rylie, who has a thin blanket draped over her shoulders, and she's visibly shivering. "Are you okay, hon?" the firefighter asks Rylie.

She nods, tears streaking down her cheeks. I stare at her

incredulously, my mind trying to put together what she's doing here. None of the answers are good.

"Rylie," I start, and she lifts her head, her eyes going wide when she sees me, as if she didn't notice me standing by her for the last couple of minutes.

Weird.

"Oh, thank God! There you are! I was so worried. Once the fire started and I couldn't see you, I thought...I thought I lost you." She fling herself at me, the blanket sliding off her body, and I realize she's dressed for bed, wearing a thin nightshirt that hits her right at the knees.

I set her away from me, shaking my head. "What are you doing here?"

"You told me to come here. Remember? I was in your room. With you." Her eyes are huge, and her expression is downright frantic.

"No, you weren't in my room," I say slowly, frowning at her. Something is way off with Rylie. Why is she saying I asked her to meet me in my room?

The firefighter is watching us, suspicion in her eyes. "You two know each other?"

"Yeah," I say at the same time Rylie exclaims, "Yes! He's my boyfriend!"

My head whips toward her at that. "No, I'm not."

"Yes, you are," Rylie says, laughing like I'm making a joke. "Stop being silly."

I glance over at the firefighter, who appears vaguely alarmed. "I'm not her boyfriend," I tell her.

"Then what is she doing here? Does she live here?"

"No." I glance over at Rylie, who's started to cry. "What are you doing?" I ask her. "Are you okay?"

"No, Ash. No, I'm not okay. You keep ignoring me, you deny everything I say, and it really hurts. You didn't believe me when I told you I was pregnant, and now I lost the baby.

317

And it's all your fault. You ruined everything. You ruined us. You ruined our baby. You ruined my life!"

The firefighter—the nameplate on her shirt says her last name is Ramirez—takes out a pen and a tiny notepad and flips it open, taking notes. Like she's some sort of cop who wants to mention that Rylie's behaving as if she's unhinged.

Shit.

What the hell is going on right now? I feel like I'm living a dream. Or a nightmare. But I'm not waking up, which means it's all real. This is actually happening.

The fire is put out quick, solely contained to my room, specifically my bed and the table beside it. The firefighters were efficient and the cleanup won't be bad, though there's a lot of smoke damage. An arson investigator shows up within twenty minutes of the fire being put out, picking over the charred and burned stuff in the room, and Drew and I stand outside in the hall, watching him move through the room silently.

"Were you smoking in there?" Drew asks, his voice low. "I won't be mad if you were. Accidents happen."

I believe him. He sounds sincere, though it's hard to believe any adult when they tell you you won't be in trouble. They always say that right before they call you out for doing something stupid.

"No. I haven't smoked since the night I got my face punched in," I tell him truthfully. My chest still hurts, and I start coughing again. The smoke damage in the room is bad, I can still smell it in the air. It was more destructive than the actual fire, and I just know all my shit is ruined.

And I have no money to replace any of it. Meaning I'm completely screwed. I'm also thinking that's the least of my worries tonight.

"What's this?" Drew stoops and grabs something off the

floor, and when I spot the wadded up tissue in his hand, I want to snatch it from him and throw it as hard as I can.

Fuck me, he's holding my used condom. The condom I used when I had sex with his freaking daughter.

"I'll take it," I offer but he doesn't give it to me. He stares at the tissue, and I know when his lip curls that he's realized what exactly was wrapped up in that Kleenex.

"Why is that girl still here?" Drew asks as he starts walking toward the open door that leads outside, his steps brisk.

I follow after him. "I don't know."

Drew stops right at the door, turning to face me. "Who is she? Do you know her?"

Swallowing hard, I nod once, looking away. Shame hits me hard, spreading over my skin, sinking deep inside me. I don't want to tell him what happened. I don't want to admit any of it. It's embarrassing. Hell, I don't even know if what Rylie says is true.

"Were you using this?" He holds out his hand, the tissue still resting there. "With her?" He nods toward Rylie.

She's standing next to Ramirez the firefighter, the blanket still around her shoulders. Rylie looks very small, very pale, and very confused.

"No," I tell Drew. "I don't know why she's here."

"Ash! Asher!" Rylie's shrill voice calls for me and I wince, glancing over my shoulder to see she's running toward me, the blanket flying behind her. "There you are."

"Ry—" I start but she cuts me off, throwing herself at me.

"I'm so glad you're okay. I was so worried. The fire was so scary, I thought I lost you." She clutches me tight and it feels like she's suffocating me.

"Hey. It's okay," I tell her, trying to disengage myself from her hold. But every time I push her hand off me, she settles it

319

somewhere else. I glance up to find Drew watching us, his dark brows pinched together and I feel...caught.

Trapped.

"Sir, could we have a word?" Ramirez asks Drew.

He sends me a look before he leaves with the firefighter, and I'm alone with Rylie. She finally lets go of me, her smile serene, her expression, her gaze blank. Like a doll's.

"Why are you doing this?" I ask her, my voice tight.

"What are you talking about? I'm doing nothing. Just like you want me to do." She blinks, her smile fading. "You don't love me anymore."

"I never did love you," I say bluntly, trying my best to fight the panic that wants to take over. Where's Autumn? Where's Fable and the rest of the family?

What is Ramirez telling Drew about Rylie?

"My mom will be here any minute," Rylie says, her voice hollow. "Maybe she'll bring me back up here later so I can get my car and we can talk."

"There's nothing more we need to talk about, Rylie," I tell her and her entire face turns red.

"You fucking coward!" She lunges toward me. Her hands curled into fists as she starts pummeling my chest. I grab hold of her wrists, holding her off as best as I can, but she's stronger than she looks. She tries to kick at me, punch me, and I just take it, wincing when her foot makes connection with my shin, her fist socking me right in my still sore ribs making me double over.

That's when Ramirez and Drew run over to us, pulling us apart. "Come on now, Rylie. Let's go wait for your mother over here," Ramirez tells her.

She leads Rylie away, who's shaking and breathing heavily. I watch them go, curling my arm in front of my chest, trying to work past the pain that Rylie's fist caused.

"The firefighter told me that girl said she was pregnant with your baby."

I turn to find Drew studying me, his expression impassive. "What did you say?" I ask carefully.

"Ramirez said that girl admitted she was pregnant with your baby, but she lost it." Drew tilts his head. "Yet I'm finding used condoms in the hall, so that doesn't make much sense."

I part my lips, unsure of what I should tell him. Do I clear myself and risk getting Autumn in trouble? "I don't believe she was ever pregnant in the first place."

The moment the words fall from my lips, a sheriff's deputy car pulls into the driveway, no siren on but the yellow lights flashing.

Great.

I would call bullshit on this entire situation, but Rylie's behavior isn't right. She's completely fixated on me, yet she's also trying to beat the shit out of me.

It doesn't make any sense.

Everything gets chaotic once the deputy arrives. The arson investigator deems the fire an accident, started by an unattended candle that they found in the middle of my bed, a waxy lump left behind as evidence. Since I've never had a candle in that room, nor have I seen one, I tell the investigator that I have no idea where it came from when he questions me, Drew still standing with us and listening to every word I say.

"I brought it," Rylie calls from where she's still standing with Ramirez, her gaze meeting mine, eyes wide and her pupils dilated. "Remember? For our romantic night?"

The disappointed look Drew sends my way guts me. "What the hell is going on here, Davis? Is she telling the truth?"

"Sir, let me explain." I have never called Drew Callahan sir in my life. I don't know why I do it. As a sign of respect? Out of desperation in the hopes he'll actually listen to me versus Rylie, who's spouting nothing but a bunch of nonsense?

"You can explain yourself later," he says with a shake of his head before he walks over to where the firefighters are clustered together, and they all glance in my direction before they start talking among themselves.

I wonder where Fable and the kids are. And Autumn. She has to be awake. Worried about me. Maybe she already knows that Rylie's here, and someone told her what she said. Maybe she'll believe her.

But how could she? I was with her right up to the moment I first discovered the fire. There's no way Autumn will believe Rylie. We were together. Autumn's my alibi. Not that I can tell Drew that.

Hey, I didn't start that fire. And I definitely wasn't with Rylie. Where was I? Yeah, I was with your daughter, taking her virginity in her bed. You have the used condom that's evidence, so that means I'm off the hook, right?

The grim thought almost makes me want to laugh, but I don't. That won't go over too well.

"We're going to need to talk to you a little more, son." I turn to find the fire investigator standing in front of me, his expression serious.

"Right now?"

He nods. "We'll just take you to the station and interview you real quick before we bring you back here."

He's lying. He was probably given orders by Drew to never bring me back here again.

"Can I get some pants on? And some shoes?" I ask him. Though I really don't know if I have any pants or shoes that aren't either burned or damaged by smoke.

"I'll get him some stuff to wear from my son," Drew says, his tone clipped before he leaves, heading for Jake's room.

Great. I'm borrowing more of Jake's clothes. That guy must thoroughly hate me by now.

"I'm not in trouble, am I?" I ask the fire investigator.

"As long as you tell the truth, you'll be fine," the man says, patting me on the shoulder.

His words, the way his hand clamps my shoulder, heavy and tight, feels like a prison sentence. Will he believe me?

No one ever has before, so why change now?

CHAPTER 38

AUTUMN

I come into the kitchen to find my parents talking, their voices low and serious, so wrapped up in what they're saying, they don't even notice me enter the room. They wouldn't let me talk to Ash earlier, when the fire was first discovered. Mom made all of us go outside and wait it out in the front yard on the opposite side of the house where the fire started. She said she wanted to keep us safe, but I don't know.

It also felt like she wanted to keep me away from Ash.

After a while Dad came out front to talk to Mom, and when the house was deemed safe, she sent us all to our rooms with strict orders that we couldn't leave. Sleep wouldn't come, so I paced my room, bit my nails down to nothing and stress ate the rest of the bag of kettle corn I left in here a few days ago. Finally I couldn't take it anymore and sent Ash a text. Then another one, but he never responded.

I have no idea where he is.

Giving up, fear propels me downstairs, where I find my parents. They're talking so intently, I have to clear my throat in order for them to notice me.

"Oh. Autumn." Mom gives me small smile. "Come sit with us. We need to talk."

Dread makes my steps slow and I settle onto the empty barstool that's in between my parents. Mom gives me a side hug while Dad just glowers. He's mad. Upset. I'm upset too. I want to know where my boyfriend is. I want to know that he's okay.

"We don't know how to tell you this," Mom starts, and I turn to look at her, fear making my insides quake. "We think Ash started the fire. By accident. But—he had a girl there with him. In his room."

My mouth drops open. "*What?*"

"Her name is Rylie Altman," Dad bites out. "Do you know her?"

Oh. My. God. "Yes, I know her. I go to school with her. She was here? At the house?"

"She was waiting outside when the fire engine showed up, frantically waving them down. She told them she was inside with her boyfriend and they fell asleep. She said they must've knocked over the candle that was sitting on the bedside table that they lit for their romantic encounter," Dad explains, his voice harsh and full of disappointment.

"But that's not true. None of it is. Ash is with me," I tell them.

It's like he didn't even hear what I said. "Apparently he's with this Rylie, and it's serious. She claimed she was pregnant with his baby, but recently lost it," Dad continues, driving the invisible knife up to the hilt, sticking me right in my heart.

"Drew," Mom chastises, but Dad shakes his head, cutting her off.

"She deserves to know the truth, Fable. Ash Davis is nothing but a con man who used us and our daughter."

I start to laugh. Seriously, this is hysterical. I can take care of this ridiculous story with the truth. "He definitely wasn't with Rylie."

"Autumn, this isn't funny," Mom says, reaching out to rest her hand over mine. She ducks her head, looking me in the eyes, her expression dead serious. "The arson investigator called just a bit ago. He said one of the deputies called to let him know that Ash's mom heard about the fire and said her son should be investigated. She claimed that he started another fire near the lake eleven years ago that went unsolved."

"Mom." I'm laughing again, and my parents are glaring at me like I've lost my mind, which I sort of feel like I have. "Ash told me about it. He was *six*. He stole a lighter from his dad and set a bush on fire. His father felt so guilty when he found out, he gave up smoking for the rest of his life and got rid of all the lighters in the house. Ash isn't a serial arsonist. He was a curious six-year-old who mistakenly set a fire because he thought lighters were cool."

They say nothing for a while until Dad asks, "What about the girl? She was there, Autumn. I saw her. I talked to her. She said they were together, in his room, and they fell asleep. She told everyone that. All the firefighters that were there heard the same story I did." He hesitates. "I found proof that they were together."

"What proof?" I ask incredulously.

He sends Mom a look before he breathes deep and says, "I found a used—condom, wrapped up in a tissue, on the floor in the hallway just outside the guest room."

I hang my head, fear filling me and making me shaky. That condom was the one Ash and I used, but how do I admit that without disappointing them completely? I don't want my parents to be mad, or to think less of me. We broke their rules. What Ash and I did violated their trust—this may ruin everything for him, for us.

But what am I supposed to do? He's already in trouble with the fire, and with Rylie being here, which makes absolutely no sense. Why was she at my house? How did she get here? When did she get here?

Did she start the fire?

I can't let this go on. I have to tell the truth.

"Ash—like I just said, he was with me. Last night. Well, early this morning," I say, staring at my hands as I twist them together in my lap. "We were together in my room for…a couple of hours, and he was returning to his room when he must've discovered the fire. He—he probably dropped the condom then. He took it with him when he left my room."

My parents are deathly quiet and I start to tremble, tears stinging my eyes.

"So he couldn't have been with Rylie when he was with me," I say, my voice small. "I don't know why she was at our house, but I think maybe she started the fire."

"Autumn." I look up to meet my father's stern gaze. Oh, he looks angry. Angrier than I've ever seen him. He also looks concerned and maybe even a little…hurt? I did that to him, which kills me. "Are you lying for Ash so he doesn't get in trouble? Because you don't have to do that. If he did sneak off with this girl and set that fire, even if he did it by accident, he has to face the consequences."

"But you see, he didn't *do* anything. He definitely didn't set that fire. How could he be two places at once?" I shake my head, the tears coming, sliding down my cheeks, one after the other. "I know you probably don't want to hear this, and I can understand why, but he was with me, Daddy. He spent the night with me in my room, he wasn't with Rylie. We're in love, Ash and me. And we wanted to be together—but we didn't think it would end up like this."

I start crying hard, burying my face in my hands, and I feel Mom smooth her hand over my back, trying to offer me

327

comfort. Dad curses under his breath before storming out of the kitchen, and I just start crying even harder.

It was right to tell the truth, but now I've completely lost my parents' trust. And I've probably sealed Ash's fate. He won't be welcome in my house any longer. Dad won't help him.

I've ruined everything.

* * *

"AUTUMN. WAKE UP."

Somehow, I fell asleep. After the embarrassing discussion with my parents where I made my father so upset he walked out and didn't come back, Mom accompanied me to my room. I was a crying, sobbing mess the entire walk up the stairs and into my room. She told me to lie down and then she joined me, where she held me while I cried, until I fell asleep in her arms. She must've eventually left me alone, and I have no idea how long I've been sleeping, but it's my dad who's trying to wake me up, and he's the last person I want to see.

Rolling over on my side, I face the wall and pretend to still be sleeping, hoping he'll go away.

He sighs, reaching out to give my shoulder a gentle shake. "I know you're awake."

Can't he pretend I'm asleep too? That's what I'm trying to do.

When I still don't move, he starts talking. "Ash has been released. Your mom is going to pick him up right now." He pauses for a moment before he says, "We thought it best I don't go. I'm afraid I might say or do something I'll regret."

The relief I feel at hearing Ash isn't in trouble anymore is so strong, I can't pretend I'm sleeping any longer.

"Oh, Daddy." I turn and sit up, slinging my arms around

his neck and holding him tight. "Do you hate me?" I ask, my words muffled against his neck.

"Of course I don't hate you." He wraps his arms around me and it feels so good, so comforting, to have my father holding me. I used to love Daddy hugs. That's what I called them. I was so little and he was so big. I thought he was a giant. I don't want him disappointed in me, though I know he must be. "But you know you two shouldn't have been sneaking around. So did Ash."

I pull away from him so I can look into his eyes. "Am I in trouble?"

"Yes." He doesn't even flinch when he says that. "You definitely are. I just don't know what your punishment will be yet."

"What about...Ash?"

"I don't know what we're going to do about him either. I spoke with Weldman earlier, and he said he could have Ash stay with him," Dad explains, referring to one of the assistant coaches of the football team.

"So he can't stay with us any longer?" I'm sad. I knew if we got caught Ash would be sent away. I hate that he'll have to leave us, but I couldn't stand by and let him take the fall for something he didn't do.

"Not if you two are involved and are going to sneak into each other's rooms behind our backs." The pointed look Dad sends me has me bowing my head in shame. "Hey, I was a teenager once upon a time, you know. I know what's going on, and why you feel the need to sneak around."

"Oh my God, this is so embarrassing," I mumble.

"Just promise me you'll be safe, okay, sweetheart?" He lifts my chin so I have no choice but to look at him. "That's all I ask. Now let's change the subject."

Gladly. "Did you hear anything else about Rylie and why she was here?"

Dad sighs, his expression softening. "The deputy said she confessed to setting the fire to her mother, who called in to let them know. Since we don't want to press charges, nothing's going to happen. Though I do believe they're going to seek help for Rylie. I guess her mom said she's not been doing well for some time now."

"Oh." I feel terrible. Poor Rylie. She's not a terrible person. It just sounds like she's having a hard time processing stuff. I don't know. Maybe she's depressed and what happened with Ash pushed her over the edge? "Is she going to be all right?"

"I hope so."

"What about Ash? Is he really going to stay with the Weldmans?" I don't know their family very well, but Dad always says he's a nice guy. And their kids are older than me, so I never went to school with them.

"I think it might end up being a better atmosphere for Ash there. No other kids to deal with, and Weldman's wife is retired, so she's home all day. She'll make him homecooked meals and fuss over him, help him with his homework. Give him some motherly attention, something he's been sorely lacking the last few years." Dad offers me a small smile. "And after a while, when I'm not so mad at him, Ash can come over and hang out with us."

"How long will that take?" I ask.

"I don't know," he answers truthfully. "You'll have to be patient with me. You two will also have to work hard to earn my trust."

"I'm sorry, Daddy," I whisper, gazing at him. "I'm sorry I disappointed you."

"It's not the end of the world. We'll work through this." He squeezes my chin gently before he releases it. "Now I have to go put a call in on an insurance claim. Looks like we have a couple of rooms we'll need to redo."

I'm thankful my parents believe me. I've never really lied

to them before, not like this, and I've given them no reason not to trust me up until now.

Stupid boys.

Stupid hormones.

I love that boy, though. So much, I'll do anything to make sure he's safe. I told the truth even though it got the both of us in trouble. It's okay.

He's worth it.

CHAPTER 39

ASH

*M*y girl is a blubbering mess.

"I don't want you to go." She flings herself at me and I have no choice but to hold her tight, not that I'm protesting. Honestly, I don't want to let her go, though I have to.

"I'm only a couple of miles away," I murmur into her hair, breathing deep the sweet fragrance of her shampoo. "And I'll see you every day at school."

"Thank God. My parents have turned this place into a jail."

Exactly what Fable wanted to avoid has now come true. Oh, they didn't put the cameras in the house, but Autumn is on lockdown for the next two months. We're not allowed to go on dates on the weekend or see each other after school. We can hang out during school hours, and we can give each other a quick hug after the games, but that's about it.

Two months. Two long months.

I guess we deserve the punishment.

I've already spent a little time with the Weldmans, who

I'm going to live with for the rest of my senior year. They're nice people, much older than Drew and Fable, and Mrs. Weldman—Laura—has a grandmotherly vibe. She's already baked me a giant plate piled high with chocolate chip cookies and they were fucking delicious, but I told her I couldn't indulge too much since it's still football season.

The lady just laughed at me, which says she's going to keep on making cookies, and I'll probably keep on eating them.

I'm going to miss living with Drew and Fable. They took me in, they listened to me, and they tried to help me. They're still helping me, but at a distance. I guess I deserve that, since I had sex with their daughter and they found out in the worst possible way.

"The two months will go by fast," I tell Autumn, clutching her tight. I'm grateful they allowed us a little alone time before I left. Most of my stuff was ruined by the fire—which Rylie most definitely set—and I was left with pretty much nothing. Not even a phone.

Fable took me shopping and bought me new clothes. They also gave me one of the latest iPhones and set me up on their plan. They may be disappointed in me, but that doesn't mean they stopped caring about me. That's the difference between Autumn's parents and my mom.

She hates me and is disappointed in everything I do. She doesn't love me either. I will never make that woman happy no matter what I do, so fuck her.

Fuck her.

Fuck Rylie too, though Autumn says I shouldn't be so hard on her. But I can't help it. Turns out she came to the house, broke into the side door and went to my room. How she figured out that was my room, I don't know. We can only conclude that she'd been spying on me, on all of us, for a while. When she discovered I wasn't there, she set the giant candle she brought with her on the bedside table and lit all three wicks, then promptly fell asleep while waiting for me. The candle knocked over, and *whoosh*. A fire started.

All that nonsense about us being together and her being pregnant with my baby? All untrue. Her parents said that she was acting more and more unstable this school year, and when I broke up with her, that's when she seemed to snap. Her erratic behavior concerned them, and they started taking her to a psychologist, but I guess it wasn't enough.

Last I heard, they put her on medication and she's going to start seeing a counselor twice a week. I hope it helps her.

"Two months is going to be an eternity." Autumn glances over her shoulder real quick before she returns her attention to me. "Kiss me before they come over here."

I do what she asks with no hesitation, sealing my lips to hers, parting them with my tongue. The kiss turns deep in an instant, and I know I shouldn't do this, but damn, it will be my last time kissing her like this until...

Tomorrow, when I see her at school and we can leave for lunch. Thank God we're seniors and haven't lost that privilege.

Hey, I might not sneak around at the Callahan house, but no one said we can't sneak around off campus and find a private spot so we can spend our lunch hour doing...other things.

I'm going to hell for my dirty thoughts, I swear.

Autumn pulls away, a reluctant noise sounding in her throat. "We should go to the front. I think I just heard a car pull up."

I follow after her as she leads me to the front of the house, her fingers entwined with mine. We don't hide how we feel about each other to her parents, but we are respectful. No obvious displays of affection. I'm not about to piss off Drew Callahan again.

The Weldmans are standing outside of their car, a silver sedan, and when they spot me, they both smile. "There he is," Laura says, beaming at me. I think she's happy to have someone back in the house, someone for her to take care of.

And I'm not going to turn her down. It's nice, having someone treat me like they actually care. Now that I've witnessed what a real family is like at the Callahan house, I don't ever want to lose it.

I've already started on my community service, volunteering at the local Boys and Girls Club. I hang out with the kids and play games with them, or just listen to them talk. It's fun. And...enlightening. Some of them remind me of myself when I was that age. A little lost, a lot pissed off. All I wanted was for someone to believe in me back then. While I know I can't offer too much to these kids, I'll do what I can to help out.

It's kind of nice, to feel wanted. To help someone who didn't ask for it.

All the Callahans are out in front of the house, ready to send me off. I hold out my hand and Beck slaps it, extra hard. "See ya later!" he yells, beaming up at me.

Damn, the kid can pack a punch. That kind of hurt.

Ava gives me a shy hug, keeping her gaze averted. Shit, Drew is in trouble with this one. She's going to be beautiful. Not as pretty as my girl, though.

Jake and I do some complicated knuckle shake we all made up at football camp over the summer, his expression impassive. We've come to a sort of peace, though I know he's not my biggest fan. But he'll get over it.

I'm not going anywhere.

Fable wraps me up in a hug, holding me tight, and whispers in my ear, "Don't fuck this up, okay?"

I start to laugh as I pull away from her. "I won't."

Nerves make me jittery as I approach Drew. He watches me, a serious expression on his face, his lips thin, and I wish I could rewind time and fix all of this.

But I can't.

"I'm sorry I disappointed you, sir. I hope I can one day earn your respect and trust again," I tell him, sounding like a complete suck-up.

But fuck it, I mean every word.

"You don't disappoint me on the field, that's for damn sure." Drew holds out his right hand for me to shake. I take it, giving him a firm shake, and then he hauls me in at the last second into one of those slapping on the back bro-type hugs.

I'm so grateful for it, my knees get wobbly.

"See you at practice tomorrow," he tells me, and I nod my response before I turn to Autumn.

She's standing before me in a thin little summer dress, and she's never looked more beautiful. Though I always think that. Every time I see her, I think, *how'd I get so lucky to find her? To find all of them?*

I don't know what I did, but I'm fucking grateful.

"We're acting like I'm moving away, when I'm only moving down the road," I say, loud enough for everyone to hear, and they all start to laugh.

Then they all shift away from us, taking their conversation closer to the Weldmans' car, giving Autumn and me one last bit of privacy.

"I'm going to miss living here with you," I tell her.

She's not crying anymore, which is good. Breaks my heart when she cries like that. I hate it. "I'm going to miss having you here."

"I'll see you tomorrow, though. And in two months, we're free to see each other on the weekends," I tell her.

"I seriously can't wait." She steps closer, slipping her arms around my waist, and lifts up on tiptoe to press a sweet kiss to my lips. "I love you."

"I love you too." So damn much, I don't know if she'll ever understand how I feel.

I'm just going to do my damnedest to show her, every single day.

For the rest of my life.

EPILOGUE

AUTUMN

Nine months later...

"What do you think?" Ash throws his arms up into the air, slowly turning in a circle as he stands in the middle of the empty football field.

"I think you look good out there," I call out to him. I'm sitting on one of the sideline benches, sweating under the hot summer sun as I cup my hand over my eyes to shield them so I can witness the boy I love have a total moment.

"Really?" He turns to look at me, an adorable smile on his face. He looks so happy. Downright boyish. After witnessing a scowling Ash for so many years, this constant smiling Ash is a more than welcome sight.

I know I've contributed to putting a smile on that handsome face, but the reason for today's happiness is the meeting he just had with his new team coach. He's so excited to play college football, he can barely contain his emotions.

"Really," I say as I rise to my feet and start walking toward him. The stadium is huge, and I've watched a few games here before with my family, though it's been a while. The stands were always full when I attended, the fans wearing red and white in support of their team. It was exciting, even as a spectator, and I can't imagine the adrenaline rush the players must experience when they're out on that field during a game.

Ash meets me halfway, his arms slipping around my waist so he can lift me off my feet and twirl me around. Squealing, I grab hold of his broad shoulders, then slip my arms around his neck when he gently sets me on my feet. We hold each other for a moment, the only two people on this field, and it almost feels like we're the only two people on this entire college campus. I press my head against his chest so I can listen to his heart's steady thumping rhythm, and I close my eyes, savoring the moment.

"All my dreams are becoming real," he whispers. "I sound fucking ridiculous, but it's true. This is all I ever wanted, to play football in college. The fact that I even got in…"

I pull away so I can look into his eyes. "You got in on your own merits," I remind him, my voice firm. "You don't owe my parents anything."

He feels obligated toward them, and it's understandable. Especially my father, who did ask a recruiter to come out and watch him play—and that recruiter just so happened to come from this very university. But Ash earned his spot on his team fair and square, and while he'll be a backup the first year or two, the fact that he's on this team is everything to him.

"They helped," he says, his expression serious as he studies me. "You know they did. If I would've stayed with my mom, I wouldn't be here right now."

He's right. He was on a path of complete self-destruction, living with his mother. She tried her best to ruin him.

Look at him now.

"And you helped too," he continues, his voice soft, his eyes glowing, full of love and affection. All of it for me. "You're everything to me, Autumn. I don't know what I'm going to do when you leave."

"Stop." I rise up on my toes and kiss him, silencing his depressing words. It's weird to think how I will never know what it's like to cheer on the sidelines of this team while my boyfriend is playing.

I'm going to a different college. I put on a positive front, but deep down, it scares me a little, to think of us separated while we're in school. But we're not going to let anything bad happen to our relationship. We've been through so much together. I love him, he loves me. We trust each other.

And that's all we need.

"What do we got?" he asks after he breaks the kiss. "Six weeks?"

"Seven," I say. "Seven long, glorious weeks until I leave."

I won't give up my dreams for him, and I don't expect him to do that for me either. He wanted to come to the local university, while I'm headed south, to Santa Barbara. It's not that far, a little over a five-hour drive one way. We can see each other on weekends. Meaning I'm the one who has to come up to see him when I can during the fall semester, since he'll be playing on Saturdays—or at the very least, bench warming.

Though I would never put it like that to him.

"I'm going to have to work extra hard then to make the next seven weeks count," he says just before he settles his mouth back on mine.

His kiss is warm and sweet at first, then with one swipe of his perfect tongue, it deepens. His hands wander, and so do mine. Until I'm gasping and clutching at his shirt, desperate for more.

Ash sets me away from him with a chuckle, reaching down to readjust himself before he glances around the stadium one last time. "Don't know if I'll get used to this," he says with a slight shake of his head.

I take his hand and we head for the exit. "Someday, you're going to be a superstar out on this field."

"We'll see." His tone is cryptic.

"You will," I reaffirm. "And once you graduate, you'll go on to even bigger and better things."

"Stop talking so much, Callahan. You're gonna jinx me," he teases, squeezing my hand.

"Never," I say. I have faith that he will accomplish whatever he sets his mind to. And I will be right there beside him.

Every step of the way.

WANT MORE? Jake's story is out now in Falling For Her, the second book in The Callahans series! Keep reading for a sneak peek!

FALLING FOR HER

Chapter One
Jake

"How about that one?"

We all snicker when we see who Diego's discreetly pointing at as we walk past her in the hallway. Some freshman who looks about ten, with big blue eyes and a mouth full of metal. She's cute enough, but way too young.

"I don't think so," I tell my friends as we stride toward the quad.

It's lunchtime. Our senior year. We're able to drive off campus now, but not today. Coach wants us to watch game film of the team we're playing tomorrow night. So we have about fifteen minutes to grab food before we all meet in the team room to study our opponents. Learn their weak spots, their strengths. See if they're better defensively or offensively.

When I say Coach, I'm talking about my dad. I just try to keep that shit separate. It's easier that way.

"Check her out," says Diego—one of my best friends—

nudging me in the shoulder and now not-so-discreetly pointing at a group of girls sitting at a nearby picnic table.

"Which one?" Again, they're young. Maybe sophomores? I don't really recognize any of them. If they're a couple of years younger than me and not friends with my sister Ava, who's a junior, or on the football team, I don't bother getting to know them.

That makes me sound like an asshole, but I don't have the time. I have my circle of friends. I even have my circle of acquaintances. This year, my last year in high school, I don't need to add to either group. I'm perfectly content with what I have.

"Any of them." Diego slaps me on the back, a giant grin on his face. "You need to find someone, bro. This single, I-don't-bother-with-any-girl business is getting old."

I don't bother with any girls anymore because when I do, they tend to take my heart and rip it to shreds. It's ridiculous, but when I fall, I tend to fall hard.

Sophomore year I got my heart broken twice, once by Cami Lockhart. We got back together the beginning of junior year only for her to cheat on me—and I found out via Snapchat.

That sucked.

I've never bothered with a girl again. Fuck 'em. I'd rather focus on football and my friends and school, exactly in that order.

"Too young," I tell Diego, and Caleb, my other best friend, bursts out laughing.

"Oh come on. She's cute. I'd bet she's down," he says with a smirk.

Caleb is an actual asshole. He hooks up with an endless stream of girls, yet most of them don't complain. It's like they're proud to be a Caleb fan girl.

"Find him a senior then," Diego says, stopping in the

direct center of the crowded quad. He settles his hands on his hips and turns in a slow circle, scanning the area with a narrowed gaze. Diego has a girl and they're supposedly madly in love. I mean, good for him. They seem totally into each other—for the most part. They've been together for over a year, and Jocelyn treats him like a god, while she's his princess, as he calls her. I'm pretty sure they've talked about getting married, which is just…insane if you ask me.

"Her."

We all swivel our heads to see Tony—our quietest friend —inclining his head toward a table to the left of where we're standing.

There's a girl sitting there, her back to us. Alone. She's wearing a black T-shirt, her reddish-blonde hair spilling down her back in loose waves. Her elbow's propped on the table and she's resting her cheek on her fist, an open book in front of her. Like she's reading. For fun.

What the hell?

"No way," Diego says with a dismissive wave of his hand. "Jake's not into smart girls."

I'm immediately offended. "Who says?"

"You, with the choices you've made in the past," Diego points out.

He's got me there. Cami wasn't that smart. None of the girls I've dated were. Not really.

"I like her hair," Tony says, his tone, his entire demeanor impassive, like we're talking about the weather. "She's cute."

"You should go for her then," Caleb suggests to Tony.

"Nah. Not my type." Tony's gaze meets mine and he tilts his head, like he's giving me permission to talk to her.

Huh.

"How do you know she's a smart girl?" I study her, taking in her narrow shoulders, the elegant slope of her back. She brushes her hair back from her face, tucking the strands

345

behind her ear and offering me a glimpse of her profile. She's pretty in an understated way, I guess. Upturned nose. Pale skin. Freckles.

I don't recognize her at all.

"Because she's reading a book, dumbass." Caleb sounds enormously pissed off, though I know he's not. That's just how he always sounds. "If you don't ask her to wear your jersey, I think I'll ask her instead."

Yes, this is what we're doing on a Thursday afternoon during lunch. Trying to find a girl for me to ask to wear my jersey on game day. It's a big deal at our high school, and so far during my reign as the varsity team's quarterback, I've only had one girl ever wear my jersey, and for only one time. It was Cami Lockhart, right at the beginning of our junior year, when I thought there was a possible chance we could work shit out and be a couple again.

But then someone sent me her private story off Snapchat —a video of her making out with motherfucking Eli Bennett, the quarterback for our rival school's team, and I was done. Finished.

For some reason, this year my boys want to see me make a claim. Find a girl. They tell me I'm too grumpy. That maybe if I'm getting some on the regular, that'll mellow me out. Some of them even complain I'm too focused, which I don't get. Why wouldn't they want me focused?

Focused wins games. I've had that drilled into my head over the years by my dad.

"No way," I tell Caleb when he acts like he's going to approach the mystery girl sitting at the table. "I'll do it."

I don't know why I'm bothering with this. I don't know her, but I'm guessing she knows me. Most girls would probably be flattered if I asked, but I'm not that sure if she's into football, or if she even goes to the games. But it would be cool to see her wear my number around school all day.

Maybe I could make it a thing. Give it to a different girl every week. They'd start fighting for their chance. It could turn into a contest. Maybe it would go viral...

"Go ask her." Diego gives me a shove in the girl's direction, his hand right in the center of my back. "Before you chicken out."

Okay, that shit's annoying. And it's just the incentive I need to make it happen. Glancing over my shoulder, I glare at my three best friends, but all they do is make clucking noises at me in return like they're a bunch of chickens.

Assholes.

Slowly I approach the table, wondering what I should say first. I don't have a problem talking to girls. I never really have. I almost wonder if this is because I grew up in a household full of women. Don't get me wrong, Dad is a strong personality and is a big influence on me, but he wasn't around much when I was little. He was busy working all the time.

Growing up, I was always with Mom, my older sister Autumn and my younger sister Ava. Our little brother Beck didn't come along until years later, and by then I was resigned with the idea that I'd never even have a brother.

So I was constantly surrounded by girls. Autumn and Ava used to fight like cats and dogs. Now that Autumn's gone, away at college in Santa Barbara, we don't see her that much. Ava is happier with Autumn gone, I think. Having an older sister trying to boss you around all the time gets old.

I know I got tired of Autumn's bullshit. Now, I miss her. Not that I'd ever tell her that.

Deciding I need to approach this mystery girl straight on, I walk around the table, keeping a wide berth so she doesn't get suspicious or think I'm a stalker. And once I'm facing the table, I take a good, long look at her.

She's vaguely familiar, so I'm assuming she's a senior like

me, or maybe a junior. Our school is small, so most of the time I feel like I know everyone, but I can't place her. I don't remember her name. Her hair is this burnished, reddish-gold color and her eyes are big and blue. Her features delicate—except for her mouth. Full, bee-stung lips that fill my head with dirty images.

Every one of them involves my dick.

Not that I'm actually interested in this girl. I don't even know her. But as far as my first choice to wear my jersey this week, it's not a bad one.

Not a bad one at all.

One of my friends, I'm not sure who, makes a bok-bok noise and I send them all a menacing look before I march right up the table and clear my throat. "Hey."

The girl lifts her head, sky-blue eyes meeting mine, her expression open. Friendly.

Until she keeps looking at me, her gaze narrowing, that open, friendly expression disappearing within seconds. Almost as if she realized who she's looking at and doesn't like what she sees.

Damn.

When she still hasn't said anything, I decide to keep talking. "What's your name?"

Her eyebrows shoot up. "You don't know my name?"

I know this sounds weird, but I like the sound of her voice. A lot. "Should I?"

"I know yours." She sniffs, shutting the book she was reading. "Jacob Callahan."

Ah, see? She knows me. She'll totally agree to wear my jersey. "You have the advantage then."

"Because you still don't remember my name?"

I shrug helplessly and flash her a smile that's hopefully equal parts bashful yet charming. "Guilty."

She rolls her eyes, resting her arms on top of the table. "Did you have a question or something?"

Her tone is short. Dismissive. This girl is totally trying to get rid of me. "Yeah, as a matter of fact, I do have a question for you."

"I'm waiting on pins and needles," she says, her voice going up a notch, those blue eyes of hers extra wide.

They're pretty, I'll give her that. *She's* pretty. There's a sprinkling of freckles across the bridge of her nose and she has very white teeth.

"I was wondering if you wanted…" I let my voice drift and I glance down at my shoes, kicking at the base of the picnic bench. I'm trying to up the anticipation a notch. Going for the golly, gee bashful vibe. Girls seem to like it.

"Wanted what?"

Huh. Guess she's not one for anticipation.

"If you wanted to wear my jersey tomorrow." I lift my head, my gaze meeting hers straight on, and I see the surprise in her eyes. I've shocked her with my request.

Come on, I can see why. I'm me and she's…whoever she is.

She studies me for a while, and now it's my turn to wait with anticipation. Her full lips part, like she's about to say something, but instead, she looks away from me, grabs her things and starts shoving them into her backpack.

As if she's about to leave.

When she shoots me an irritated glare, slides off the picnic bench and walks away without another word, I chase her, surprised by how quick she is. My friends are laughing, I can hear them as I follow after this chick—still don't know her name—but I can't worry about them right now.

Even though they're total assholes for laughing at me.

"Hey!" I call out, but it's like my voice only spurs her on. She's practically in a full jog as she heads toward Adams Hall, and I wonder if her plan is to duck into a classroom and hide from me.

Putting a little speed behind my step, I catch up with her easily, hooking my fingers around her upper arm and stopping her escape. She turns to face me, the look on her face so full of disgust I immediately release her and take a step back.

"Why are you chasing me?" she asks breathlessly. Her cheeks are pink, and she's practically panting. I get the sense that maybe she doesn't exercise much? I mean, I'm not even winded.

"You never answered my question."

She lifts her chin. Blows out an exaggerated breath, like what I'm asking is too damn much. After enduring the last five minutes with this chick, I don't even want her to wear my jersey now. She's making way too big a deal about this.

But for some weird reason, I have to know what her answer is.

"My name is Hannah," she finally says, and it all hits me at once. I do know her. Barely. Hannah Walsh. Senior. Moves in a completely different crowd. As in, she doesn't really move with *any* crowd. I've never had a class with her ever, because she takes all the advanced courses. My friends were right.

She's a smart girl.

"Right. Hannah." I nod and smile. "I know you."

She smiles in return, though it doesn't quite reach her sky-blue eyes. "Uh huh. Sure you do."

"I do. You're friends with…" My voice drifts. I don't know who she's friends with. I can see their faces, but at the moment, I can't recall their names.

"Please." She reaches out, settling her hand on my forearm, and it's like a spark of electricity between us the moment our skin makes contact. She snatches her hand away like I burned her. "Stop trying so hard."

I almost want to laugh. This girl is telling *me* to stop

trying so hard? Does she even know who she's dealing with? The power I wield at this school? I'm the most popular guy in the senior class—maybe in all the classes. This is my year to shine. My year to reign.

And this Hannah nobody is telling me to stop *trying* so hard?

Get the fuck out of here.

Can't back out now, though. I'm fully committed.

"So what do you say, Hannah? Are you in? Do you want to wear my jersey tomorrow?" Not like I want her to anymore. She's been rude from the moment I started talking to her.

"Gee, I sure appreciate the offer, but…" She scowls at me, her lush lips pursed. "No."

ACKNOWLEDGMENTS

Big ol' thanks to Drew + Fable for having kids so I can write about them later. So crazy, right? When I set out to write ONE WEEK GIRLFRIEND, I had zero plans on writing about their children.

Well, look at me now.

I hope you enjoyed this book. Ash and Autumn's story was easy to write, and I can't wait to explore this world even more. This is my way of telling you there will be more books.

I want to thank all the readers, reviewers and bloggers who gave shout outs about this book – thanks for shouting about all of my books, actually. I can't do this job without you, I swear! I want to thank my Facebook reader group—I love hanging out in there every day. From cat memes to book recs, it's where we share all the good stuff.

Thank you to Nina for the encouragement and for all the hard work you do. To Brittany for wanting to read this book because she still suffers from a #TuttleHangover and maybe Ash will cure it.

Finally, I want to acknowledge the girls on my cheer team. I never in a BAZILLION YEARS would've thought I'd be a coach for my daughter's high school cheer team, but I am. With zero cheer or coaching experience, my friend and I took on this job and while we went through some real crazy, difficult times, it's also been a lot of fun. And while sometimes all those girls make me (us) nuts, and all the practice and games and camps take up a lot of my time, I wouldn't trade this experience for anything else. You guys are AWESOME! Oh and to Brandy—she's Autumn's coach and she's my friend and fellow coach in real life. She's also my homegirl. My BBG. Go Badgers!

ALSO BY MONICA MURPHY

BILLIONAIRE BACHELORS CLUB (REISSUES)

Crave & Torn

Savor & Intoxicated

NEW YOUNG ADULT SERIES

The Liar's Club

KINGS OF CAMPUS

End Game

LANCASTER PREP

Things I Wanted To Say

A Million Kisses in Your Lifetime

Birthday Kisses

Promises We Meant to Keep

I'll Always Be With You

You Said I Was Your Favorite

New Year's Day

Lonely For You Only (a Lancaster novel)

THE PLAYERS

Playing Hard to Get

Playing by The Rules

Playing to Win

WEDDED BLISS (LANCASTER)

The Reluctant Bride

The Ruthless Groom

The Reckless Union

The Arranged Marriage boxset

COLLEGE YEARS

The Freshman

The Sophomore

The Junior

The Senior

DATING SERIES

Save The Date

Fake Date

Holidate

Hate to Date You

Rate A Date

Wedding Date

Blind Date

THE CALLAHANS

Close to Me

Falling For Her

Addicted To Him

Meant To Be

Fighting For You

Making Her Mine

A Callahan Wedding

FOREVER YOURS SERIES

You Promised Me Forever

Thinking About You

Nothing Without You

DAMAGED HEARTS SERIES

Her Defiant Heart

His Wasted Heart

Damaged Hearts

FRIENDS SERIES

Just Friends

More Than Friends

Forever

THE NEVER DUET

Never Tear Us Apart

Never Let You Go

THE RULES SERIES

Fair Game

In The Dark

Slow Play

Safe Bet

THE FOWLER SISTERS SERIES

Owning Violet

Stealing Rose

Taming Lily

REVERIE SERIES

His Reverie

Her Destiny

BILLIONAIRE BACHELORS CLUB SERIES

Crave

Torn

Savor

Intoxicated

ONE WEEK GIRLFRIEND SERIES

One Week Girlfriend

Second Chance Boyfriend

Three Broken Promises

Drew + Fable Forever

Four Years Later

Five Days Until You

A Drew + Fable Christmas

STANDALONE YA TITLES

Daring The Bad Boy

Saving It

Pretty Dead Girls

ABOUT THE AUTHOR

Monica Murphy is a New York Times, USA Today and international bestselling author. Her books have been translated in almost a dozen languages and have sold millions of copies worldwide. Both a traditionally published and independently published author, she writes young adult and new adult romance, as well as contemporary romance.

- facebook.com/MonicaMurphyAuthor
- instagram.com/monicamurphyauthor
- bookbub.com/profile/monica-murphy
- goodreads.com/monicamurphyauthor
- amazon.com/Monica-Murphy/e/B00AVPYIGG
- pinterest.com/msmonicamurphy
- tiktok.com/@monicamurphyauthor

Printed in Great Britain
by Amazon

43842977R00212